The critics on Anita Burgh

'A blockbuster . . . an excellent reading experience'
Literary Review

'The mix of suspense, romance, humour and good old heart-tugging pathos is irresistible'
Elizabeth Buchan, *Mail on Sunday*

'A blockbusting story of romance and intrigue'
Family Circle

'The perfect beach book' *Marie Claire*

'Sharp . . . wickedly funny' *Mail on Sunday*

'Ambition, greed and manipulation add up to a great blockbuster' *New Woman*

'You won't be able to put it down' *Good Housekeeping*

'A well-written contemporary story that has all the necessary ingredients to make a great read – and it is!' *Oracle*

'Anita has the storyteller's gift' *Daily Express*

'Sinister and avaricious forces are at work behind the pious smiles . . . Gripping!' *Daily Telegraph*

'A sure-fire bestseller' *Prima*

Anita Burgh was born in Gillingham, Kent, but spent her early years at Lanhydrock House in Cornwall. Returning to the Medway Towns, she attended Chatham Grammar School, and became a student nurse at UCH in London. She gave up nursing upon marrying into the aristocracy. Subsequently divorced, she pursued various careers – secretarial work, as a laboratory technician in cancer research and as an hotelier. She divides her time between Gloucestershire and the Auvergne in France, where she shares her life with her partner, Billy, a Cairn terrier, three mixed-breed dogs, three cats and a bulldog puppy. The visits of a constantly changing mix of her four children, two stepchildren and six grandchildren keep her busy, happy, entertained and poor! Anita Burgh is the author of many bestsellers, including *Distinctions of Class*, which was shortlisted for the Romantic Novel of the Year Award. Visit Anita Burgh at her website: www.anitaburgh.com.

THE VISITOR

Anita Burgh

ORION

An Orion paperback

First published in Great Britain in 2003
by Orion
This paperback edition published in 2003
by Orion Books Ltd,
Orion House, 5 Upper St Martin's Lane,
London WC2H 9EA

A CIP catalogue record for this book is available
from the British Library.

ISBN 0 75285 881 5

Typeset by Deltatype Ltd, Birkenhead, Merseyside

Printed and bound in Great Britain by
Clays Ltd, St Ives plc

For Steve Collie with love.
Welcome to my family
and good luck!

Chapter One
September 1899

I

It was fear that propelled her. Fear that he was close behind her. Fear that if he caught her he would surely kill her this time.

Phoebe kept looking over her shoulder, checking he was not there. She knew it slowed her and made her stumble, but she was unable to stop. Her legs ached as she pushed herself to hurry, needing to get as far away from the cottage at Cowman's Combe as she could. Despite the rain, she was more vulnerable on this open stretch of moorland. With no trees, her hurrying figure stood out against the vast emptiness.

In the contrary way of the moor, the rain stopped abruptly. Sunshine broke through and beat down on her. She loosened the thin blanket from her shoulders and tied it round her waist. When the sun was out it made her hot; as soon as it went in she was cold again. She looked up at the sky, alarmed to see that the sun was further down the horizon than she had realised.

'Hot or cold, it's not good to be out on the moor in the dark,' she said aloud, although there was no one to hear – at least, she hoped there wasn't.

'What a stupid thing to say. I know that,' she answered herself.

The rain had made a quagmire of the track. She was sliding on the mud as if she were wearing skates rather than her serviceable boots. At any other time this would have made her laugh but not today. Twice she fell and her skirt, not clean at the best of times, was soon caked and heavy with mud. The hem slapped coldly against her calves.

Another sudden downpour, common in these parts, made her race towards an isolated tree. It was so bent from the relentless wind that she had to double up to shelter beneath it. She crouched there reassuring herself that it was only rain: there was no thunder and lightning.

When she had set off from her home, terror had dulled the pain. Now, as feeling returned, she ached all over. There was a stabbing sensation in her ribs, she'd ricked an ankle, her head hurt where his boot had landed, and she was sure her knee was swelling and badly grazed.

The rain subsided, and although she wished she could stay and rest she made herself set off again. At last she reached the lane, which dipped steeply down into the valley. It was bounded by trees, bowed low by the constant wind, that formed a tunnel of greenery. When it was dry and hot such lanes offered welcome shade, but Phoebe knew that on a day like this the trees would drip on her even though the rain had stopped. She undid the blanket, placed it over her head and plunged into the darkness made by the canopy of trees. 'If it rains any more, I'll catch a chill,' she announced.

'Then you should have thought of that. It's always raining on Dartmoor!'

Either side of her, water tumbled in the ditches. Ruts in the soil, made by the constant passage of carts and wagons, were awash. She had to concentrate hard on where to place her feet. At the bottom of the dark lane, the water in the ford had changed from a trickle into a torrent. She would have to wade across or manoeuvre along the banks to find an easier place to cross. She chose to remove her boots. She tied the laces together, then placed them safely around her neck – she wore no stockings since she owned none. She pulled up her sodden skirt, knotting the fabric in front of her. Clutching that, her blanket and the small bundle she had been able to bring with her, she waded into the water, pushing against the current that was hungrily pulling her sideways. She looked down and saw her slim legs coloured a ghostly green in the crystal clear water. 'At least there's no snakes – too cold,' she said, to cheer herself.

Once on the other side, she shivered. Her teeth were chattering now, making her sound, she was sure, like a woodpecker. She paused to wash her face, which must look a sight, and rearranged her clothes.

Ahead there was a fork in the road. The left she knew would take her straight to Widecombe; the right would circle the village and was the longer, steeper route. Since she feared meeting someone who knew her father, she look the longer way, and started wearily up the steep hill in front of her.

At the top she paused to catch her breath and looked down into the valley. The shadows were darkening rapidly in the village, and she could smell the sweet scent of burning wood spiralling up from the cottages. It made her long to be cosy and warm. Then she saw a storm lantern swaying back and forth, being lifted to swing in the breeze. That would be the pot-man hooking up the light outside the Old Inn. Perhaps she had been over-cautious: maybe she should rest there – the landlord's daughter might let her sleep in the barn. Phoebe barely knew the girl but she always smiled kindly at her – not like most of those hereabouts who, fearing her father and his wrath, avoided her and her brothers.

'Not much sense in thinking that. How do you know you could trust her?' she asked herself.

' 'Er wouldn't tell on me.'

'Oh, no? What if her father beat it out of she?'

She stared down at the welcoming light, imagining warmth, good food . . . Not that she'd be given any.

The lane's hedges protected her from the stiff breeze that was blowing up now. There was a maze of such pathways around every village on the moor, snaking out like green capillaries, but the trees and bushes that bordered them soon became sparse as the moor once more encroached. No trees grew there and only the tufted grass was hardy enough to withstand the weather.

Within minutes it was as if the valley, with its cottages, gardens and mighty trees, its dogs barking and women calling, had been a figment of her imagination, except for the pungent scent of woodsmoke that still lodged in her nostrils.

Now the moor took control again. This was unfamiliar territory for Widecombe was the furthest she had ever travelled in this direction. The wind, colder here at the top, was whipping at her clothes, as if it was playing with her – 'Or trying to tear them off!' her other voice said. Bitter cold would quickly follow. She looked anxiously to the north and saw angry black clouds.

'That's a big storm brewing and no mistake.'

'You should have waited until morning.'

'I might have been dead by then.'

She began to warble 'Onward Christian Soldiers' to give her courage. She couldn't remember all the words – it had been such a long time since she had sung them . . . when her mother had been alive and they had walked each Sunday to the parish church.

'Oh, Mum . . .' She sighed, and the longing for her mother returned as it so often did.

'No good thinking that way,' she told herself stoutly. 'She's gone and you're on your own, Phoebe, my girl!'

She liked to sing, and that was the reason she was trudging across the inhospitable moor now. Remembering what had happened made her sing louder, as if in defiance of her father who had banned it long ago. 'Ungodly', he called it, as he called so many things – colours, pretty hair combs, ribbons, lace on petticoats. Whistling was for the devil, he'd said, as were cards, alcohol, stained-glass windows, dancing, bonnets – in short anything pleasurable. The church was too papist.

She missed the hymns and the rituals but not, she had to admit, the sermons, which were invariably too long. Instead she had been made to attend meetings in the homes of others like her father. The whole of Sunday was devoted to praying and listening to the Scriptures. No food or even water was allowed.

How could such things be ungodly, Phoebe had wondered, when God had made everything? But it was a thought she should have kept quiet. Today her father had crept up behind her when she was singing softly to herself as she cleaned the parlour.

'Stop that noise!' he had bellowed.

'God gave me a voice, so I'll use it.'

'What did you'm say?' He had glowered at her.

'Nothing.'

'Don't lie, you spawn of Satan! I demand to know.'

She looked up at him and her insides felt as if they were turning to water. His stare bored into her. 'Pity it was your mother went to her Maker and not you.'

Don't mention my mother. I grieve for her, but she's better off where she is, than living in this hell-hole with you. She wanted to say it but she hadn't the courage.

'What did you'm say?' He took a step towards her, arm raised.

'Very well. You asked.' She had put her hands on her hips, in a show of defiance she was far from feeling, and taken a deep breath. 'Why did God make nice things if He don't want us to enjoy them?'

'Blasphemer! Whore of the devil! Godless bitch!' And so began the worst beating she had ever endured. As the blows rained down on her, her father's face distorted so that he himself looked like the devil. His eyes bulged, his colour was choleric, and as he screamed to God to deliver her he showered her with spittle. She thought he had finally gone mad. She tried to escape him by slithering away across the stone floor, scraping her knee, twisting her ankle, but he caught her and began to lambast her

5

with his belt, then a stick and finally his boot. 'I'll beat the devil out of you if it's the last thing I do!' he roared.

She rolled over to avoid him and he lost his balance long enough for her to scramble to her feet. 'Then I hope it is!' she had screamed back, as he lunged for her again. From somewhere she had found the strength to push him away and he had fallen backwards, struck his head on the old wooden dresser and crumpled in a heap at her feet. She hoped he was dead, but he got to his feet groggily. She had the wit to move out of his way as he took up the small axe he used to chop the firewood. She had backed away from him into the scullery, and slammed the door shut as the axe crashed into the other side.

She had bolted it and pushed the heavy table against it. Her brother was cowering in the corner by the copper. 'Big help you were, Jim!' She opened the small cupboard in which they stored their food and grabbed some cheese, then took a loaf from the bread crock. She tipped the salt out of its tin and scrabbled for the few pennies she had hidden there.

'What you doing?'

'Leaving. I can't stay here a moment longer.'

'But you're all bloody!'

'It'll wash off.'

'Where you going?'

'As if I'd tell you and have you sneak on me!'

'I never would.'

'And pigs might fly.'

'Can I come with you?'

'I'll send for you one day when I'm rich and famous.' Despite everything, she grinned at him.

She had moved speedily out of the back door, across the yard and down the lane. If she rested she would stiffen – she knew that from past beatings. It would be best to move off the path and cut across the fields.

She had no way of telling the time, but she thought at

least four hours must have gone by since she'd left home. She had wanted to be off the moor before nightfall. She stepped off the path towards a huddle of rocks. Few would come this way but she didn't want to be seen: gossip was rife among the folk round here, and her father would find out which direction she had taken.

With night falling, she walked gingerly, for fear of stepping into a bog. A mighty crag loomed in the distance. She wondered if it was Haytor, which she knew only from afar. She sat down on one of the rocks and began to tear at the bread and cheese.

Her brother Dick had run away after a similar beating. 'If I don't go I'll kill the evil sod,' he'd explained to Phoebe, when she begged him not to leave her.

'I wish you would,' she said, and stood on tiptoe to kiss him goodbye.

'And be hanged? For him? He's not worth it.'

'You'm right. Let him live. After all, he bain't happy. Let's keep him in his misery. Where will you go?'

'I've asked Mrs Benson if I could send her messages for you. I'm sure she won't tell. She and the vicar are no friends of Father. I'll send for you and Jim when I'm settled. That's a promise.'

In the beginning she had gone every day to the vicarage to see if there was anything from him, but there never was. Then she'd gone once a week, and eventually once a month.

After two years she had given up all hope of hearing from him when a letter came. Dick had not written it himself, because he could neither write nor read, and Mrs Benson had read it to her since neither could Phoebe. It told her that he was in the army and happy with his lot.

'Dick a soldier, well I never! He'll be a general before we know it,' Phoebe had said, bursting with pride.

'Most certainly, dear Phoebe.' Mrs Benson had smiled kindly.

'Does he say when we're to join him?'

'No, my dear.'

Another six months passed before another letter arrived, which had told her he was being shipped to the Cape. 'And where's that?'

'Africa.'

Phoebe had never heard of Africa either. 'Mrs Benson, can we keep about Dick and the letter a secret?'

'Yes, Phoebe. Unless, that is, your father asks me a direct question. I cannot lie.'

Why not? Phoebe had thought.

Now she took a small bite of cheese. 'Surely there are good lies? Why shouldn't she lie for me? 'Twould only be a little one.'

'A vicar's wife has no choice.'

'Seems daft to me.' She wrenched a piece of bread from the loaf.

'You shouldn't have left Jim.'

'And what would I have done with him in tow? Dad won't hurt him. It's Dick and me he hates.'

'He'll be lonely.'

'When I've made my fortune, when I've met and married the man of my dreams, when I'm rich, I'll send for him.'

She grinned.

She leaned back against the rock and looked up at the darkening sky. What wouldn't she give for some hot water and her bed? 'If wishes were horses, beggars would ride.'

Phoebe had always talked to herself. It was another of the many things about her that annoyed her father. He said she communed with the devil but Phoebe knew better. From the day she had learned to talk she had held long conversations with herself.

'It bain't the devil in me, Mum, honest,' she had said one night after her father had shouted that it was just that. Now he was snoring in the room over their heads, and the two women were huddled over the dwindling fire, whispering to each other for fear of waking him.

'I know, my maid ... Perhaps it's time I told you something.'

'What?'

Her mother beckoned Phoebe closer. 'If I tell, you might be afeared.'

'I won't.'

'And promise never to tell?'

'I won't.'

Her mother lowered her voice even further and Phoebe strained to hear what she said. 'You'm a twin.'

Phoebe sat bolt upright. 'A twin? But where is her?'

'Shush, he'll hear.' She motioned nervously to the ceiling above. 'You came first and then your sister, but she was dead.' Her mother's eyes filled with tears. Phoebe wanted to hear more immediately but she had to wait for her mother to compose herself. 'I've often wondered when I've heard you chattering away if her soul stayed in your body and it's her you talk to.'

'I always knew it was something like that,' Phoebe said, with quiet satisfaction.

'Then it doesn't frighten you?'

'Not a bit. It makes me feel ...' she searched for the right word '... Peaceful with meself. But why must Father never know you've told me?'

'He thinks my carrying two ... well, that it was—'

'The devil's work!' Phoebe interrupted, and laughed. 'You know, Mum, for someone who loves God he never gives Him any credit for the good things.'

'Guard your tongue, my dear heart, or it'll be the death of you.'

'I'll try,' she said, then asked, 'Did she have a name?'

'Of course, and laid to rest in a Christian burial – not that your father would have anything to do with it.'

'What did you call her?' Phoebe prodded.

'Phyllis. The ancients thought that Phyllis died for love . . . and became an almond tree.'

'That tree in the garden, the one you love so much?' It never failed to amaze Phoebe how much her mother knew, uneducated as she was.

Now to Phoebe her sister was not dead: she was always with her, a companion when she needed her – as she did now, alone on the moor and trying not to be afraid.

It would have been better if she had lived, but this was the next best thing. And she knew that, without Phyllis to talk to, the loneliness after her mother died would have been much worse. She had often been drawn to one grave in the churchyard, and was convinced now that it was where her sister lay. The family had been unable to afford a proper grave and the baby had been placed in the coffin of an adult who was to be buried that day, 'so she won't be lonely,' her mother had explained.

'Where is she buried?'

'I'll show you tomorrow afternoon.'

But the next day, on the way back from the market, her mother had been struck by lightning. Her injuries were so dreadful that none of her children was allowed to bid her farewell.

Phoebe regretted that she hadn't dared risk visiting the graves to say goodbye before she had left home.

'What would have been the point? I'm here, aren't I?' said Phyllis's voice.

'Of course. No need.' But there was, really.

'Come on, it's getting dark.'

'Shall we stay here for the night or carry on?'

'Best keep moving.

Phoebe packed up the rest of the bread and cheese, and wound the blanket tightly round herself.

Once it was dark she began to enjoy herself. It was a

clear night and she could see every star in the sky. For the next two hours she made good progress. Eventually she saw lights in the distance. Perhaps it was a village or, even better, a town. She did not know which because she had never been so far across the moor before. Everything now was unfamiliar. The wind was loud, not that it frightened her – she was used to it – but it prevented her hearing the rattle of the coach behind her. The snort of a horse and a curse made her move quickly to the side of the road. She looked up just in time to see in the window a ghost-like man smiling at her. He looked eerie, but she smiled back and waved.

A little further along the road the coach drew to a clattering halt. The door opened and the man stepped out. He was smartly dressed, smarter even than her father when he donned his Sunday suit, and his hair was white. In the dark he looked even more ghost-like, with his pale skin and colourless lips . . .

'What is a pretty young woman like you doing walking on the moor at this time of night?'

'I felt like a stroll,' she said. He didn't sound like a spirit.

'Cheeky too.' He laughed, as if her reply had pleased him. 'Have you run away?'

'No,' she lied.

'No angry father or brother out searching for you?'

'I'm an orphan,' she lied again.

'How convenient. Would you care to ride with me?'

It was dark, she was tired and her feet hurt. 'That'd be nice,' she said, although she felt unsure.

'Up with the coachman, I think. You're somewhat dishevelled for the inside of my coach.'

'I expect I am.'

She climbed up beside the coachman, who moved pointedly to distance himself from her. She laughed. It didn't matter to her.

Arnold Randolph-Smythe was walking to his office as he did every morning when the weather was fine. If it rained, his coachman would be at the door at seven forty-five on the dot, but he preferred to walk.

He liked to vary his route each day from his fine villa, built to his own specifications eighteen years ago, overlooking the Devonshire market town of Barlton. During his walk he checked the neighbouring houses – he found that he learned much that way. He was not comparing them with his own: he knew without doubt that his was the finest. Rather, he was looking for the first signs of neglect – an untended garden indicated that things were not well with the inhabitants. When fiscal problems arose the gardener was invariably the first to go.

If he knew the occupants of a house and they were his customers, a neglected garden told him to watch their accounts, and perhaps take the ultimate action – cease offering them credit. This was always a delicate matter. He did not wish to offend them in case their fortunes recovered.

If he did not know them he would endeavour to meet them and become friendly with them, which was not difficult in this town of sixty thousand souls where he was well respected. For the most part his offers of financial help were gratefully accepted, and even when they weren't he knew to bide his time, for eventually they would be. He was not of the middle classes, although he hoped no one had realised this, but he understood them. They found it less shaming to deal with him, their 'friend', than banks or money-lenders. And it was easy to make them think he was doing them a favour. In their panic they never queried the interest rate or how it compounded. If his loan got them out of a mess they were far too grateful to mention the amount he had made from them. If it made matters worse his constant demands for settlement ensured they were drummed out of town. If the problems were too great, and a loan too risky, all was not lost: he was the first to ask if he might buy their jewellery, paintings, furniture, houses and even their businesses.

He did not restrict himself to the villas in his own area. Once down the steep hill, he cast his eye over more rows of houses. Property here went for a song, and he was accumulating it at a satisfying rate.

'Good day to you, Cooper.' He had reached the street where the shops began and had spoken graciously to the butcher, who was manhandling a life-sized wooden pig, painted an alarming pink, on to the pavement.

'The same to you, Mr Randolph-Smythe, sir.'

Arnold passed along the row of shops uttering a word of greeting to all with whom he traded. He was well known for prompt payment of his bills, which ensured that he was greeted as befitted an upstanding citizen.

Not that he had always been such. Neither had his name always been Arnold Randolph-Smythe, but 'Arnold Smith' was not nearly as impressive. He had been amused by the change in attitudes to him brought about by a *y*, an extra *e* and a hyphen.

'A fine day, Mrs Fanshaw.' He doffed his top hat, bowed, and bestowed a charming smile on the simpering woman as she emerged from her front door.

'You're late this morning Mr Randolph-Smythe.'

He removed his half-hunter from his pocket and flipped open the lid. 'Why, by five minutes only, Mrs Fanshaw.'

'But, Mr Randolph-Smythe, we set our clocks by you.'

'Is that all? You disappoint me. I had been hoping you had been waiting for *me*.'

'Oh, Mr Randolph-Smythe!' She tittered.

He strode on, certain that her greedy eyes were on him.

If he were king he'd pass a law forbidding middle-aged and ugly women to flirt. How could she think he might be interested in her gross, bloated body? He swung his silver-topped cane through the air as if slicing away the idea. He was sure that women like her only saw in their mirror what they wanted to see and not what was there. Each morning he stripped naked and studied himself at every angle with the professional eye of an artist. Each day he checked dark brown hair for the first sign of grey, but it was still as dark as it had been on his wedding day, twenty-three years ago. Nasal and ear hairs were ruthlessly torn out: neglect in these areas betrayed a man of scant self-respect. He preferred to shave himself: he had not trusted a man with a razor since the day he'd seen his father slash his mother's throat. He kept his moustache short but immaculate, and his firmly muscled body in trim.

Sometimes fat on others had to be ignored: the patronage of women like Mrs Fanshaw was essential to his wallet. He treated her as she wished to be treated – he was aware that his fortune was based on his charm.

Soon he turned into St Mary's Close. He attended church, although he felt no need for the Almighty's help. After all, he did well enough on his own. It was a shame St Mary's was not a cathedral, but one day perhaps . . .

He had every intention of becoming mayor of this town and then he would apply for a charter. When it was granted his name would be spoken with awe a hundred years from now. He was already a councillor, had been an alderman for two years, and some were pushing him to accept the mayoralty. But he was waiting for the old Queen to die: he wanted to be associated with the new, not the old. But the old girl was still going strong. Had he been her son he'd have helped her into paradise a long time ago. With a new king there would be changes a-plenty, not least socially: the Prince was far more liberal than his mother in his choice of friends. When Edward was on the throne shopkeepers, such as himself, upstanding citizens, such as himself, rich men, such as himself, might even be elevated to the peerage. That was his aim. And, like everything in his life, he expected to achieve it.

Meanwhile he worshipped Society rather than God. He was a member of the County Club, which gave him access to the gentry – who were now his clients – if not local aristocrats, but it would happen. He would like to know the latter socially but was less sure that he wanted them as customers: he had discovered long ago that the higher the stratum of a customer's class, the more loath he was to pay out his money.

He often reflected on what a wise choice Barlton had been. There was money in these parts. 'A wise man looks for sheep,' he had told his startled wife before they moved. 'Where there's sheep there's money to be made.' And he had been right. In the twenty years they had been in the town he had watched his shop grow from a small haberdashery into a magnificent department store. With the greater frequency of trains people travelled more, with the advent of automobiles on the roads they would begin to travel even further. Clothes and accoutrements had to be purchased to match those of their city friends. Entertaining was on the increase as people were able to move more easily from village to village – and this was just the beginning of a new era of transport. He had been right. But then, he thought, wasn't he always?

He paused on the corner of Coxswain's Passage and the high street, as he did every morning, and looked to the right. There it was, smartly painted in black, the swirling gold lettering standing out in bold contrast: Randolph's Emporium. It was a sight that never failed to impress him, and he glowed with satisfaction. He crossed the street and walked past all of its windows – large, well lit, modern – inspecting the merchandise displayed, considering what needed changing, brightening, subduing.

'Mr Randolph-Smythe, sir!' The uniformed doorman lifted his hand to his gold-braided cap, then jumped to attention like the soldier he had been.

'Good morning, Shepperton.' The door was held wide for him to enter. It was his practice to show politeness to those he employed, no matter what he thought of them. It was easy enough, cost nothing, and he was repaid in their loyalty.

His progress through the shop was the high spot of his day: it assured him of his own importance. He could sense the atmosphere of anticipation, the frisson of tension in the air. His staff were wondering if he had noticed anything lacking, whether he would compliment or chide them as he passed their polished counters.

He had installed armchairs, with low tables beside them near to the door for customers to study the pattern books at their leisure. Then, as he did now, they would walk between the long mahogany counters, on which were laid the bolts of fine fabrics in every colour known to man.

'How is the chartreuse silk selling, Miss Fitch?'

'Very well, sir. We shall need to order more.'

He wrote this down in the notebook he always carried with him. 'I am gratified but surprised, I must admit. It's a bold colour.'

'Quite difficult for some to wear, I fear.'

'You should never sell it to someone if it is unsuitable, Miss Fitch. They will blame us, not their own colouring.'

The woman blushed alarmingly. 'But I never do, sir. I always try to guide my ladies to what is most becoming for them. Some cannot be moved from their choice, sir, and then what am I to do?'

'A dilemma, but I rely on your diplomacy, Miss Fitch. Why, you are like a spiritual adviser – you are their salvation.'

'Oh, Mr Randolph-Smythe!' Miss Fitch gushed, showing her teeth. A mistake.

He turned abruptly and entered Haberdashery. 'A button.' He pointed with his cane. Two young assistants raced at the same time to pick it up.

'It must have rolled there, sir,' the prettier of the two told him.

It was always the same, he thought. The better-looking they were, the more confident and cheeky. He liked taming that sort. 'Buttons cost money.'

'I'm sorry, Mr Smythe.'

'And lost buttons mean less profit.'

'I understand.'

'And less profit means a cut in your wages.

'Yes, sir.' The girl looked close to tears now. That was better: she was far less confident and far more malleable.

'What is your name?'

'Rosie Grainger, sir.'

'Well, Miss Grainger, I shall remember your name, and I would like you to do me the courtesy of remembering mine. It is Randolph-Smythe. It always has been and always will be.' He chose then to smile at her.

'Sir,' she said, in confusion. An hour later she was even more confused when he passed again and arranged an assignation with her. She longed to tell the other assistants, but he had been adamant that their meeting should remain a secret. It would be more exciting if only the two of them knew about it.

Haberdashery was a particular favourite with him: he had begun his career counting buttons. No one knew except Dulcie, of course – he made sure of that: the small shop had been in a seedy part of Chatham, a part of his life he would prefer no one knew about.

There was a cunning logic to the layout of his store that was lacking in others. He had planned it long before he had acquired the premises. A woman would enter and purchase a pattern. Then she would see the display of silks, arranged close by, and enter the fabric department. From there it was a mere step to selecting the buttons, hooks, eyes, cotton and ribbons needed to complete her outfit. She was moved effortlessly along without realising it. It was so simple, yet other shops were invariably cluttered chaos. Arnold liked order.

The other departments were arranged in a similar manner. Ladies' Fashions was on the first floor. When the shop was open he rarely ventured there – for decorum's sake – but now he climbed the wide, carpeted staircase, checking the brass rail for fingermarks. He walked through the sections just as his customers would. Having selected their garments and been advised on their lingerie, the ladies were led unsuspectingly through the shoe, handbag, hat and glove departments, and left the shop with everything they needed.

Ladies' Fashions was a great success. Long before his competitors, Arnold had moved into ready-made garments. Here, there were rows of gowns, jackets and coats, which meant that women could be better dressed than they had ever dreamed possible at half the price. Yes, he was an innovator and proud of it.

He was continually expanding his stock. He had recently begun to sell furniture to go with the curtains he had been making for some time. This had meant buying the building adjacent to the main shop and, unfortunately, had led to an unpleasant scene in the County Club with old Markham, who owned the largest furniture store in Barlton. But it couldn't be helped. 'Business is business,' he had explained, not that the man had listened. And Agnes, his daughter, had not been pleased either: unbeknown to Arnold, she had set her cap at Markham's son, Robert. 'Just as well I caused a furore,' Arnold told his wife. 'I've plans for Agnes and they do not include a shopkeeper's son.'

'But what is she if not a shopkeeper's daughter?'

'And what a shopkeeper, Dulcie. I'm a cut above the rest, don't you think?'

Dulcie had bestowed on him her usual cynical expression. It was difficult to remember that once she had looked at him with adoration. Now it was with dislike that sometimes verged on hatred. Not that it bothered him.

At one time, falling out with Markham would have upset him. Not any longer: he had wealth, and he had learned that nothing made a man more popular and acceptable in small-town society than a fine house, a spanking carriage and a packed wallet. Money was power.

3

Every weekday morning, at eight twenty-five, Lily Howard's skin tingled and her stomach fluttered. In five minutes exactly she would see the man she loved. She checked her watch against the clock on the wall, and checked it again seconds later. The watch, bequeathed to her by her grandmother, hung on a long gold chain over her meagre cleavage. It was the only thing of value she possessed. She glanced surreptitiously into the mirror over the fireplace to check her mouse-coloured hair, then swung round sharply at a suppressed giggle. Edith, her assistant, was bowed over a ledger. 'Yes?' Lily demanded.

'I'm sorry?' Edith looked up, blue eyes wide with false innocence.

Lily hated those eyes. 'You were amused? By something I did?'

'No, Miss Howard. I'm not sure what you mean.'

Her smile was insufferably smug and Lily felt an almost uncontrollable urge to slap her hard. 'You laughed.'

'Me? No, Miss Howard. I stifled a sneeze.' She fiddled with a blonde curl and returned to her bookkeeping.

Cheeky slut! 'I haven't finished speaking to you.'

'I'm so sorry, Miss Howard. Yes?' She was attentive now, her skin glowing with youth and health.

Lily eyed her with loathing fuelled by jealousy. 'Get on with your work.'

'I was, Miss Howard . . .' Edith muttered something more that Lily didn't catch. Sense, at last, told her to ignore the girl.

She returned to her desk. The room was small and she longed for the days when she had worked here alone. Then it had been her sanctuary, and *he* had been just a few feet away, his presence such a comfort, such an excitement. It had all been spoilt when this – this *whore* had been foisted upon her.

She tidied her desk. At the sound of footsteps in the corridor outside she stood up, smoothed down her skirt, patted her bun and ignored the snigger that, this time, was unmistakable. The door swung open.

'Miss Howard. You look particularly well this fine morning.' Lily felt her colour rise as she thought frantically of words with which to respond. 'And you, Miss Edith, look positively beautiful,' he continued, before, sadly, she had found them.

'Why, thank you, and you look particularly handsome yourself, sir!' Edith's long lashes fluttered. Life was so unfair, thought Lily. Those clear blue eyes were augmented by such perfect curly dark lashes.

Lily felt bleak. Why had *she* not thought of such a reply? 'The letters you asked for, Mr Randolph-Smythe, are on your desk awaiting your signature,' she said briskly, determined to regain his attention.

'Thank you, Miss Howard. A cup of coffee would be most appreciated.'

'I have already ordered it, sir.'

'The newspaper?'

'At your desk.'

'Biscuits—'

'With your coffee.'

'But you didn't let me finish, Miss Howard. I don't want any biscuits this morning. I would prefer a poached egg on toast.'

'If you so wish, sir.' She felt destroyed, as if she should have known what his choice would be.

'I *very much* wish,' he said, a little too pointedly for comfort.

'I shall attend to it immediately.'

'I thought you would, Miss Howard.'

This time Edith Baker made no attempt to hide her grin. But for Lily, when he entered his office, it was as if the sun had disappeared. 'Get his poached egg, Edith. Three minutes not a second longer, and hurry,' she ordered.

'He asked you, not me.'

'Miss Baker! Do I hear you correctly?'

'I'm not his cook.'

'You won't be his clerk either, if you don't do as I say.'

She watched Edith's upright figure glide across the room. So undignified the way she moved, insinuating herself, like a snake or a lizard. The girl obviously thought it attractive – how could she be so stupid?

She checked his diary, which was pointless since she knew every entry she had made for him. But when she was angry with the girl she always found it better to keep busy. It was a sure way of damping down the irritation she had felt constantly since Edith had joined the firm four weeks ago. She had protested to Arnold – in her mind she always thought of him by his Christian name – that she needed no assistant.

'We can't have you overworking, can we?' he had replied. 'I insist. And I want no more disagreement.' He had wagged his finger at her in the delightful playful way that always made her feel quite skittish. She had had to give in to him, but planned to ensure that he knew how bad Edith's work was. Yet each time she pointed out the girl's mistakes he brushed them aside.

'A spelling error? She has an elderly widowed mother to care for, *dear* Miss Howard . . .'

'Sixpence? A small mistake. She needs this employment, *dear* Miss Howard . . .'

'A blot on the ledger? She will learn. We must be patient, *dear* Miss Howard . . .'

On hearing those words Lily had been in turmoil. On the one hand she felt a frisson of joy at the endearment, but on the other she wanted to tell him that she, too, had a widowed mother, needed the work and the little money she earned from it, but he'd never had cause to be patient with her.

However, such reflections would not get her through the day and the mountain of tasks she had to do, as well as having to check everything Edith did. She opened the wooden cover of her writing machine. Arnold called it 'the stenographic machine', but she preferred her own name for it. She checked that the revolving wheel was moving freely, then cleaned the keys, which tended to clog with ink from the reservoir. Edith envied her and Lily knew she longed to try it, but she would never allow that: it was Lily's, *she* had the skill.

Arnold was always so progressive. As far as she knew he was the only member of the business community in Barlton who had female office staff; all the others had male clerks. He had been to America to seek out new ideas for his shop, and had brought back the writing machine for her. She always felt that her fine copperplate hand was faster and that the finished correspondence looked better, but he had been so excited by his purchase that she had struggled to learn.

She could still remember the day, nearly fifteen years ago, when she had applied for this position. Her mother had been dismissive. 'What sort of man employs women in his office?' she had asked suspiciously, when Lily had shown her the advertisement – to which only 'ladies' might apply. 'No doubt he's a white-slave trafficker – not that you've got anything to fear. He'd have to pay them to take you!' She had laughed. Not for the first time, Lily had longed to kill her.

She would always remember the nervousness she had felt as, with the other applicants, she had sat in the hot, fusty waiting room and waited her turn. Three were so attractive that she had resigned herself to failure: who would want to look across their desk at her when they could have a vision of beauty each morning? She was just about to leave when her name was called.

The minute she entered his office her life changed.

Standing by a large mahogany desk, a warm smile on his face, his hand out in greeting, stood the man of her dreams.

She felt her heart pitter-patter in a most unfamiliar manner, and she blushed. She found herself wondering if this was love – she had so often imagined and wondered about it.

When she was told that the position was hers she was sure that he must have made a mistake. Of course, it was somewhat marred for her that his wife had been present at the interview, which had been disconcerting, and even more so since the woman barely spoke. Consequently Lily often wondered if she had been chosen because she was the plainest applicant. But she kept the thought locked away in the back of her mind.

Now, at thirty-three, she had long given up any hope of romance, let alone a husband and children. She was too lacking in beauty and self-assurance. Her hips might be slim but, unfortunately her chest was flat. A prettier face might have compensated for her lack of womanly curves, but her spectacles made her eyes – pale grey and her best feature – look unattractively watery.

It was sad that Arnold was married, but Lily's hopes reawakened when she considered Dulcie. She was never too sure what she hoped for: he couldn't marry her, and the alternative made her break out in perspiration even to think of it. But there was no doubt that she was better-looking than his wife. While Lily veered towards plain, Dulcie Randolph-Smythe was downright ugly, with her thin hair, hooked nose, lack of chin and the wart on her cheek. As if this was not enough, she was fat – not plump, not motherly, but gross, which Lily abhorred. 'When she moves, her flesh takes time to catch up,' she had told her mother gleefully.

Unfortunately for Lily, though, Dulcie had the one commodity that blinded all suitors: money. And she was kind and generous, so it was impossible to hate her. She never forgot Lily's birthday, there was always a gift for her at Christmas, and she never failed to ask after her mother.

One of the kitchen staff brought in the coffee she had ordered, ending Lily's reverie. She took it and bustled into his office. 'Your coffee, Mr Randolph-Smythe,' she said.

'Thank you, Miss Howard . . . This letter, I think you have made a mistake.'

'A mistake!' She moved to his side of the desk, light-headed at her proximity to him.

'Here.' He stabbed at the page with a perfectly manicured finger. 'Surely it should read "comiserate", not "commiserate" as you have written it.'

She was in a quandary. Should she point out that he was wrong? Should she change it even though it was correct?

'How remiss of me, sir.'

'Only angels can be perfect, Miss Howard. And how often do you make mistakes? Rarely.'

Wrong, Arnold, she thought, I *never* make them. 'I shall correct it immediately.'

'Thank you, Miss Howard.'

She returned to her desk as Edith appeared with his

breakfast tray. She put out her hands to take it, as she did whenever he ordered food. Today, on seeing that the egg yolk was broken and the toast had been scraped, she changed her mind. 'You give it to him. I don't want him thinking I was responsible for such a disgusting-looking dish.'

She flounced to her desk, feeling better now that Edith would be in trouble. But the darkness returned when she heard laughter in the next room.

4

Phoebe had been awake for a good half-hour. She was stiff and every part of her body ached, but even if it hadn't she wouldn't have wanted to get up. This bed is what Paradise must be like, she thought. She did not know what to do or where to go, and after the housekeeper's unfriendliness last night she was afraid to do anything to annoy her.

Mrs White was almost as fearsome as Phoebe's father and, no doubt, could hit nearly as hard. She had been reasonable when Phoebe's rescuer had been present, but as soon as Mr Bartholomew – as she had learned he was called – had left the room, she had pushed, pinched and scolded her. 'Filth, that's what you are. And filthy. A bath for you, young woman, before you're allowed to set one foot upstairs, make no mistake.'

She had been plonked into a tin bath in the scullery, and Mrs White had seemed to take pleasure in scrubbing her flesh with a hard brush and carbolic soap. She was quick to learn that the more she squealed the harder the woman scrubbed, so she bit her lip. It was as if Mrs White was angry with her, though why that should be when Phoebe had done nothing was a mystery. When soap got into her eyes from the torrent of water poured over her soaped hair she could not stop herself. 'Then you should have kept your eyes shut, no good yelping at me, you silly girl!'

'I can dry myself,' she protested, when Mrs White approached her with a skimpy towel.

'Shut your mouth!'

The towel felt like brambles. 'Funny you'm called White when your hair and everything else is so black.'

The slap stung, but it was worth it for Phoebe had enjoyed annoying her. She would have liked to add, 'Even your moustache!' but she didn't have the courage.

She had been pushed up the back stairs, Mrs White muttering and prodding her until she stumbled, whereupon the housekeeper kicked her.

'Hold hard! Who do you think you are, shoving a body about like that?'

'And who do you think you are, then? Miss Hoity-Toity.'

'I didn't come here to be treated like this. I'm going.' She turned and stared angrily at the woman.

'Oh, no, you don't!' Mrs White barred her way.

'Don't you tell me what I can and can't do! You tell His Nibs I don't like it here. And I don't like you.' Phoebe pushed her aside – and, with the intuition she had needed to survive living with her father, knew that the woman was suddenly afraid.

'You can't. You've no clothes!' Mrs White wailed. 'And on a night like this!' As if to underline her words there was a flash of lightning followed by a clap of thunder. Phoebe screamed and covered her ears with her hands.

'Changed your mind, have you? Come along with me.' Meekly she followed.

Expecting an attic room, she had been astonished to be shown into this one. She had not been aware that such grandeur and luxury existed. Until now, the finest she had seen was the vicar's parlour, which was nothing like this. This room had lights that were controlled by a knob at the door. It had frightened her so much she had refused to touch it, so Mrs White had plunged her into darkness. She had hidden under the pillows, cowed by the mighty storm that raged outside, convinced that the same fate would befall her as her mother.

Now, however, with the sun stealing in through a gap in the curtains, the fears of the night were forgotten. Phoebe saw that the room was even more splendid than she had realised. The wall above her bed was covered with paper over which had been painted colourful flowers and exotic birds. The walls at home were rough-cast and whitewashed. Even more extraordinary, the birds and flowers were in a pattern that was repeated all over: when she found the blue bird she knew there would be mauve flowers beside it. It must have taken someone ages to paint.

Curtains hung at the windows; they were made of a shiny fabric with gold thread woven through it. 'Blimey! I bet even the Queen don't live like this.' At home there was sacking.

She hauled herself out of bed and padded across the thick carpet – more colour, more flowers – how soft it felt, how wonderful. She yanked at the curtains with effort since they were heavy and her ribs still hurt. The sun blazed into the room. She peeked out of the window. Below, she saw an enormous garden, not like the small one they had. It was surrounded by a high wall, not a rickety fence to be seen, and planted with hundreds of bushes and flowers – there wasn't a vegetable anywhere. Beyond the wall there was a park with huge trees, they'd be worth a bob or two when felled she decided. Beyond the park she could see the purple and mauve smudge of hills. It was the moor, stretching into the distance as far as she could see. The sight of it made her shudder: she had hoped to be further away than this.

She turned back into the room and studied the large paintings on the walls, all of nude women. 'Look how fat they are. Have you ever seen such great big arses?' she asked herself. 'Imagine what Dad would say if he saw them!'

'"Filth, evil nudity, work of the devil!"'

'I'd give anything to see his face.'

'I wouldn't. Don't want he here, spoiling everything.'

She heard a noise outside the door, leaped back into bed, covered herself and pretended to be asleep.

Someone entered the room and she heard the clink of china. 'You're to eat and then dress.'

Phoebe stretched in the bed, still feigning sleep.

'I know you're awake, you can't fool me.'

Phoebe opened her eyes to find Mrs White in aggressive stance. She tried to smile engagingly, which did not work judging by the woman's expression. 'Eat and dress.'

'But you took my clothes away.'

'Burnt the lot, I did too. Filthy with lice they were.'

'They never were. How dare you?'

'I dared. And don't you *dare* to speak to me in that tone! Dress. Mr Bartholomew wants you to take luncheon with him. Understand?'

'Yes, Miss.'

'Mrs White to you.'

'Yes, Mrs White.'

'Be ready by noon.'

'Yes, Mrs White.'

'Can you tell the time?'

'No.'

'Stupid child! Then I shall call for you. I know every item in this room – in the whole house, come to that – so don't you think about pocketing anything or I'll have the constable on to you faster than you can say "knife". Understood?'

'Yes.' There seemed to be no point in protesting at the implied accusation. She had no intention of getting into a row with anyone.

'Those clothes there.' She pointed at a neat pile on an ornate gilded chair. 'And wash.'

'Again? But I had a bath last night.'

'And haven't you pissed since then? Make sure you wash – *everywhere*. Mr Bartholomew is a very particular man.' At which she turned on her heel and would have flounced, had she not been so heavy. Instead, she trundled out and slammed the door.

Phoebe picked up the dress. 'Look at this, will you?' She held it against herself. It was of the finest blue wool and the bodice had stays sewn into it. There was a fine lace modesty collar to go with it, and a short-waisted jacket in a darker but toning blue, made of a silky material she did not recognise. The sleeves were puffed at the top, but they tapered down to the wrists and were so narrow she wondered if they would button up. 'It's even got a bustle, just like the vicar's wife! And look, petticoats, a corset, a chemise . . .' Phoebe laughed with excitement.

'You realise there are no knickers?'

'What's that mean?'

'I'd rather not think.'

'Careful does it.'

'But the clothes are lovely . . .'

'Phoebe!'

She'd been told to wash – but where? There was no bucket, no bowl. She noticed a door to the side and knocked. When no one answered she pushed it open. What she saw astonished her: a gleaming white lavatory, a basin, and a huge china bath set right in the middle of the room. She ventured in and used the lavatory quickly. Then, finding no jug of water to sluice it down, she was unsure what to do. The bath was encased in shiny mahogany and beside it was a table on which there were bottles and pots, soaps and powder. Should she wash or have another bath? Perhaps a bath would help the aches and pains.

But where were the jugs of water? At the foot of the bath there were two metal handles. She turned one and squealed when hot water gushed out. 'Well I never!' she exclaimed. Hastily she turned on the other as well. They must be taps. She'd heard about them but never seen one. You could fill a bath without hauling hot water out of the copper – always such hard work, and the reason Phoebe only bathed a couple of times a year. But how to keep the water in? She found the plug.

This bath was different from the one she had endured last night. She poured in a mixture of oils, lay back and allowed the water to flow until she was submerged to her chin. 'This is the life!'

The towel with which she dried herself was enormous, soft and wrapped round her twice.

Then she got dressed. When she looked in the long mirror in the room, she barely recognised herself. She brushed back her curly dark brown hair, but as she could find no clips she let it flow loose. 'This is the life,' she repeated, and twirled in front of the mirror again. Proud of herself, she crossed the thick carpet and tried to open the door. It would not budge. 'For pity's sake, I'm locked in!'

An hour later Phoebe was bored. She had studied every picture in the room, she had peered into the cupboards and leafed through the books – only a few had pictures and, since she could not read, they held no interest for her. She had solved the mystery of the lavatory by gingerly pulling a chain then jumped back from the torrent of water that resulted. 'Well, here's another marvel and no mistake!' Where did the water go? she wondered. And how was it there were no smells? How the privy at home had hummed! She smiled to herself. When she ventured to the lavatory at night it was wise to take a hefty stick since rats resided there. And then there were the cockroaches, monsters they were, not like the ones in the kitchen, the thunder box favoured them that was for sure.

Now she sat in the luxurious bedroom. 'I think what's going on here might be – well, dangerous. I keep thinking of white-slave trafficking.'

'No, not that Mr Bartholomew. He's a kind toff, that's all. He saw a young girl in distress and wanted to help her, that's what.'

But there was something wrong here, something frightening, something ... 'Oh, fiddlesticks, I'm not going to waste my time worrying about something that hasn't happened and might not. Think of the Good Samaritan.' Phoebe stood up, crossed to the window and tried to open it. She wanted to know if there was a handy creeper she might be able to climb down if she needed to. 'Better safe than sorry.' But, like the door, the window would not budge. 'Blow me! What if there was a fire?'

Then she became aware that the door was opening and let out a squeal of alarm.

'Mr Bartholomew wants to see you. Push your hair back – it looks untidy,' Mrs White complained.

Phoebe brushed at her hair with the palm of her hand but it did little good: the curls just bounced back. She followed the fat housekeeper dutifully.

'You're to curtsy.'

'Yes, Mrs White.'

'And don't speak until spoken to.'

'No, Mrs White.'

'What do you mean by that?'

'That I won't say anything.'

It seemed a long way from the bedroom to wherever *he* was. She wondered how many people lived in the house: there was enough space for all the inhabitants of her hamlet a hundred times over. They passed through one big hall, and two little ones, and swept through three sitting rooms. She spied one room full of books. The corridors went on for ever, lined with doors – how many rooms, used for what purpose, lurked behind them? Treasures were everywhere, too many to take in, which seemed to her to be a waste since how could you concentrate on looking at one picture when there were another six hanging beside it? She gave up trying to look at them: each time she lagged behind, Mrs White shouted at her to catch up.

Eventually, the housekeeper stopped so abruptly that Phoebe all but cannoned into her. With a flourish, she pushed open double mahogany doors. 'Phoebe, Mr Bartholomew.'

Well, *she* hadn't been spoken to before she spoke, that was for sure. She felt herself being propelled into the room.

They were in a dining room. In the centre there was a long table with the whitest cloth imaginable and a collection of silver that took her breath away. It was made to look even brighter by the sunshine that poured into the room. Mr Bartholomew was seated at the far end and stood up. 'Come here, my dear.'

Phoebe's heart was in her mouth and she suddenly wished she had used the lavatory again before coming downstairs. She felt another shove from behind and wished she was anywhere but here. 'There's no need to be afraid. I shan't eat you,' he said, in a pleasant tone. She tried to smile, but it was as if the muscles in her face had seized up. 'Are you hungry? You must be. See? A place has been laid for you. Come, sit. Relax.'

Relax! she thought. Fat chance of that. Slowly she walked towards him.

'Charming,' he said, and smiled at her. 'That's better,' he added, as she slid into the seat to his right.

'Thank you,' was all she could think to say.

There was a bustle behind her. She looked over her shoulder and saw that two male servants, footmen, had come in with trays of dishes. A plate was placed in front of her by one and the other man cracked open the napkin she had not known what to do with. The plate was covered in a swirling gold, red and blue pattern, the most lovely thing she had ever seen. She touched the rim with a finger.

Then one of the footmen came across with a tureen, and the other ladled soup into a bowl. They served Phoebe first. While they attended to Mr Bartholomew, she picked up one of the many spoons before her, scooped up a mouthful and sucked it in loudly. It was delicious, like nothing she had ever tasted before.

'It is customary to wait.'

'Pardon?'

He winced with a pained expression. 'We don't say "pardon".'

'Why not?'

'Never mind.' Mr Bartholomew waved his hand in a gesture of irritation. 'Mrs White, attention is needed here.' Then he began to eat his own soup. The spoon moved away from him, dipped into the bowl and then, only half filled, was transported to his mouth from which issued no sound. She wondered how he did that and tried it herself.

'Phoebe, you come along with me,' Mrs White hissed.

'But I—'

'Now.'

'Thank you for my soup, sir.' Her politeness was rewarded with a shove from the housekeeper.

'Perhaps another time.' Again he waved his hand. 'And nails, Mrs White.'

'Yes, Mr Bartholomew, sir.' Mrs White bobbed, then yanked Phoebe out of the room.

'Not up to scratch, then?' one of the footmen asked, with an unfriendly snigger, as they scurried past.

'You could be right!' Mrs White laughed.

Phoebe was marched back through the house. They paused only when Mrs White told one of the maids to fetch a Mrs Lingford. 'And she's going to have her hands full with you,' she assured Phoebe.

Finally they were back in the room in which Phoebe had woken up. As they entered her stomach rumbled. 'He might have let me finish my soup,' she said.

'And listen to the disgusting noise you were making? He's a sensitive man, Mr Bartholomew.'

'But I'm hungry.'

'You'll be fed when you've learned some manners.'

Phoebe flounced into the room and slumped into the nearest easy chair.

'And you needn't act like that with me, young woman. That won't help.'

'I don't know what you mean. I wasn't disgusting.'

'Oh yes, you were, and if you want to stay here, things will have to change. And you do want to stay, now, don't you?'

'I suppose so,' she answered, but she was not sure that she did. She did not like Mrs White, but the house and the bed—

'What have we here, Mrs White?' A tall woman with a back so straight it looked as if it were made of wood had walked in. She had the blackest hair and the darkest eyes, and a frown so deep it looked as if she carried the problems of the world on her shoulders.

'The worst one yet, Mrs Lingford. He seems to be going for the scrapings of the barrels, these days.'

'You know me, Mrs White, I enjoy a challenge. Would you mind standing up, young woman? Turn round.' She studied her for what, to Phoebe, seemed an eternity. The woman's gaze seemed to bore into her and Phoebe hoped she could not see how scared she was. She had learned long ago that to show fear was to attract anger.

'I feel like a prize heifer the way you're gawking at me,' she said.

'Not a prize heifer yet, but perhaps one day you will

be, if Mrs Lingford has her way with you!' Mrs White snapped.

It sounded like an ominous warning.

5

'I would like to add a raspberry jelly to the desserts, Mrs Bramble, and woodcock to the savouries.'

'Yes, Mrs Randolph.' The cook scribbled in her notebook.

'And the fish?'

'The fishmonger sent a fine salmon.'

'And the beef?'

'The best – as you would expect from Cooper.'

'I've arranged for extra help in the kitchen.'

'That's most kind of you, ma'am.'

'A butler will be arriving at noon. I trust Bee has been helping with the silver? Good. That will be all, Mrs Bramble.'

Having dismissed her cook, Dulcie turned back to the paperwork she was doing at the small Queen Anne desk in the morning room. Dulcie Randolph never used the name 'Smythe'. She thought it pretentious, and false. She preferred to use her maiden name, which her husband had purloined – fortunately for her as it transpired: her continued use of it allowed her, when he was not with her, to pretend that she had never met and married him.

She had no one but herself to blame. No one had forced her into marriage – in fact, she had had to use all the wiles of which she was capable to persuade her father to agree to the union. She looked at the photograph of her stiffly posed parents, set against an arch leading to a sumptuous garden, which stood in pride of place on her desk.

'He's not good enough for you,' her father had said.

'How sweet of you to say so, dear Papa. But, you see, I don't feel I'm nearly good enough for him.'

'He's a thief. I am almost sure he stole from my till. And if he steals from me what will stop him stealing from you?'

'*Almost* sure, Papa? That's not fair. But if he had, it would make no difference. If he was a murderer, I would still love him. I can't help myself.'

'I wish I'd never given him employment.' Her father had been grey with worry, and it had been her fault.

She shook herself with annoyance at the memory of her own stupidity. Why had she not listened to her father? Instead, strong-willed, knowing that in the end her father would let her have what she wanted, she had succeeded.

Once he was married to her, Arnold's rise in her father's firm had been inevitable: Fred Randolph felt he had no alternative but to promote his son-in-law to manager of his store in Whitechapel, London. However, unknown to the couple, he had also changed his will. He had previously left everything outright to his only child, but now everything was put in trust for her to ensure that there would be no question of Arnold getting his hands on the shop, that it would always be Dulcie's. Not that he had expected his end to come so swiftly. Within a year of her marriage, Dulcie was an orphan: both of her parents had succumbed to a virulent attack of food poisoning.

At the time she could not fault Arnold's behaviour: he was assiduous in his kindness and concern for her. He held her when she wept for the parents she had adored, and she had felt confident in leaving all legal matters in his hands while she dealt with her grief.

When she emerged from mourning it was to find he had sold her father's shop and the house in nearby Spitalfields. 'I didn't know about all this, Arnold,' she said.

'But, light of my life, we discussed it.'

'Did we?'

'You can't remember, my dove, because your grief has erased the memory.'

'Yes, it must be so.'

'You don't think I would do anything without your agreement, do you? I explained it all when you signed the papers.'

She remembered signing a large pile of documents, 'Minor matters,' she had thought he said, but she must have been mistaken. 'No, of course. I know you always have my best interests at heart.'

'Especially now.' He looked at the slight swelling that her dress could no longer disguise.

While she was pleased to be having his child, she wished it was not so soon: she feared her sadness over her parents' death might transfer itself to her baby, and she didn't want it ever to know such misery.

'Remind me, why did we decide to sell? Father's shop has always been so prosperous.'

'Because we decided it was wrong for you to stay here. That you will regain your spirits only when we are far away.'

'I can't imagine why I agreed to it.'

'Because, my love, you understood it was what I wanted. I don't want to live my life in your father's shadow. He was a great success, but I need to be a success for you in my own right.'

'I must appear selfish but all my fondest memories are here in this house, in the shop.'

'It's time for us to build our own store of joyful memories far away from sadness, in Devon.'

'Why Devon?'

'I explained it to you. Sheep.'

'I'm not sure I want to move so far from London, from my friends, the few family I have, the life I know.'

'I do . . .' And she was so much in love with him that she had been deaf to the sharpness in his voice.

Dulcie rearranged her papers on the desk in the morning room of her fine house in Devon. She could see clearly now how she had thought at that time. What Arnold had wished, so had she. And there was reason in his argument: she had been deeply depressed, but she could not mourn her parents for ever – it was not fair on him.

'A new life and a new beginning. It's a good idea, Mr Lockyer,' she had reassured her lawyer, whom she had known all her life, when, concerned at the speed with which things were happening, he had called on her. 'The idea of moving to the West Country appeals to me. This house is too sad for me now.'

'I understand, but sometimes it is not a good idea to act too soon after a bereavement.'

'It's six months, Mr Lockyer.'

'But to go so far?'

'Sheep, Mr Lockyer.' The lawyer looked just as perplexed as she had been, and the memory still made her smile. 'I don't think there is ever a "right" time. I shall always mourn them.'

'Quite so. But the shop as well?'

'We thought it was for the best.'

'I have to tell you that I am concerned. I had asked to see you but your husband refused me permission.'

'He, too, was concerned for my well-being. He felt I needed solitude. I understand his concern, but what was yours?'

At this Mr Lockyer looked trapped. He coughed and shuffled papers, and she had known he was finding the courage to tell her what he thought. 'Whether you had willingly signed the papers pertaining to the sales,' he had said rapidly.

'Really, Mr Lockyer! Did you think my husband stood over me with a shotgun?' She had laughed light-heartedly.

A long silence followed, of the sort that always troubled Dulcie. She scrabbled for something to say.

'I'm not sure how to put this, Miss Dulcie,' Mr Lockyer said eventually, 'but I feel, in memory of your father who, as you know, was a dear friend of mine, that I must tell you your husband tried to overturn the terms of the trust your father set up for you.'

'Really? If he did it would only have been for my benefit.'

'There would have been no benefit for you, Dulcie. Quite the contrary.'

'Then I'm sure there must have been a mistake. He would never do anything to harm me.' And that had been her belief.

'But the change in the trustees?' Mr Lockyer had continued.

'Yes, my husband told me.' It caused her such pain to lie to an old friend.

'He did?'

'But of course. Didn't the others retire?' She was groping in the dark.

'Yes, somewhat abruptly.'

'And that implies?'

'I am loath to say this to you, of all people, but perhaps they were suborned into doing so.'

'Oh, Mr Lockyer! What a thing to say!' She had laughed.

She knew better now.

When Chauncey, her son, was born, she loved him with an intensity that took her by surprise. Even her love for Arnold paled by comparison with this avalanche of emotion. It was as if she was suddenly alive. Chauncey monopolised all of her waking day and her thoughts.

Her wish had been that he should be called Frederick for her father, but Arnold, with his fascination for all things American, fancied Chauncey, a name she privately thought outlandish. They compromised and gave the baby his grandfather's name as the second. It was at this time, when they were about to move to Devon, that he had announced he was changing his name by deed poll to Randolph. How could she object? It was a kind gesture, made so that her family name would continue. She was not consulted on the change of Smith to Smythe.

It had been a shock to her to discover that her husband had no interest in his son. There was no fondness, no pride. When she had queried his feelings, she had not been sufficiently alarmed by his reply: 'He has enough affection from you, he's no need of me,' Arnold had told her.

Why did she constantly go over the past in this way? Why keep remembering the sadness? She dipped her pen into the inkwell. She had letters to write. She looked at the engraved paper, her mind blank. Letter-writing was not her favourite occupation. A watercolour of her father's house hung over her desk. She looked at it dreamily, and sighed. She still missed it.

Arnold had quickly found them a suitable shop in the market town of Barlton, south of Exeter and close to Dartmoor. It was a pleasant place and the clean air was good for the baby. Their first home was a villa overlooking the harbour and she had been content there, even though Arnold paid her scant attention. He was busy so he was tired when he returned home, she reassured herself.

A year after their arrival, they moved to a larger house in the best part of town, Hangman's Hill. It had once been a cottage, but over three hundred years had been gradually extended until it had become a house with six bedrooms and a servants' wing. Arnold had added to it too: a fine conservatory and a music room. He had also built a lodge at the end of the drive to house their newly acquired coachman.

Dulcie's morning room was in the original cottage. Two rooms had been made into one and the small window converted into a glazed door that led out on to the terrace where she had planted wisteria, clematis, camellias, honeysuckle and roses. She liked this room best: it was cosy in winter and cool in summer, and she had made it her own, filling it with the knick-knacks, paintings and bibelots that Arnold did not like.

Sometimes she felt sorry for the cottage, swamped now by all of the additions. There were times when she was sure it would like to revert to how it once had been – rather as she wished she could be young again, at home and adored by her father.

Dulcie rarely defied her husband, but over this house she had. Arnold had wanted to change its name to Barlton Grange, but Dulcie had felt this was ostentatious and insisted the old name remained – December Cottage. He had agreed reluctantly once she had pointed out that since they had taken possession in December it was a good omen – Dulcie no longer believed in omens.

Her problems had begun with the move, she thought. She picked up her pen again. She must get on with the letter, but it was difficult. When Chauncey was here she could talk to him about anything, but it was much harder to write. If she told him how much she missed him he might be upset. If she told him about what she had been doing it would be as stale as last month's newspapers by the time he received it in South Africa.

When she studied the atlas her heart sank at how far away he was. Why had he chosen that wretched regiment? He wasn't a soldier, he was an artist. And the danger was mounting daily: she could no longer read the newspaper for fear of what she might learn about the bloodthirsty Boers, the skirmishes, the wounded ... Think of something else, she told herself.

Her mother stared out at her from the photograph. She'd been such a pretty woman and had tutored her daughter well in housewifely skills. But as Arnold's plans for their future unfolded Dulcie had feared that she was not nearly skilled enough. He wanted to rise in society, and the new house was suitable for the scale of entertaining he envisaged.

Until then Dulcie had rarely entertained but now she found herself planning sumptuous dinners for the smartest set in town and often felt inadequate for the task. She read every book on etiquette and entertaining she could find, and scoured the ladies' magazines for tips on what to wear. She had purchased every new edition of *Manners and Tone of Good Society*, written by a member of the aristocracy, no less, just in case there might be something new to learn.

She needed more staff to run such a large house, but she was uneasy in her dealings with them, and unsure how to treat them or win their respect. She was always afraid they were laughing at her behind her back.

Sadly, her efforts were never good enough for Arnold who, after each party, would sit late into the night pointing out to her what had been wrong, where she needed to improve. She had often wished he was less ambitious.

She stood up from her desk and arched her back, which ached. She glanced in the mirror. She had new clothes, a new hairstyle, but she never looked right for him. With elocution lessons, her London accent had disappeared, as had his, but within months of arriving here she had known she could never be what he wanted.

Her weight was a constant problem. Like her mother, she had always veered towards plumpness but now she was downright stout. She would have liked to be thinner but every time she annoyed him she ate to ease her misery. His distaste for her size grew in parallel with her inadequacy. Insidiously his attitude towards her changed. He no longer pretended he loved her, and on some evenings he barely spoke to her, which added to her feelings of inferiority.

She could still remember the shock she had felt when Chauncey was nearly two, and a friend had told her that while she was pregnant Arnold had been unfaithful to her. That had wrecked what little confidence she had left. 'Why? Because you don't love me? Because I am unattractive to you?' She had dared to confront him.

'My sweet, I am a weak-willed man. I did not want to bother you, in your condition. This woman meant nothing to me. I have forgotten her. Forgive me.'

She believed him and forgave him, but there was no question of them resuming physical relations, which had ceased at Chauncey's birth.

It was about then that she discovered there were always 'friends' eager to inform her of his other indiscretions: that woman had not been the first or the last.

'You never loved me, did you?' she asked him one day.

'No.'

It was the answer she had been expecting ever since she had met him, but she had thought he would never say it. It did not break her heart, but her trust in him dissolved. If he could deceive her thus, in what other way might he?

He had taken her on a trip to America – to make amends he had told her. They were away for four months, during which she ached to see her son. Despite that, though, she had enjoyed the excitement of that country, the new experiences, the new people – so much easier to get on with than the English. And Arnold was happier, more relaxed and kinder to her. But she was glad to return home.

When Agnes arrived he could not have been a more doting father. She watched him bestow on the little girl the love she yearned for, but the betrayals continued. She felt so humiliated. As depression took hold, she detached herself from both of them.

'I have been informed that you have a couple of houses in which you keep your mistresses?' She had felt embarrassed, six years on, as she asked this question, as if it were she who had done wrong.

He looked at her coldly. 'That's right.'

'Then I feel I must inform Mr Lockyer and have these creatures evicted. The property must be sold.'

'They are not your houses, but mine.'

'Yours? How can that be? It is *my* money.' This was the first time in their years together that she had reminded him of it.

'What a charming woman you are. *My* money. Who works all the hours? Who provides? Who pays the bills? Me. These houses are mine, in my name and nothing to do with you.'

'You've stolen from me!'

'No, Dulcie, I wouldn't stoop so low. I've *earned* them – something you wouldn't understand – not only by my toil but by putting up with you.'

That was when Dulcie had written to her lawyer and asked for a duplicate set of detailed accounts of her stocks and shares, the rentals from the other land and properties she owned to be sent to an accommodation address in Barlton. She had never understood them but they were filed away now, some in the small safe in the morning room and others in a strongbox at the bank, in case she ever needed them.

She had had one triumph: she remembered how jubilant she had been when she had extracted from him a promise that, if she made no more mention of his mistresses, he would not embarrass her by pursuing anyone they knew socially.

Dulcie returned to her desk, took up her pen, then laid it down again. Why had she stayed with him? It was a question she often asked herself but she knew the answers well enough. The most important had been that she could not contemplate losing Chauncey, and the law would have seen to it that she did. Second, there was the question of the social ostracism that separation would bring on her: she was sure that would destroy her. Third, she could not run the shop an eighth as well as he did. And, fourth, most pathetic of all, she did not want to live alone.

In the intervening years, there had been changes. Her love for Arnold was long dead, and now she hated him because of Chauncey.

Perhaps, looking back, it would have been better . . .

'Papa is very excited about tonight. Who's coming?' Agnes had entered the room.

Dulcie jumped. 'You startled me! I was miles away.'

'Nice day-dream?'

'I was thinking of the past.'

'You know what Papa says. "Yesterday is dead and gone, think only of today and tomorrow."'

'Yes, but I treasure my long-gone yesterday, as you will one day.'

'Not me!'

Dulcie smiled at her confidence – she would learn. She was a beautiful young woman . . . and it was a shame she was not easy to like.

'We shall be twelve. Several of your father's friends from the County Club are coming. And an Edward Bartholomew-Prestwick. Your father met him at the club and took a liking to him. I gather he is young and handsome.'

'If this is to help me forget about Robert Markham, it won't.'

'Of course not,' Dulcie lied.

'Is that a new table?' Agnes pointed at Dulcie's latest acquisition, the bright colours of the inlaid marble. 'Not another! It's impossible to move in here for rubbish and clutter.' She looked disdainfully around the room even though she knew that these were some of Dulcie's most loved, if not valuable, possessions. Then her tone changed: 'Silly Papa! Always so enthusiastic about new people – he's such a dear,' she said fondly.

How she loved her father, and how he loved her. If only things could have been different.

'Such a deep sigh, Mother. What were you thinking?'

'Nothing, really . . . of how unfair life can sometimes be.'

'What a thing to say. You have everything you could possibly want. A lovely home, clothes, jewellery. Food whenever you want it.' Did Agnes glance pointedly at her waistline? 'I think you're the luckiest woman in the world to have Papa as your husband. He is *so* good to you – why, he gives you whatever you want.' Dulcie had to look away to prevent Agnes seeing the annoyance on her face. 'If I find a husband half as wonderful as Papa I shall be a lucky girl.' She placed on her head the bonnet she had been carrying and admired herself in the mirror as she pinned it into place. 'I am meeting Adeline Salter now. Might she come this evening? Her dreary parents have gone away so I suggested she should come here and Papa *adores* her.'

'If she wishes.' He liked most of Agnes's friends – a little too much at times.

Dulcie heard Agnes trip across the hall floor – tessellated with the finest stone from Italy – open the stained-glass front door and close it. Then she heard the stout oak outer door bang. It was studded with large nails as if it had come from a castle and not from the joiner on the other side of town.

She looked out of the window at the sunlight on the immaculate lawn and the copper beech, her favourite of all the trees in the garden. They had had one at home in Spitalfields. Her father had hung a swing from it . . .

She brushed her eyes as if ridding herself of the memory. She had wasted the morning in mooning about the past when she had a dinner to plan. At the thought the familiar gripe of nerves clenched her stomach.

'Phoebe, I'm tired of telling you that we do *not* eat peas from our spoon. That spoon is intended for your dessert, as you are fully aware. Are you being wilfully obtuse?'

'How would I know when I don't know what obtuse means?'

'Being rude is not going to help us.'

'I'm not, I'm telling you'm the truth. If you'm use words what I don't know, what can you expect?'

Lynette Lingford sighed. 'Not "you'm", Phoebe. How many times do I have to tell you? You must try harder to rid yourself of your accent – Mr Bartholomew does not like it.'

'Then he'll have to lump it. That's how I've always talked. If it don't suit him then why don't he move?'

'Because he speaks correct English and you do not.'

'Who says I don't?'

'Sometimes, Phoebe, I have an almost uncontrollable urge to slap you.'

'I don't advise that, Mrs Lingford. I reckon I could finish you with one whopping flop on the gills.'

Mrs Lingford burst out laughing. 'Now it's my turn not to understand!' Try as she might to be stern with the girl it wasn't easy. She had such spirit and could be so amusing.

The two women were in the breakfast room eating their luncheon, which Phoebe had already learned was no longer her dinner: she had that when she used to eat her supper. In the couple of weeks she had been there, she had begun to like Mrs Lingford and was no longer afraid of her. When she was cross, which was often, Phoebe sensed that half the time she was pretending.

'You see, Mrs Lingford, I don't understand something like this. Peas are truly fretful things to eat. *You,*' she grinned, as she emphasised the pronoun, '*you* said I couldn't mash them. They roll off the fork, which you say I should use. So what's left but to scoop 'em up with a spoon? Meself I likes them mashed.'

'*Myself*, Phoebe. But don't you see that it's more elegant to eat them this way?' She indicated her own fork. 'You agreed with me that it was best not to make noises when you ate, and it's the same with peas.'

'I reckon that if I'm eating with His Nibs I'll refuse peas.'

'That, of course, is an option. And perhaps, in the circumstances, simpler.' She smiled as she watched Phoebe chase a scattering of peas across the table – once again, she had failed to balance them on her fork. 'Often, Phoebe, when a rule of etiquette appears foolish to you, think about it and you will find it exists for a very good reason.'

'Like what?'

'Like a gentleman always walking on the right side of a lady so that his right hand is free to protect her.'

'To protect her?'

'He must keep his sword arm free.'

'But men don't carry swords no more.'

'No, but the tradition continues. In that position he protects her from any mud or wet thrown up by passing carriages.'

'I see. But what if when they did have swords a man was left-handed?'

'Well, he'd . . .' She paused to think. 'To be honest with you, Phoebe, I don't know. But probably he would still have been taught to fight with his right hand since to be left-handed was regarded as sinister.'

'Like, in league with the devil?'

'Yes, probably.'

'My father would approve. He goes on about Satan all day every day.'

'Is that why you ran away?'

'Who said that? I never did. I just left of my own free will.' But her blush identified the lie.

'You told Mr Bartholomew you were an orphan.'

''Twas a fib.'

'Do you often lie?'

'If I think it will keep me out of trouble.'

'Isn't that wrong?'

'Not if it stops problems.'

'I'm not so sure of that.'

'I am.'

Mrs Lingford was perplexed at the best way to deal with her: Phoebe had an answer for everything. 'Did your mother not mind you going when you are so young?'

'She's dead.' Phoebe shook her head once, sharply. Mrs Lingford was sensitive to the gesture and did not pursue the matter, even though she had been told to. 'And I'm not young, I'm sixteen.'

'Are you, Phoebe? I would have thought fourteen.'

'What?' Phoebe stood up with agitation. 'Fourteen? Me? Are you blind? I'm sixteen, nearly seventeen.' She sat down again with a bump not prepared to admit she wasn't completely sure.

'As you wish, my dear.' But Mrs Lingford was not convinced, despite Phoebe's full-breasted figure. In this house she had observed that a country maiden's body matured far faster than that of her city cousin.

'In any case, it's unlikely I shall ever meet a gentleman so I won't have it happen to me.'

'You can't be sure of that, Phoebe. You're very beautiful and when you're older, say, sixteen . . .' she said slyly '. . . why, then you could attract any man you wanted.'

'Me? Beautiful? Are you just saying that? When I'm sixteen? You think so?'

'It's true. You are.' She hid a smile behind her napkin: for once she had outsmarted Phoebe.

'I think you need spectacles, Mrs L.' Phoebe had

blushed with pleasure. 'But, as I keep telling you, I'm already sixteen. It hasn't happened yet – and you thought you'd tricked me but you hadn't.'

It was always a relief to Phoebe when her meal-time manners lessons were over. She was always hungry: it took her so long to eat correctly that invariably her food went cold, or she had to pretend she had finished because Mrs Lingford's plate was empty and, out of her own natural courtesy, she did not want to keep her waiting.

To her astonishment she was enjoying everything else. She was amazed that so much was involved in her *toilette*, that so many soaps, unguents and perfumes were required – her ablutions until now had been a splash under the pump in the yard. Mrs Lingford had taught her how to manicure her nails and she had to buff them every day for at least twenty minutes. Already they were looking pinker and shinier.

'That's much better,' Mrs Lingford said, inspecting them.

'But all this titivating don't leave any time to do much else, does it? And these,' she flapped her hands, 'they won't stay looking like this with cows to milk and weeds to grub up.'

'But what if you never had to do those tasks ever again?'

'Paradise.' Phoebe sighed.

She was learning to dress her hair so that it no longer looked wild, and enjoyed sitting in front of her mirror each night and rhythmically brushing it for one hundred strokes. It had an extra gleam now, the curls were no longer unruly, and the ritual had a soporific effect on her: instead of lying awake worrying about why she was here, and what was to happen to her, she fell asleep quickly.

Mrs Lingford had also promised her that, if she listened to and acted on all she was told, she would teach her to read and write, and how to make conversation.

She was looking forward to the reading and writing but couldn't see the point of learning how to talk. She was a natural chatterbox anyway.

'Some topics are never discussed in polite society – money, religion, politics.'

'That's not difficult. I have no money, no religion, and I know nothing about politics.'

'I won't even say what I think about you not having a religion. Everyone needs religion.'

'Not if you've heard as much of it as I have,' was Phoebe's sharp response. 'So, what is there to talk about?'

'The weather, shopping, the arts.'

'Food?' Phoebe asked helpfully.

'Food is never mentioned, not even in a compliment to your hostess on the meal you have just eaten. That would imply you were surprised by the quality.'

'That's silly. My mum loved it when we said her apple pie was the best in the world.'

'That's different.'

'Why?'

'It just is.'

'Everything was much simpler at home. There wasn't much of what you'd call conversation there.'

'Are you homesick?'

'Not me.' She laughed at the very idea. 'I shall never go back.'

'What would you like to do?'

'Go to Exeter or Barlton, of course.'

'Not London?'

'Too far away – but perhaps one day . . . Who knows?'

'And how do you think you will get there?'

'I thought I'd find work and save.'

'Doing what?'

'I thought of going into service but I don't think I'd like that.'

'Why not?'

'Serving other people. I'd end up telling them how lazy they were.'

'Yes, Phoebe, I fear you might.' Mrs Lingford chuckled.

'Perhaps I could work in a shop.'

'But that would be serving, too, wouldn't it?'

'Yes, but not like having to empty slops. That's what a friend of mine does. Every morning she has to empty the chamber-pots.' She shuddered. 'Let them empty their own, I says.'

'What a little radical you are.'

'What's that?'

'Someone who holds extreme views.'

'What's extreme about not wanting to empty someone else's piddle? I want a different life. I want these fine clothes all the time, the lovely food and wine we have here. Before, eating was for staying alive, but now I know what a pleasure it can be. And then there's the warmth. And a bath with water from the taps. Perhaps if I was in a shop I could find a rich husband and have all those things.'

'Or perhaps a protector?'

'What's a protector?'

'A man who looks after you and buys you pretty things but doesn't want to marry you.'

'And what would he want from the likes of me?'

'Your body.' Mrs Lingford said it so quietly that Phoebe was unsure if she heard her correctly and asked her to repeat what she had said.

'Seems a good bargain to me,' she said, but she thought, No man is going to touch *me*! 'Do you know why I'm here? What the old man's going to do with me?' There! She had finally found the courage to ask.

'Mr Bartholomew is a kind man. He likes to educate and make the lives of young girls easier.'

'And boys?'

'No, just girls. He's what we call a philanthropist.

Other than that, I have no idea what his intentions are.'
At that she looked away, and Phoebe wondered why.

'So, Mrs Lingford, tell me what are you making of
Phoebe?'

'She's very bright and spirited. She knows her own
mind. She is eager to learn, although she questions
everything. She is beginning to take an interest in caring
for her physical well-being. I think you will see a big
change in her.'

'She is very beautiful.'

'Indeed, sir. I would go as far as to say the most
beautiful we have ever had.'

'And her speech?'

'It improves slowly. She's rather attached to her
accent.' She allowed herself a little smile. 'But I think she
exaggerates it to tease me.'

'I sense you like her?'

'Very much, sir.'

'And what have you gleaned?'

'Certainly she's from the moor. A smallholding. Her
mother is dead, and she hates her father. He is a religious
man and she has rejected his religion. She wants a rich
husband but is not averse, I believe, to the idea of a
wealthy protector.'

'Excellent. You do well, Mrs Lingford, as always.'

'Thank you, sir.'

7

'Agnes, I have told you time and again that you lace
your corsets too tightly. It is injurious to your
health.'

'Fiddle, Mother, it isn't. Everyone I know laces tight.'

'But not you,' Dulcie said. 'Jane, loosen them,' she told
the maid, then busied herself about the room. Try as she

might she could never get Agnes to be tidy or considerate towards the servants.

'Mother, stop fussing. Don't do Jane's work for her. If you do everything there would be nothing left for her to do. Isn't that so, Jane?'

'Yes, Miss Agnes.' Jane smiled, but it looked forced.

'I've never understood why it is necessary to make such clutter. And it is most inconsiderate of you, Agnes. Jane has enough to do.' Dulcie smiled sympathetically at the long-suffering maid.

'Thank you, ma'am.'

Agnes had gone quite pale.

'You see? Just look at your colour! Loosen those stays a fraction more, Jane. Only last week I heard of a woman who had sliced her liver in two with tightening. She's dead, of course,' Dulcie added, somewhat unnecessarily.

'Jane, do no such thing.' Agnes stepped back from the maid. 'You can go now.' She waited for the girl to leave the room. 'Really, Mother, you make me so angry you force me to say something. I feel such mortification when you correct me in front of the servants.'

'So, you admit you're in the wrong?'

'I do no such thing. It is wrong of you to criticise me in front of the girl.'

'If you were more considerate I would have no need to.'

'The truth is, Mother, you don't know how to treat them.'

Dulcie stood still, clutching a chemise. 'And you do?'

'Better than you. They're not our friends, they're servants. You lack finesse.'

'And you lack manners.' She bent to retrieve a ribbon. 'Do you really need to try on four chemises? Do you need six pairs of stockings all at the same time? How many legs do you possess?'

'You're changing the subject.'

'No, I'm not. Who will wash and iron these? Jane.

Who will have to press and rehang all the garments you have rejected?' She pointed at the pile of dresses cascading from the nearby chair and over the bed. 'Jane. Who will put away your sketching materials, your books, your papers?' She swung her arm wide to indicate the untidy surfaces and the floor. 'Jane.'

'It is what she is paid to do.'

'Yes, she is, but a little consideration goes a long way. A little gratitude.'

'I should thank a maid?' Agnes snorted.

'If you continue like this you will never be a lady.'

'Oh, yes, I shall. But you won't.' Agnes smiled indulgently at her reflection in the ornate mirror on her dressing-table.

'Do you think that girl feels any loyalty to you, would put herself out for you? Of course not. No doubt she loathes you and moans about you behind your back.'

'Not as much, probably, as she moans about you.'

'She must despise you for your lack of good manners.'

'What?' Agnes stopped gazing at herself. 'She'd better not – I shall dismiss her immediately.'

'You will do no such thing. The staff are my responsibility, not yours.' I take them on and dismiss them, not you.'

'Good God, Mother! You so frequently allow your base origins to show.'

'Not nearly as often as you.' Dulcie glanced about the tidier room with satisfaction. 'That's better, Jane has a busy evening ahead of her.'

'And it's mortifying the way you insist you are called Randolph! It's not your name and it's not fair on Papa – it hurts him dreadfully.'

'Nor is it your father's. But at least it *was* my name. Would you prefer that I call myself Smith, which is his real name if he wasn't so ashamed of it? Do you think that would please him?'

'You know exactly what I mean, Mother.'

'I don't like falsehoods, I never have. And loosen those stays,' she said, as she finally left the room.

This morning Dulcie was not in a good mood, which was rare for her: she tried at all times to remain equable. The large glass-fronted cupboards that contained the dinner services were in the corridor outside the kitchen and she was deciding which to use tonight. The kitchen door was open and the staff were taking a well-earned break. Should she let them know she was there? She decided against it: it might make them feel they shouldn't be putting their feet up. Maybe, in Agnes's eyes, she didn't know how to treat them, but she always tried to imagine herself in their place and to be considerate towards them. It might be wrong but it was her way.

'Thank you, Mrs Bramble. This is fine cake,' she heard Jane say. 'But Mrs Randolph told her fair and square – she hires us and gets rid of us, she said. And she likes me, feels oh-so-sorry for me.' Jane laughed rather unpleasantly.

Dulcie looked up from her task.

'Yes, Jane, but family loyalty is another thing. She might castigate her daughter but she wouldn't like to hear you doing so.'

Dulcie smiled: how wise of Bee – her maid and, perhaps, her truest friend.

'What? You going to tell on me, Bee?'

'No, I don't go in for tittle-tattling. But you never know who would. And sometimes people keep information in reserve in case it should come in handy, and that's a fact.'

'She told Agnes she'd never be a lady.'

'Listening at doors were you?' Annie Bramble said sharply.

Dulcie was abashed – she was doing the same but it was all most interesting.

'No, I was not! She said it with me standing there, holding her daughter's pantaloons.'

'I don't believe you.'

'You calling me a liar?' Jane bristled.

'Yes, I am.'

Something fell on to the tiled floor.

'Those boots are too tight for you, Annie,' Bee counselled.

'They give lovely support though, like Miss Agnes's corset. That's when all the fuss started. She was making me lace her tighter and tighter but we can't get her less. She's never going to have a sixteen-inch waist like her friend Adeline, built like a little sparrow she is.'

Dulcie stood transfixed. She shouldn't be listening to her servants' gossip. But, then, most of the women of her acquaintance wouldn't think twice about doing so.

'I wish His Nibs wouldn't keep inviting people at the last minute, like he does. I don't know where I am with my numbers. I think it's insulting to the guest, like they're an afterthought.'

'Robert Markham wasn't insulted though, was he? Miss Agnes got her way as usual.' That was Jane again.

'His Nibs didn't get where he is today without understanding people. If they ban him, our Miss Agnes is likely to elope. Encourage him, welcome into the bosom of the family, and she'll tire of him.'

Dulcie could imagine her cook nodding at Arnold's wisdom.

'Actually, it was Mrs Randolph insisted. I overheard them.'

'So *you* were listening at doors, were you, Bee?'

Really, thought Dulcie, moving a plate quietly so as not to be heard.

'She likes young Robert, if you must know,' Bee continued. 'It's Himself doesn't think he's good enough. You can never say the mistress is a snob, now, can you?

She's trade herself, and knows it. She's got her feet firmly on the ground, and no mistake.'

'No doubt weighed down with all that money in her pockets.' Annie Bramble guffawed.

'What they having for dinner?'

'What aren't they? We've turtle soup, and then pâté, the fish is salmon and lobster, we've chicken and beef and a turkey pie, then seven puddings, not counting the sorbet, savouries and fruit.'

'Pigs, all of them, that's what they are.'

'You won't last if you carry on like this, Jane.'

'If you ask me, in this household they're trying to ape their betters and it don't work, does it?'

'I hadn't noticed anyone *had* asked you, Jane,' Bee said cuttingly.

'When I was at Lord Smedley's they did things proper.'

'As does Mrs Randolph. You don't know the half of her, my girl. And how dare you be so cheeky about your employer, a good one at that?'

'I know she is, but that don't stop me seeing her as a social climber.'

'I don't think that's kind or accurate. What's wrong in bettering yourself? You did when you came here and went from being a tweeny to a lady's maid – well, trying to be one.' Dulcie heard Bee's almighty sniff of disapproval.

'But you can't compare this house with the Smedleys'. Why, theirs was three times the size.'

'Wasn't much use to you, though, was it? You still got dismissed when you took a shine to his nephew,' the cook said slyly. 'And who took you in with no testimonial? Our Mrs Randolph. Ever heard the phrase "Don't look a gift horse in the mouth", Jane? Perhaps you should take note.'

How interesting this all was, thought Dulcie, to hear them talking honestly. She shut the cupboard, her decision made, and turned to go back to the main part of the house.

'I hear that whore Sophie Franks is dining tonight. How she has the nerve!'

Dulcie stopped to listen.

'Bee – never! The brazen hussy! Poor Mrs Randolph.'

'Disgusting, isn't it? Flaunting his mistress in front of his good wife. No breeding, that man!'

Dulcie could not have moved if she'd tried. Sophie Franks! The young friend she'd helped. And Arnold had promised! She felt angry, humiliated, lonely and sick in turn. This time he had gone too far.

8

'Such a pleasant way to spend an afternoon.' Arnold looked down at the girl beneath his own sleek body. He stroked her full breast, admiring its gentle curve. He cupped it in his hand, then allowed it to fall back on her body, and laughed as it quivered. 'Just like a jelly.'

'Oi, don't you be so bloody rude! You implying I'm fat?' Edith Baker tried to sit up but his weight was too much for her.

'Indignant, are we?'

'Too bloody right I am.'

'Are you in any position to be indignant?'

'No one's rude to me, not even you. Understood?'

He grabbed her wrists, yanked them above her head and smiled at her yelp of pain. 'Now, let's get one thing straight, Edith. I am in control here. You are my whore and I do with you and insult you as I wish.'

'Just a tick—'

He twisted her wrist, making her cry out. 'Just a tick what? You weren't about to give me orders?' He bit her ear-lobe.

'No, nothing like that.'

'You like this, don't you?' He was biting her neck, and she closed her eyes against the pain. 'Don't you?' He nipped her breast and she screamed. He smiled and thrust into her so brutally that she cried out again. His lust was fuelled by her anguish as he rode her. Finally he rolled off her, then took his gold cigar case from the bedside table. Slowly he unwrapped a cigar, pierced it, struck a match and lit it.

'Can I have one?'

'Ladies don't smoke.'

'Haven't I just proved I'm no lady?' She rubbed at the numerous bruises that now marked her body.

'That could be said. You enjoyed it, didn't you?'

'I like a man who's in control.' She simpered at him.

'Then we understand each other.'

She sat up, not bothering to wrap herself in her gown, and positioned herself at the foot of the bed, looking at him. 'Open your legs,' he ordered. 'Wider.' He looked at her coldly, then blew a plume of smoke at her most intimate parts. He glanced up at her and, seeing excitement in her eyes, took her again . . .

It had been a long day for Lily Howard. There had been no help in the office, with that lazy girl disappearing at noon. She claimed she'd a bad headache – a lie, Lily was sure. Then Arnold himself had gone: he had to collect things for his wife's dinner party, he'd said. That was appalling. If she was his wife she would never ask such an unmanly thing of him. It was a wife's duty to have everything prepared. How could she treat him as if he were an errand boy?

Her bag was heavy with shopping. Her aunt Cherry was coming on her annual visit from London to see her sister. Lily was in two minds about this. In the past she had always enjoyed her aunt's company. She was friendly and cheery, with a rich stream of stories about the public house she ran in Whitechapel. A boozer, she called it, which always made Lily purse her lips. 'Inn' would be a nicer word, she always felt, and the one she used when she told people about her aunt. However, she always got on well with her, and looked forward to her visit – so it had come as a hurtful surprise when Lily discovered what she had said last year about her behind her back. Her appearance and lack of a husband topped the list her mother had taken pleasure in relating to her, but these did not bother her. How could Aunt Cherry think she neglected her mother? She had been so annoyed that when she had read the letter announcing her aunt's arrival, she had nearly written to tell her not to come. Instead Lily had decided to have it out with her when they were together. Perhaps she'd end up killing both old women. Topping her mother was her favourite daydream!

There couldn't have been two more dissimiliar sisters. Her mother, Pansy, was dark and thin, while Cherry was blonde and fat. Her mother took no pleasure in anything; Aunt Cherry enjoyed life to the full. She could, of course, be quite frightening, what with the coarse language she used, and Lily didn't understand some of her jokes, but she was fun. So why was she two-faced, and cruel about her?

She wished Uncle Alf was coming – she liked him and he never said horrible things about her. Unfortunately he loathed Pansy, and had stopped coming five years ago when she had ranted at him about the amount he was drinking. Since he was a publican this was hardly fair.

As she trudged along the road she marshalled her thoughts on what she would do if her aunt had said what her mother claimed. She'd put her straight, of course, but she couldn't row with her. That wouldn't do. She and Uncle Alf were childless and, as her mother said *ad nauseam*, they were worth a pretty penny. The last thing anyone in Lily's position would want to do was argue with the one person in the world who, one day, might leave her a legacy.

She was near the harbour now, close to her home. This part of the town bore no relation to the area of Barlton she had just left. There, it was clean, with road-sweepers tending the streets each day, scrubbed steps, pristine net curtains. The people were well dressed and strode about; here they were dowdy, some in rags, and they scuttled, always reminding Lily of rats caught out in daylight. Here, there were no whitened doorsteps, no front gardens: the houses huddled together as if supporting each other. It smelt of rotting rubbish, of malfunctioning sewers, of illness and degradation. How she hated it – and how she envied Arnold his house on the hill. One day ... Where would she be without her dreams, she wondered.

She had just turned into Turner's Lane, a street she disliked intensely. An unsolved murder had been committed here so she always felt edgy walking along it, and there was a gang of rude boys who plagued her with insults and threats, but it was the shortest route to her house so she braved it. Someone came out of number forty-five.

Arnold!

Lily almost stopped in her tracks but managed to keep walking, her heart pounding harder the closer she came to him. Should she invite him home for tea? Her pulse raced at the idea. But what if her mother had been incontinent? Perhaps it would be better not to. He looked so proud, so handsome – his clothes, his demeanour were out of place in this mean street.

'Good evening, Mr Randolph-Smythe.' She was proud of how normal her voice sounded.

He swung round sharply. 'Miss Howard! What a pleasant surprise.'

'Isn't it?' she said. 'You're a long way from your home.'

He tapped his attaché case. 'Some laundry my wife wanted me to pick up.'

'I see,' she said, although she didn't.

He doffed his hat to her, which made her blush with pleasure. What a gentleman he was! If only someone she knew had seen. She watched him as he strode ahead of her. When she reached the corner it was to see him getting into his brougham, which he had left round the corner. How strange.

A laundress at number forty-five? Who could that be? she wondered, as she walked, slower now for she was tiring. Then she stopped dead. Forty-five Turner's Lane! She knew that address. Edith Baker lived there!

'No!' She wasn't sure if she had said it aloud. She had to lean against a wall. She felt faint as myriad emotions battled inside her. She had been overjoyed to see him because she loved him so much. If he was happy she should be pleased for him. 'No!' She had shouted it this time. The joy she had felt was gone and anger rushed to take its place.

She began to walk again, but now she was striding, muttering as she did so, her anger making the heavy bag in her hand as light as thistledown. How could he? With that tart! He'd get diseases! 'And serve him right!' she shouted, startling the passers-by. 'I hope he does.'

How could he do this to her? She worshipped him, would die for him. She would make him suffer. Hate was rapidly quenching love now.

Five minutes later she reached the wretched row of houses where she lived. 'I'm home!' she called, forcing herself to sound light and happy. 'Aunt Cherry, how lovely to see you, and looking so well.' She kissed her aunt, which she didn't normally do, not liking to touch fat bodies. 'That hat suits you. You should always wear dark blue.' She hoped she sounded sincere. And normal. She didn't want them to know what she had just discovered. She couldn't bear anyone else to know the hurt she was feeling.

'You're late,' her mother whined.

'Sorry, Mum, the shopping was heavy. Did you have a good journey, Aunt Cherry?'

'The train was on time but the omnibus was late getting here. A horse dropped dead in its harness. Poor old nag.'

'How vexing for you when you've come so far.'

'It wasn't so bad. I'd packed a sandwich so I didn't go hungry.'

No chance of that, thought Lily. She was hardly likely to starve with all that blubber on her, that was for sure. 'Just as well I got a nice bit of pig's liver for our tea.'

'I don't like liver.'

'Yes, you do, Mum.'

'Not pig's liver, I don't. When your father was alive we fed that to the cat.'

'When Father was alive you could afford calf's liver. I can't. Pig is what you'll get.'

'Stop complaining, Pansy. You should be grateful you've a dutiful daughter to take care of you and cook for you.'

Two-faced bitch, thought Lily.

'Well, you've changed your tune and no mistake. Only five minutes ago you were saying what a lazy girl she was!'

'I never did, Lily. Pansy, how could you say such a thing?'

'Because it's the truth.'

'It's all right, Aunt.' Certainly her aunt looked genuinely cross, Lily thought. But who could she trust? 'Mother likes upsetting people, don't you?' She looked at her mother with loathing. 'I'll just get this on the stove.'

'If you soak it in milk you won't be able to tell the difference,' her aunt called after her, as she left them to go to the kitchen.

A couple of hours later, the liver, smothered with onions and bacon, had been demolished – her mother had even had a second helping – and so had the apple crumble. Then she'd washed Pansy, carried her upstairs and put her to bed.

'You do too much, you know, Lily. You should think more of yourself.'

'That'll be the day. How can I? She's helpless.'

'Not so helpless that she can't look after herself when you're not here.'

'What do you mean?'

'She can totter down to the King William and get herself a pint of stout.'

'But that's a good hundred yards. How do you know?'

'I was so late getting here she'd given me up for lost. I met her coming out of the pub as I passed it. She had the grace to look ashamed and made me promise not to tell you. And I wouldn't have, until I saw you carrying her up to bed. You'll be doing your back in at this rate.'

'Aunt, when you were here last year, did you tell her I neglected her?'

'No! Whatever gave you that idea?'

'She said you did. Why?'

'God knows. I don't like to speak ill of anyone but she's really needled me today. Lily, you're very dear to me and I never said those things – you must believe me. But Pansy was always making trouble even when we were only knee-high. No, I told her what a good daughter you are, Lily, better than she deserves.'

'I've spent this past year hating you.'

'I'm not surprised. I hope you don't any more.'

To Lily's astonishment – and her aunt's – she burst into tears, and once they had started she couldn't stop: ugly, wrenching sobs shook her. She was crying from anger, rage, exhaustion but, most of all, from the thought that twice today she had been deceived.

'There, there . . . Don't take on so . . .' Aunt Cherry

fussed over her, which Lily found quite pleasant. When her aunt put her arms about her and cuddled her to her ample bosom, Lily found she enjoyed it and was comforted.

'You need a holiday, my girl,' her aunt said, when Lily had calmed down. 'Couldn't you get time off from work and come to Alf and me? Let your mother stew for a couple of days.'

'I don't see how.'

'Here, try this.' Her aunt was holding out a glass of bright yellow liquid. 'That'll cheer you up faster than you know.'

'I don't drink.'

'Then you don't know what you're missing. Here. Have a sip. It's my home-made egg nog – it's medicinal.'

Lily took a sip and then, liking the taste, another. A warm feeling seeped through her as she accepted a second glass.

Maybe it was the drink that emboldened her. 'Aunt, tell me, you're from Whitechapel. Did you ever know anything about a family called Randolph-Smythe? They might have owned a shop?'

'I knew a Fred Randolph. Lovely man. Dead now, of course.'

'No, it was an Arnold I was asking about. He's my boss.'

'No, don't know anyone called Smythe. You sure you got the name right?'

'Oh, yes. I do the books for him. I was working late one night and I needed some papers and, well . . .'

'You just happened to find something?' Aunt Cherry chuckled.

'A letter. It was from a firm of solicitors about a shop in Whitechapel and certain payments which, well, hadn't been met. I'm curious, that's all.'

'Arnold Smith. That's who you're talking about. He employs you? Then you look out for yourself, my girl.

I've never met him but, from what I've heard, he's a nasty bit of work.'

'Really?' Lily leaned forward and held out her glass for more egg nog. She wondered what on earth had made her sign the Pledge all those years ago.

'Inveigled his way in, he did. Married Fred's daughter. She was no oil painting but the sweetest creature in the world. No sooner were they married than Dad pops his clogs, shop was sold and they left. It's all coming back to me now. They went to the West Country. I didn't know the family that well, you understand, it was your uncle knew Fred well, not me. Member of the same lodge, you see. But there was a lot of talk at the time.'

'Such as?' Lily had to put her hand out to steady herself. She felt dizzy – was she drunk? If so, it was a pleasant sensation.

'Food poisoning. Well, I ask you, that can cover a multitude, can't it?'

'I don't understand.'

'Who's to say? Attack like that out of the blue, the doctor not called until morning when it was too late? Dead as doornails, both of them.'

'You mean there was talk of foul play?'

'That could be said.'

'That he poisoned them?'

'I never said that,' Cherry demurred.

'But where was the daughter, Dulcie, when this was going on? If he's under suspicion, so is she.'

'Lord love you, no. She was away, nursing a sick aunt. Most convenient.' Cherry pursued her lips. 'Makes you think, circumstances like that. If I was Dulcie, I'd watch what I ate and drank when he was around, if you take my meaning.'

Lily slumped in the armchair. 'Well I never! And him so handsome.'

'They usually are.'

Lily looked long and hard into her glass as she swirled

the yellow liquid around it. 'I think I will come for that visit, after all. You're right. I can ask the lady next door to care for Mother. Maybe we could even travel back together, Aunt.'

9

Phoebe was looking out of the window. The room was hot and the early-morning air outside was cool so she could draw in the condensation on the glass. At least it was something different to do.

'Stop that! You'll smear the window-pane.' Mrs White bustled in with a pile of laundry, a young maid in tow. Phoebe looked with interest at the girl: normally she only ever saw the housekeeper and Mrs Lingford.

'Hallo.' She smiled at the maid, who blushed to the roots of her hair.

'Don't speak to her, Sylvia.'

'Why can't she? Hallo, Sylvia.' She looked pointedly at Mrs White as she spoke.

'Hallo,' the girl whispered.

'I told you to ignore her.' Mrs White gave Sylvia a push. 'Get on with changing the linen. And you, stop causing trouble,' she said aggressively to Phoebe.

'What's troublesome about being polite? What's the matter with you? I'm not infectious.'

'You mind your lip, my girl!'

'And you mind your manners. Why do you never knock when you come into my room?'

'Why should I?'

'Because it's polite, that's why. Mrs Lingford does.'

'More fool she.'

'She's not a fool, and don't you dare say she is!' Phoebe put her hands on her hips, her whole body rigid with defiance. Sylvia was clutching the clean sheets to her scrawny chest, her expression an odd mixture of awe and fear.

'It isn't *your* room. It belongs to Mr Bartholomew, and don't you ever forget it.'

'Whoever it belongs to, I'm in it for the time being and you should knock. It may not be convenient to me to have you just stalk in.'

Sylvia had to stifle a giggle. She turned away to concentrate on the bed in case Mrs White saw.

'My hand itches to slap you good and hard.'

'I know the feeling.' Phoebe scratched at the palm of her hand.

'Mrs White?' Sylvia was still whispering so the housekeeper did not hear her. 'Mrs White,' she said, more loudly, but still there was no response. 'Mrs White!'

'Good God, girl, I'm not deaf! Do you have to shout so loud.'

'Sorry, Mrs White, but you've not put in any pillow-cases.'

The housekeeper lifted her chatelaine, which habitually clanked against her thigh, and unhooked a key. Then she changed her mind. 'No, you stay here. I'll go and get them – you'll only make a mess of my linen cupboard.'

Once Mrs White was safely out of the way, Sylvia giggled. 'She's frightened I'll find her secret store of sherry,' she confided.

'So that's why her nose is so red. I might have guessed. I haven't seen you before. How long have you worked here?' Phoebe crossed the room to the bed and, to Sylvia's astonishment, helped her with the bottom sheet.

'Two weeks.'

'You've been here the same time as me. Do you know what goes on here?'

'No, Miss.' She bit her lip.

'You do.'

'I don't.'

'You're lying.'

69

'I'm not.'

'You'll burn in hell fire for eternity.'

'Miss, don't!' Her cry was anguished.

'Well, then, tell me.'

'Honest, Miss, I'm not sure, only I think it's something to do with the master and you young ladies, like. But I don't know more and that's the honest truth. They always stop talking in the servants' hall when I come in.'

'There's someone else here?'

'Yes, but she's not like you. She cries all the time.'

'What happened to her.'

'I don't know, honest I don't, but they said it was her own fault and she probably enjoyed it.'

'Couldn't you find out more? Ask her what's happened, why she's crying?'

'I'm not allowed in there no more. She tried to hand me a letter to take out, to her mum she said it was, over Exmoor way, though how I was supposed to get it there, I don't know. But I needn't have worried. Mrs White found out.' She fussed with the corner of the sheet. 'Mrs White's very particular about the corners.'

'I don't give a tinker's curse about the sheets.' Phoebe leaned over the bed and grabbed and maid's wrist. 'What did she say? What did the old crow do with the letter?'

'You shouldn't talk like that, you'll get into trouble.'

'Not nearly as much as you will if you don't tell me.'

'She tore it up.'

'The old witch!'

'She said it was from the girl's lover, and that's not nice, is it, a girl of her age having a lover? Not right at all.'

'How old?'

'Same as you, I should guess.'

'Sixteen?'

'Thereabouts. But you look younger than that.'

Phoebe grabbed the girl's other wrist. 'Mrs White

never found it, did she? You gave it to her, didn't you? You're not to be trusted, are you?'

'You're hurting me.' She looked as if she was about to cry but then her expression became cunning. 'Here, don't you live over at Cowman's Combe? Only I'm from Southcombe. That's only a mile or two away.'

'Not me. You're muddling me with someone else. I'm from Exeter, born and bred.' She let go of Sylvia's arms just as the door flew open.

'You were talking. I heard you. What have I told you, Sylvia? You're not to speak to the likes of her.'

'She made me, Mrs White. She was hurting me.'

Phoebe rocked on her feet as Mrs White slapped her hard across the face. 'How dare you hurt my girls?'

Phoebe slapped her back. 'And how dare you hit me? I'll tell Mr Bartholomew about you, and that's a promise.'

'Come, Sylvia, out of this room! You shouldn't be near the likes of her – you're a respectable girl.'

'So am I!' Phoebe raced across the room to the window and scrawled patterns all over it. 'So am I,' she shouted.

'So am I,' she said softly, and began to cry, now that the door was shut and she was alone.

'I gather you had an altercation with Mrs White this morning.'

'If you mean I shouted at her and slapped her, yes, I did. But she did it first.'

'She shouldn't have done it, of course – but you should not have reacted as you did. It cannot help your time here.'

Phoebe glanced up from the picture book she had been looking at. 'You mean I won't always be here?'

'I didn't say that.'

'No, not exactly, but it's what you meant.' Carefully she laid the book down on the table. 'You never answer anything I ask you. Why not? Have you been told not to?

Are you frightened to answer?' Lynette Lingford looked away. 'I'm still here. There's no point in looking out of the window and pretending I don't exist.' She walked round, stood in front of the other woman's chair and bent forward, pushing her face at her. 'Answer me! How long will I be here? What am I here for? What is going to happen to me?' She sank to the floor with unconscious grace and grabbed her hands. 'Please, Mrs Lingford, I need to know.'

The older woman looked from right to left, as a trapped animal does. Then she looked into Phoebe's eyes and paused as if to say something. She shook her head. 'Child, you've nothing to fear. Really. You learn so much. Shall we go for a walk?'

Phoebe stood back. 'A walk? Wonderful!'

'I asked Mr Bartholomew if this were possible. I explained that as a country girl, you were in need of exercise.'

'Thank you, Mrs Lingford. I feel as if I've been shut up in this room for a million years!'

'You'll need a cape and your bonnet. A young lady must never be seen outside without her bonnet.'

'A minute, that's all I need. Sun! Air! Wind!' she cried with glee, and dashed off to find what Mrs Lingford had prescribed. At the door she paused. 'Young lady, yes, that's me, isn't it? Who would have guessed it?' Then she moved in a more sedate manner, as she had been taught.

Outside the house, Phoebe scampered across the grass throwing back her head to feel the sun on her face.

'You must protect your skin from the sun's rays. We don't want you becoming brown, now, do we?'

'I'm always brown in the summer. Like nutmeg, my brother Dick always said.'

'A brother? Older than you?'

'Yes, he's eighteen and built like a shite-house—'

'Phoebe! Language! Is he at home?'

'No. He's a soldier,' she announced proudly. 'He

72

joined the Devonshire and Dorset Regiment. He's been sent off with the others.'

'To the Cape?'

'He says it's hot there.'

'I can show you on the globe when we return to the house, if you like.'

'I know where it is. Mrs Benson – she's the vicar's wife at home – showed me on her atlas.'

'It must be a great worry for you.'

'Not really. He wrote that he was happy, and that's all that matters to me.'

'Have you not heard of the Boers?'

'Of course.'

'And still you're not concerned?'

'I know lots of bores. Most of my father's friends in fact.'

'Not that sort of bore, Phoebe. Boers. They are people of Dutch origin who settled in South Africa.'

'Never heard of them.'

'Explaining things to you can be nigh impossible sometimes. If you stand still for a moment I will tell you. The Boers want a war with England—'

'My Dick? In a war? I don't like the sound of that, Mrs Lingford. What war? Why would anyone want a war with us?' She was serious now.

'They say the land is theirs when, of course, it is ours.'

'Is it?'

'Yes.'

'How can two lots of people own the same land? If our neighbour claimed our land my father would set him right.'

'How would he prove it?'

'Because he was there first. That's fair. So who was on this land first? Them or us?'

'It's more complicated than that. There is trade, the railway to be built, and investments, gold, a myriad reasons, all of which these people are being difficult about.'

'So it's not just about land, it's about gold too.'

'Well, yes, but . . . I told you. They think it should all be theirs. It's not reasonable of them.'

'And is it reasonable of us to want it too? Especially if they were there first?'

'Phoebe, why do you argue every single point?'

'I wasn't. I'm curious.'

'These are brutal, ruthless people who will stop at nothing. Where is your brother garrisoned?'

'A place called Wagon Hill. That's easy enough to remember.'

'You still don't seem worried.'

'I don't mind. No, I'm not worried. If we're not fighting now why worry about something that might not happen? And what can I do about it? Nothing. In any case, Dick is a lucky person. We used to tease him that if he fell into a pile of dung he'd come up smelling of violets. And if anything happened to him, I'd know. Straight away. That's when I'd worry.' Phoebe felt nervous at this turn of conversation. Dick in danger was something she did not want to think about. She glanced up at the imposing mansion, which she was seeing from the outside for the first time. 'Do you feel as if we're being watched?'

'One of the maids, I expect.'

'It's a lovely house. Just look at all those turrets and towers. It's like the picture in the book you lent me.'

'*The Sleeping Beauty*?'

'Yes, that's the one. Not that I'm sleeping, nor no beauty.'

'I wouldn't say that. Shall we take the Long Walk? It's always so pretty and the trees will protect your complexion.'

They walked along in companionable silence, Phoebe delighting in the fresh air, taking great lungfuls of it as if she was storing it up for when she was cooped up in her room again.

'You never answered my question. And I won't walk another step until you tell me.' She sat down on a stone bench at the side of the path, a vantage-point for the view that was spread out before them.

'I told you several days ago. It amuses Mr Bartholomew to make poor young women such as you into elegant young ladies.'

'Why?'

'As I said, because it pleases him.'

'No one does anything for nothing.'

'He does.'

Phoebe looked at her with a shrewd expression. 'All this . . .' she made a sweeping gesture with her hand to encompass the house in the distance, the gardens '. . . I mean, just look at the room I'm in. Well, I've been thinking it's all got to be paid for one way or another, hasn't it?'

'There are people who worship beauty. Mr Bartholomew is one of them. While you are here you need not fear.'

'And what happens to make me have to go?'

'If he tires of you.'

'Does that always happen?'

'He seeks perfection, and perhaps it will be you.'

'Me!' This idea made Phoebe laugh. 'And after?'

'That is entirely up to you.'

Try as she might Phoebe could not find out anything of value from Mrs Lingford. 'I can sit in my room any time, so if you won't tell me nothing, there's no point in me wasting a walk sitting here.' She jumped abruptly to her feet and sped down a path that criss-crossed the steep bank on which they'd been sitting. She was aware that Mrs Lingford was hurrying after her, calling her name, but she ignored her and quickened her pace. From her bedroom window she had noticed an enormous square of high bushes, neatly trimmed and planted in a complex pattern. It was a maze, Mrs Lingford had told her, and had then explained what it was.

All that planting, pruning and cutting just to create somewhere you could get lost in on purpose? It was the stupidest thing Phoebe had ever heard of. It was easy enough to get lost on the moor, and that was free.

Today, wanting to get lost, she headed for it swiftly, her companion some way behind her.

'Wait for me!' Phoebe heard Mrs Lingford call as she found the entrance and dived in. She ran along the green corridors, turning left, then right, uncertain where she was. At first it was fun, especially as she could hear Mrs Lingford calling her anxiously. 'Phoebe, answer me, where are you?' She did not reply.

The fun dissipated as she realised that the voice was getting fainter. Then, for the third time, she noticed the same weed. The place was so well tended there were no others. Panic set in as, also for the third time, she reached a dead end.

'I'm over here,' she called, but how could she know where 'here' was when everything looked the same?

'Only a bloody lunatic would build a trap like this,' she told herself.

'I agree!' she answered.

She was running now, up one path and down another, and suddenly she found herself in a square. In the centre a fountain was spurting water in a small pond – and a man was sitting on a stone bench, looking at the water, lost in thought. She began to back away when he turned and, seeing her, stood up. 'I hope I didn't startle you?' he said, doffing his hat and bowing. She stood transfixed. He'd bowed – to her! And he was handsome, and *young*!

'Are you a ghost? A beautiful young wraith?' He smiled, which made him look even more handsome.

'I . . . I'm . . .' Why on earth could she not form any words?

'Ah! There you are! Really, Phoebe, you must not . . . Why, Mr Edward! What a pleasant surprise. Phoebe, may I introduce Mr Edward Bartholomew-Prestwick. This is my friend, Miss Phoebe . . .' Mrs Lingford paused.

'Drewett,' Phoebe said, dropping a neat curtsy, with such grace that she might have been doing it all her life.

'Miss Drewett, I'm charmed.' He bowed again and Phoebe refrained from laughing, but her face was pink. He was the most beautiful man she had ever seen. She felt a strange melting feeling, as if her insides were made of honey. 'May I join you?'

'It would be our pleasure.' To her relief, Mrs Lingford answered. 'Especially for me. I confess I loathe this maze. I'm always afraid I shall never find my way out and weeks later my skeleton will be discovered!' She laughed in a girlish manner. To her shock and annoyance, Phoebe realised the woman was flirting with him.

'Disgusting!'

'Did you say something, Phoebe?'

'Nothing, Mrs Lingford.'

'You should not fear, Mrs Lingford. If you failed to return, the gardeners would climb the lookouts – there are four, you know.'

'I'd never noticed. How unobservant of me.'

'I don't think that could ever be said of you, Mrs Lingford.'

No! thought Phoebe. He's flirting too!

'And there is a simple way to escape.'

'Pray, don't tell me, Mr Edward. You'd spoil the fun.'

'You ladies are so contrary. Charmingly so.' He smiled again, but at Mrs Lingford, and Phoebe felt a strange new emotion. Jealousy! She wanted them to stop flirting, but she didn't know how to make them. If only she could think of something to say.

They fell into step. 'We don't often see you here, Mr Edward.'

'I have business in Barlton. This way, ladies. Shall I

77

take the lead?' Phoebe followed them: the path was only wide enough for two. 'I felt I should combine it with a visit to my uncle.'

'But, of course, how convenient.'

'I dine with a Mr Randolph-Smythe. Do you know him?'

'Only *of* him, his emporium is a wonder. His wife is a kind woman. She . . .'

Phoebe was not listening as they talked. She was content to walk behind him, listening to his voice. How deep, how refined it was. That was how Mrs Lingford wanted her to speak. Perhaps if she did he'd notice her. He was so tall, and what shiny boots! Phoebe was smiling to herself now. In the few minutes she had been in his company all her fears and worries had disappeared. Without doubt she had fallen in love. She had always known it would feel just as lovely as this. But what to do about Mrs Lingford?

'Break her neck!'

'Did you say something, Phoebe?' Mrs Lingford turned to look at her. But so did he.

'Nothing, Mrs Lingford.' Now why couldn't she have thought of something witty to say? She smiled at him. Her heart felt as though it was about to stop as he returned the smile, and looked so intently at her that she was sure she would swoon if she were a lady.

10

For one as shy and lacking in confidence as Dulcie, entertaining was a nightmare. To ensure everything went to plan she approached such occasions with meticulous care.

Whenever Arnold announced they would be having a dinner party, a reception, a dance, her mind whirled with decisions to be made. The guest list was the first thing to tackle. She would leaf through her address book, grown large over the years deciding who would like whom, who would be stimulating, then balancing the serious person with someone more frivolous.

Like many shy people, she loved watching others who weren't. She envied their ease. She, who found conversations terrifying, would listen enthralled to others. She, who could never remember a joke and did not know how to be witty, appreciated the skill of others. Never wanting to hold centre stage, she was more than happy to let others shine.

While she could not play a musical instrument, or sing, she enjoyed listening, and always encouraged those with even minimal talent to perform. A quintet she had employed for years always performed at her soirées. Some of her happier moments were spent with its leader, discussing which pieces should be played and in what order. She had acquired, without noticing it, an almost encyclopedic knowledge of music. Frequently she had a lady harpist to play, even though her husband's interest in the young woman exceeded her ability with her instrument.

She planned the meal like a military operation. She would open her personal receipt book, crammed with favourites she had collected over the years, and consult with Annie Bramble. Her cook loved food as much as she did, and was happy to talk about it for as long as Dulcie liked. She and Mrs Bramble enjoyed working together for both respected the other's abilities – something Agnes could never understand. And Dulcie knew a lot about wine, too, for someone who rarely drank it. Good wine had been one of her father's passions and he had taught her well.

Over the years she had evolved her own filing system of who had attended which dinner, what they had eaten, which china had been used, what colours she had chosen, so there was no risk of repeating what she had served them previously.

The morning of a day of entertainment would find Dulcie in the flower room, her dress protected by a green overall, secateurs in hand, fretting over great vases of blooms that, for her, never seemed to wilt. She made delicate arrangements for her table, twining long garlands of flowers to drape over the cloth. Not for her the convention of only two colours in a vase: she filled them with an array and, daringly, she had been known to include weeds!

Unfortunately people never thought to tell her how delighted they were to receive her undivided attention, which made them feel far more important than they were. Although her guests commented to each other on her kindness, her charm, her formidable talents as a hostess, and congratulated Arnold on his paragon of a wife, the compliments never reached her ears.

Dulcie feared she was the dullest, most incompetent creature alive.

Dulcie looked at her watch. It was nearly six. If Arnold didn't come home soon he would not have time to bathe and change as he always liked to do before dinner. Where was he? An avid reader of the society columns, she had tried once or twice to move her dining time to later, like the Prince of Wales, but in these rural parts the innovation had not been well received, and seven was the latest she could serve the meal. Her guests would be here in less than half an hour.

Tonight she felt even more nervous than usual. She did not know how she was going to react when Sophie Franks, her betrayer, appeared. She had even toyed with the idea of a sudden indisposition, but duty made her dismiss that comforting idea.

She had dressed with particular care, and she had asked Bee to pin ornaments in her hair, which normally she never bothered with. She took one last look in the mirror on her dressing-table. She would have to do: no amount of primping and fussing could make her look any better.

'There, ma'am, you look a treat.'

'Thank you, Bee.'

She stood up and studied herself in the long cheval mirror. She had chosen a sea-green dress – they could manufacture such wonderful colours, these days. What would her dear father have said? She patted her frock, cut cleverly to minimise her bulk, and sighed. She often wondered what it would be like to be slim and pretty. Sophie was both, and young too, which only added insult to injury. She selected a silk chiffon scarf, admiring the way one green complemented the other, and draped it round her neck to hide the lines and her double chin. Sophie, of course, had neither.

'How do we look?'

The door had opened. Agnes and her best friend, Adeline Salter, stood waiting to be admired. Dulcie clapped her hands.

'Perfection,' she exclaimed. Both girls looked beautiful, one in blue, the other in yellow. In her day she would never, at their age, have dared to wear anything but white.

'Perhaps the *décolletage* is a little too daring?'

'Mother, everyone is wearing low this season.'

'Are they?' Dulcie was the first to acknowledge that she knew little of fashion, which changed with such speed that it was impossible to keep up with what colours, fabrics and cut of sleeve were in vogue. Consequently she was invariably dressed in the style of five years ago. 'Your hair is beautifully dressed.' *There* was another difference: how she had begged her own mother to let her put up her hair, but these two had curls and fringes and tresses brushing their shoulders. 'You have such a tiny waist, Adeline.' Agnes scowled. 'As have you, Agnes,' she added hastily.

'No, I haven't. You said that to hurt me. But at least I have a waist! Not like some.'

'You look lovely, Miss Agnes,' Bee interjected.

Dear Bee, thought Dulcie, always so protective of me. 'As do you, Miss Adeline,' Bee went on, after a noticeable pause. So Bee doesn't like her either, thought Dulcie, who despised herself for not having taken to the girl, especially since the child was always polite and helpful. Perhaps she was *too* polite and helpful. She smiled to herself. Compared with Agnes, that would not be difficult.

'Mama, I was hoping you'd lend me your pearls since you're not wearing them,' Agnes wheedled. 'Please.' The girl's ability to switch from spite to sweetness in a second always amazed Dulcie. 'Be careful if we have dancing.' She handed over the string, her wedding present from her parents.

'*If*, Mother? Of course we shall, and I shall guard your pearls with my life.'

'There's your father. Leave us now, he'll be in a flurry to change.'

She heard Agnes greet him, the laughter, the kisses. Agnes could do no wrong in his eyes, as he couldn't in hers. If Dulcie disappeared overnight she doubted that those two would notice.

In the doorway Bee drew back to let the master of the house into the room. He passed her without a word. 'Dulcie, my sweet, you look lovely.'

He bent to kiss her cheek and she moved quickly so that his lips met air. 'You're very late,' she said.

'Held up by business, my dear.'

'I've laid out your diamond studs.'

'You always know exactly what I want. You have such a genius for pleasing a man.'

Dulcie bustled about and, not for the first time,

wondered why he had bothered with the compliments, especially when there was no one but Bee to hear. She didn't need this charade to know that he had been with another woman. She could smell the stench of cheap perfume and sex.

'Your bath is drawn. I'll go down in case our guests are early.' At the door she turned, as he was about to enter his dressing room. 'Might I suggest something, Arnold?'

'What's that, dear heart?'

'Buy your whore some decent scent. I find hers cheap and offensive.'

Bee clapped her hand over her mouth to suppress a cry of astonishment.

Dulcie sat in the drawing room awaiting her guests. She hoped Sophie and her husband would not be first to arrive: to be alone with them would be difficult tonight. She wondered if Basil Franks knew about his wife and Arnold. Some women in her position would have made a point of telling him. She wouldn't. Why disseminate the shame and humiliation?

Of all the women in their circle Sophie was the one friend she had least expected to deceive her.

Now, wasn't that a strange thing for her to think? She sat even straighter from the surprise of it. Had she known deep down that this affair, his breaking his pledge, was inevitable?

But Sophie! When the girl had been introduced to her two years ago, Dulcie had gone out of her way to befriend her. Sophie's husband was a good thirty years older, a rich seed merchant, but he was gruff and mean, no companion for a sweet girl of twenty. At least, she had thought her sweet. Dulcie took a sip of the sherry that, unusually, she had poured for herself.

She had lost count of the times she had helped the young woman pay bills she had run up and was afraid to tell her husband about for fear of a beating. She had even paid for a couple of dresses the child had had made in the hope that she could persuade her miserly husband to buy them. All Dulcie had achieved was to help a perfidious creature ensnare her own husband. It was not his unfaithfulness that hurt, it was the betrayal among their set. For if the servants knew, how many others were aware of her humiliation?

The butler announced the first arrivals, then the second, and finally there was Sophie, resplendent in a mauve dinner dress Dulcie had purchased, wearing diamond earrings she had lent her, hair dressed by Mr Emil, whose bills Dulcie often paid.

'Dearest Dulcie, how fine you look.' Sophie swept towards her and bent to kiss her, but Dulcie moved her head sharply to one side. 'Such a pretty colour.'

'Mrs Franks,' she said coldly. She stared at Sophie and received a measure of satisfaction in seeing her look ashamed and, for once, ill at ease.

Dulcie found now that a steely core had formed within her. She would be passive no longer. It was time to act.

Despite Sophie's presence, the dinner was going well. She had purposely placed the young woman between the two most tedious men of Arnold's acquaintance. After her cool welcome, Dulcie had reverted to her normal self. She was not ready for Arnold to learn that she knew of the liaison. She saw Sophie looking confused and this evening the girl did not sparkle. Dulcie was sure that no one, including Sophie, was aware of how angry she was.

She sat at the head of the table, watching with pleasure as her guests ate greedily. She beckoned to the butler. 'It would be better if Miss Agnes's glass was not replenished quite so frequently,' she whispered in his ear. The silly child was looking quite flushed and was on the verge of becoming noisy. She watched the butler pass her by as he topped up the other guests' wine. Agnes looked annoyed and turned her empty glass to attract his attention, without success. Robert Markham had been invited for her, yet she had eyes only for the guest of honour, Edward Bartholomew-Prestwick. Was she smitten with him or just trying to make Robert jealous? Or was it just that she had drunk too much wine?

This made Dulcie smile. She was a fine one to criticise. On top of the sherry, she'd had three glasses of wine, far in excess of her normal intake. Was that why she felt so calm, yet strangely elated?

'Are you staying in these parts long?' she asked Edward Bartholomew-Prestwick. Fortunately she had discovered just before dinner that he was an Honourable, and had had time to change the seating so that, as the man of highest social standing, he sat on her right. Arnold must have known, and should have told her.

'My visits to my uncle only ever last three days. It's the maximum amount of time he can tolerate me.' The young man laughed good-naturedly.

What a winning smile he had. 'I can't think that is true. I should think you the most charming companion.'

'My uncle prefers his own company.'

'I gather he is somewhat reclusive.' She had heard a lot more but didn't like to dwell on it. 'And I am told his skill as a translator of ancient texts is considered most erudite.'

'They're all Greek to me.'

She laughed at his little joke.

'But you like books too?' he continued. 'Have you not founded a library for the poor?'

'A modest affair. I enjoy reading so much and for the poor it might be an escape from the hardships of life. Why should they not have the opportunity too?'

'Very commendable. That's if they can read.'

'We offer lessons in reading – in the evenings, to avoid interfering with their work.'

'And your husband is involved?'

'Arnold?' She laughed. 'Good gracious, no. He thinks I

waste *my* money.' She had used the emphasis deliberately, for the first time in her married life. 'Do you live here?'

'No, in Exeter. We used to – but it's a long story.'

She wondered why he looked sad when he said that. 'Such a charming city. I enjoy visiting it when I can find the time. What brings you to Barlton?'

'Your husband wished to discuss business with me and that was another reason to come. I am having such a delightful evening, and in such wonderful company.'

He can't mean me, she thought, so he must be taken with Agnes. Was that a good idea? Yet he may not have the same tastes as his uncle and, in any case, he was young. Arnold would be pleased, of course – a young man with a title, and even Dulcie had thought that Robert Markham was too soft and sweet a man to control Agnes. And Edward Bartholomew-Prestwick would have all that land and money, should he inherit from his uncle. Or did his parents have land too? And why did he have a title if his uncle didn't? There was much she had to find out. Still, didn't she herself know that all the money in the world would not make Agnes happy unless she was loved?

'You frown, Mrs Randolph-Smythe. I trust I haven't offended you?'

'Of course not, and please, Mrs Randolph is sufficient. I was curious what business my husband wishes to discuss with you.' She attempted to look arch but was not sure if she had succeeded. She was not good at wheedling anything out of anyone, let alone a handsome young man such as this one. What she really wanted to say, but her courage failed her, was, 'What is it that my husband wants me to invest *my* money in this time?'

'My uncle owns some property in Gold Street. Your husband wishes to purchase it. I look after my uncle's affairs for him and that is the matter to be discussed.'

'Oh, I see. And what is he purchasing it for?'

Edward looked nonplussed. 'Has he not said?'

'My husband rarely tells me anything. He thinks me stupid.' She smiled. What a liberation the truth could be! But the young man looked even more baffled. 'He thinks discussing business is not for the delicate ears of ladies,' she explained, more gently.

'I often think that most unfair, Mrs Randolph.'

'I very much agree with you.'

'I'm not sure what his plans are – I presumed to expand his shop.'

'My shop, you mean?' There! She had said it! Told the truth! She found it quite intoxicating. What else might she say before the evening was out?

'Forgive me ... but of course – I was not aware ... I simply assumed.'

The poor young man looked so confused. 'And what is the expansion for?'

'I'm not sure, but he was asking me about antiques for furnishing it.'

'Really? How interesting.' What *was* Arnold up to? Well, she wasn't moving, and that was certain. And Bartholomew House, which was on Gold Street, was far too big for them.

'Judging by your beautiful home he has no need of advice. He has a connoisseur's eye.'

'Everything you see is mine.' She smiled sweetly. 'He just likes people to think it is his.' She laughed, almost girlishly.

'Quite.'

Poor man, he was puzzled again. She was not being fair to him. 'In a marriage who owns what is immaterial,' she said.

'Naturally.'

'Are you interested in the subject?'

'Marriage or furniture?'

'Why, both!' She was laughing again, a mite loudly,

and was gratified to notice Arnold frowning at her from his end of the long table.

'At the moment, neither of those two. Porcelain is my passion.'

Dulcie clapped her hands with joy. 'Mine too,' she said, almost as if it was a conspiracy. 'Perhaps you would like to see my collection after dinner?'

'I would be overjoyed.'

The meal over, Agnes demanded of her father that they dance. The servants began to move the furniture and Edward approached Dulcie. 'Your collection, Mrs Randolph, would this be a good time?'

'You don't wish to dance?'

'I'd rather look at porcelain.'

'It would be my pleasure.' Ignoring Agnes's thunderous look, Dulcie took Edward into what she fondly called her china room. Glass cabinets covered three walls, each lined with silk, and lit by the wonderful electricity Arnold had had installed. 'Here we are.' She opened the double doors with a flourish.

'What treasures!' he exclaimed, when he saw the Spode, Meissen, and the Chelsea ware she had just begun to collect.

'I'm never sure if displaying it in this manner is right. It looks a little like a museum.'

'I think it wonderful.'

'Really? Only . . .'

'Yes?' he asked politely, when nothing was forthcoming.

'I was in the Moll tea shop a little while ago, and I overheard two persons . . . I shouldn't be bothering you with this.'

'Please, continue.'

'They, of course, were unaware of my presence, but they said my way of displaying my china was vulgar, but what could one expect from the *nouveaux riches*, such as us?' She said it in a rush, for fear that otherwise she would never say it. And wondered why on earth she had unburdened herself to him.

'They sound as if they might be jealous.' He smiled kindly.

'Do you think so?'

'I am certain of it. I think it most original. In fact, with your permission, I would like to emulate you.'

'I should be proud if you did. I don't know why it upset me so. I don't pretend to be anything that I'm not. And, really, I hardly knew those women, so why should I have been so upset?'

'Because they were criticising your most precious possessions.'

'Perhaps. I was wondering,' she said shyly, 'if you would care to see my dinner services? I have so many that Arnold has banned me from buying more.'

'It would afford me enormous pleasure.'

'I collect famous people's dinner services. I've one of Lord Nelson's and . . . But come and see. They are at the back of the house, if you don't mind?'

Half an hour had gone by, and they were admiring the set that Napoleon had had made for his stepdaughter Hortense, which Dulcie had only recently acquired. She knew she would never tell a soul what she had paid for it – just thinking about it kept her awake at night. Still, Arnold had his secrets, why shouldn't she have hers?

'Here you are! Dulcie, you neglect your other guests.'

'My fault, sir. Your wife graciously showed me her collection when I asked if I might see it. We were too engrossed to realise our rudeness.'

How diplomatic he is, she thought, as they walked back to the main part of the house.

Arnold was furious with her. 'What on earth got into you? Taking our most important guest to view your stupid collection of dinner plates! By the *kitchen* of all places! What must he have thought of us?'

'He was most interested and very knowledgeable.'

'You took him to the *kitchen*!'

'He didn't seem to notice.'

'Of *course* he noticed. He must have thought I was married to a madwoman. You were drunk.'

'I was not drunk.'

'God knows if he'll do business with me now.'

'Don't you mean with *us*? Is he not doing business with *us*?' She allowed her irritation to show.

'What do you mean?' Arnold looked astonished.

'You know exactly what I mean. You know, the one reason you stay with me. No, that's wrong, there are two. One, you could not afford the scandal of separation or divorce if you are to be mayor. And, two, there is always the money.'

'You are an evil-minded woman, Dulcie.'

'But not nearly as bad as you, Arnold.'

Agnes, too, was furious with her. 'How could you, Mother? How could you keep him all to yourself? I longed to talk to him, dance with him.'

'I'm sorry, my dear. I thought you wished to dance with Robert.'

'And what did you say to him that he left almost as soon as you came back from your stupid china?'

'He didn't think it stupid. He was most complimentary. He had a long distance to ride to his uncle's at Courtney Lacey.'

'Do you think he noticed me?'

'I'm sure everyone noticed you.'

'I didn't mean everyone, I meant him!'

'I really couldn't say.' She hoped not. She liked Edward and sensed he was too good a person for Agnes.

'Mama, if I tell you something, will you keep it a secret?'

'I'll try.'

'I love him, Mama. I saw him and I knew he was the one. I shall marry him, Mama. I have decided.'

'Have you?' Dulcie said, as equably as she could. But she had noticed the sudden switch to 'Mama', which meant that Agnes wanted something from her.

Chapter Two
October 1899–November 1899

I

Phoebe had glimpsed Edward twice from her window. Both times he had been walking alone in the garden – towards the maze, she was sure. Just seeing him, even at a distance, had excited her so much that she thought she might melt into a pool on the floor. The second time she had tapped bravely on the glass. At first he hadn't heard, so she had rapped again, which made him look up. He waved, and she blushed furiously.

The blush had deepened when he doffed his hat and bowed. Phoebe was not sure what was happening to her: the sight of him dressed for riding in his tight breeches had made her feel oddly weak. She was certain she was in love, but she had not realised that his breeches might be connected with that. 'Love's an odd thing,' she said.

'And you are odder,' she replied.

He beckoned to her to come out and join him. *He* wanted her to walk with *him*! Her heart was beating alarmingly and she hoped it wouldn't burst. She shook her head sadly and made a locking motion with her hand. She could only hope that he understood the gesture. Regretfully she watched him stride away.

After this she pestered Mrs Lingford every day to walk with her in the grounds, but even though she cajoled her into staying out far longer than she had intended, she didn't see him again. If only she could persuade Mrs Lingford to visit the maze at the same time each day perhaps she would bump into him. But she never knew at what time she would have her outing, for Mrs Lingford came at varying times.

Nor, to her disappointment, did she see Sylvia. She had asked Mrs White about her, but the woman's bad-tempered reply told her that it had not been wise to do so.

'Mrs Lingford, do you know a maid called Sylvia who works here?'

'I know none of the maids. I have no contact with them,' she answered. Phoebe didn't believe her. 'I only come to the big house to see you.'

'It was pleasant to meet someone my own age – for a change.' She had added the last phrase because she was feeling irritated. She often did, these days.

'It must have been pleasurable for you. Did you talk much to her?'

'There was hardly time.' They were on the Long Walk now, her second favourite place after the maze. There was no reply, and she must not alienate Lynette Lingford, Phoebe realised. 'So you don't live here?' she asked, more pleasantly.

'No, I have a cottage.'

'Where?'

'Do you see the oak – the one I told you was in the Domesday Book? To the left of that.' She was pointing across to the park. 'Now, do you see a small copse? That's where our cottage is.'

'Ours, you say. Do you have children?'

'I have two, and three stepchildren. Such a handful but a joy, all of them. And my father-in-law lives with us.'

When she had spoken of her children her voice was light, but it changed when she mentioned the man. She didn't like him, Phoebe concluded.

'And you have a husband too? What a squash it must be!'

'It's certainly is, but I am a widow.'

'I'm so sorry, I shouldn't have asked. How rude of me.'

'Why should you not? He's been gone a long time. I

can talk about him now, although it was hard for a long time.'

'Was he ill?'

'No.' She looked so sad that Phoebe wanted to hug her and wished she hadn't been so nosy. 'I might as well tell you before someone else does. He killed himself.'

'Never! How awful for you! How sad.'

'He was in prison.'

'Prison!'

'He was innocent.'

'Of course.'

'It was the shame, more than he could bear.'

'Certainly. But how . . . ?'

'How was he imprisoned? Because he refused to allow the real villain to be arrested. He had a great sense of loyalty – if misplaced.'

'If that was so, he wasn't very loyal to you, was he? Leaving you with all those children to care for, and his father.' Phoebe felt quite indignant for poor Mrs Lingford.

'You have a wisdom far beyond your years, Phoebe. Not many people see it that way.'

'Then they can't be very kind.' She longed to ask who the real criminal was, but didn't like to. Instinct, and the change in Mrs Lingford's tone when she mentioned him, made her wonder if it had been her father-in-law.

'Still, I must not complain. Our cottage might only be small but we are fortunate, thanks to Mr Bartholomew's generosity, to have a roof over our heads?'

'What's generous about it? If you work for him of course he should give you a house to live in.'

'I don't work for him all the time.'

'When, then?'

'When he requires me.'

'To do what?'

'To teach you.'

'And before me?'

'You ask so many questions.'

She was laughing but Phoebe knew it was the false laugh people used when they were embarrassed. 'Do I?'

'All the time. But it's a sure indication of an intelligent mind.'

'And before me, who did you teach?' Phoebe was not sidetracked by the compliment. Mrs Lingford walked on, without answering. 'Who?' Phoebe persisted.

'No one,' said Mrs Lingford, but Phoebe was quick to notice how pink she had become.

'Is Mr Edward here?' she asked, with such nonchalance that she felt like congratulating herself. She had changed the subject because she knew the woman was determined not to answer her question. Far better to drop it and resume later.

'He left this morning for Exeter.'

'Oh!' Suddenly her world seemed immeasurably bleaker.

'Don't dream, Phoebe. There's no point.'

'I'm sorry? I don't understand.'

'The likes of Edward Bartholomew-Prestwick are not for you.'

'What a thing to say, Mrs Lingford. I thought no such thing. He was a nice man, and young too. I need young people, I only meet old ones.'

'We all age.'

'But I shan't for some time!'

They walked on in silence. She shouldn't have said that, Phoebe thought. If Mrs Lingford took against her, then where would she be? 'I'm sorry. I was rude.'

'It's all right, Phoebe, I understand.'

'After all, you're not *that* old!'

'Phoebe, you're such a character.' Mrs Lingford was laughing now.

They reached the end of the Long Walk, turned and retraced their steps. 'Why does Edward have two names?'

'Mr Edward, to you, Phoebe,' but she said it gently.

'Prestwick is his father's name. He adopted Bartholomew because our Mr Bartholomew has no heir.'

'What does that mean?'

'Mr Edward is his nephew, on his mother's side. It is to ensure that the name will not die out with Mr Bartholomew. When his time comes, Mr Edward will inherit all of this.'

'All of this?' Phoebe looked around her. 'He's lucky – and all he had to do was add a name. I wouldn't mind doing that!'

'Of course, should Mr Bartholomew marry and have children it will not happen.'

'I expect Mr Edward hopes and prays it never does.'

'I doubt he would have such a base thought.'

'I would.'

'But you are not of his class.'

'More's the pity.'

'Phoebe! What did I say?'

'I'm sorry.' Phoebe grinned. 'What does Mr Bartholomew do?'

'His work, do you mean?'

'Yes.'

'Some people don't work. They have investments and property that pays them money.'

Phoebe stopped dead in her tracks. 'Do nothing and still they have money?'

'Yes.' Mrs Lingford chuckled.

'I'd like to be like that.'

'As I. But there are not many who are so fortunate.'

'Do you think he gets bored? I mean, I'm doing nothing at the moment and there are times I could scream.'

'Like today?' Lynette Lingford smiled slyly at her. 'He has his books, and his translations. That is a form of work.'

'What's a translation?'

'It means changing something from one language into

another. In his case it's Latin, Greek or French into English.'

'When you told me there were people who couldn't speak English, I found that so hard to believe. Poor things.'

'Have you never met a foreigner, Phoebe?'

'Oh, yes. At Widecombe fair you meet lots of people from all over the place. Exeter, Somerset, Cornwall, even.'

It was Mrs Lingford's turn to stop. 'Dear Phoebe, you know so little.'

'That's true, but you're teaching me so much and I'm enjoying it.'

'It's a pleasure to teach someone who is so keen. I don't think I've ever met anyone who learned to read so quickly.'

'But there are so many words and I don't know what they mean.'

'Then I must show you how to use a dictionary. That will help you.'

They neared the house. Phoebe looked up at the south-facing façade where she knew her bedroom was, and was sure she saw a face at one of the windows. 'Tell me, Mrs Lingford, is there another girl here?'

'Another girl?' Mrs Lingford repeated, in a way that made Phoebe think she was playing for time.

'Yes, near my room – a girl who cries a lot.'

'Did Sylvia tell you this?'

'No, I heard her,' she lied. No point getting Sylvia into trouble.

'Then you dreamt it. There's no one except you.'

'I think there is.'

'That is very impertinent of you, Phoebe.'

'I'm sorry.'

'As you should be.'

They entered the house in silence. She had been right.

Mrs Lingford's face was as red as a beetroot and Phoebe didn't think it was from indignation.

'You are pleased with her progress?' Kendall Bartholomew asked.

'She is as bright as a button, sir. She is hungry to learn.'

'That is good. It would be wonderful for me if I could converse with her.'

'I think that might take more time than she will be here.'

'Not necessarily, Mrs Lingford. If she is as you say, she might stay a very long time.'

Lynette shuddered inwardly. 'I fear she knows that Coral is here.'

'How?' He frowned.

'She says she heard her.'

'Impossible.'

'That's what I thought.'

'Then someone has been gossiping. Who?'

'I have no idea, sir.' It had more than likely been the maid, but if she told it would mean instant dismissal and she was desperately in need of work.

'It is not a problem. Coral is leaving tomorrow. One of our failures, Mrs Lingford. She wearied me with her sniffling.'

If only she herself could escape from this place, this man! 'She has an elder brother, I gather. A soldier.'

'Coral?'

'No, Phoebe.'

'Is he likely to come galloping to her rescue?' he asked, with amusement.

'No, sir, he is in the Cape.'

'A dangerous place to be. And if, as seems inevitable, there is war, he might be killed.'

The coldness with which he said this made her shudder again, outwardly this time.

'Are you cold, Mrs Lingford?'

'No, sir.'

'Have I said something to shock you?'

'No, sir. Perhaps someone walked over my grave.'

Phoebe was in her favourite place, sitting on the window-seat staring outside. She must have been in this house for a month at least: the days and nights were getting colder, and there was winter in the air. She prodded her stomach: she must be getting fat from such inactivity. She still had no idea why she was here, what Mr Bartholomew's plans were, but since nothing but pleasant things had happened to her she no longer felt afraid. Her apprehension had disappeared. There seemed no point in worrying, especially when she didn't know what to worry about. And now that she knew Mrs Lingford and Edward, her earlier fears appeared ridiculous: they were both such normal, charming people. There could be nothing bad here – they wouldn't have allowed it, of that she was sure.

Her time here was a great opportunity, she realised. Not only was she dressed in lovely clothes – and what girl wouldn't like that? – she was learning so many things that would help her find employment when she left, as she would one day. Not only could she read and nearly write, she knew how to eat politely. She understood how important it was for a woman to look after herself so that she always looked attractive. She knew all about personal hygiene and had vowed she would never go unwashed again: she liked to smell nice. She had learned to swish her skirts when she walked, so they made that frou-frou sound. At first she had thought this silly, but she was told that gentlemen found it delightful, and gentlemen meant Edward. Now she was proud of her skill at it.

Mrs Lingford had begun to teach her how to make conversation. Before, she had chattered, not knowing that talk could be about so many interesting things, and that it was polite to tailor what she said to the person she was talking with.

She also knew more about the world and other countries. But so much learning in such a short time was bewildering as well as exciting, and some knowledge was unwelcome: she had been told why poor Dick had had to sail away to fight. However, knowing now that he had gone to defend the English settlers and having had patriotism explained to her, she was aware that he must be proud to be there, helping them. This helped her a little, but she'd much rather he was here.

The oddest thing was that, these days, she rarely spoke to Phyllis, her dead twin. She no longer felt the need. She could pinpoint when this had happened. Edward! She didn't want to share him with anyone, not even Phyllis – she might be jealous.

She looked up as she heard a key grate in the lock. Mrs White bustled in with a newly laundered lace-trimmed blouse over her arm. 'You're to have lunch with Mr Bartholomew tomorrow. You've a new set of clothes for the occasion, as if you don't already have enough!' She hung the blouse in the wardrobe. 'Now, young woman, don't let us down. You understand?'

'I won't, I promise.' Phoebe leaped down from the window-seat. At last. Now she could show him what a fine lady she was becoming. She was mortified at how she must have seemed to him when she had first arrived. And, if she sensed it was the right time, she had every intention of asking him why she was here.

2

'But, Mother, you don't understand. I want to see him.'

'I understand perfectly, but wanting something doesn't necessarily make it right. I most certainly cannot do as you wish.'

Dulcie did not respond to Agnes's exaggerated sigh, or ask what she had muttered. That was what Agnes wanted her to do. She continued with her task.

'Are you not speaking to me?'

'Of course I am.'

'Then why don't you answer me?'

'I have. I cannot possibly invite Edward Bartholomew-Prestwick so soon after his last visit.'

'I don't see why not.'

'It would not be correct, Agnes. It would appear to him that you were pursuing him, and that would be unseemly.'

'You always think you know everything.' Agnes pouted.

'I thought you believed I knew nothing, due to my humble station in life.' Dulcie spoke so sharply that Agnes looked at her, as if she had not heard correctly.

'There! You are in a temper with me.'

'I'm tired of this constant complaining, that is all.'

'Are you ill?'

'I've never felt better. Now, excuse me, I have numerous matters to attend to.' Agnes stood back to let her pass with a stack of linen in her arms.

'That blue suits you, Mama.'

Dulcie smiled. Agnes was wheedling again.

'I think I shall die if I don't see him soon, Mama.' The girl flopped into a chair, flapping her hands agitatedly while admiring her slender fingers and perfectly buffed nails.

'I doubt it. You look in remarkably good health to me.' Dulcie continued to fold her best damask napkins, putting tissue paper between each layer.

'I'm in love, Mama.'

'But two weeks ago you were in love with Robert – such a nice young man.'

'He's dull. And he has red in his hair.'

'You did not notice it before.' Dulcie could not keep the chuckle out of her voice.

'It probably means he has a bad temper. You know that, Mother.'

'He is the most equable of young men.' The more formal 'Mother' had slipped back in.

'But not exciting.'

'And Edward is?' She knew the answer. Of course he would be a preferable choice for most young women. Handsome, intelligent, a fine figure, charming – oh, such charm. He had even made *her* heart flutter, until she had berated herself for being an ugly old fool.

'Adeline tells me he's rich.'

'He might be one day. It is his uncle who is rich, not Edward.'

'But he has expectations.'

'I always fear that expectations are never enough. One should never rely on expectations, Agnes. They may not be forthcoming.'

'But his uncle is a bachelor.'

'And don't bachelors marry?'

'But he's too old to find anyone.'

'Since he is so rich I doubt he would find his age an obstacle.' She smiled to herself.

'But he's ugly, too, from what I hear.'

'And nor is ugliness an impediment to marriage, if one is wealthy enough.' As I know to my cost, she sighed to herself.

'Don't you want me to be happy, Mother?' Agnes pouted again, which she thought made her look adorable. In fact, it increased Dulcie's determination not to give way.

'Of course, Agnes. But it doesn't mean I am about to defy convention and embarrass the young man by inundating him with invitations that he might feel obliged to accept. Now, if you wouldn't mind running along, I have much to do . . . Unless, of course, you're going to help me?' Dulcie returned to her task of checking linen but had to laugh at the speed with which Agnes left the room, swishing her skirts as she went and slamming the door in a most unladylike manner. She was an idle young woman, often unpleasant, and showed her such scant respect. But what was Dulcie to expect, given Arnold's example?

Half of the napkins would have to be laundered and ironed one more time, she decided, putting them to one side. They had the merest hint of a crease in the wrong place. She would have to reprimand the proprietor of the laundry she had patronised since her laundress had died – from exhaustion, Dulcie was sure. 'Poor people,' she said aloud, to the empty room. Agnes was lucky with her life yet she was not aware of it. Worse, although her father doted on her and gave her whatever she wanted, and although she had no worries, she was not happy.

Dulcie looked out of the window. If only creating a happy life was as simple as making a lovely garden or sorting linen. Recently she had been feeling different for some reason: sadness had been part of her life for so long that she was accustomed to and accepted it. But the shadows of melancholy were slipping away, leaving her feeling light-hearted. If Chauncey came home safe and sound she might even be happy.

Her anger over Sophie and Arnold had faded. She felt a curious sense of liberation, almost of freedom. But for Chauncey . . .

Sometimes, in the past, she had dallied with the thought of what might have been, had she been beautiful. Would her husband have strayed? She would have liked to take a lover, pay him back, show she did not care. But she had no beauty, only money. Then, such a conclusion had added to her dejection. But today she thought, what does it matter? She had integrity and her pride. And the money, which sometimes she felt had been a curse, she could see now was a blessing. She had founded the library, she was a stalwart of the local orphanage and a patron of a home for waifs and strays. These were worthwhile causes and she would no longer help undeserving women like Sophie.

There was an old mirror in the corner of the linen room. She pulled it towards her and studied herself. What could she do to make herself more appealing? It would be nice to have someone love her, a man in her bed – but not Arnold!

'Just listen to yourself, woman!' Why, she should be blushing at such ideas. She sighed. She would go to her grave never having been loved, never having been held with tender passion, never having had someone to care for her.

She replaced the mirror. Such self-pity! Anyway, Chauncey loved her unconditionally. Just thinking of him made her insides turn to water, her heart palpitate, fear almost paralyse her. Why had he run away and joined the army without coming to talk to her first?

If only he had, she might have dissuaded him. She would have given him money to set himself up somewhere safe. But, then, Chauncey had not known this was possible. It was her own fault. She should never have promised Arnold that she would allow their children – everyone – to think that everything they had was his. Still, she had been young, stupid and in love when she had vowed this, and Dulcie was not the sort of person who broke her promises – until now. Surely his betrayal negated any pledge she had made?

She fished in her pocket and took out Chauncey's letter to her, explaining his need to go, begging her forgiveness. The writing was streaked with her tears, the pages crumpled from the many times she had read them in the past six months.

. . . Forgive me, sweet Mama, but I could not stay and watch you, the loveliest, dearest woman in the world suffer and be humiliated any more. If I stay, I would kill him, of that I'm sure . . .

Kill his own father! As if Chauncey would! As if her gentle son could hurt any one. But now he had to. Now he was a soldier at the Cape, already fighting and killing the Boers who were trying to kill him. Dulcie lived with a fear that had become part of her and it had sired another emotion of which she had not thought herself capable. Hatred. She hated Arnold. If anything happened to Chauncey she was afraid of what she might do to him. Last night she had dreamt that Arnold was dead. She had woken with such happiness, which was shattered when she realised the truth.

'Papa, Mother doesn't understand. Speak to her, please!' Agnes was holding her father's hand.

'And what am I to talk to her about?'

Really, Dulcie thought, it was as if she wasn't in the room with them. She buttered her toast thickly, looked at it, then decided not to eat it. You don't care, she told herself.

'Papa, I want to see Edward, I need to see him. And she says it's impossible – that we have to wait for him to return our hospitality, that it wouldn't be proper . . .'

'Undoubtedly she is right. Your mother knows about such matters.'

'But if one waited until it was *correct* to contact him he might find someone else!'

Arnold laughed. 'You are so like me, my darling. If you want something, you must have it immediately.' He leaned forward and stroked her cheek. 'I applaud your passion – and also your perspicacity. He is a far better catch than young Markham.'

'Mother says one should not rely on expectations, don't you, Mother?'

'I think it unwise.'

'Your mother always sees matters in a bleak way – it's her nature, more's the pity.'

Don't react, Dulcie told herself, as she rang the small handbell at her side for the plates to be cleared.

'But if he didn't have a penny I should still feel the same way!'

'Now, now, my darling. One should never fall in love with a pauper. Lack of money kills love.'

'You married Mother when she had nothing.'

'That was different.'

'What was different?'

'I am a man. It's more difficult for a woman.'

Dulcie was aware that he did not even glance in her direction as he lied. She often wondered if he had persuaded himself that everything of hers was his.

'Yes, it was different, Arnold, wasn't it?' She looked straight at him and was glad to see she had made him a little edgy.

'At least Edward is handsome.'

'Agnes!' He sounded shocked, but his eyes, filled with merriment, belied the sternness in his voice. 'You should be more polite and dutiful. Your mother has much to do.'

'That's not fair, Papa! I wore myself out before the last dinner. I helped, didn't I, Mother? You enjoy organising the house, don't you? You don't need me. I think it is unkind of you to accuse me thus.'

'That is true. I don't need you.' And again she looked at her husband. He was even edgier. 'And something else, Agnes. I'm tired of your rudeness and lack of respect towards me.' She stood up, placed her napkin on the table, collected her papers and moved, head held high, to the door.

'What a huff!' she heard Agnes say, with an uncertain giggle.

Safe on the other side she listened at the still open door.

'It would be politic to be kinder to her.'

'Why, when I have you? What can she give me that you already don't?' Dulcie could imagine the pout she would be giving him.

'Such a pretty mouth,' he said. She imagined him touching the moist pink lips gently with his forefinger. 'It will be a lucky swain who has this to kiss.' Sometimes he behaved more like her lover than her father. Dulcie frowned with distaste.

'It just so happens that I know something about Mr Bartholomew-Prestwick,' he continued.

'What, Papa, what? Tell me, do!'

'He will be in my office at four on Friday. And if my lovely daughter should visit me . . .'

'Dear Papa.'

'Of course, I might leave instructions that I am not to be disturbed, even by members of my family.'

'You wouldn't, Papa!'

'I might not, if I got a kiss.'

'Papa. I love you!'

Dulcie could listen to no more.

3

Lily Howard was appalled by the company her aunt and uncle allowed into their public house in White-chapel. She had not known that such base people existed. They were noisy, they smelt, they spat and they swore.

'You'll get used to it, Lily. Why, I no longer hear the swearing. It's as if my ears have learned to block it out.'

'I've heard words today I didn't know existed,' said Lily, determined that she would not stay long enough to become inured to the goings-on.

'So long as you don't know what they mean there's nothing to worry about.' Her aunt laughed as she poured them another cup of tea. Already, even though it was only five in the afternoon, they could hear that the bar below the parlour was filling up.

'And the women!'

'Some are a bit colourful, it has to be said.'

'Are they . . . ?' Lily's face coloured as she wound herself up to ask the question that had haunted her since their arrival last night. 'They seem to me, well, not what you could call *nice*.'

'They're not that, to be sure. And don't get on the wrong side of any of them. Their language can be worse than the men's.'

'Are they . . .' How best to put it? '. . . ladies of the night?' There! It was out in the open. She sat back in the chair, her face bright pink.

'And the morning, afternoon and evening. Whenever they can pick up the business.' Her aunt chuckled.

'It's disgusting! I don't know why you allow them in your establishment, Aunt Cherry.' Lily was pious with indignation. 'I don't know what my mother would have to say about it if she knew.'

Her aunt bristled – alarming to witness. She appeared to expand, first her cheeks, then her breasts, and her fingers resembled sausages about to split out of their skins as she banged them on the table. Lily wished she hadn't spoken quite so bluntly.

'I don't give a tinker's cuss what your mother thinks. She's not that angelic herself.' Lily did not have the courage to ask what she meant. Perhaps she would later, when her aunt was not so cross.

'And I give even less for your opinion, Miss. You didn't have to come here, and if you don't like it you can scuttle back to Devon and never come back.'

'Aunt Cherry, I've made you angry.'

'That's near the truth.'

'I didn't mean to.'

'Then you should not be concerning yourself with matters you know nothing about.'

'Yes, Aunt. I'm sorry, Aunt.'

'As you should be.' She sounded mollified.

'I was concerned for you, Aunt, that was all. I'm afraid that such persons might keep respectable people away.'

At this her aunt laughed until her colour rose to a shade of magenta. Feebly she waved her handkerchief in front of her face, untill fat tears of mirth rolled down her cheeks, cutting runnels through the powder and rouge – which, to her horror, her niece now saw she was wearing.

'Aunt Cherry! Are you all right? Aunt, you frighten me . . .' She looked with dismay at the woman who was now holding her sides as if in pain. Lily ran to the kitchen and fetched a glass of water.

Her aunt waved it away. 'Gin,' she said hoarsely. 'Get me a glass of gin!'

Against her better judgement Lily ventured down the stairs to the saloon bar, a mite more genteel than the public bar from which alarmingly raucous noises were issuing. She was thankful to find it empty. She jumped at a loud rap on a wooden partition in the wall that backed on to the street. Gingerly she opened the flap.

'Apple fritter.' A filthy urchin peered up at her. He had to stand on tiptoe to plonk the tin jug on the shelf.

'I'm not sure we have any.'

'Gawd almighty! Don't say yer've run out! My mum'll knock the daylights out of me!'

'I won't be a minute.' She slammed the partition shut and went into the public bar. There, she found her uncle Alf and a vulgar-looking barmaid. Lily realised she could now be seen by the customers and that a silence had descended. All eyes seemed to be watching her.

'Ah, Lily,' Alf said, 'let me do the honours.' He faced his clientele. 'This 'ere is my niece. A respectable woman so mind your Ps and Qs.' For some mysterious reason this invoked laughter. 'And what can I do for you?'

'There's a child wants some apple fritters but I told him I wasn't sure we had any. He seems upset.'

At this her uncle laughed. Not him too, she thought, looking about her desperately.

'Did you hear that everyone? My niece thinks we might not have any bitter. Lawks, Lily, if we ran out there'd be a riot.' The assembled company brayed at her, mouths wide open, the stench of their drink-laden breath making her step back sharply only to crash into the bar and send a stack of pewter tankards flying.

'Bitter?' She began to pick up the tankards.

'Apple fritter – *bitter*!'

'Why couldn't the boy have asked for that in the first place?'

'Because that's the way we talks in these parts.' She realised from his tone that she was not alone in her irritation. 'Nelly!' he yelled. 'Jug and bottle needs attending. Now, what can I do for you, Lily? Come down for a nip yourself?'

'No, of course not, Uncle. It's Auntie. I think she's having a seizure. I tried to give her water but she wants gin.'

'Quite right too. Don't drink the water hereabouts, nasty stuff to be sure.' He was pouring gin into a jug as he spoke. 'Best take some Jack-a-dandy while you're about it.' And he proceeded to fill another jug. 'By the way, Lily, there was a girl in earlier, knows someone who might tell you a think or two about that friend of yours, Arnold, the cove you asked me about.'

'He's no friend of mine. He's my employer,' she said, with immense dignity.

'Gotcha. Want some dirt on the old bugger, do you? Very wise.'

Lily did not answer but picked up the jugs and made her way back up the stairs. She sniffed at the second jug she was carrying. It was brandy. This place was a madhouse: they were incapable of calling anything by its given name.

'Here, Aunt.' She placed the two jugs on the chenille

tablecloth. Her aunt had stopped laughing but looked exhausted.

'Bless you, child.' She began to drink the gin in great gulps straight from the jug, not waiting for a glass. Lily began to clear the tea-things so she didn't have to witness such excess. How could Cherry and her mother be sisters, she wondered, as she carried the tray to the kitchen. She returned in time to hear her aunt burp loudly.

'Uncle Alf says there's a woman might tell me something about Arnold.'

'Really? Could you bring yourself to speak to her?' Aunt Cherry looked up at her with a cunning expression.'

'I don't understand.'

'You want to know what made me laugh? It was your idea that respectable people frequented this pub. Respectable people in these parts are as rare as a spotted zebra. Don't you understand? Whoever's coming she'll be a pussy-pedlar, make no mistake. Be careful she don't have a pimp in tow. They can get nasty. And if you're about to make some money from this Arnold, he'll want his cut.'

'Oh, Aunt. I don't know if I can be in the same room with her, let alone speak to such dregs of society.'

'Look, girl, let me tell you a thing or two.' Her aunt shifted in her chair and wagged her finger at Lily. 'You're lucky. You've a respectable job, a home, a family what cares about you.' Lily was not too sure if that was the case with her mother but forbore to speak. 'You don't have to sell yourself and I hope to God you never will. But these girls didn't choose this life. They don't do it for pleasure, believe you me. Some have been forced out on the streets by the parents – yes. You needn't look so shocked, it happens when there's mouths to feed. Sometimes it's their husbands because they're too idle to look for work themselves. And if the women earn nothing, do you know what happens?' Lily shook her head. 'A beating. Oh, yes. And some gets a taste for the old white nectar.' She tapped the jug of gin and took another slurp.

'Or worse. Others have children to support, fathered by men who conned them and then did a runner. Others were corrupted by gentlemen.' Cherry had whipped herself up into a fine old dander. 'Do you think they enjoy being out in all weathers, going with whoever turns up? Ugly men, brutal men, men who stink, whose breath would knock your wig off.' Another gulp of gin. 'And not knowing if you'll even go home again. Worrying if you're about to have your throat slit or your guts torn out. Wondering if each man could be the Ripper back to his old tricks.' Her aunt slumped into her seat, as if the lengthy tirade had weakened her, and Lily saw that her eyelids were drooping. She got up to return to the comparative safety of her bedroom. But her aunt sent a parting shot after her: 'So don't you be so high and mighty, young woman. If you had to peddle yourself, it's unlikely you'd earn much, not with them tits you've got.'

Lily wanted to go home – she wanted to feel safe again. She didn't feel it here, and what her aunt had just said was unforgivable. She folded her arms over her breasts, and looked at her. But Cherry's head was lolling. She was about to fall asleep from the excess of gin. Thinking it politic, Lily removed the brandy.

'Lily! You've visitors,' her uncle bellowed up the stairs. Lily, who had been sitting on her bed awaiting this summons, felt her stomach clench with nerves. She checked herself in the mirror. At least she looked tidy.

'How do you do?' she said, politely enough, as she entered the saloon bar. She did not proffer her hand – she had no desire to touch one of these creatures. The two women might have been mother and daughter. The older one was raddled; the rouge on her face was uneven, making her look like a clown, and she was filthy. The younger was pretty and, though her dress was stained, she had made some effort to smarten herself. The smell of body odour was overwhelming. Lily pretended to sneeze so that she could hold her scented handkerchief to her nose.

'Miss Howard? I'm Iris, this is my sister, Constance. Pleased to meet you.' Iris smiled.

Lily registered that she spoke with a West Country accent. 'You have information for me?' she said, without preamble.

'Hold your horses. Not so fast.' It was Constance who spoke. 'There's ways of doing things. Aren't you going to ask us to sit down?'

'Of course. Do.'

The two women sat side by side on a bench.

'So, what is it you know?'

'Now, now. Keep your wool on. It's difficult for folks to talk when they're parched.'

'You'd best order what you want. I don't know about these matters.' Lily had barely finished her sentence before Iris was at the bar, calling for Alf.

'I trust you're paying for this lot?' Alf said, when he appeared at the table with a tray on which were four glasses, two small ones and two pint-sized ones.

'Of course,' Lily said, with marked irritation.

'I thought I'd better check. These two have thirsts an ocean wouldn't quench.'

'I said I'd pay, Uncle.'

'Right yer are.' A minute later he returned and plonked a bottle of whisky and a jug of beer on their table.

'We don't need all that!' She was aghast.

'You want to take a bet?' Constance laughed, not a pretty sound.

'Very well,' Lily said, once the drinks were sorted and she had refused one for herself. 'Now, will you tell me what information you have for me?'

'There's terms to be decided first.'

'How can we do that when I don't know what you have to tell me?'

'Well, then. We ain't going to get very far, are we?'

'Who has this information? You?'

'She has.' Constance nodded at Iris who, from the speed with which she was drinking, would not be sober for much longer. 'I'm here to look after her interests. Make sure she ain't cheated out of what's rightly hers.'

'Iris, what is it?' She chose to ignore the implied insult.

'Not so fast, miss. Constance is right. We're losing money sitting here talking to you. We've got to be recompensed for that.'

'I understand. What amount is it that you . . .' she coughed delicately '. . . normally charge for your services?' Dear God, she thought, was she really having this conversation?

'An Oxford scholar.'

'Pardon? I don't understand.'

'Five bob.'

'Don't be so ridicilous.' Lily allowed herself a ladylike laugh. 'Five shillings! I've never heard such rubbish.'

'Well, it was worth a try.' Constance grinned good-naturedly. 'All right then, a tossaroon.'

'We shall not get far if you persist in not speaking the Queen's English.'

'No need to get all high and mighty with us. Come, Iris.' Constance was on her feet but grabbing at the bottle. Iris picked up the jug.

'Please, I didn't mean to annoy you. I was just explaining that I don't understand the language you use.'

'Apologise, then.'

Lily longed to slap her and tell her to go to hell.' 'I'm sorry,' she said instead.

'Half a crown.' Constance sat down again, looking smug.

'My aunt said you got a shilling – if you were lucky.' She regretted adding that but it was too late.

'Your aunt talks too much. Very well, let's split the difference, one shilling and sixpence. We ain't going lower than that, are we, Iris?'

'No. We've got our pride.'

'Very well, one and sixpence it is.' Lily delved into her purse and laid the coins on the table.

Constance tapped it. 'Three bob, if you don't mind. There's two of us.'

Lily would have liked to point out that the way she looked and smelt it was unlikely she would earn anything, but instead she returned to her purse and added the extra coins. 'So, now we're fair and square.'

'Are we? That's just our expenses. The information will cost you more.'

'More? I'm not made of it, you know.'

'Then borrow from your aunt. She's rich.'

'How much?'

'A white one, a fiver.'

'Oh, really!' It was Lily's turn to stand up. She scooped up the coins on the table.

'All right, all right. Two pounds ten. That do you? Not a penny less. She's got a load on him.'

'Very well.' Lily sat down again.

'Come to think of it. That's for half what we got. You want the whole lot, it's got to be a white one.'

'What do you think, Iris?' Lily asked.

'Constance is right. You put your money back, I'll tell you half. You like what you hear you can pay me the rest.'

She extracted the money from her purse, pushing the five-pound note she had there deeper inside so that they could not see it. 'So?' she asked calmly, but feeling sick with excitement.

'Arnold's a pervert.'

'That's not sufficient to pay good money for.'

Iris drank deeply of the whisky. 'It was he taught me to like this stuff.'

'You know him?'

'Oh, yes. Very well. He bought me, you see, at an auction . . .'

4

'The weather is unseasonal for September, is it not?' Phoebe patted her lips delicately with the napkin, as she had seen Lynette Lingford do, even though she was certain that nothing was lurking there. She was sitting bolt upright at the dining-table with space enough for a cat to pass between her back and the chair, as she had been taught. She'd also been told to think she had a metal rod at her back. It couldn't be any more uncomfortable than this if she had, she thought.

'Very. And which of the seasons do you prefer?'

'I like the summer when it doesn't rain, when it's hot.' How she longed to lean forward. Why couldn't she put her elbows on the table? She shifted in the chair trying to get more comfortable. 'But, then, spring is lovely with the little birds – and the excitement when you see the first primroses. Even winter, if it's not too cold. I hate the cold. The truth is, I love them all.' And I'd be more comfortable if I didn't have these wretched corsets on, she thought. How was she supposed to eat when she was encased in such a monstrosity? She'd have loved to alter the position of an intrusive stay, but knew it would be frowned upon – every normal action was.

'And autumn? You haven't mentioned it.'

'No, perhaps I don't like that one. All foggy and slippery with dead leaves.' It was all right for him. He didn't have to sit like a soldier at attention. He wasn't held in by bits of dead whale. He could let his stomach expand as much as he wished. She wondered if she really wanted to be a lady.

'But the smell of autumn is pleasant, don't you think?'

'What? All that decay?' She laughed. 'You must have a funny sense of smell, Mr Bartholomew.'

'Do I?' He looked puzzled. 'I meant more the smell of

woodsmoke. When I'm abroad if I smell wood burning it always reminds me of home.'

'You travel often?' She had perked up. Perhaps if she behaved herself and did exactly as she was told he might take her with him. She sat even straighter. Just don't eat, she thought.

'Not so often now. But when I do I prefer to go to Rome.'

'Ah, yes, the antiquities. I should love to see the statue of David . . .'

'That's in Florence.'

'Is it? Well, wherever it is I'd still like to see it.'

'Maybe you shall, one day.'

'And beggars might ride.' She looked hopeful but he did not respond. 'Do you go to the gardens of the Borghese?' she asked politely, glad that Mrs Lingford had tutored her only this morning on Italy and its treasures. It was the right question to ask for he spent the next quarter of an hour extolling Rome and all things Italian. In fact, he went on rather too long and she could feel the muscles in her face ache as she continued to look interested and smile.

He wasn't nearly as old as she had first thought him, she decided. In fact, she thought him nearer fifty than seventy. He wasn't handsome, far from it, not like Edward, but he was not ugly either. And when he smiled he looked much better, less stern, almost kind. But there was still something about his eyes that scared her. They were blue but not a clear colour like a summer sky, rather as if a snippet of white cloud had been added to them, giving them a strange, opaque look, not helped by the pure white eyelashes that matched his hair. They were the only colourful thing in his face, for his skin, very smooth for a man of his age, not gnarled and wrinkled like her father's, was as white as if God had forgotten to mix in some pink.

However, she approved of his clothes. There wasn't a

speck of dust on his black jacket, and she thought his striped trousers the smartest she had ever seen. His shirt was the whitest imaginable with no marks at all round the collar and cuffs. At his neck he wore a cravat of Paisley silk, fixed by a gold pin set with a glittering stone. She wondered if it might be a diamond – she had had no idea that men could wear jewellery too. What would her father have to say about that? And he smelt nice too, of cloves. She had got a whiff when he bowed over her hand as she was shown in. At least this time the footmen weren't sneering at her – in fact, she'd noticed them looking at her with what bordered on admiration. One was very good-looking – not, of course, like Edward, but nobody on earth could be. She had been sorry when they were dismissed and she was left alone with Mr Bartholomew.

'But I must stop wearying you. Never ask me to tell you about Italy, Phoebe. I am likely to talk the whole day long.' He poured more port into the tiny glass in front of her. She liked the taste and wished the glass was bigger.

'But it is so interesting,' she lied, and took one of the sweetmeats he offered her, which she liked even more. 'You must teach me.' She hoped he wouldn't: he wasn't nearly as interesting as Mrs Lingford.

'I have to congratulate you, Phoebe, my dear. The improvement in your demeanour is outstanding.' He was studying her intently from the large oak chair at the head of the table. 'You are unrecognisable as the little waif who arrived here.'

'There was room for it, Mr Bartholomew.' She grinned, then remembered that Mrs Lingford had said it was vulgar to show your teeth. 'It's Mrs Lingford who should be congratulated, not me. She did all the work.'

'Are you pleased with yourself ?'

'I am. I can't believe I'm me!' She giggled. 'I have to pinch myself every day.' And she pinched the back of her hand – she couldn't have done it anywhere else since the cuffs of her leg-o'-mutton sleeves were so tight.

'My dear, don't harm yourself.' He laid his hand gently on hers. She wished he wouldn't: it felt dry and scaly, like a snake. Then he looked at her so intently that she felt alarmed and had to look away from him. After what seemed an age he took his hand from hers, but then, to her horror, he lifted it to his lips. She was glad he didn't kiss it, just the air above it, or she might have snatched it back, and he would have been offended. She didn't want that. Apart from locking her door – which she *must* speak to him about – he'd only shown her kindness with the lovely things he showered on her.

'I wasn't at first.' She thought it might be safer if she talked.

'I beg your pardon?'

'You asked if I was pleased with myself. I didn't like it at first. To be honest I thought it was an infernal liberty wanting to change me.' She laughed, to let him know it was a joke.

'And why was that?' He was smiling, so he must be amused by her forwardness.

'Because I thought I was fine as I was. But now I see I wasn't. Now, well, I can read – not very fast but I improve every day. And I can eat properly. And I love the clothes and my room. And the food. Well, just about everything.'

'Do I detect reservation in your voice?'

Should she say what she was thinking? It was worth the risk. 'Please don't be cross with me, but I hate being locked up. I get this horrible panicky feeling. What if there was a fire? How would I get out?'

'That is highly unlikely. A man patrols the premises night and day.'

'But it's a horrid feeling. And it's not necessary.'

'And why might that be?'

'Because I wouldn't run away, if that is what you're

afraid of. Why should I? I like it here. I love all the things you give me. I'd hate to go back to what I left.'

'What would make you run away?'

'If someone was cruel to me.' And if there was any hanky-panky, she thought, but kept this to herself.

'No one will be that. Good gracious!' He looked offended.

'I never meant—'

'I'm sure you didn't, my dear.'

'Mrs Lingford says I must think before I speak and that way I won't offend.'

'What a wise woman she is.'

'So what do you think?'

'About what?'

'Not locking me up?'

'Let's start with perhaps an hour a day.'

'Or two?' She smiled cheekily at him.

'Very well. One hour today and two tomorrow.'

'And can I go outside? On my own?'

He frowned.

'Just in the gardens?'

'You may.'

At this she leaped up and kissed his cheek. 'Thank you so much!' She kissed him again enthusiastically and then, realising what she had done, gasped and slapped her hand over her mouth. 'I'm so sorry, I shouldn't have done that.' To her surprise she had found that the skin of his face was not unpleasant to touch: it was so soft that it had been like touching the new kid gloves Mrs White had brought in yesterday.

'I don't know, I found it rather delightful.' He put his hand with the shiny nails to his cheek where her kiss had landed.

Phoebe had enjoyed her walks with Lynette Lingford, but she enjoyed being on her own far more, even though she still felt she was being watched. Every time she looked up at the windows, however, she saw no one.

'Imagination,' she said.

'Probably,' she answered.

She went along the Long Walk. It was chillier higher up on the hill than it was in the valley. She pulled her coat closer to her and stuffed her hands deep into her pockets, even though she knew now that a lady never did that. The air was crisp and, despite the full sunshine, she could smell autumn.

'No one to see.' She dug her hands deeper into her pockets.

'Exactly.'

She paused at the place where the walk curved and a large monkey puzzle tree towered. She looked down at the maze, its pattern clear from high on the hill. 'It was at that very spot I met him.'

'No good mooning about him.'

'I doubt I'll ever see him again.'

'You might.'

'If he visits.'

'Which he probably will do.'

'And then?'

'Who knows?'

She would like to go into the maze but, restricted for time as she was, she dared not. What if she couldn't find her way out? If she was late she was sure this little bit of freedom would be taken away from her.

Telling the time was an accomplishment she had not yet mastered and, in any case, she hadn't a watch. However, like so many country people, she had an instinctive feel for time. She knew when to turn back towards the house. Today she did not mind: she was confident that if she kept to Mr Bartholomew's rules, he would allow her out again. And next time for longer, until she was never locked up at all. She entered the house with five minutes to spare.

'I went for a walk this morning on my own.'

'So I heard. And you were sensible and returned before the hour was up.'

'Who told you?'

'It was noted.'

'So I *was* being watched? I thought so.' It took the sheen off the outing.

'Perhaps as you kept the rules you won't be next time. And how was your luncheon?'

'I didn't slurp, I didn't speak with my mouth full, I took only tiny morsels of food. I conversed. He seems nice but a bit boring.' She laughed. 'Like my father's friends, not like them in South Africa.' She laughed again, quite pleased with her little joke. 'But you frown. Why? Is there bad news from there?' Her heart raced with fear and she had to sit down.

'The Boers become more aggressive. There have been skirmishes. They have made guerrilla raids on some British farms. I'm afraid the tension is mounting.'

'I'm not going to think about it!' She put her hands over her ears. 'If I don't, it'll go away.'

'Yes, dear, that's by far the best thing to do.'

It was easy to say, but difficult to abide by it. Dick kept popping into her mind even when she begged him to go away. And that added to her worry that he had been hurt and was trying to tell her. Was he dead and coming to her from the other side? At that thought she cried out with terror.

'What is it, Phoebe?'

'What if my brother has been killed?'

'There are no reports.'

'Everything takes so long to find out.'

'There would have been telegrams.'

'But no one knows I'm here. And, as much as I long for news, I don't want to leave. I want to stay here. I can't go home, not ever again.'

'It would have been in the newspapers.'

'The newspapers? My Dick in the newspapers? He'd be so proud.' Her eyes widened with amazement.

'Not if he was dead. He wouldn't know. So, since he hasn't been, I think you can relax.' Mrs Lingford smiled encouragingly. 'Now, Mr Bartholomew says you showed a keen interest in Italy. He wishes for you to be taught much about that country and its antiquities. I have borrowed these books from his library.' She spread the large leatherbound books on the table at which they were sitting. 'Perhaps he plans to take you there.'

'Me? To Italy? On a boat?'

'He has done so in the past.'

'Done what?' Phoebe looked up from the book on Michelangelo she had taken from the pile.

Mrs Lingford looked flustered. 'Taken a companion,' she answered, neatly sidestepping what she had been about to say.

For a week Phoebe had been allowed out. The hour had been stretched to two and then she had been told that she could go for as long as she liked, provided she was back and changed in good time for luncheon or teatime. With so much time she had dared to venture into the maze. There, she felt Edward's presence so strongly, that she almost expected him to appear. She had sat on the bench, in the centre, where he had sat. She stroked the stone as if she could feel him. When it was time to leave, it was simple to find her way out – as if he was guiding her.

Her room was still locked at night and she had determined that it should not be, but she was willing to bide her time before asking. She had learned that, with her benefactor, there was no point in trying to rush anything.

She had not seen Lynette Lingford for two days. She had asked Mrs White where she was but the woman had said she did not know. Phoebe thought she was lying. Mrs White had been much nicer to her once she had been given some freedom, and she wondered what might be the significance of that.

This morning she went in the opposite direction to the route she normally took. She crossed the knot garden, went through the small gate beyond the rose garden, crossed the ha-ha, and struck out across the meadow to the copse of trees where she knew that Mrs Lingford lived.

The cottage was pretty, if on the small side. She didn't know why she had expected her to live in something bigger, but she had. Perhaps because to her it didn't seem right that someone who knew so much should live in such a tiny house, like ignorant folk.

She knocked on the front door. There was a lot of noise the other side, and much scraping of bolts and keys. It must be like at home: the only time she remembered the front door being opened was when her mother's coffin had been carried out. Eventually the door creaked open. A pretty girl, younger than herself but taller, peered out.

'I've come to see if Mrs Lingford is all right. I trust she is not poorly?'

'You'd better come in.' The door was opened wide.

'I'm Phoebe.'

'And I'm Freda.' Solemnly the two girls shook hands just as Mrs Lingford entered the passageway that led from the front door.

'Phoebe! What on earth are you doing here?' She looked anxious rather than cross.

'I was worried you were ill.'

Mrs Lingford's shoulders slumped with relief. 'That was kind of you. I am well, it is my son who is ill. I couldn't leave him, you understand.'

'Of course not.'

'Mr Bartholomew is vexed with me.'

'What for?'

'That I neglect you.'

'But your son must come first.'

'Unfortunately he doesn't see it in that way.' She spoke with uncustomary bitterness. 'Come in. Some tea? Lemonade?' She ushered Phoebe into a room so small that, with all the chairs, sofas, cabinets, pictures and books, it was difficult to manoeuvre.

'You were worried when you saw me?' Phoebe said.

'Was I? I thought perhaps something had happened. That you had . . .' Her voice trailed away.

'Run away? Now why should I do that? I'm very comfortable and privileged.'

A door at the back of the house banged and Mrs Lingford tensed again. The parlour door opened. 'This is my father-in-law. This is Phoebe, Mr Lingford.'

The old man who had been bent double stood remarkably straight at the sight of the pretty visitor. 'How do you do, Miss . . . I didn't catch your name.'

'Because I didn't give it, Mr Lingford.'

'Oh, I see. One of them!' He appeared to lose interest in her, which intrigued Phoebe. She watched him collapse into a worn but comfortable leather chair. He opened the newspaper he had been carrying.

Mrs Lingford put another log on the fire.

'I see we get another log if the likes of *her* are here.' Mr Lingford did not speak in a pleasant tone.

Phoebe looked about her to see whom he had referred to, then realised it was herself.

'It gets chilly, doesn't it?' Mrs Lingford rubbed her hands together.

'I think winter will be early this year. Did you see how large the blackberries were? That's always a reliable sign.'

Silence descended, and Phoebe was puzzled that Mrs

Lingford of all people seemed as uncomfortable as she was and appeared unable to make conversation, which was odd when she had been so adept at teaching her. 'I'll get the tea,' Mrs Lingford said. 'Come, Freda, you help me.' To her discomfort, Phoebe found she was left alone with the old man. She glanced at him. He looked like an angry frog sitting there all scrunched up, his pince-nez sliding down his rather flat nose.

'What are you gawking at?'

'If you'd excuse me, sir, I was wondering if there was anything in your newspaper about South Africa?'

'What's it to you?'

'Someone I know is there. I was only asking.'

'More fool him, then.'

'Thank you,' she said, with heavy irony.

'You one of those whores up at the big house?'

'I beg your pardon?'

'You heard.'

'I'd have preferred not to.'

'Well, are you?'

'Of course I'm not. Do I look like one?' Phoebe had no idea what a whore should look like, never having met one, but she knew what they were and what they did, and she could feel her anger growing.

'That means nothing. The old man is rich enough to choose the best.'

'My, my, Mr Lingford, take care. That was almost a compliment.'

'Don't you be cheeky with me, you little tart.'

'Then don't you be so rude to me, you filthy-minded old beggar!' She stood up and swished out of the room. She met Mrs Lingford in the corridor. 'Thank you for the tea, Mrs Lingford, but I think I'd better be going. Otherwise, old as he is, I might just slap that old sod.'

As she slammed out of the door she heard Freda laughing and Mrs Lingford joining in.

Two nights were long enough, Lily could not wait to be home. She could not relax on the railway journey back to the West Country. On the trip to London, with her aunt for company, she had hidden her nervousness: she had been determined to appear a seasoned, sophisticated traveller, rather than the nervous wreck she was. Now, alone, it was harder to hide her terror at the inordinate speed at which they were travelling.

The Ladies' Only carriage had been fully reserved, which was vexatious. Her aunt had recommended it as safer for her, implying that the rest of the train was full of robbers and rapists, which had not helped settle her nerves. She was not happy in the second-class carriage in which she found herself. The woman next to her was fat, and smelt of mothballs which made Lily sneeze. And each time she did, the wretched woman turned to her necessitating the rearrangement of her mountain of flesh, and with each 'Bless you,' showered Lily with a fine spray of saliva. Her two children sat beside her and, with the amount of food they were consuming, would soon be as fat as their mother.

A seedy man sat opposite Lily: he was emaciated and his complexion was so sallow that Lily's mind was filled with images of coffins and shrouds. At the slightest movement of his head so much dandruff was scattered that she was convinced he was disintegrating before her eyes and would no doubt have disappeared by the time they reached Taunton.

She tried to read but the rocking of the carriage made the words dance before her eyes and it was not long before she had a dreadful headache. The hard-boiled eggs were the last straw. Before she knew where she was, she was fighting with the strap to open the window, then sticking out her head. As vomit gushed from her mouth it was blown back into her face.

When she finally sat down again she was unsure whether to apologise or pretend it had not happened. She opted for the latter.

'You should never be sick into the wind,' the woman advised. 'Perhaps you ate something that didn't quite suit.'

'Or was off,' the man suggested.

'It's easily done.'

'Oysters, never eat oysters unless there's an R in the month.'

'There is,' snapped Lily.

'Then it must have been something else.' At the mention of food Lily's queasiness increased and before she could control herself her head was hanging out of the window, but at least facing the right direction this time.

'Better out than in,' was the received wisdom.

'I missed you, Lily.'

She hid her astonishment at her mother's greeting. 'But I'm here now and glad to see you too.' It was the truth: after her experiences in London she was glad to be back in Barlton.

'And about time too.'

Lily sighed. For a second she had allowed herself to think that perhaps her mother had missed her for herself, but she had missed Lily caring for her. Although how she was to carry on as before after all she had discovered was a quandary. She'd think about it later.

'So, have you learned that I don't look after you so badly?' Lily's question was met with silence. 'Well?' she persisted.

'Better than that woman you got in for me, that's for sure. Mind you, that's not saying much.'

'Thank you, Mother,' she said, with heavy irony, but she might as well have saved her breath.

'You smell.' Her mother sniffed deeply. 'Of vomit.'

'I was unwell.'

'I trust you're better now. I don't want to catch anything. And I hope you'll clean yourself up before you get my supper.'

'Mother, really! You are so uncaring.'

'Me?'

'Yes. And Aunt Cherry says you're deceiving me, that you can walk. She says she saw you at the pub. She says you lie.'

'What? The evil bitch. Me? Lie? *Pretend* I'm a cripple? Why should I do that?' Her mother bristled with anger and indignation.

'So that you won't be expected to do anything, Mother. So that you have me waiting on you hand and foot. She says you were born idle.'

'She's always hated me. She was always jealous of me because I had you.' The anger had been replaced with whining.

'She's not. She wouldn't swap her life for yours. And she never wanted children.'

'Drunk, was she, when she said that?'

'No, and I didn't see her drink once while I was there,' Lily lied. She looked down at the top of her mother's head where the hair was thinning and the pink skull showed through, and imagined what joy she would feel if she swung a hatchet right on it. She touched the place.

'What are you doing?' Her mother shook her head.

'Just straightening your hair.'

It wasn't until after she had cooked her mother's supper and got her to bed that Lily had time to think. In this she showed the same methodical disposition that she did with most other things. Mentally she would lay out all her findings, as if on an imaginary table, and go through them one by one.

At last she sat in blissful silence, a cup of tea beside her, the gas light hissing. The sound was always a comfort to her. She put her feet up on the ottoman and began to plan. One thing was certain: with the information she had she was not going to live in this slum for much longer.

First, there was her mother – or, rather, Pansy – to consider. How interesting, if hurtful, it had been to learn that her mother was not her mother. She had been two when the woman who had given birth to her died, so she had no memory of her and had simply accepted that Pansy was her mother. Admittedly her aunt had told her when in her cups and had apologised fulsomely in the morning for telling her such tittle-tattle.

'Is it true, Aunt Cherry? That is what is important,' Lily had asked.

'The cat's out of the bag now, no point in denying it. Your mother was your father's first wife. My sister is your stepmother. Are you hurt, Lily? I feel so badly about telling you.'

At this Lily laughed, to her aunt's astonishment and relief. 'Hurt? Good gracious me, Aunt, not a bit. I'm relieved. I never liked her and now I need not feel guilty about it.' But the hurt she denied was already established. She was not sure if it was because she was now truly an orphan, or because she had been deceived. Or, and this seemed unbelievable, that she had now lost the only mother she had known.

However, whichever it was, it was an unexpected luxury for her to be able to plan her future without the mother-who-wasn't. The prospect even diluted her anger that her so-called mother had done worse than lie about their relationship. Lily had insisted on Aunt Cherry telling her everything.

She had been eight when her father had died, old enough to remember him and feel sad, but not old enough to understand the financial significance. At first their modest but comfortable life, which his wages as a clerk had afforded, had continued unaltered. When she was ten, the house was sold and they had moved into something smaller, then smaller again, until they had finally been driven to this slum. Pansy had always set the blame squarely on her father's shoulders for leaving them almost destitute. That was the part that angered Lily most, even more than losing the money. How dare she accuse an innocent man when it was Pansy who had, in her sister's words, 'pissed the lot away on drink, men and betting'. She had *stolen* Lily's inheritance.

Lily poured herself another cup of tea and this time added a tot of brandy. What bad habits she had acquired at her aunt's! Ever practical, she could see that, despite everything, there were advantages in the situation for her. She could contemplate setting up home on her own.

She began to plan how this was to be achieved. As she did so, she was unaware that a small self-satisfied smile kept flitting across her face. It had gone two in the morning before she extinguished the gas and made her way to bed.

'Miss Howard, you have no idea how much I missed you.' Arnold's smile, she thought, was genuine, as he entered her office. She was not standing, ready to welcome him, as she usually did, but sitting steadfast at her desk. 'I trust you are better?' The smile made her heart flutter in the old way even though she hated him now.

'Thank you for enquiring, Mr Randolph-Smythe. It was a mild indisposition.' She looked at him, and felt as if she was seeing him for the first time. She must have been blinded by love, she decided. He was handsome, to be sure, but in a somewhat vulgar way. Though his eyes were of the finest ... And his full mouth ... the soft lower lip. She closed her eyes to blot out such thoughts. He was smart, but wasn't he a little *too* well dressed in a manner that no true gentleman would allow?

'You were wise to take a few days to recover. One can

never be too careful with one's health.' Such a melodious voice ... Yes, but listen to the dreadful accent lurking there, reminiscent of her aunt's clients, which he tried so hard to hide.

'It was most considerate of you not to mind my absence. I see Miss Baker is not here.' She nodded towards the girl's desk, which was empty, not even an inkwell in sight. Without both of them, especially herself, he must have been in a dreadful pickle, she decided.

'No, it was most unfortunate,' he said, entering his own office and placing his hat on the stand in the corner of his office. Lily joined him there. 'She, too, was ill.'

'How inconvenient for you, sir.'

'Perhaps it was some infection you both succumbed to.'

'It might have been.' She had to turn her head away so that he could not see her smile – a superior one, she knew. If Miss Baker were ever ill it would be from syphilis or worse. She sincerely hoped that he had caught it too. That would show him! 'Let's hope that her recovery will be as speedy as mine.' She had to look at her shoes as the smile broadened into a grin.

'Sadly, she will not be returning.'

'Oh, no. How regrettable.' She was sure there had been a bubble of laughter in her voice. Oh dear. 'She has found another position?'

'I gather so, yes.' He began to look at his mail. Normally she would have opened it and placed it for his attention. Not so today: let him sort it himself. 'By the way, Miss Howard, my daughter might visit us this afternoon. Will you look after her until I am free?'

'My pleasure, sir.' She turned to leave.

'But my coffee, Miss Howard?'

'How forgetful of me. How remiss.' She waited.

'If you would be so kind?'

'Of course, when you ask so nicely.' She left him looking puzzled. And there won't be coffee waiting tomorrow, or the next day: he was going to have to ask every time, she had decided. She had been taken for granted for too long and by too many people.

6

Lily tutted as she checked Arnold's diary. She had only been away three days and it was a mess! Couldn't people make entries without smudging, crossing out and writing virtually illegibly? She liked things neat. It was his writing not Edith's – so she hadn't been here the whole time Lily had been absent. She was glad to see the back of her but she doubted she had a new position – except that Lily knew she had, and with whom. It hurt just thinking of them together.

She should be thankful, she supposed, that he hadn't neglected the diary altogether. She turned to today's page and made out the entries for this afternoon. A couple of travelling salesmen had appointments. She never had any bother from them. Once they had registered that she was not a mere clerk but an important person in this office, they treated her with the respect she deserved. Most brought her little presents, which she always accepted but with a measured distance. She did not want them to think they could be familiar with her. The entry for four o'clock was harder to read. She was shocked, curious, excited and apprehensive to see that the appointment he had was with none other than a Mr Bartholomew.

'Miss Howard.'

She jumped eagerly to her feet, then sat down abruptly. Old habits died hard. 'Yes, sir?'

'I think I should have some Madeira this afternoon when my guest comes, and perhaps you would go to the shops and purchase a cake. It would be so kind of you.' He smiled at her, and she felt her treacherous limbs weaken. 'Here,' he rootled in his inner pocket, withdrew his leather wallet and gave her some money. 'You may keep the change.' How dare he? she thought. He was treating her as if she were a barmaid. 'Buy yourself something pretty.'

'That won't be necessary,' she said coldly, glad that she was angry with him again. She must hold on to the anger.

As he reached the door, he turned and smiled at her once more. 'I hope it won't mean too much hard work for you, Miss Howard, but I have to say it's rather nice, just the two of us again, isn't it?'

She was speechless as she sank back on to her chair. That had been a moment of exquisite intimacy, the like of which they had never had before. She felt she was on a swing, rushing high with excitement and love at one minute, and sinking low with loathing and anger at the next.

It is all so confusing, she thought, as she put on her hat and found her galoshes, since it was raining, then made for the door. She didn't want to forgive him, she wanted to hate him for preferring that tart to her. She swung out of the main door of the shop, oblivious to the doorman's surprise and greeting. She normally never used this door, staff were confined to the back entrance, but today was different. Today she must assert herself, or she would lose the advantage she had.

The tap on the door was light, not authoritative. Lily always noted how people knocked: it said so much about them. 'Enter,' she called.

'How do you do?' A tall, handsome young man was proffering his hand. Lily was overwhelmed: she was usually ignored by gentlemen – only the lesser mortals took any notice of her. 'I have an appointment with Mr Randolph-Smythe.'

'Mr Bartholomew?' she said uncertainly. From what she had heard he was an old man, but this one could not have left his twenties behind.

'Bartholomew-*Prestwick*. Yes. Am I too early?'

'I apologise, I hadn't seen . . .' She was flustered by her lack of efficiency. Too much on her mind, she presumed. She peered myopically at her watch – fortunately she had removed her spectacles just as he had appeared. 'On the dot, Mr Bartholomew-Prestwick.' She gave an apologetic smile. 'I shall tell him you are here.' She felt quite self-conscious as she walked across the office, certain he was watching her – or, rather, hoping he was.

She duly informed Arnold that his appointment had arrived. She knew that he would bide his time for five minutes, then come hurriedly into the outer office as if pressed for time in his busy schedule.

Still unspectacled, Lily rearranged her ledgers and papers. She could do no work since she could not see things close up, but that didn't stop her surreptitiously admiring the young man reclining in the easy chair. He sat with such loose-limbed elegance, she thought. How well dressed he was, how charming his smile. His dark brown eyes were like a puppy's. If her plans worked out as she hoped, she would have money: she could dress differently, have her hair styled by Monsieur Emile in the new salon that had opened in Gold Street with all the latest equipment. 'Monsieur Émile of Paris and Mayfair' – it said on the window. She would bathe in expensive perfumes and then anything was possible.

'Bartholomew-Prestwick, my dear chap. Sorry to keep you waiting.' Arnold breezed into the room, hand outstretched, dynamic and forceful and handsome—

'Stop it!' Lily said to herself.

She knew exactly how long to wait before entering with an excuse. This time it was an imaginary telephone message. Arnold always liked new people to know he had the instrument.

'Excuse me, sir, but I thought you should see this telephone communication.' She handed him the paper on which she had written, 'I trust I do right?'

'Why, thank you, Miss Howard. Most important. I'll be straight with you, Bartholomew-Prestwick. This,' he waved the paper in the air, 'is from another party keen to sell me property.'

Liar, thought Lily.

'I can't say my uncle is *keen* to sell to you, Mr Randolph-Smythe. He was interested because he never uses his town-house . . . It would depend on the terms we can agree. Of course, if others are offering you premises at a better price then, rest assured, we shall feel no ill will if you choose to go with them.'

Clever! That's right, my handsome one, play him at his own game, she thought as, reluctantly, she left them.

Five minutes later she was back with a tray of tea, the cake and the Madeira. She carried it carefully so that no china rattled or silver clinked. She had purposely left the door ajar so that she could push it open silently and steal back in, hopefully unheard – she had often picked up interesting snippets by moving stealthily.

'It was not necessary to tell my wife about this purchase, Edward.'

Two points made her prick up her ears. If they were on Christian name terms already the relationship had moved on rapidly. And what was this about his wife? She moved furtively behind Arnold who, as yet, was still unaware of her presence.

'I apologise, Mr Randolph-Smythe. I just presumed she would know since—'

'Since what?'

'Nothing, I was embarrassed by my indiscretion, that was all. I can't think what else I meant to say.'

Yes, you can, thought Lily. You were about to say, 'since it was *her* money'. Despite Arnold's efforts to hide it she had discovered easily enough who owned what, and she couldn't be the only one who knew the true state of affairs. This was becoming interesting. What could Arnold be up to? And he had been presumptuous over the young man's name. It was always a mistake to become too familiar too soon, and he should have known that. A teacup rattled.

Arnold swung round in his chair. 'How long have you been there?'

'I had just entered, sir,' she lied, and hoped the young man wouldn't correct her.

She fussed over serving them until, with an irritable wave, Arnold shooed her away. She left, apparently shutting the door, but she had held on to the knob so that even though it sounded as if it were firmly closed she was able to reopen it the inch needed to hear everything that was said.

Before listening, however, she took the precaution of wedging a chair against the outer door in case that stuck-up Agnes came earlier than she was expected. Thus she could relax and listen to Arnold's plans. He was negotiating to buy the fine Bartholomew mansion next door but one. Well, well! What for? Also she had learned that he already owned the premises next door. That indicated he had papers stored elsewhere than here. What else was she unaware of? He was going to convert Mr Bartholomew's house into a hotel, but a grand hotel, which certainly Barlton lacked, and with a ballroom for dances and assemblies. How exciting. And in his name? No, she heard him say, it was to be called Bartholomew's, should the young man's uncle agree. That was slyly clever: it was always a good idea to pander to these old families' egos. And, of course, no immediate connection to Arnold would be apparent – which would explain his irritation that his wife knew. What was he about? He could pretend to Dulcie that the deal had not materialised. Yes, she thought, that was probably what he would do. What a perfidious man.

Lily's head reeled as she listened to the figures the two men bandied about. She always enjoyed listening to men bartering; first the ridiculous demand, and the equally ridiculous offer. On to the negotiating, trimming here, compromising there, young Mr Bartholomew-Prestwick extolling the virtues of the property, Arnold denigrating it. There were times when she longed to have been born a man: she felt she would have good at business.

Now, she thought, these were extraordinary amounts of money. Where had Arnold acquired such large sums? One did not have to be a genius to guess: he had purloined them from his wife. Still, Dulcie had plenty more. If she hadn't already missed it she couldn't need it. If it had been Lily's money, she would have known where every penny was. In a way, if he was stealing from Dulcie, his wife had only herself to blame. Lily would have kept an eye on what was hers.

And his wife was not to know! Better and better. She had heard all she needed. She moved across her office and removed the chair just as Agnes swept in, ignoring her, not even answering when Lily welcomed her. Not that she was surprised: it was how Agnes always behaved towards her. What a contrast she made to Dulcie, who always went out of her way to be polite and kind. Lily knew she was not alone in being treated in this manner: she had heard the impolite and inconsiderate way Agnes spoke to her mother. It was not right. When she had thought Pansy was her mother, she had *never* been rude to her. Without a by-your-leave the girl unbuttoned her top coat and dropped it on to the floor. She smoothed her peach silk tea dress, pinched her cheeks, patted her hair, then crossed to the door of her father's office.

'Come, darling Papa, you work too hard. Take me—' Here, she put her hand prettily to her mouth. 'I am *so* sorry, Papa. I didn't realise you were otherwise engaged. I wasn't told.' At this she cast a sweetly cross look at Lily. 'Fie, Miss Howard, you should have told me Papa was busy. And with Mr Bartholomew-Prestwick. What a wonderful surprise. May I join you? Please don't get up, and pay no attention to me. I shan't understand a word of your clever business talk.' She flashed a stunning smile at the young man, who, to Lily, seemed to be in a daze.

The fool! Can't he see through her? He doesn't stand a chance now, Lily thought, as she closed the door firmly.

She picked up the coat. It had a fur collar and she lifted it to her cheek, revelling in its softness. Mink, she was sure. She inhaled the smell of lily-of-the-valley, which permeated the fabric. An expensive smell . . . Still, not long now.

7

While bursting with pride that her father had pur-chased one of the first automobiles to be seen on the streets of Barlton, Agnes could have wished that Edward had not been with them for this ride. For one thing there was no protection against the rain and the winter chill that was in the late October air. To look attractive was almost impossible, wrapped up as she was in her thick tweed coat. Admittedly it was topped with a fur collar, but it was so bulky it made her look shapeless and enormous. Her mother had insisted she wore it. Her hat was held in place with a veil, to protect her complexion from the elements. She had hoped it would make her look mysterious and seductive. Instead she appeared to be in purdah. She felt like an Egyptian mummy and, no doubt, looked like one. Also, it would have been better if her father had mastered the controls before taking someone as important as a Bartholomew for a ride.

As they lurched up the high street, two men waved their umbrellas angrily at them, and a gaggle of people laughed at their kangaroo-like progress. The noxious fumes that belched from the back were making her feel sick.

Their humiliation was complete when their carriage, in

which she had ridden to the shop, passed them at a spanking rate, the horses tossing their heads as if they were laughing too. The coachman gave them a cheery wave with his whip. She hoped her father would have a strong word with him.

'Isn't it exciting?' she said, trying to make the best of an impossible situation. Edward was sitting close beside her in the back of the contraption. That was the only good thing: their progress was so rocky that their bodies kept inadvertently touching, which excited her.

'I'm sorry?'

'The ride. It's so exhilarating.'

He shrugged an apology, so she leaned towards him and shouted in his ear – just as they hit a rut in the road, which threw her into his arms.

'Thrilling!' he replied.

At that moment they began the descent of Hangman's Hill. It was steep, and the automobile whirred along at an alarming rate, Agnes clutching her hat with one hand and holding on to the strap beside her like grim death. 'Not so fast, Papa! Pray not so fast!' But by the time she had got the words out they were zooming up the other side, and she found that going uphill fast was not nearly as alarming as going down. Her father made a sharp right turn into their driveway, forcing two neighbours to jump smartly out of his way.

By the time the vehicle shuddered to a halt, Agnes was in love with driving. 'So uplifting!' she declared, once Edward had helped her down from the high vehicle. 'So elevating.'

'It was most certainly a different mode of transport.'

Agnes swept back the veil with a dramatic gesture, hoping he was longing to see her face again, but he was looking the other way. She hoped he wasn't one of the strange men her brother had told her about who did not care for women.

The front door burst open and an anxious Dulcie

appeared on the steps. 'Such a noise! The neighbours will be complaining.'

'Let them.' Arnold removed his goggles and clambered out of the driver's seat, not easy when he had so many bulky clothes on.

'Do you have such a vehicle, Mr Bartholomew-Prestwick?'

'Not yet, Mrs Randolph, but after that little trip I shall most certainly view them with greater respect.' Was he laughing at her husband's driving, Dulcie wondered. From her own experience in this vehicle yesterday she knew he was alarmingly rash.

'My dear chap, go and see my fellow, George Sadler. Used to be a coachman for old Biggleswade when he was alive. He's very sound on the combustion engine. What he doesn't know isn't worth bothering about. Don't part with a penny until you've spoken to him. Tell him I sent you and he'll give you a fairer deal.'

'Thank you, Mr Randolph-Smythe.'

Oh dear, thought Dulcie. She wished Arnold wasn't so forward. No doubt he had an arrangement with this man Sadler, and money, to her husband's advantage, would be involved, of that she was sure. She wished he had told her he was bringing guests back.

'I trust you do not mind me appearing uninvited in this manner?'

'You *were* invited – I invited you.' Arnold slapped Edward on the back, knocking the wind out of him.

'It's a pleasure to have you here, I do assure you.' Dulcie shepherded them into the house, fretting about the rain, soaking clothes, chills and pneumonia.

'Don't twitter, wife,' Arnold remonstrated.

He really was showing off for Edward. He had two ways of talking to her when they had guests: either he was over-effusive in his endearments, or he was sharp with her as now. She thought she preferred the latter – it was the more honest of the two.

'Your coat, Mr Bartholomew-Prestwick, let me have it to dry. Agnes, go and change immediately. A hot drink? Soup?'

'The man wants a whisky. Come, Edward, we've matters to discuss. You'll stay for dinner, of course?'

'I fear I must decline all of your kind offers. I must leave – my uncle expects me. I have much to discuss with him.'

'Then I'll drive you back.'

'No, no. That won't be necessary. I asked my coachman to follow us. He'll be outside.'

'Another time?' Dulcie smiled, relieved that she was not going to have to arrange a sudden dinner.

'I wonder if I might call again?' he asked her.

'Any time,' Arnold answered for her.

'If I might have a word, Mrs Randolph?'

'I'll see you out.' She was pleased to see Arnold frown with displeasure.

At the door, Edward turned to shake her hand. 'I was wondering if you would care to come and meet my father. I told him about your collection of porcelain and he would like very much to meet and talk with you.'

'I would be delighted.' She watched him walk down the short drive. Strange, she thought, but highly amusing – there was no carriage waiting for him. She wouldn't tell Arnold: she always enjoyed it when she had a little secret like that.

In the hall she met Agnes flying down the stairs, looking particularly fetching in a pale blue linen tea gown. 'You let him go?' she accused Dulcie.

'He had to leave.'

'Why didn't you stop him?'

'He had other things to do.'

'No!' Agnes stamped her foot. 'How could you?'

'Angel child, he asked your mother's permission to call again. And that, my dove, can mean only one thing.' Arnold chucked her under the chin.

'Papa!' she squealed, and flung herself into his arms.

Dulcie so rarely did anything other than care for her house that her announcement at breakfast that she would need the carriage to take her to the railway station took Arnold by surprise.

'Why on earth would Lord Prestwick want to see you?'

'Porcelain,' she replied.

'Yours? He's interested in that?'

'Apparently.'

'I shall drive you there.'

'That won't be necessary, Arnold. I have already made my arrangements.' And you weren't invited.

'And Agnes?'

'She wasn't invited.' That was cause for more joy. 'And in any case she is to visit Adeline and her family. It is too late for her to cancel.'

'She will be sorely disappointed.'

'There will be other times.' Briskly she put on her gloves.

'Where are you going now?'

'Into town, to meet young Mr Bartholomew-Prestwick. We shall catch the train together.'

'Is he not calling?'

'I said I would meet him. It will be easier for him if—'

'You didn't want Agnes to know your plans. Why not, for heaven's sake? This is a golden opportunity for our child to better herself. Why, she might even become a Lady.'

In name, perhaps, if not in reality. Dulcie enjoyed her malicious thought. 'Don't be silly, Arnold. I was being considerate, that is all.'

'But not to your own daughter. How callous you are.'

'If he is interested in Agnes, he will eventually show it. My meeting him in town will not change how he feels about her one jot. Just in case I'm late, I've arranged your dinner with Mrs Bramble.'

In the carriage she pondered this conversation with her husband. He had been right, of course: she had wanted to keep this visit to herself. If Agnes was with her she would demand to be the centre of attention, to monopolise Edward and, most certainly, she would have grasped any opportunity to make Dulcie look inadequate, the better to shine herself. What the silly girl was unable to understand was that such behaviour only emphasised her unpleasantness.

She leaned back on the soft leather cushion, closed her eyes and acknowledged that she wanted to be free of them – if only for a few hours. Dulcie had put up with so much for so long and she was reaching the end of her patience. Since Chauncey had felt forced to leave she had disliked being in the same room as her husband, and now that she knew of his liaison with Sophie Franks she was loath even to remain in the same house. Did she want to continue in this way?

If she were separated – just thinking of that sent a shiver through her. Of excitement or fear? 'Anticipation,' she said aloud, and smiled to herself. Separation, like divorce, would certainly make her an outcast, which once she could not have endured. But the importance to her of Society had diminished. What had it to offer her but endless anxiety that she was not doing things correctly, that she was letting Arnold down?

'I don't give a fig!' she declared, which gave her added courage. The other women in their circle had never accepted her. Often, she had the uncomfortable feeling that they laughed at her behind her back. She had so little in common with them and their endless chatter of fashion, shopping and servants. Would Dulcie being a pariah affect Agnes's marriage prospects? It was possible, hidebound as Society was by etiquette. Should she stay miserable for Agnes's sake when she never gave her a thought?

Dulcie knew many people, her address book was full to

overflowing, but she had no friends. If she left her marriage Arnold and Agnes would be content with each other. She would not be missed, with Chauncey gone too.

If anything should happen to Chauncey! She could never bring herself to think the dreaded word. She always used 'anything' when she meant death. At that she put her hand to her mouth to prevent herself crying out. But, if anything did happen to him, and she must be realistic, she would be desperately lonely and isolated. It was up to her to make a life for herself, not to be dependent on her family.

She opened her eyes and looked out of the window as they clattered over the cobbles of the high street. She could not get out of her head the notion that she wanted to protect nice young Edward from her rapacious husband and the manipulative Agnes.

'I can't tell you what a pleasure this is for me, Mrs Randolph-Smythe, to meet another collector – and of Meissen too. My own collection is sadly depleted these days.' He did not elaborate on why this was so but, given his very modest house in Exeter, the paucity of paintings, Dulcie could guess that lack of money must be the reason. 'We must compare notes,' he said, ushering her into the drawing room, whose curtains and upholstery needed replacing.

This was the second surprise: at the railway station they had had to take a hackney carriage since, as Edward explained, they had none of their own. Neither did he have a horse, but hired one when necessary. She had presumed that all lords must live in grand houses, own spanking *équipes*, the best horses. In a way she found it comforting that this one didn't.

'It's an equal pleasure for me, too, Lord Prestwick. And, please, Mrs Randolph is sufficient.' She smiled and was surprised by how emboldened she felt.

'Hyphens make such a mouthful. Poor Edward has the

same problem. But he does it to pander to his uncle. I said to the boy, "If a hyphen means the difference between nothing and an inheritance, then pop in as many as you want, dear chap."' He laughed, a most delightful sound that rumbled about the room and would surely make even the most disgruntled soul smile. He was not at all as she had expected. With such a handsome son she had expected him to be good-looking too. But he wasn't. In fact, he was rather plain – not ugly, for Dulcie believed no one to be ugly except perhaps herself, although people did comment on her dark brown eyes. He was short too, only a couple of inches taller than she, well upholstered around the middle and scruffily dressed in a fashion more suited to fifty years ago. He did not look or sound as Dulcie had imagined a lord to be. She liked him on sight, and what made her like him even more, was that right in the middle of his left cheek he had a wart the mirror image of her own.

'My husband insists on his to pander to his own snobbery,' she heard herself say. Her hand flew to her mouth. 'Forgive me. I don't know what made me say such a disloyal thing. What on earth must you think of me?' She was flustered with embarrassment.

'If it's the truth, can it be disloyal?'

'To my shame I fear it is.'

'Then here we have a meaty ethical problem, Mrs Randolph. I like nothing more. Let us be comfortable and consider which is the worst sin: disloyalty or dishonesty?'

'I couldn't really say. What a conundrum.'

'Why do I sense, Mrs Randolph, that you have most definite views on them both? And views I am eager to hear.'

'My opinion, Lord Prestwick?'

'Most definitely, Mrs Randolph.'

And Dulcie, for the first time in many years, found herself blushing with pleasure that anyone should think enough of her to seek *her* opinion.

'You see, Phoebe, here the artist has used this blue colour, and that sharp, almost chartreuse green there. Why do you think he painted it so?'

Phoebe enjoyed looking at the paintings in the large folder of watercolour sketches that Kendall Bartholomew had spread out on the round library table beneath a lamp on a weight and pulley, which he had lowered over the book, the better for them to see it. She didn't like being questioned about the pictures and her opinion of them. 'To balance the work?' she said tentatively. It seemed so unnecessary to her, this studying, this analysing. Why couldn't they just enjoy them?

'Correct. Well done. But there's another reason.' He looked expectantly at her.

She didn't like it when he spoke to her as if she was a small child, but supposed, given the difference in their ages, that she was to him. 'I don't know,' she said sulkily.

'If you don't try, you won't learn.'

'I can't see any reason in it.' This morning's session had gone on too long. If they looked at any more pictures she would scream, she was certain. At this rate she wouldn't have time for her walk before luncheon. She looked forward to the days when she wasn't summoned – the meals could be very long, the conversation tedious.

'Because it will give you another topic about which you will be able to talk with confidence.'

'I only ever see you, so does it matter?' The sullenness was increasing.

'Don't I matter to you?'

Don't bite the hand that feeds you. That was Phyllis – inside her again after so many weeks' absence – making her see sense. 'Of course you do. I'm grateful that you try. But you know me, who I am, what I know and what I don't know. Why do I have to pretend to you?'

'But if you know how to appreciate paintings it won't be a pretence. You will have knowledge. Phoebe, I can buy you fine clothes, a carriage, jewellery,' Phoebe perked up, 'but the greatest thing I can give you is knowledge.'

Phoebe smiled, and thought that *that* was a matter of opinion.

'Mrs Lingford tells me you are hungry to learn. But not with me?' He looked wistful.

'I've been here eight or ten weeks and me head is bursting with knowledge. I think it needs a rest.'

'*My* head, Phoebe. You must try to remember. And a young brain such as yours, hardly used until now, needs no rest.'

'I did use *me* head,' she said, to annoy him. 'How do you think things grow? They get sown, weeded, hoed, gathered, stored. That all needs thinking about. And all the things my mother taught me about what herbs are for what – when to pop the St John's wort into me dad's tea, when to use fever balm and camomile. How do I remember *they*, if I'm not using *me* brain. There's learning and learning, Mr Bartholomew. What you think is important might not be so to some. I know that what *I* think is important *is* important, because without it the likes of you would starve.'

Mr Bartholomew laughed. She had known he would. She had learned that he liked it when she spoke her mind. '*Touché*,' he said, bowing slightly from the waist. 'But, just to please me, couldn't you think, Why has the artist used this green and this blue and in those positions?'

Phoebe gave an exaggerated sigh so that he would know she was obliging him at cost to herself. She looked down at the picture, pursed her lips and frowned. 'To make you look deeper into the subject? It takes the eye to that there, that pastoral scene.'

'Excellent, Phoebe. The answer I hoped for. That wasn't so difficult, now, was it?'

Phoebe stabbed at the painting with her forefinger. 'Just look at them sheep. Either he can't paint sheep or they'm got scrapies, if you'm ask me.' Lapsing into her West Country dialect was always her way of showing she thought she had won.

Each day, even if it was raining, Phoebe walked in the grounds. Mr Bartholomew would fret when she did – in case she caught a chill, he said. She wasn't bothered. 'If you can survive a Dartmoor winter you can survive anything,' she had explained. Not that she enjoyed walking in all weathers but she felt that she should stick with the routine lest it be taken away from her. She certainly didn't want to be out in the fog, which swirled around her today like a winding sheet of grey dampness. Bushes and trees loomed out at her, making her jump. 'It's got to be done, though.'

'Better than being locked up.'

Phyllis only spoke out now if Phoebe was scared or worried, rarely at other times. On the moor people got lost in fog, fell into the mires, went mad, were found weeks later, just skeletons, their flesh eaten by carrion birds. Oh, yes. Fog was scary.

The odd thing was that, despite the way she lived, she wasn't lonely, even on the days when she saw no one but Mrs White, who had continued to mellow towards her. Phoebe realised that this wasn't because she liked her but because Mr Bartholomew did.

He was a rum old cove, she thought, as she hugged her new coat with its fur collar to her and plodded on. Some days she enjoyed his company, others he bored her witless. The learning could be interesting, but equally it could seem pointless. And while her manners were improving by the day she could not understand why they had to improve even more when there was no one but him to see her. Sometimes, at night, she wondered about the wisdom of staying any longer. It would be easy enough to escape, since she was locked up only at night now. But where would she go? And how would she survive? Those were the two insurmountable questions that always stopped her doing anything. And there was something else too: she loved the luxury of her life and did not want to go back to the old one. If she left, that might happen.

She wondered what advantage her new skills could be to her. Certainly they would be useless back home. She could go to a city and see what happened: as she'd never been to one she did not know what might be available to her there.

She hardly saw Lynette Lingford, these days, and missed her. She had been the nearest to someone of Phoebe's own age, except the maids who were still banned from talking to her. Kendall Bartholomew had taken over most of her tuition. She looked across the grounds to Lynette Lingford's cottage, but she wasn't going to venture there again to be insulted by that old father-in-law. She had her pride, after all.

Her handwriting and reading had improved beyond all measure. She couldn't think now why she had always found it so difficult. Now she could read her brother's letters, which she always carried in her pocket, although they were tattered and torn now. She would have to keep them in a box. Several weeks ago she had written to him. She had been so proud of her first letter. It hadn't said much – she wasn't yet up to writing reams:

Dear bruther Dick,
I am well
I hope you are well look after yourself don't get shot
your luving zister
Phoebe

She was particularly proud of her signature, which

swooped large and confident across the bottom of the page – she had spent a lot of time practising it.

'Mrs Lingford, would it be possible for you to post this letter to my brother? I've got the money for the stamp.' She had taken the coins from the precious store she had brought with her, which she had had no need to touch so far.

'To South Africa?'

'No, to his regiment in Exeter. That's what he said I was to do.'

Mrs Lingford looked at the envelope with a deep frown.

'I didn't say anything I shouldn't have. Just I was well. You can read it if you want.'

'No, I couldn't do that. Letters are private. Can you assure me that that is all you have put?'

'Yes.'

'You didn't write the address here?'

'No,' Phoebe answered truthfully. There had been no need: the address was printed at the top in a lovely black type, which, when she felt it with the tips of her fingers, she could feel was raised. Very smart it looked.

Each day since the letter had been sent she hovered around the table in the hall where the mail was put on the off-chance that she might one day get a letter of her own. She knew it was unlikely. First, the letter to Dick would take weeks to reach him, if it ever did, and if he replied the war would probably be over before she received it.

'Mr Bartholomew wants you in the library, this instant.' Mrs White met her in the hall, as if she had been lurking there in wait for her. Phoebe didn't like the way she had said it – as if she was in trouble.

As she hurried to meet him she tried to think of how she might have displeased him.

'Phoebe, sit down.' He didn't look cross, rather mournful.

'Yes?'

'I'm afraid I have some bad news for you.'

'Me? What? My brother?' Seemingly of its own accord her hand shot to her mouth.

'You told Mrs Lingford he was in the Devonshire and Dorset Regiment?'

'Yes. That's what his letter said.'

'I fear I have to tell you that the town of Ladysmith is under siege by the Boers, as are Mafeking and Kimberley. And that your brother's regiment are engaged with the enemy.'

'Like Carthage? And like they did in the Middle Ages?'

'You have learned your lessons well. Yes, just like them.'

'They'll be eating rats and cats. They'll be dying of disease.' Her eyes filled with tears.

'We don't know that.'

'Are they fighting?'

'Yes. Poor Phoebe.'

'No, poor Dick and all those innocent people.' She shook her head. 'He's be all right. Dick will survive, he's that sort of person.'

She insisted then that Mr Bartholomew get out the atlas the better for her to understand. It was not until she was alone in her room that she allowed her fears, worries and tears free rein.

The gong sounded, summoning her to luncheon. She splashed cold water on her face, but had no time to do more. When she entered the drawing room she wished she hadn't been crying: her eyes were all pink and swollen, and Edward was standing in the middle of the room. Her knees weakened at the sight of him and she blushed.

'Here she is. Phoebe, this is my nephew, Mr Bartholo-mew-Prestwick. Edward this is my little companion, Phoebe Drewett.'

'We've already met, haven't we?' Phoebe grinned, and wished she had remembered in time to smile.

'How, pray? And when?' Mr Bartholomew was frowning.

'Out walking one day, in the maze.'

'Alone?' There was an edge to his voice, and she was aware that Edward looked uncomfortable.

'No, Mrs Lingford was there.'

Mr Bartholomew visibly relaxed. 'How strange that she did not say.'

'Perhaps she forgot.'

'It was a brief meeting, Uncle.'

'I understand. We must be gentle with poor Phoebe today, Edward. She has had distressing news.'

'I'm so sorry. Is there anything I can do to help?'

At his kindness Phoebe felt certain she was about to start crying again and had to turn her head so that no one would see.

'We think her brother is engaged in fighting at Ladysmith.'

'Oh, the poor fellow. Miss Drewett, I am so sorry. You must be so anxious.' His voice brimmed with concern and sorrow for her.

'Don't worry for me, Mr Edward. He'll be all right, he's such a brave person, always into scrapes, but he gets through . . .' She had to stop for tears were welling. She must keep hold of the conviction that nothing would happen to him.

'I could check with the army for you. I have contacts.'

'Would you? That would be so kind.' She smiled at him radiantly.

'Luncheon is ready,' Mr Bartholomew said abruptly.

The summons came in the middle of the night. She awoke to find a footman beside her bed, shaking her and smiling oddly at her. 'His Nibs wants you. You're for it now.'

'What do you mean?' she asked, bleary-eyed. She was

already out of bed, placing a shawl around her night-dress. 'Dick!' she said, and needed no second bidding to follow him.

They went along the landing, down the stairs, along another corridor, and finally stopped. The footman tapped on the door and Phoebe entered a large bedroom, in the centre of which was a heavily curtained four-poster bed. Her heart lurched and instinct made her take a step back, but the footman propelled her forward.

'You wanted to see me, Mr Bartholomew?' She was aware that the door behind her was closing. She stepped forward, the light from the flickering flames of the banked-up fire, making her shadow dance across the ceiling of the room ahead of her.

'Come here, my dear.' He held out his hand to her. She approached the bed, feeling sick with apprehension. Either he was going to tell her that Dick was dead or he had plans for her. Bad plans. 'Sit.' He patted the satin coverlet. She did as she was told. 'There's something I want you to see.'

'It's not Dick?'

'Your brother? No. What gave you that idea?'

'It's the middle of the night.'

'The best time. Look, see this.' He had a leatherbound book. He leafed through it, and paused. 'Delightful,' he said softly. 'What do you think, Phoebe?'

In the light from a candlestick – no lamps in here, she registered – she looked at the drawing. A woman was lying supine with a gaggle of men around her, all naked, all with enormous erections. 'See.' He turned the page. Now one of the men was entering the woman as the others watched. 'See.' On the next page there were two men, then three servicing her. 'What do you think?'

'Bet that hurts,' she said, with a nervous giggle.

'Do you feel anything?'

'No,' she lied – for she did. It was as if the butterflies

that sometimes inhabited her stomach had migrated further down her anatomy.

'Let's look at another, then.'

And so it went on, picture after picture, and then his most prized possession he told her, photographs, each one more grotesque than the last. The pleasant feeling had disappeared quickly. She didn't like these pictures: they frightened her, disgusted her. She wanted to be out of here. But at each picture he asked her how she was feeling and his eyes were glinting with a strange look, like excitement but more so. Finally she realised he wanted her to be as excited as him.

'It's like my insides are full of honey,' she eventually said – to please him.

'Ah.' He lay back on he pillows. 'Divest yourself of your garments.'

'I beg your pardon?'

'Take your clothes off. Let me see you naked.'

'No.'

'Phoebe, do as I say.'

'I won't do that for anyone.'

'You'll do it for me, or tomorrow I will return you to your father at Cowman's Combe. Now, do as I say.' There was a steely look to him now, a look that said he would not brook any argument.

Phoebe felt sick. He was going to take her – rape her! What could she do? As she lifted her nightdress she looked about her for an escape route. There was none. Only the door, and who was on the other side?

'Let me see you.' His voice had changed, was deeper, huskier. She stood naked and vulnerable, her arms folded across her chest. 'Take your hands down.' She did so. 'Turn.' She did. 'Again.' She did. 'Dance.'

'What?'

'You heard me. Dance.'

She felt stupid, dancing naked with him watching her from the bed and no music, just the spluttering of the fire.

She tried to imagine she was somewhere else. She began to move . . . She was in a glade in a wood, Edward was watching her, the sun was shining, she was free. She moved her body rhythmically, swaying to imaginary music, throwing back her head in an abandoned manner. It wasn't so hard, she realised.

She looked at the bed. But Edward wasn't there, only her captor. The coverlet rose and fell as he pleasured himself.

'You can go now,' he said, as he collapsed back against his pillows. 'Thank you,' she heard him say, as she fled from the room.

9

Lily was confused. She wavered about what action she should take against Arnold. In the morning she would awake and lie in her narrow bed, imagining his body thrashing about in a large one with that unspeakable tart groaning and flailing with passion. Her heart swelled with anger, jealousy and hatred.

All the way to work she planned her revenge. She told herself what a duplicitous cad he was, what a fool, what a conceited idiot. He didn't deserve her. He didn't appreciate her. She fostered her loathing carefully.

'Good morning, Mr Randolph-Smythe,' she would say, upon seeing him enter the office, her treacherous heart a-flutter, her longing for him unabated. Who was the fool? Who was the idiot? she would ask herself, sitting at her desk, certain she would never be able to put her plans into action.

It was his presence that confused her. When he was not there she could resurrect her anger, build on it, nurture it. Alone in the office, first thing in the morning or late at night, Lily delved into ledgers, checked bank statements that went back years, opened the safe – to which, unknown to him, she knew the combination – and added to her dossier on him. She had also found where he had hidden other papers, to do with property he had bought. There was a secret drawer in his desk that hadn't remained secret once Lily had determined to find it. Her notebook was now half filled with valuable information she would take home with her at night. She slept with it under her pillow and carried it to work with her the next day, never letting it out of her sight.

'Miss Howard, you have changed! Please don't think me presumptuous, but this new style suits you.'

Lily blushed at the unexpected attention and patted her fringe. It was a false one she had bought. It had taken her days to learn how to pin it in place so that it looked as if it was her own hair. Emboldened, she purchased several more false hairpieces and soon had a luxurious head of curls, which necessitated her rising an hour earlier in the morning to fix it in place, but he did not comment further.

The hair, however, had given her a confidence she had not possessed before. Normally she wore black to the office, thinking it appropriate for work. Now she tried a darkish grey skirt with a white blouse and a tumble of lace trimming. The dark grey became light, and one morning she ventured out in blue, with a matching feathered hat.

'Whatever next? What *do* you think you look like?' Pansy snorted.

'I felt like a change.'

'Not for the better.' She sniffed. And then she sniffed again. 'What's that you've plastered on yourself? It's scent. There's only one reason for that – to cover up other smells. Given up washing, have you?'

'Mother!' Exasperated, Lily spoke through clenched teeth.

'Looking for a husband, are you? Always the optimist!' She cackled. Lily decided it was more dignified to ignore her but she slammed the front door of the small terraced house as she left, and felt marginally better.

He noticed. 'Why, Miss Howard, blue suits you. You must always wear it. Banish black and dull grey!'

And she had. She had gone home, parcelled up all her black clothes and put them into a trunk, which she manhandled down to the cellar. It was working: he was noticing her, seeing her for the first time as a woman. It would only be a matter of time and their relationship would change: he would see what a gem he had in her, how intelligent she was. Why, she could be almost his intellectual equal.

'Any news of Edith Baker?' she asked one morning, with heavy innocence.

'I've no idea where she is.' She wondered if she could believe that. 'She wasn't a very good clerk, was she?' Certainly she agreed with *that*.

She looked frequently at her notebook. Sometimes she thought of destroying it, but something always stopped her. He had been audacious, and he should be more careful. He needed her, that was certain: he had made little attempt to hide any of his misdeeds. She could show him how to do it, and then no one need know. Except her.

November was upon them. Thick fog swirled outside the office window. It was a busy month, when many of the accounts needed to be watched carefully. With the festive season approaching, the Mayor's Assembly on New Year's Eve and many parties, some of the women in the town went mad with their purchases. She wondered if, one day, Arnold would become mayor. In her dreams she was always his mayoress.

Lily's experience of working at the shop was invaluable: she knew which families must be chased for money, their credit curtailed, and which could be left to run up even larger bills.

This was the time when complaints multiplied too. Often the manageress of the Ladies' Fashions department came to ask Lily's help. The most common were that the dressmakers were not working fast enough, or that a dress hadn't evolved as it had been envisaged, even that it did not fit. Then Lily would venture out to the shop floor. If a poor or infrequent payer was complaining she had no compunction in pointing out that they had put on weight. If they were rich with a large account she blamed the seamstress and ordered a new one made. It never was – they simply let out the seams: the stupid rich never noticed.

She returned from one such exercise, feeling pleased with herself, and opened her office door to find Edith Baker standing in the middle of the room, a picture in primrose yellow, her tiny waist emphasised by the cut of the heavily embroidered jacket, a fur cape thrown casually over her shoulders, diamonds at her ears, neck and fingers.

'Hallo, Lily. What *have* you done to yourself?'

'Miss Howard to you.'

'Hardly!' Edith laughed at the idea. 'What do you think you look like?'

'I beg your pardon.'

'Talk about mutton dressed up as lamb!' Her laugh was a coarse trill.

Lily stalked to her desk. She had allowed herself to believe that Edith was no longer in his life. That perhaps she had gone away. Even, sometimes, that she had never happened in the first place. But to see her there, gloating in all her finery, was too much.

'You really should take advice on what to wear,' Edith said.

'What are you doing here?'

'Waiting for *my* Arnold as you are well aware.'

'He never said.'

'I decided to surprise him.'

'He won't be pleased.'

'He'll be ecstatic. Tea, Lily. I fancy a cup while I wait for darling Arnold.'

'Get it yourself. You know where things are kept.'

'You ordering me, Lily?'

'Something like that, yes.'

'We shall see about that. I shall tell him.'

'Do as you wish.'

'He won't like it. Still soft on him, are you?'

'I don't know what you mean!'

'Don't you?' Edith leaned far over her desk so that Lily had to move her own head to avoid contact with her. 'I suggest you listen. You are a dried-up old prune. An old maid. You're just a convenience to him, nothing more. He thinks you're pathetic. He told me about the false hair. We laughed about it in bed together. What a waste of time! You're nothing to him.'

Lily pushed herself into the back of her chair. Each insult struck her as if she was being whipped. She felt a lump forming in her throat, wanted to cry, refused to allow Edith the satisfaction of seeing her do so. Instead she got to her feet, lunged across her desk and sent Edith sprawling, just as the outer door opened and Arnold walked in.

'Arnold, she's mad! Help me! Save me from her!' Edith was scrabbling to her feet, then flung herself at him, clinging to him like a limpet. 'What have I done for her to treat me so?' She began to cry, pretty tears trickling down her cheeks.

'Miss Howard, what is the meaning of this?' He looked at her with anger.

'Edith was rude to me. She said the most dreadful things.'

'Arnold, I never did! She's lying! Why would I do something like that?'

'There, my sweet. Don't upset yourself.'

'I only wanted to surprise you, Arnold.'

'As you did. Now, Miss Howard, I demand an explanation for your appalling behaviour.'

'It was not I who behaved badly. I told you why I pushed her.'

'If you won't explain yourself I have only one alternative. You will be dismissed.'

To Lily it was as if the floor had rushed up to hit her in the face.

'Oh, yes, Arnold! Sack her! Get rid of her! She called me a whore!'

'I never did!'

'She said she was going to tell your wife about me.'

'She lies!'

'Miss Howard, such remarks are insupportable. And no one blackmails me. You are dismissed. Kindly vacate this office forthwith.'

'I don't think—' she began, but he did not hear her. He was already shepherding the sobbing Edith, whose tears would have melted the sternest heart, into his office.

10

Summoned to the library by Mr Bartholomew, and told by the footman she was to hurry, Phoebe dawdled. Why should she? There was still an hour before lunch. Also, she was tired and far from inclined to hasten anywhere.

It was not that she went to his room every night to perform for him, but on the nights when she wasn't called she lay awake, unable to sleep for wondering if she *would* be called. When she went the routine was always the same: first the silly pictures – she was amazed that he wasn't bored with looking at them because she was – and then the dancing. She no longer minded this. In fact, she quite enjoyed it, although she wished she didn't have to take off *all* her clothes: she was sure it would be much more artistic if she was allowed a little covering – muslin, feathers, silk, she could think of many things she could use to effect. She pretended she was an actress: it made it easier for her to feel detached from what was happening if she imagined an audience of hundreds rather than one, and as if she was choosing to do this for herself, not him. Her 'Attitudes', she called them. She had read in a history of Nelson that Lady Hamilton had done much the same for him and his friends, though it hadn't said she was naked, or that she was expected to dance. But it comforted her to know that she was in such exalted company. And if *Lady* Hamilton had done it, it couldn't be wicked, as she had at first feared.

She dallied at the window overlooking the knot garden from which she could see the outer bushes of the maze, her favourite place on the whole estate. Every day she hoped Edward would come but she was always disappointed.

The footman appeared. 'There you are! His Nibs is furious you're taking so long.'

'In my own good time,' she said, waving her hand as she imagined a grand lady would. She couldn't care less if old Ken was cross with her. Knowing what she knew, seeing what she saw on those nights, made her feel as if it was she who had power over him, not he over her. The respect she had had for him was long gone. A poor, stupid old codger was how she saw him. Still, if it meant this life was to continue, who was she to complain? Although she had resolved that if he laid as much as one finger on her, the very idea of which made her shudder, she would be out of this house fast. And no amount of lovely things would stop her.

'What kept you?' He was standing by his desk, drumming on the surface with his fingers.

'I didn't know there was a fire.'

'Wipe that stupid grin off your face. I've been waiting a good ten minutes!' The drumming ceased and he began to bang on the desk with his fist so that the inkstand rattled, a book went flying and an ornament toppled over. He didn't seem to notice. He was really angry and she'd never seen him like this before.

'I was admiring the garden.' Her voice was thin and reedy with nerves.

'When I order you to come you obey immediately. Is that understood?'

'Yes, Mr Bartholomew,' she said. Who does he think he is, talking to me like that? she thought, but she knew she was only trying to buoy up her morale, which was sinking fast.

'What is the meaning of this?' He waved a sheet of paper at her.

'If I knew what it was I might be able to give you an answer.'

'How dare you?' And before she knew what was happening he had slapped her hard across her cheek.

'Here, hold your horses . . .' She put her hand up to her smarting face, sorely afraid: she had been beaten so many times in her short life and the fear that she was to be beaten again made her want to run.

'Answer!'

'What is it? I don't know.'

'Don't you? Don't lie. It is a letter addressed to you.'

'From my brother.' Her voice lifted with excitement, the slap forgotten. 'Please let me see it.' He held it higher aloft. 'I'll do anything you want, if you let me read it.' She stood on tiptoe trying to grab it.

'You did not have permission to write to anyone.'

'I didn't think I had to ask.'

'Of course you did, fool.'

'I'm not. And don't you call me names.' She sidestepped the blow this time. 'Please, Mr Bartholomew, I beg you.'

'What did you write about me, about my house, about your life here?'

'Nothing. I promise you. All I said was that I was happy. What does he say?'

'Nothing.'

'Then why can't I read it?' She made to grab at it again. 'If you won't let me see it, then for God's sake tell me what is in it!' She was virtually screaming at him now.

'The more hysterical you become the less inclined I feel to do so. And I repeat, you did not ask my permission.'

'I was not aware I needed it. You had me taught to read and write, so I didn't think there was any harm in it. I wanted Dick to see I could write.' She forced herself to speak calmly, to compose herself.

'And how did you post it?'

She had to think quickly, not wanting to get Mrs Lingford into trouble. 'I met a man out walking. I asked him to post it for me. I brought a few pennies here with me.'

'You lie. You taint yourself by lying.'

'I do no such thing,' she said weakly.

'Mrs Lingford posted it.'

'Her never did!' Distract him, she thought. Get him correcting your speech! Her mind was racing.

'She has admitted to it and she has been dismissed for it.'

'No! That's not fair. It had nothing to do with her.'

'She knew the consequences of disobeying me. Your concern is as false as you are. And, you lied to her too.'

'I never did.'

'You told her you had not enclosed your address, but you must have done or the reply would never have come here, would it?'

'She asked me if I had written the address and I said I hadn't, which was the truth. It's not my fault if you have it printed at the top of the paper.'

She was knocked sideways by the whack across her

head, which made shards of light dance before her eyes. 'You have ruined everything,' he shouted.

She sat down suddenly. 'I don't see what I have done that is so wrong.' She began to cry. 'He is my brother, not my lover! Please . . .' She held out her hand towards the letter. 'Please, give it to me.'

With no warning he turned from her and approached the fire, the letter still in his hands. He threw it into the flames. Despite her dizziness, despite the pain in her head, Phoebe dashed forward, dived to the side of him, put her hand into the fire, grabbed the paper and burnt herself. She cried out.

'If you do wrong you will be punished. I had such hopes for you, but you are just like the others.'

The scrap of letter she had rescued was charred, the writing indecipherable. 'How could you do that? How could you be so cruel?' She leaped at him and, oblivious to the pain of the burn, pummelled him with her fists. 'You had no right!'

He held her from him, a disdainful expression on his face, until she realised the futility of what she was doing and stopped. As she had hoped, he let her go.

'So there *were* other girls here? Who lies now? Everyone lies in this house, everyone but me!' She stabbed passionately at her breast. 'I'm leaving.'

'You will do no such thing. You will stay here until I decide you can go. And we will revert to a locked room. I have finished with you!'

'I hate you!' she screamed, and turned towards the door.

'Stay there.' He leaped in front of her, barring the way.

'You stupid old fool!' Nimbly, she lifted her knee, aimed it at his crotch and raced from the room leaving him doubled over in agony.

It was raining outside and bitterly cold, but she ran out of the door and down the drive, so fast that she developed a stitch, which forced her to slow, then cramp in one calf. She collapsed on to the grass verge, her dress soaked and clinging to her, her teeth chattering with the cold. 'Don't cry!' she ordered herself, as she rubbed her leg. 'Whatever I do I'm not going to cry!'

'Miss Phoebe?' She jumped. She hadn't heard anyone approach.

'Mr Edward!' And all her good intentions not to weep came to nothing as she burst into tears.

He, oblivious of the rain and mud, knelt at her side. 'Dear Miss Phoebe, what is it? What has happened? What can I do to help you?' He put his arm about her and Phoebe felt wonderfully safe as he held her close.

'My brother . . .' she hiccuped. 'I had a letter.'

'What has happened?'

'I don't know – he wouldn't tell me.'

'Your brother?'

'No, your uncle. He burnt it!' And she opened a clenched palm to show him the ashes. 'That's all there is left. And he won't tell me . . .' Her voice trailed off.

'I don't understand. Why not, pray?'

'He is angry with me because I wrote in the first place.'

'Because of a letter to your brother? Surely not.'

'He is. He frightened me. He says he didn't give me permission and I didn't know I should ask.'

'Then that is easily rectified. You must explain to him just as you have to me. He won't be unreasonable then. It is not in his nature.'

'You don't know him.'

'Of course I do, he is my uncle. But you have hurt yourself. Let me see.' He looked with concern at her hand. 'Allow me.' From his pocket he took a pristine handkerchief, which he bound round the burn. 'We need to get Mrs White to put some salve on this—'

She snatched away her hand. 'I'm not going back there.' She clutched the burnt hand with the other. 'Never.' And she stood up abruptly as if about to take flight.

He caught hold of her arm. 'Miss Phoebe, do not distress yourself so, you will harm yourself. No one is going to hurt you. There has to be an explanation. My uncle is a kind man. He would be distressed to see you like this. And you're soaked! How stupid of me not to notice immediately.' He removed his thick ulster coat and wrapped it about her. She clung to the fabric, which smelt warm and comforting – his smell? For another moment she enjoyed a sense of security. 'Please, Miss Phoebe, come with me.'

'I can't.'

'But I shall be with you. I won't let anything befall you. Trust me.'

She looked up at him, into his eyes – which were full of concern, she was sure. She pulled the coat tighter and the feeling of safety returned. 'I won't stay.'

'That is your decision.'

'You won't leave me?'

'Not until you are happy for me to do so. But that hand must be treated. And you need dry clothes. See how sensible I can be.' It was his smile that gave her the confidence to agree. 'Would you care to ride on my horse?'

Phoebe looked up at the snorting beast and decided against it. 'No, I'd rather walk.'

'Come, then.' He put his hand under her elbow.

They walked back in silence. She enjoyed his close proximity, his coat about her, but as the house drew nearer, her fear took control.

'I don't want to go in.' She stopped at the bottom of the main steps.

'But if you don't, you won't know what was in the letter.'

She tried to make up her mind whether or not to climb the steps. He sounded so reasonable. 'He'll lock me away.'

'Uncle Kendall! Hardly!' He laughed, and for a second

she wondered if he was in league with his uncle, but then she looked at his handsome face, his outstretched hand. He couldn't be . . . Even as she made up her mind, the door opened. There stood Mr Bartholomew and she thought her heart would stop.

'There you are, Phoebe! I was getting worried – walking in this weather, you'll catch your death of cold.'

'I found her half-way down the drive in a pitiable state, Uncle.'

'It was a good thing you came along when you did, Edward. Now, let's get this poor dear child into the warm.'

'No . . .' Phoebe put up her hand as if to push away him and the house. 'No,' she said again, then fainted dead away.

Phoebe was aware of voices talking. She felt as if she was at the bottom of a deep well. Then she remembered where she was and fear brought her round. She was lying on her bed. 'There, my lovely, is that hand better now?' she heard Mrs White ask.

'The patient wakens, Mrs White?'

'That she does, Mr Bartholomew.'

'Miss Phoebe, what a fright you gave us.' Edward's voice was brimming with concern. 'Shall I help you sit up?'

Phoebe felt groggy. 'I'm dizzy,' she complained.

'Mrs White gave you a small amount of laudanum for the pain. Miss Phoebe, there's nothing to be afraid of. My uncle has explained. The letter wasn't from your brother, it was from his regiment. Your letter didn't even get to South Africa. He isn't in Ladysmith as you feared. He was out on patrol when the town was invaded.'

'Not in Ladysmith? Then where?'

'Phoebe, it's good news and bad. He's on his way home.'

'Dick's coming here?'

'Yes, and my uncle says he will find work for him on the estate. But Phoebe, he was wounded. Not seriously, but badly enough for the doctors to decide he should be sent home.'

Phoebe struggled with this information, and tried to pull herself up. 'Why couldn't he have told me that? Why burn the letter? Why hit me?'

'Oh, really, Phoebe, it must be the drug distorting your mind. Edward, can you imagine me hitting anyone?'

'No, Uncle, I must say, I can't.' Edward was even laughing.

That made her angry. 'I was not dreaming. He burnt the letter.'

'Miss Phoebe, he didn't. I've read the letter. It is just as we tell you.'

'You're in league with him!' she cried. 'How could you deceive me?'

'I don't understand what you're saying, Phoebe.'

'I think our young friend needs rest, Edward. We should leave her with Mrs White to tend her. Come, luncheon is imminent.'

'I'll come and see you before I go.'

'Leave me alone! I don't want to see you. I don't want you near me!' she screamed at the astonished young man.

When she next awoke it was dark. Her mouth felt as if it was full of cotton, and her head ached. When she sat up she gasped. By the light of a candle she could see Kendall Bartholomew standing at the end of her bed.

'What a stupid girl you are, Phoebe, shouting at my nephew in that way, upsetting him as you did. He was your one hope, and now he has gone.'

'I don't need him and I don't need you.' She moved to get out of the bed.

'I suggest you get back into that bed and rest. You're not going anywhere – for the moment.'

'So, you're going to lock me away again?' she said, in a defiant tone.

'No.' He turned and made for the door.

'Good.'

'You will be leaving here later tonight.'

'And where am I going?'

At the door he faced her. 'I had hoped you were the one who could remain here, be my companion for life. But it is not to be.'

'Thank heavens. Spend my life with you!' She managed to laugh.

'Maybe you will come to wish you had. I am going to sell you, Phoebe, at auction, to the highest bidder.'

Chapter Three
December 1899

I

Phoebe had no idea where she was. The journey, in the dark, was terrifying. The horses were being whipped into a frantic speed and she was thrown this way and that as the carriage rocked and pitched along rutted roads. She banged on the roof and yelled at the coachman to slacken his pace, but either he had not heard or did not wish to. Finally she sat on the floor and braced her back against one seat and her feet against the other. Not a dignified way to travel, she thought, but she was convinced she would be brained if she did not.

An hour later, she estimated, the coach clattered to a halt, and she could hear the horses snorting and pawing the ground as if wishing to be gone again. The coachman opened the door and, with scant ceremony, yanked her out. She could feel the cobbles through the soles of the satin slippers she wore. She had no coat, since she had not been given time to put one on, and a chilly wind blew. She wrapped round herself the fine woollen shawl she had been wearing when banished from the house, but it was no protection.

She sniffed. She could not smell the clear air of the moor with its distinctive scent: instead there was an unpleasant odour of tar and soot – and something else, something unfamiliar. She took a deep breath: it reminded her of how the moor smelt just before a thunderstorm.

'Not so rough,' she complained, as the coachman manhandled her over what she saw was the yard of a large building. 'Is this a town?' she asked. 'Where am I?'

But he didn't answer. 'Cat got your tongue?' For her pains she was pushed harder, which only made her more recalcitrant. 'Born dumb, were you?' She nearly fell flat on her face from the shove he gave her.

'The latest from Courtney Lacey,' he said, to the woman who opened the door almost immediately to his impatient rapping.

'So you can speak?' Phoebe said.

'Shut your gob,' the coachman snarled.

'Less of your cheek,' the woman added. 'Come here, you.' Instead of being pushed from behind, Phoebe found herself yanked from the front. 'It's been some time since we had one of his. Then two in a month. Evil old sod! There's food in the kitchen for you.'

'Good, I'm hungry.'

'Not for you, for the coachman.' To Phoebe the woman's voice sounded like a rusty iron gate opening. She could see her clearly now in the light from a lantern hanging in the passageway into which she had been pulled. She was middle-aged, her grey hair pulled back so tightly that the skin on her face looked as if it was being stretched to its limit. A clay pipe hung from her mouth and her teeth were stained as brown as mahogany. 'Up them stairs.' She pointed, and gave Phoebe a push.

'You needn't prod me like that. What happened to "This way, please"?'

'Get a move on.' At least she wasn't poked this time. 'We've got a spirited 'un 'ere.'

'Mrs White said as to keep an eye on her – she wasn't frightened of nothing.'

'We'll soon see about that!' The woman cackled, a discordant sound.

Phoebe was shown into a comfortable but shabbily furnished sitting room on the first floor. 'You're to wait here.'

'What for?'

'You'll find out.'

'Is everyone as pleasant as you?'

'Watch your lip, girl, it'll do you no good.'

That woman would be quite at home as the superintendent of a workhouse, Phoebe decided, and stuck out her tongue at the closing door. She had intended the childish action to make her feel better, but it hadn't worked. If anything, it had made her feel worse. She realised that, once again, she was virtually a prisoner, at the mercy of others, and she didn't know where she was or why.

'There's no point in feeling sorry for myself.'

'I think you're in a right pickle now.'

'That's all I need, Phyllis. Couldn't you be just a mite more cheerful?'

'What's there to be cheerful about?'

'I think you enjoy being gloomy.' Phoebe flopped on to one of the easy chairs and jumped up again when a spring bit into her. She chose another chair and sat down gingerly. 'He said I was to be auctioned. What's he mean by that? Cattle, sheep and pigs are auctioned. And where am I? That's what I want to know.'

'Then look.'

Despite the headache she had and the nausea that Mrs White's laudanum had brought on, she began to explore the room, but found no clues as to where she was until she saw a newspaper sticking out of a wastepaper basket. She snatched it up and smoothed it out.

'The *Barlton Globe*! Bartholomew sometimes had this newspaper. So this could be the town! That's good news. The more people there are the safer I'll be.'

'Or the more there are to do you harm.'

'Shut up.'

Barlton had been one of the places she had hoped to go when she had set out on her journey. It was 2 December, she noted, from the paper. 'It'll soon be Christmas!'

'And when did you last enjoy Christmas? When Mum was alive.'

Just saying that made her want to cry. Until Mr Bartholomew, that had been the last time she was given a present. 'No, that's not true. Dick made me a workbox last year. Oh, Dick, if only you were here.' Tears were close to the surface. 'You could hardly call what Mr Bartholomew gave you presents. He took them all back.'

Her father wouldn't even notice Christmas Day: he did not approve of such *papist* festivals. She wondered if he had looked for her, or missed her – probably not. 'What on earth made you think of him?'

'Because I don't know what's happening. Or what my fate is to be. Even he's better than . . .'

'Don't think that! And it's best not to dwell on what might happen, Phoebe.'

The date was a shock, however: she hadn't realised how long it was since she had arrived at Courtney Lacey. She had been there for over three months. Time had passed so quickly, yet there had been days that seemed to go on for ever.

She sat down again, intending to read the paper. Her reading was still slow: she hadn't been practising without Mrs Lingford to chivvy her into it. But even if she could have read faster she doubted that she would have been able to concentrate long enough to absorb it. Her nerves were scudding about all over the place and, try as she might, she could not calm herself.

Where were Mrs Lingford and her family now? Such a nice girl that Freda, and so pretty.

'Why worry about her? She didn't care about you. She knew what was going on, she must have, and did she warn you?'

'No.'

'Did she try to stop him?'

'No.'

'So why should you care about her and her stupid family?'

'Exactly.'

She laid the newspaper on the table. And then there was Edward. She felt a pain in her chest, as if her heart was held in a vice.

'Was he concerned?'

'Not a jot.'

'Probably in league with his uncle.'

'No doubt of it.'

'And I thought I loved him.'

'Fool!'

'That's true. But if I ever see him again, if ever I'm in the same room as him, I shall . . .'

'What?'

'I don't know, but it'll be horrible.'

There was a sudden roar of male voices from the room beneath her, which made her jump. The noise was deafening. She stood up and eyed the door with wild-eyed horror.

She started again when the door opened and a young girl was thrust into the room with such force that she stumbled across it and fell into Phoebe's arms. She was so thin and weighed so little that Phoebe didn't lose her footing.

'Oh, Miss, I'm that sorry.'

'It wasn't your fault. I'm Phoebe.'

'Ethel.' She wiped the back of her hand across her nose, leaving snot on the sleeve of her musty-looking black dress.

'Do you know why we're here?'

'To be sold.'

Phoebe had to sit down. 'Auctioned? Like the animals at market?'

'That's right.'

'Are you sure?'

'Oh, yes. I was last here in September. I didn't suit so they sent me back.'

'Why didn't you suit?'

'I'm too thin and I couldn't do the work they wanted.'

'What work?'

'Scullery-maid.'

At this Phoebe let out a great sigh of relief. So that was what her fate might be. 'Exaggerating as usual,' she said aloud, before she could stop herself.

'Sorry?'

'Ignore me, I'm going mad, I was talking to myself.'

'I do that all the time.'

'Do you?' Phoebe was interested.

'When I get lonely, and there's no one else to talk to.'

The door opened again and another girl entered. This one wasn't pushed: she walked in, upright, proud and defiant. Phoebe admired her. 'Hallo.' Phoebe smiled and introduced herself, then did the same for Ethel, who was looking at the new arrival with awe. She seemed to have been struck dumb by her posture and her prettiness.

'I'm Rosie Grainger, how do you do? Isn't it warm in here? Such unseasonable weather.'

It struck Phoebe that this was the oddest situation she had ever been in. Here she was, about to be sold, if Ethel was right, and here was Rosie, talking as if they were at a social gathering. She watched her sit. She didn't do it properly, not as Phoebe had been taught, but she wasn't bad.

The dragon reappeared with two diaphanous dresses in her arms. 'You two, you're to put these on.'

'Which two?' asked Phoebe, taking the dresses. Ethel looked too scared and Rosie looked too grand.

'Not her, she's too ugly.' The dragon pointed at Ethel, who grinned as if she didn't mind being described in such an uncomplimentary manner. With no further explanation, she left them.

'Ethel, why have we got to change? What's wrong with what we've got on?'

''Cause you're going to have to perform. Rather you than me. There was a girl here called Coral. She had to but she couldn't, and then they all threw pennies at her and spat at her and she cried and she couldn't go on—'

'Perform what?' Phoebe asked.

'She wasn't sold. No one wants a misery guts, do they? They shoved her out on the streets when it was all over.'

'What happened to her?'

'Gawd knows! On the game by now, I should think.'

'What game?' asked Phoebe.

'Really, there's no point in pretending to be so innocent here.' Rosie yawned, as if everything was of scant interest to her, which Phoebe did not believe since she'd noticed her listening intently.

'Perform what? And for whom?' Phoebe was exasperated. 'Why won't anyone tell me?'

'For them.' Ethel pointed at the floorboards. 'This is a club. They're watching bare-knuckle fighting at the moment. Then you'll have to dance, and you'll be bought. It's in God's hands who you end up with. At least I know where I shall be, in someone's kitchen.'

'This can't be true. People aren't *sold*, like slaves. Why, it'll be the new century in a few weeks. There haven't been hiring fairs for ages in these parts. You're making it up, Ethel, and it isn't funny.' But she was afraid. Her own grandmother had been sold at a fair, and she had heard tales of goings-on in isolated inns that she didn't like to think about.

'You tell that lot down there, then. They do it. They've always done it. A few laws aren't going to stop they.'

'Do you believe her, Rosie?'

'I've heard rumours. My lover threatened me that if I didn't do as he asked then this would happen to me.'

'You don't seem worried.'

'Why should I be? Anything will be better than the mean, sadistic bastard who's just thrown me out. What alternative is there? The streets?'

'We could run away and seek employment.'

'I had a position – in a shop here in Barlton. I believed him when he said he'd look after me and take care of me. Such a fool I am. I'd never get work anywhere now, not without his testimonial.'

'What? Your lover? But it would have to be your employer surely, gave you papers.'

'He *was* my employer, Arnold Randolph-Smythe Esquire. Just pray *he* doesn't buy you, Phoebe. That's all I can say.'

2

The jailer, as Phoebe thought of her, returned with two more young women and food for them all. The new arrivals were friends of Ethel and ignored Phoebe and Rosie. They dived for the food as though they were starving.

'Do you want anything to eat, Rosie?' Phoebe asked.

'No, thank you, not after seeing them behave like wolves. The state of their hands and nails kills hunger stone dead. And to think people employ them in their kitchens!' Rosie's distaste was evident in her voice.

'Dreadful!' agreed Phoebe, who only a short time ago had given scant thought to hygiene. But she wasn't about to tell Rosie that. She might be in a dire position but, for all that, she was enjoying being with someone closer to her in age. And she admired her looks and her sophistication. For all that she felt a twinge of guilt that she was betraying Ethel: she should have defended her and said she knew no better. Ethel had been kind to her and was even nearer her age than Rosie.

Ethel held up some cheese in her filthy hands. 'Here, Phoebe, want this?'

'No, I'm not hungry. You enjoy it.'

'Suit yourself,' Ethel said, with a shrug.

'Who's your hoity-toity friend?' one of the others asked Ethel.

'There's no need to be like that.' Phoebe was affronted. A few weeks ago she would have been one of the first to dive for the food.

'We're too posh for the likes of them.' Rosie turned her back disdainfully.

'Posh? Me?' This made Phoebe laugh for the first time that day.

'We look different from them, we've fine clothes, we're clean, we smell nice, we speak differently.'

'Doesn't alter what we are inside, though, does it? You're still a shop girl and me . . .' She paused. 'I don't know what I am. I can hardly call myself a milkmaid, we only had one cow. A farm labourer is about all I can think of.' At least that made her feel less disloyal.

'Then your hands don't match what you say you are. Once you've tasted the good life you can never go back to the other. So, whatever you choose to think, you've changed.'

'I still feel the same.'

'I don't believe you. You want different things now. You choose different people to talk to – you're talking to me rather than them. And what on earth would we have had in common when you were a farm labourer?' Rosie smiled, but Phoebe found her attitude too superior for comfort. 'I can't think of anything worse than having to be polite and serve those fat, ignorant bitches who patronised the shop. I shall most definitely not return to my former life.' She said this with a toss of her head and an unconscious air of bravado.

'But what else is there to do? I thought I might try to go into service. At least I'd have a roof over my head, and I've learned a lot these past weeks,' Phoebe said.

'No one would take you without recommendation, and who would give you that? No, our only hope is to find a protector and hope he's not too mean, cruel, old and smelly.' Rosie shuddered.

'I couldn't do that!' Phoebe was shocked at the very idea and, even though she now hated him, found herself thinking of Edward. If it was him . . .

'That would be different,' Phyllis said, before Phoebe could stop her.

'What did you say?' Rosie asked.

'Nothing,' said Phoebe, feeling foolish.

The noise downstairs was calming into a general hum of conversation, punctuated by laughter. There were other sounds now, of cutlery and glass. Apparently the fight had finished and the men were dining.

An hour later Ethel and her friends were called. Phoebe and Rosie were told off roundly for not having changed into the clothes the woman had given them.

While she put on hers, Phoebe took a sly look at Rosie. She was lovely, she thought, all pink and blonde, strawberries and cream. Rosie would soon find someone to look after her. All the prettiest women were fair, in Phoebe's opinion. There was a mirror on the wall and Rosie stood before it to arrange her hair and pinch her cheeks. 'Rather nice, isn't it?' She twirled in front of the mirror, the sheer muslin swirling around her like white mist, making her look even prettier.

'They're like togas, aren't they?'

'I'd agree if I knew what a toga was.'

Phoebe looked at herself in the mirror with amazement. That was the first time she had ever known more than someone else. She smiled at herself with satisfaction.

'There's just one or two things I've to tell you.' The jailer was back.

The waiters carried the vast tureens into the crowded dining room. Crouched inside, fearful of being tipped over as she was rocked from one side to the other, Phoebe put her hands over her ears to deaden the noise of men shouting, which was magnified by the metal of the lid. Finally it was placed on the table.

Her mouth was dry when the prearranged tap on the tureen warned her that she was about to be uncovered.

There was a drum roll. 'Gentlemen, pray silence,' she heard a man's voice shout over the hubbub. 'It is my pleasure to introduce to you, for your delectation, Miss Rosie and Miss Phoebe.' Another drum roll and then the lid was raised. The light shining into her eyes was blinding, and she winced at the cheer as she and Rosie, in unison as they had been instructed, rose from the containers and stepped daintily on to the table.

Approximately twenty men were sitting around it, all staring at them, drunk, their mouths open wide, braying, shouting.

'Let 'em rip!' A large man banged his glass on to the table with such force that it broke.

'Dance my beauties!' shouted another. Phoebe looked at the leering faces, at the sweat rolling down them, checked every one, afraid she would see Edward, but he wasn't there.

'Shake a leg!'

Phoebe looked at the other end of the table where Rosie was already swaying to the music issuing from a pianola. She wasn't very good, Phoebe thought. Not like me. And she began to dance as she had for Mr Bartholomew, swaying, swooping on the table, using her robe like a fan, like a curtain, first hiding herself, then exposing just a little bit. She was enjoying the cheers, the compliments. She liked all the men's eyes on her – they had quickly become bored with Rosie's efforts. Her dancing became wilder, she was in control of them, she was making them happy, she was giving pleasure, delight, and in the giving she found she was happy too, happier than she'd ever been before.

'I want the altogether!' A man with a scowling face

grabbed at the hem of her robe. She pulled it away, and danced out of reach, teasing the man, hiding her face, lifting her skirt, turning her back, peering over her shoulder at him, smiling, throwing her head back, letting her hair fall. He was laughing – she had changed him, she had made him turn from temper to happiness. This was glorious – this was *power*.

'Let's have her naked! Get that off!' Another hand was tearing at Phoebe's dress, then another. They were all shouting, grasping, clutching, snatching. They were like wild animals, their eyes bulging, their mouths salivating. Phoebe woke from her pleasurable trance and fear swamped her – made worse when she looked for Rosie and saw her, on her back, her head in the cheese, with a man burrowing under her skirt and another ripping the cloth to expose her breasts.

Phoebe looked about her frantically. There was no escape: if she jumped off the table and raced for the door, they would catch her. Instinct made her step towards Rosie, to help her, but there were too many of them. She might make matters worse. She felt sick with terror as the men became more excited, their eyes glazed with lust. Was she about to be raped? Would she die?

'Pull yourself together! Make them laugh!' Phyllis shouted.

Phoebe pulled her dress back from the men's grasp, picked up a napkin, and slapped it firmly across the groping hands. 'Naughty boys! We'll have none of that, if you don't mind.' She was aware how shrill her voice sounded, quavering with nerves. 'Now you don't want Phoebe to be cross with you, do you?' She stood, hands on hips, looking down on them, trying to look stern, shaking from head to toe with fear.

She held her breath. And then they laughed. Each one saw the joke. And sat down.

'Gentlemen, gentlemen, don't let's get too carried

away. Phoebe here is a virgin, and we don't want damaged goods, do we? Wouldn't be fair.'

'And the other?' asked a man with the fattest pink fingers Phoebe had ever seen, like overstuffed sausages.

'Unfortunately, no, Folgate, old man. But she's still tight. I can guarantee that.'

'You're a card, Arnold. What they see in you is a mystery to me.'

'Money!' bellowed the youngest man there.

'So, let's begin shall we? The second-hand one first. What am I bid for Rosie here? She comes highly recommended but needs strict training.' The man called Arnold laughed unpleasantly.

Nobody bid. Rosie looked close to tears. How humiliating, thought Phoebe. What if when it was her turn no one bid for her?

'Are you mad?' Phyllis spoke too loudly and one or two heads turned in her direction.

'Not bidding for someone so lovely.' Phoebe had recovered just in time.

'She's right. Two guineas.'

'Five.'

'That's an insult. More gentlemen, please. I've promised my dear wife I shall be raising hundreds for her favourite charity.'

Women knew their men behaved like this? Well, Phoebe would rather stay as she was than be like one of them, allowing such goings-on. She could imagine them, respectable and stuck-up, with such wicked secrets.

Rosie was finally sold for fifteen guineas. A huge sum, thought Phoebe. The man who bought her was middle-aged, his stomach so pendulous it rested on his thighs. He didn't wait to witness Phoebe's fate, but swept Rosie off the table and rushed with her to the door.

'He'll be ravishing her before they reach the carriage,' Arnold told the cheering throng. 'And now our sweet, provocative, virginal Phoebe. Anyone got the clap? Need a pretty virgin to cure you? No one. Good. It would be a shame to infect her. Phoebe here is a gem. She can read, write, converse. She's such a treasure that I will open the bidding at thirty guineas.'

Thirty guineas! Such a huge amount – Phoebe couldn't imagine what it looked like. Quickly it was fifty. Then seventy-five. A hundred was reached and then fifty was added . . . Phoebe was proud that they thought she was worth so much. She looked at the faces and tried to keep up with the bidding, wondering which one would win her. There were four disgustingly old men, seventy if they were a day. She hoped it wouldn't be one of them. But then, on the other hand, what did her father do with the ram when it could no longer mate? He killed it. Maybe the older they were the less capable they would be of mating. She wasn't having anyone she didn't love between her thighs, that was certain. She'd kill herself first.

The bidding went on. It was now at two hundred. Two men, she decided, had cruel faces and she didn't want them to succeed. The man called Arnold was the best-looking and he was clever the way he was making the men spend more and more. But hadn't Rosie said he was cruel? She didn't like being hurt. No, of them all she liked the look of the man to her right. About thirty, she estimated, and he didn't shout as much as the others but watched her with eyes that glinted with excitement. She'd seen that look before, in Mr Bartholomew. Perhaps it would be best of all if there was a fire and she could escape through the flames.

'Two hundred and ten guineas it is, then. I could continue bidding, Orton, as you are fully aware. She's a fine filly, to be sure, but I bow to your seniority.'

With horror, Phoebe saw that she had been sold to the oldest man there. He was even dribbling.

The auction over, the drinking done, Phoebe and her purchaser set off, through the streets of Barlton, for the King William Hotel. While she was still full of trepidation, there was a glimmer of hope. Mr Orton was so drunk that he could barely stand. She looked about her, trying to get her bearings, wondering in which direction to run. She decided to wait until he fell down, which was inevitable, then steal his greatcoat – though how she was to achieve this, given his weight, she had no idea. All she had on was the diaphanous dress she had been given to dance in, and her shawl. She hadn't had time to collect her other clothes. Already it was cold, and as the night wore on it would get colder.

'Hey.' She had to use all her strength to prevent him toppling on to the pavement. She couldn't let him fall yet: it wasn't the ideal moment for her to escape. They were still in the high street and there were too many people about who might stop her removing his coat, perhaps even call a constable and have her arrested.

He might still have money on him, or a watch. She would help herself to both. Such evil planning took Phoebe by surprise, for she had never stolen as much as an apple in her life. 'Serves him right, wanting a young girl like me.'

'Disgusting!' Phyllis agreed.

Although it must have been past midnight, there were still many people walking about, carriages passing, horsemen. Did they never sleep? They couldn't all have been at the auction. Then a tram approached, its warning bell ringing as it trundled down the street. She had never seen anything so large and noisy, bigger than the next-door farmer's threshing machine.

As they passed a public house the door opened and a gaggle of men piled out, singing and joking. At the sight of Phoebe they shouted their opinion of her face and figure, and of the age of the man she was with. Phoebe's step faltered. She wondered if this was the moment. Should she throw herself on their mercy, tell them what had happened? Beg them to help her? But on seeing their glittering eyes, hearing the drunken comments, smelling the beer on their breath, she decided that she was probably better off with one drunk than a gang of them.

The men moved off in the opposite direction, catcalling and singing. At Cowman's Combe there were only the sounds of animals, the wind in the trees and owls hooting after six o'clock on a winter's night. Here, it was Bedlam. She looked up at the windows over the shops and wondered if people lived there, and how they could sleep with so much going on in the street below.

Drunk as he was, Mr Orton knew the way. When they reached a passageway, he pointed imperiously with his stick. Speech appeared to have deserted him. They were half-way along it when he stopped abruptly. 'Who are you?' His voice was muffled, as if he spoke through layers of wool.

'Phoebe.'

'How do you do? I'm a goat. An old goat.' He guffawed. The stench of stale ale that wheezed out of him made her reel back. He beckoned her with a finger whose nail was rimmed with black. 'Don't tell anyone, but last week I was an egg.'

'How very nice for you. Hard-boiled?'

He found this very funny but since it made him laugh and release more fumes she wished she hadn't said it. Then, without warning, Mr Orton flung himself to the ground and began to crawl around the alley in the lamplight. Phoebe stood transfixed, unable to believe what she was seeing. He tried to rise, then collapsed back on to the cobbles and lay there in a heaving, sorry heap.

She peered up and down the passageway and could see

no one. Swiftly she knelt down and felt for the buttons on his jacket . . .

'Dear me. Has our poor friend hurt himself?' She looked up to see the auctioneer, Arnold, looming over them. 'He's on the stout side to take a fall.'

'I was just checking his heart. I was afraid he'd had a seizure.'

'He'd most certainly have one if he found you searching for his wallet.'

'I never was!' She scrambled to her feet.

'This was your chance – if you weren't trying to rob him you'd be stupid. And I don't think you are.' He chucked her under the chin, and she turned her head abruptly, not wanting him to touch her. 'It's a good thing I decided to follow you in case Orton went a purler. I think I'd better escort you now. It will be safer, and we don't want you getting lost, do we, Phoebe?' The man was smooth and smiling, charming and gracious. He spoke in such a measured, pleasant manner and he didn't look in the least evil, she thought. But he had to be bad to do what he had done, she reasoned. It wasn't just the auction: she'd seen him watch Rosie being abused and he had laughed, not trying to help her.

'And our friend is too large for you to haul him up on your own, a slim little thing like you.' He put his hands under Orton's shoulders and, with one heave, had him on his feet. 'Hold on to me, Orton, old chap. I'll see you safely to the hotel.'

She walked on, looking steadfastly ahead. She could easily have outrun the old man but it would be impossible to escape Arnold. She was close to tears now.

'And if you'd thought you might take a little walk on your own, I'm here to suggest it wouldn't be a good idea.'

'I wasn't.' She hadn't meant to say anything.

'I think you might be lying, Phoebe.'

'I don't care what you think.'

'Spirited little creature, aren't you? Perhaps I should

have outbid Orton.' She felt his hand in the small of her back, and arched it to prevent the contact. 'You know, Phoebe, I like girls like you. Not afraid of anything or anyone. Full of pluck. I like nothing better than to train them, bend them to my will. A joyous pastime.'

'Like Rosie?'

'She talked, did she?'

'Said anyone would be better than you.'

With a slow deliberation, Arnold Randolph-Smythe propped Orton against a shop doorway, swung round and rammed Phoebe to the wall. With one hand he held her in a vice-like grip from which there was no escape. With the other he flipped up her skirt and his hand was on her. He bent back her head and his mouth was on hers, his tongue prising it open and exploring within.

'That was nice, wasn't it?' he said, as he let her go. She stood shocked, disbelieving. It had all happened so quickly.

She wiped her mouth feverishly on the back of his hand. She looked at him with loathing – but, to her horror, she knew she had enjoyed the experience.

'I'll have you eventually, you know,' he said, as they reached the hotel steps and, as if to emphasise the statement, he patted her behind.

'No, you bloody well won't.' She spat at him and had the satisfaction of seeing the gob of phlegm land on his immaculate black coat with its astrakhan collar.

He removed it fastidiously with a pristine handker-chief. 'You will pay for that. You see, Phoebe, I always get what I want.' He opened the door, helped Orton through with one hand and dragged Phoebe in with the other.

It was not a grand hotel but a shabby inn. There was the stench of stale food, beer and tobacco, and the carpets were dirty and worn. 'Here we are, Hodges, Mr Orton safely returned with a little friend to keep him warm.'

'Right you are, Mr Randolph-Smythe.'

'He will need some assistance, and this young woman will need an eye keeping on her.'

'I understand.' The man winked and touched the side of his nose with a key. From the corner of her eye Phoebe saw a young man sniggering at her. It was the most humiliating experience of her life.

'I will escort you as far as your room.'

'That won't be necessary,' she said, wanting to get away from him, fearful of him, remembering the pleasant feeling she had enjoyed a few minutes ago, and not wanting to feel it again.

'But I think it is.' They were led up the narrow stairs. She was conscious all the time of him behind her, Orton and the owner bringing up the rear.

'To the right, Miss. Third door along,' the owner called, as they reached the top of the staircase.

'A deplorable establishment, Miss Phoebe, isn't it? But it's the best that Barlton has to offer at the moment. Soon, this town will be having a fine hotel, thanks to me. I shall call it Bartholomew's.' Phoebe stumbled at the mention of that name. 'But then, of course, you know them, don't you? Charming people. Especially the nephew.'

'I haven't had that pleasure,' she lied, not wanting to acknowledge that Edward must know what went on in this town.

'You've another key to this lock?' he asked the innkeeper. 'We shall place this one under the mountainous flesh of my friend Mr Orton here.'

The man did as instructed.

'Good night, sweet maid.' He bowed to her. The door closed and she heard the key grate in the lock. A prisoner again. Was this her future? 'To hell with that!'

Phoebe did not sleep. Orton lay on the bed snoring – not like a pig, more like a whole sty of them. She looked down at him with disgust. He was old, fat, and smelt of unwashed flesh. And he wanted to steal her virginity – even impregnate her. What right had he? What right had anyone to buy her and do with her whatever they wanted? Did they think she had no feelings, no dreams? All those silly dreams she'd set out with. To make her fortune, send for Jim, find love. To be loved. They had all been such harmless fantasies.

'So, what are you going to do?'

Phoebe looked at Orton, afraid that in speaking her thoughts she had woken him. 'He's sleeping like the dead. The whole place could fall down and he won't hear me.'

'You could smother him. He's too drunk to struggle.'

'And be hanged? For him? No thank you.'

'Steal his money.'

'There's no way out with the door locked.'

'The window?'

Gingerly she opened it and leaned out. There were cobbles, head-cracking cobbles, too far below for her to risk jumping. She hung further out: the only drainpipe was too far away for her to reach it. There was no creeper, no ledge. And it was raining. Ice-cold rain that threatened to become snow. She began to pull back into the room. And then she saw it, stretching out into the night, oily black, making a comforting lapping noise like a giant cat. It explained the smell she had noticed earlier. It was water, more water than she had ever seen in her life. This must be the sea. She'd never seen it, but she'd looked at pictures and Dick had told her about it. She sat on the window-seat, lulled by the water slapping gently against the harbour wall. She was alone in the world. There was no one to whom she could turn, no one to help her. Finally she allowed herself to cry.

'There's no point in that.'

'Why not? There's no one to hear or to care.'

Phoebe sat all night at the window determined she was not going to share a bed with Orton until he forced her. Despite the position she was in, the stiffness that encroached, and the fears she felt, she was entranced as, slowly, the dark of night peeled away. The sea, its enormity, emerged to her astonished eyes. Never could she have imagined anything so large, so restless. It was going to be a dull day, and it seemed to her that the water, grey as an old man's beard and joining an equally grey sky, went on for ever. She fantasised about taking a boat and sailing away on it, never to return. And if she couldn't find a boat she would wade in and swim to the other side of the world.

'You can't swim.'

'I've never tried.'

Mr Orton turned over in bed. His breathing was loud and laboured and the blankets slipped this way and that.

Phoebe was holding her breath, dreading his wakening, wondering what mood he would be in, fearing he might take her there and then. She couldn't let him – she would rather die than be his. 'Kill him,' she told herself. She looked about her for a suitable weapon. There was a bottle of whisky on the dressing-table. Swiftly she crossed the room and grabbed it, hiding it behind her as she stood, a frightened animal at bay.

Then the mountain that was Mr Orton moved again making the bed springs shriek. A pillow was tossed one way, a bolster the other. The sheet rose in the air and a puffy red face appeared over the top.

'Who in God's name are you? What you doing here?' he demanded, then twisted and turned until he had located his wallet. He delved into it, withdrew the notes and counted them, his blubbery lips mouthing the amount. Then he did the same with the sovereigns in his purse. With a sigh of evident relief he fell back on the pillows but he had dislodged them and there was nothing there, so he landed flat on his back, reminding Phoebe of a stag beetle the wrong way up. Now he did not seem nearly as frightening.

She opened her mouth and was about to point out to him that he had bought her, but stopped herself in time. Maybe he had forgotten, maybe she would be able to talk her way out of here. 'Nothing,' she said. 'Just making sure you came to no harm.' She attempted a bright smile. Perhaps if she could ingratiate herself with him he might think she was a hotel employee.

Finally he achieved a sitting-up position, and yawned, an alarming sight – like the picture of the whale's open mouth with Jonah inside that she had once seen.

'Bejabers! I must have had a skinful last night.' He put his podgy hands to his head and held it almost tenderly. He peered across at Phoebe, frowning deeply. At least he no longer appeared to be mad. Perhaps the drink had made him so strange. He pointed at her. 'I remember, I bought you!' He began to laugh. 'It's all coming back to me. God in heaven, what got into me?'

'I don't know.' This sounded more hopeful, as if, perhaps, he was regretting it.

'What did I pay for you?'

'I can't remember.' Better he didn't know. If he did he might insist on getting something for his money. She eased the bottle back on to the dresser. If he registered her intentions he might get angry and, as it was, he seemed to be in reasonable spirits.

'Blowed if I can remember. Blowed if I can think why. But there was a reason, yes, there was . . .' He ruminated. 'I'm drawing a blank.' He frowned ferociously. 'Don't you know?'

'How could I? We've hardly met.'

This made him guffaw, but in mid-laugh he stopped. 'I

remember!' he said triumphantly. 'I gave that arse-crawling Arnold an IOU. For how much? That's what I can't remember.' He banged his forehead with the back of his hand, then fished about in the bed and retrieved the key. 'What fool . . . ?' She didn't explain. He stood up in his far-from-clean combinations. 'Don't watch. It's not proper, a young woman like you.'

'I'm sorry.' She turned and looked out of the window. She could see a harbour to her right, with fishing-boats lined up, and much activity on the quay. On the other side there was a sandy beach. She'd love to walk on it, feel sand between her toes. That would be a new experience. 'And cold too.'

'Pardon? What did you say?'

She turned to see him fully dressed. Relief swept over her. If he'd been going to do anything to her he'd hardly have got dressed first. 'I'm sorry, I talk to myself a lot.'

'Then don't. My wife did that, got my dander up and no mistake. I'll have you carted off to the asylum if you do. Lace my boots, there's a good maid.'

Phoebe helped him put on his boots, averting her nose from the smell of his feet. 'Right you are. Breakfast, my beauty.'

She wished she had the courage to tell him she wasn't *his* beauty and never would be, but sense prevailed and she stayed silent as she followed him down the narrow stairs they had climbed, he with much difficulty, last night. 'Service!' he bellowed, in the small hallway. A half-witted-looking maid appeared, bobbed a curtsy and showed them into the dining room, which was empty.

Phoebe realised how hungry she was. While Mr Orton ordered everything on offer, plus a pint of stout, she asked for two poached eggs and tea.

'You won't get far on a piddling breakfast like that,' he remarked.

'Won't I?' What did he mean by that? That she was going somewhere? On her own? With him? What if she just stood up, thanked him for a pleasant evening and left? Would he let her? Would there be a scene? Should she try and find someone to save her? Who was in league with whom?

'What do you think of the Randolph-Smythe fellow?'

'I don't know him.'

'Just as well, if you ask me. Randolph-Slimy would suit him better. Don't like the fellow.'

'Then why were you there?'

'Where?'

'Last night, at the dinner.'

'I went for the boxing. I didn't mean to end up with a little harpy.'

This, she thought, was her opportunity. She stood up. 'Then I'll say goodbye.'

'Did I offend you?'

'Calling me a harpy, well, it wasn't very nice. But I'm not offended. I don't know you, I shall probably never see you again. So . . .'

As she turned to leave he grabbed her arm. 'Hold on. I paid good money for you and you're not going anywhere. Sit,' he ordered, as if she was a dog. Phoebe complied, and watched him eat with mounting horror: he was shovelling the food in as if it was likely to be stolen from him. How offensive her own eating habits must have been to someone like Mr Bartholomew when she had first arrived with him. But if Mr Orton carried on eating in such a manner he'd kill himself. This thought cheered her.

The journey to Mr Orton's was silent in the main. They were in a trap pulled by a horse more dead than alive. As they laboured up a steep hill, Mr Orton lashed the beast with his whip. 'Get on, you lazy old blackguard.'

'Stop that!' Phoebe shouted.

Mr Orton looked about him in a parody of surprise. 'Is there someone else here? Is that who you're speaking to?'

'The animal can't go any faster. Whipping it will make it slower.'

'And you're the expert, are you?'

'No, but even an idiot can see you weigh too much for the poor creature. An elephant might suit you better.'

'Less of your lip, hussy.' And he hit her fair and square, knocking her sideways. 'It's my horse and I'll beat it to death if I feel like it.'

She sat huddled on the seat of the trap. She should have kept quiet. She was making it worse for the poor animal, not better. Why was it that when an opportunity arrived to say something sharp and smart she took it, as if her brain had no control over her mouth? Gingerly she put her hand to her face, and touched where his fist had landed. Just as she'd been thinking he was quite nice, if uncouth, he had turned into a bullying monster. And there was worse: with a sinking heart she had realised they were heading for the moor. She was returning to the very place from which she had first run. What if he knew her father? What if he told him he had purchased her? She knew her dad: he would take it out on *her*, not him. No doubt he would beat her to death. She pulled the shawl closer to her. She was freezing, she was frightened, she wished she was dead.

To make matters worse, and evidently to punish her for her previous rudeness, at every hill they came to she was made to get down and walk behind the trap – as if her light weight made a pennyworth of difference to the horse.

An hour later, though it seemed longer to Phoebe with her chattering teeth, they turned off the road to Barlton, and headed east. At least they weren't going closer to her father. She made herself think logically: they lived on the other side, so it wasn't likely that her father ever came this far east.

They were now passing through well-tended farmland, with large meadows and big fields. She admired the good red Devon soil. This acreage would produce abundant crops, she thought. At a gate he slowed the trap and ordered her to get down and open it. Point East Farm, a sign said. 'Shut it!'

'I know what to do. I'm not stupid!' She felt so much better when she stood up for herself.

They passed fields full of fat, contented-looking cattle. There was a large flock of sheep, the ewes already heavy with lambs. A shepherd waved his crook at them.

'Surly old fellow,' said Mr Orton, as he waved back.

It was evidently a large farm and a mixed one and, as Arnold Randolph-Smythe had said last night, Mr Orton was obviously wealthy. Which, she supposed, was something. If she was to be used and abused by anyone, a rich man was preferable.

'You've good stock,' she said, hoping to curry favour.

'So, you recognise it when you see it?'

'You don't have to be an expert to see what they are.'

He grinned. 'I like your spirit, girl. You're just what I need. I couldn't have chosen better if I'd been sober.'

They finally halted in front of a Devon long-house. Lights shone from the windows at one end, and she could hear the rustling of beasts on the straw at the other. A man rushed out of a barn to take charge of the horse and trap. Phoebe jumped down, not wanting either of them to touch her.

Mr Orton pushed open the door and ushered her into a screened cross passage.

'Lester!' he roared. 'Lester, get your arse down here.'

A tall, thin blond man scurried down the stairs, which were at the end. He looked wild-eyed, his hair in disarray as if he had just got out of bed.

'There you are. You took your time. What were you doing? Sleeping?'

'No, Father, I was reading.'

Phoebe grinned. He was lying.

'Reading! Bah, what good will that do us? Why can't

you get your arse out in them fields, do some work for a change? Still,' he divested himself of his coat, 'perhaps I should forgive you today. Happy birthday, son. I've brought you a present.'

'That's very kind of you, Father.' He looked shyly at Phoebe as he stepped past her and peered into the trap, looking, she presumed, for a parcel.

'I didn't have time to wrap her, but here she is. This is your present. This is Phoebe.'

5

Lester Orton and Phoebe stood in the narrow passage-way and looked at each other. It would have been impossible to say who was the most astonished.

'You can't give ... give ... a p-p-p-person as a present, Father.'

'Who says?'

'Those days are long g-g-gone.'

'Who says?'

'It's against the law.'

'Bugger the law. Do you want her or not? If you don't I'll take her meself.'

Phoebe semaphored her alarm to the young man with raised eyebrows.

'Well, um, she's here now ... Thank you, F-F-Father.'

'And you, don't stand gawking. Now that's settled go and make yourself useful. I need feeding.'

'You've only just had breakfast.'

'And you don't speak to me like that!' He raised his hand.

'No, Father,' said Lester, stepping forward but looking terrified. 'If she's mine, you don't h-harm her.'

'Well, blow me down with a feather, you'm changing already, my son.' With that he bellowed with laughter and ambled down the corridor out into the yard.

'It's this way.' Lester led her to the back of the house and into a cavernous kitchen. The ceiling was the colour of a meerschaum pipe her father had owned when he smoked – before he had decided it was a pastime of the devil. The range was enormous, large enough to roast an ox.

'This is the kitchen,' Lester said unnecessarily. Phoebe was feeling a little more at ease. He was frightened of his father, and she sensed that he was likely to be frightened of her too. She could use that to her advantage.

The floor was filthy. A poodle, with a litter of suckling puppies hungrily attached to her nipples, was in a basket in the corner. The evidence of their existence was scattered all over the floor.

'Oh, what dear little creatures.' She swooped on them, picked one up and cradled it.

'Father was going to drown them and I stopped him.' She heard a note of pride in his voice.

'I'm glad you did. Who could harm them? How many are there?'

'Just the three, thankfully. I've found a home for one in the village. That's Mimi, she was my mother's dog.' Tears stood in his eyes. 'She loved her so much.'

'And you loved your mother?'

'Of course.'

'Then why have you let her dog get into such a state? Just look at her.' She spoke sharply, and he looked ashamed. 'She needs a bath, a good brushing, her blanket changed. Did she look in such a mess when your mother was alive?'

'Well, no.'

'Then do something about it.'

'What?'

'I've just told you.' She was expressing irritation now, and it seemed to be working. 'Still, if your father wants something to eat . . . I can't stand gossiping.' She gave the black and white puppy back to its mother who had been watching her with beady, intelligent eyes. 'There you are, Mimi, no need to fret.'

'You like dogs?'

'Love 'em, not that ours were ever allowed in the house. There were times I smuggled one into my bed, you know, when it was cold or pouring with rain.'

'That's how I feel. She's such a gentle creature. But when Mother died, he put her out in the yard.'

'It's fine to have them in the house, but we can't be doing with all this mess, can we? Is there a bucket and mop?'

'Over here.' He showed her to the adjoining scullery, where there were more saucepans, more cupboards and, best of all, a pump over the stone sink. Phoebe filled a kettle and put into a bucket some soap shavings from a jar on the side. 'You carry that kettle – it's heavy. I'll bring the mop and bucket,' she said bossily. She was quite enjoying herself.

In the kitchen he wavered, as if unsure what to do. 'Put the kettle on the range. It won't heat itself, will it?' she said, with exaggerated patience. 'This place looks as if it hasn't been cleaned since your poor mother passed on.' Once he'd put down the kettle he made to leave the room. 'Here,' she called out, 'where do you think you're going? They're your dogs, you clean up after them.'

'But—'

'No buts. If I'm to cook for your father you can't expect me to clean up first.' Seeing his alarmed expression she stopped frowning and smiled at him instead. She mustn't get carried away and antagonise him.

'I doubt I'll make a good job of it,' Lester said.

'You can try.' She went in search of food in the large larder. There were stores in there enough for an army, she thought. What it was to be rich! She found a basket and sorted through the vegetables, rejecting any damaged potatoes and onions.

'You haven't got very far, have you? You might just as well be back at Cowman's Combe,' she said to herself.

'It's a bigger kitchen, and pumped water. It could be worse.'

'You've got to run.'

'Where to?' She selected some meat from the mesh-covered cupboard. 'Anyway, it could be worse.'

'You keep saying that.'

'At least he's young.'

'You can't let him *do* it. He looks as if he's been sieved through muslin.'

'I'd rather him than that smelly old man.'

She moved back into the kitchen.

'Who were you talking to?' Lester asked. 'I heard voices.'

'Myself. And you needn't think of carting me off to the asylum.' The water was boiling, so she poured it on to the soap and swirled it around to make a froth.

'I wouldn't have you taken away.' He looked at her shyly. 'I talk to myself all the time. It annoys my father no end. He says if I have anything to say I should be saying it to him. Have a care when he's around.'

'And he's the last person you'd want to talk to.'

'Exactly.'

'And it stops you being lonely when no one else sees how you're feeling.'

'Yes!' He looked at her with what amounted to wonderment. She handed him the mop.

'And don't you think there would be more sense if you picked the mess up first, then washed the floor? . . . Why are you looking at me like that?' she asked.

'Because you understand. I didn't think anyone else did.'

'Get on with you! The world is full of people as soft as us.' She began to peel the potatoes. 'Well, get on with it,' she ordered, since he was still standing looking unsure what to do. What a ninny. She must watch herself or she would bully him unmercifully. Still, he seemed to expect it – perhaps his mother had hectored him too. The potatoes finished, she stoked the fire in the range then turned to the meat. 'You've cleared up nicely. Thank you very much.' He looked grateful for her smile. 'When I've done this I'll bath the dog.'

The meal was a success. Phoebe was glad to see that Lester ate neatly and noiselessly. She minded about such things now – manners, prettiness, clothes, books. She had changed so much – yet in other ways she hadn't: she was washing up the debris of the meal, just like in the past; she was afraid of Mr Orton, just as she had been afraid of her father; and she had nothing and she still wanted to run away.

Now she could hear Mr Orton snoring in the next room. She looked at her hands ruefully: those nails were not going to remain pretty for much longer, not the way the old man had been talking over supper. He'd plans for her to take over the dairy, just like her own mother, and the kitchen garden. Then there would be washing, ironing, preserving and the dogs. The house was bigger, the food more plentiful, but was this the fulfilment of her dreams? 'No,' she said, with emphasis.

She stacked the last of the dishes on the wooden rack over the sink in the scullery. Lester didn't seem that bad, if a bit on the wishy-washy side. But to lose her virginity to him and spend the rest of her days with him? She felt immeasurably sad and thought of Edward. The contrast couldn't have been greater. Edward was a man, Lester was a boy. Edward had courage, Lester was frightened of her. Edward was—

'A traitor! He never helped you.'

'True.' Just acknowledging it made her want to weep. 'Which wouldn't do much good.' To delay joining Lester in bed and the inevitable she began to clear out the kitchen cupboards. Busyness, in her experience, kept too much thinking at bay. But first she laid newspaper on the newly washed floor, a trail that led to the back door. 'See, puppies? This is where you go, until you learn it's done out there.' The three puppies wagged their tails, but she resisted the temptation to cuddle them. She had to get on with the cupboards.

Some time later she heard a voice behind her. 'What are you doing, still here? It's midnight.'

'Mr Orton, you made me jump.' She looked up from the floor where she was surrounded by jars of marmalade and jam, some more than ten years old.

'My wife made all of them.'

'Should I keep them?'

'No point, I suppose, if they've gone off.' He sat down abruptly, as if he was too tired to continue standing. Maybe he was ill – perhaps he would soon be counting worms. She shuddered at how unkind she'd become. Still, he hadn't been kind to her, so why shouldn't she wish him dead? 'No!'

'What?' He looked at her with rheumy eyes.

'Nothing,' she said hurriedly, and concentrated on the jars. 'I can wash these out and use them again.' She looked up to see Mr Orton wiping what looked suspiciously like a tear from his eye. 'Are you all right, Mr Orton?'

'She was a good woman.' Now they were running down his cheeks and, unheeded, plopping on to his lap.

'You miss her?'

'Every day, and it gets worse.' He blew noisily into the most disgusting handkerchief she had ever seen.

'Has it been long?' Her voice brimmed with a sympathy she wished she did not feel.

'Five years.' He allowed himself a good bellow.

'Early days,' she said, although she had expected him to say five months, the way he was carrying on.

He stood up abruptly. 'So, what are you waiting for? Go and make a man of my son.'

Phoebe blushed to the roots of her hair, got to her feet and scurried from the room. She climbed the stairs, her mind in turmoil. She had left the old man blubbing and this was her opportunity to run. She turned on the stairs and looked out of the window on a half-landing. It was teeming with rain and a bitter wind straight off the moor was howling around the house seeking chinks to invade it. 'Go on, make a bolt for it.'

'I can't.'

'What's stopping you?'

'Look at the weather.'

'There's always some excuse. Run – this is your chance.'

'How long would I last in these clothes? How long before I collapsed, fell asleep and died?'

'Rubbish? You're young and fit. You're afraid, that's nearer the truth.'

'Yes, I am. I think I'd be safer here.'

'With that feeble creature?'

'At least he wouldn't hurt me.'

'Do you want to go to bed with a man you don't know and you'll never respect?'

'What choice have I got?'

She heard a door open above her. 'Phoebe?' She looked up the stairs. Lester was at the top, in a nightshirt, holding a candle. 'Phoebe, my father thinks you should join me. If you don't mind, that is.'

'Yes, Lester.' She felt weary as she climbed the stairs towards him. *'Run! Escape!'* Phyllis was shrieking at her, but Phoebe chose to ignore her.

6

Phoebe was sweating as she followed Lester back into his room. She had seen animals mate, had heard the females, fighting, squalling, crying, screaming. It might be natural but it was not something that appeared to be all that pleasant, and she didn't want to be hurt. She didn't want to have him in her either, and she didn't want his babies. She wanted to be anywhere but here.

Since the rest of the house was plainly furnished and lacked anything of beauty or interest, this room was a surprise and, for a minute or two, distracted her from her fears. The walls were covered with what looked like rich red silk. There were large embroidered cushions on the floor, which sparkled with sequins, and gold and silver embroidery. A fine mahogany bookcase and desk were overflowing with books and papers. The bed was large, she noted, out of the corner of her eye, covered with a luxuriant fur. There was a pleasant smell as if the room was filled with lilies, although Phoebe could see none. The walls were dotted with lovely watercolour paintings, which, from her time with Mr Bartholomew, she recognised as skilfully executed if a shade amateurish.

'Everything was my mother's,' he said, as if reading her thoughts.

'She liked nice things?'

'When she was allowed them. Most of these she brought with her when she married. He would never allow her to spend money on fripperies – that's what he called them, to hurt her.'

'But he misses her. He just told me so.'

'Like a bull misses a cow,' he said bitterly.

'Did he not love her, then?'

'Love! He doesn't understand the word. He brutalised her. And she was the gentlest of creatures.' He held out a finely engraved silver frame, inside which, in sepia tints, was the likeness of a pretty young girl, fair-haired and with a sweet expression.

'She's lovely. You take after her, not him,' she said. He was not as good-looking as his mother had been but there was the same gentleness and blondness. 'It's the eyes, I think.'

'I'm glad I don't look like him.'

'You don't like him?' She smiled at the absurdity of her question.

'I hate him. For what he is. For what he did to her.'

'Why didn't she run away?'

'Where to?' he said, with a defeated air.

'I wouldn't stay.'

'Then why didn't you run away just now?'

'You were listening?'

'Yes.'

'Then you know why.' She coloured: he would have heard her refer to him as 'feeble' and he would know she did not respect him. 'I'm sorry for what I said.'

'It doesn't matter. I know I am not a young girl's dream.' He smiled, which transformed his face so that he looked almost handsome. 'I understand your reluctance. Fear is debilitating.'

'Are you afraid of him? You don't stammer when he's not there.'

'I know. He has succeeded in destroying much of me, or what, perhaps, I might have been.'

'Then why do you stay? You're a man – it would be easier for you to run than for me.'

'Where else can I go? I have no money, no skills.'

'There must be something you can do. My brother ran away – he joined the army. He wouldn't stay to be bullied by our father.'

'He bullies me less now since I hit him.'

'You hit him!' Before she could stop herself, she laughed at the idea. 'Now, that was brave. After all, he's twice your size.'

'It wasn't courage. I lost my temper and hit him with the poker. He's been a little better since then.' He allowed himself a small smile. 'I only wish I'd done it when Mother was alive.'

'You'd have been too young.'

'But I should have done something.'

'I still don't understand why you stay.'

'The dog.'

'Mimi?'

'Yes. I vowed to my mother, you see, that I would never leave the dog alone with him. He'd kill her, split her head open with the axe like he did his own sheep-dog.'

'I've seen that done. Horrible cruel, with its poor brains everywhere.' She shuddered. 'Take her with you.' She saw defeat in his face again. 'I know, I know, you've nowhere to go.' But she grinned at him.

'It's not just that. My mother's money bought this farm. Why should I go and let him leave it to someone else when it's rightfully mine?'

'I can't help you there. I'd put my happiness before thinking about who owned what. But, then, you see, it's different for me. I wouldn't be left anything by my father anyway – even if he had something to leave, which he hasn't.'

'You don't like him?'

'He's come straight from hell . . .' She began to tell him of her life, of her pain and misery, of Dick and Jim. She wasn't even aware that she was sitting on the bed and feeling quite at home. The fear had gone. He was so understanding, so sympathetic. And then she told him of Mr Bartholomew and the auction.

'That's appalling – feudal! And with a new century dawning. The authorities should be informed. And my own father was involved!' He shook his head in disbelief. 'But, then, I shouldn't be surprised, he's capable of anything. I'd heard of Bartholomew – people say he's mad. They say he kidnaps young girls, has his way with them, then throws them out. Evil.'

'He didn't touch me. He made me dance for him, that's all.' She felt too embarrassed to tell him about the dirty pictures. 'In a way he was kind to me until I made him angry by writing to my brother. He wanted me to be his companion.' She felt proud, then shocked with herself. 'Not that I wanted to be, you understand.'

'You must have been frightened when my father bought you.'

'I nearly died. I've been planning how to run away, how to kill him if need be.' She laughed.

'It would be most kind of you to oblige me like that.' And he was laughing too.

How strange this was, she thought. She must have been sitting here talking for over an hour and nothing had happened: he had made no advance on her. What was more, she was enjoying herself, talking to someone who had suffered too, and who evidently understood her and wanted to know about her. It was a heady experience. She liked him, and she'd been wrong: she knew about fear, and would never hold that against him; she respected him, and felt that liking and esteem would grow as she came to know him.

Maybe, in the flickering light of the candle, he wasn't bad-looking, and he looked so weak he was unlikely to hurt her . . . Then she remembered his tale of attacking his father with the poker and decided that she might as well mind her manners with him too, just in case.

She jumped when his arm slid round her waist and he pulled her towards him tenderly. He smelt reasonably clean, she thought. He touched her neck with his lips and nuzzled her – she could feel the feather-like touch of his breath. She leaned towards him, but there was no strength in him, no solid body to lean against, not like . . . Perhaps this would not be so dreadful.

He took hold of her chin and turned her face to him. She felt his lips on hers, not rough, not prising. It felt as if a butterfly were kissing her. She felt nothing. Perhaps if she allowed herself to think of Edward . . . but nothing happened. There was no lovely feeling, no excitement as there had been when Edward had held her arm, and nothing like she had felt when that pervert Arnold had kissed her.

'I'm sorry.' Lester pulled away from her. 'Forgive me. I can't . . .' He put his head in his hands as if in despair.

'Lester, what is it? What's the matter?'

'I don't want to kiss you.'

'Don't you like me?'

'Very much.'

'Don't you find me pretty?'

'You're not pretty, you're beautiful.'

'Is it something I've done? Do I smell?'

'No, nothing like that.'

'Then what?'

'You're lovely and I wish I could enjoy kissing you, but I don't. I don't wish to insult you. Can you forgive me?'

'I'm not insulted,' she said, but of course she was. 'I don't mind if you don't kiss me.' Which was true.

'Really? But my father will be furious.'

'What business is it of his?'

'He wants me to make love to you to prove I'm a man.'

'I can see that you are.'

'No, you don't understand. I can see you're attractive and pretty. I can appreciate that, but it . . . Well, it doesn't excite me. *You* don't excite me.'

'I see.' She felt ridiculously affronted and began to slip off the bed, folding her diaphanous dress close to her.

'No, you don't. You're offended.'

'Not at all. I'm being stupid. It's my vanity that's hurt. If you must know I don't find you attractive either. See, now I've offended *you*.' This made her feel marginally better.

'No. That's what I wanted you to say. I want us to be friends. Not enemies, not lovers. You see, Phoebe, it's not you, it's me. I don't find any women attractive.'

'Really? No one?'

'Never.'

'Ha, I see. Well, I don't, really.' She'd heard the way

Dick and his friends talked about the girls in the village. Why, even young Jim said things he shouldn't.

'I only like looking at men.'

Phoebe had to sit down again. 'Men?' She knew her eyes were wide with astonishment.

'And it's men I dream about.'

'Well I never! I've not heard of such a thing in my whole life. I mean, I've seen cows but, well, men . . .' She was lost for words.

'I know it's wrong and I shouldn't, but that's how I've always been. Even as a schoolboy. It's wicked, I know. Please don't lecture me.'

'Why should I, if it makes you happy and no one else's feelings are hurt?' She meant it, but she was still trying to absorb the knowledge that anything like this existed. 'But, I mean, what do you do with a man? In bed, I mean?'

'I don't know. I've never been with a man either.' At this he managed a wan smile. 'My father has his suspicions of what I'm like. He's accused me, but I've always denied it. You're the first person I've told.'

'Then I'm honoured.'

'But it's why he brought you here – so that I would bed you and it would make a man of me. A proper man.'

'Don't upset yourself. You can't help how you are.' She put her arms round him and comforted him. 'Look, don't worry.' She pushed him a little away so that she could see his face. 'We can cheat him. We can pretend.'

'What do you mean?'

'I can sleep with you and we'll act what he thinks we should be doing. He's not going to come in and watch, is he?'

'No, I wouldn't let him.'

'It would suit me. I can stay here for a little while until I can plan what next to do. Maybe find my brother when he returns.'

'So what do we do?'

Phoebe lay back on the cover. 'Oh, Lester, yes . . .' She sighed. 'Kiss me again. Please!' And she repeated it, louder. Then she began to roll on the bed from one side to the other, and bounced, making the springs creak. At first he watched her in astonishment, then, with a grin, he joined in. 'Groan,' she whispered to him. And they sighed, moaned and groaned together.

Outside in the corridor Mr Orton pressed an ear to the door and listened. With a satisfied smile he made his way to his own bed.

Chapter Four
December 1899–January 1900

I

Dulcie's hands shook when she saw, on the envelope she held, the crest of the Devonshire and Dorset Regiment Chauncey had so foolishly joined. At the opposite end of the breakfast table, her husband was reading the newspaper. She was in a quandary: she didn't want him to know she had this letter because she didn't want to share the contents with him. So far she had not divulged what Chauncey had done or where he was because when he had left Arnold had not asked. And if Chauncey had wanted his father to know he would have written and told him so. But now? She stared at the envelope intently as if trying to read its contents. She needed to be alone to read this but if she left the table now he would know there was something afoot. And if it was the worst news, if the letter said that Chauncey was dead, she didn't want to share her grief with him. He would not grieve, he would not care. She didn't want him of all people to watch her heart break. She slipped the letter into a pocket and helped herself to a slice of toast.

It was as if it was burning a hole in her skirt. She placed her hand over it as if that would help, but it didn't. She was so foolish! If he were dead she would have received a telegram. She knew three women who had and one of them, poor soul, on learning that her twin sons had been killed by the same bullet, which had passed through one and into the other, had expired on the spot. So he was not dead! She took out the letter and ripped it open.

Chauncey was on his way home! The most beautiful

sentence in the world. Then her heart almost stopped, He was wounded! She had to steel herself to reread that sentence. His condition was not serious, but what did that mean? A wound could be anywhere and what soldiers thought was not serious she might think of quite differently. Her mind raced – arrangements for nurses, Bath-chairs, companions!

'I see you had a letter?' Her husband was looking at her. 'Was it bad news? You look faint.'

'No, it is nothing. One of the women in the sewing bee for our soldiers in the Cape cannot come this week. It's a nuisance, that's all.' She put the letter back into her pocket. At least Arnold was not like some husbands who insisted on reading their wife's post. She would hurry her breakfast: she needed to think.

'This evening should be interesting. I'm sure I'll be invited to become deputy mayor now that Smart has gone to meet his Maker.'

'Really?' she said, uninterestedly.

'You'll enjoy being mayoress when, in due course, I am mayor.'

'No, I won't.'

'Of course you will.'

'No. You had better ask Agnes – she would enjoy the role.' She stood up and prepared to leave the room.

'You are strange, these days, Dulcie, not yourself at all. You've changed.'

'I'm not aware that I have.' She picked up her papers from the table. 'This evening, you said? Had you forgotten that Lord Prestwick and his son are dining with us?'

'No! You didn't tell me.'

'But, Arnold, I did.' Once she had begun to lie she had been surprised to find how easy it was. And, in the circumstances, she found she was free from guilt for doing so.

'Dulcie! How stupid you are.'

'Thank you, Arnold.' She inclined her head. 'You say the most gracious things.' But she was wasting her breath; irony was lost on him.

'You knew I wouldn't be here.'

'I didn't,' she lied.

'The second Wednesday in December is always an important council night. You are fully aware of that.'

'I forgot.' Yet another lie!

'You have no right to forget. This is very vexing. Can you not rearrange the dinner?'

'Hardly, at such short notice, Arnold. It would be most impolite.'

'Say you are indisposed.'

'I can't lie.' Yes, you can, she thought, with concealed glee. 'As it is, it will be most impolite if you're not here. I might just as well ask *you* to rearrange your plans.'

'I can't. It's but three weeks to the Mayor's Assembly, and I am hosting it, as you know. There is much to finalise at the meeting tonight. It is imperative I attend.'

'I meant to tell you that I shall not be at the Assembly this year.'

'Of course you will, you always are.'

'I'm not even sure I shall be here.'

Arnold had risen from the table in agitation. Now he sat down again. 'And were will you be?'

'It is not decided yet.'

'And leave me in the lurch like this?'

'I suggest you invite Sophie Franks to be your hostess. I'm sure she will do it charmingly – and you get on so well. Now, if you will excuse me, I have letters to write.'

She could hear him calling her name as she crossed the hall. She had so enjoyed the look of astonishment on his face. Serves him right, she thought, as she entered the morning room and locked the door. He banged once or twice, demanding entry, but she ignored him. Eventually he left, not on the dot this morning but five minutes late because of her. So sweet, these little triumphs.

Was she wicked to lie to him? To make plans that did not include him? Yes, of course she was. But didn't his untrustworthiness justify her actions? Or was that wishful thinking? She would have liked to discuss this particular dilemma with Lord Prestwick – such an interesting man. In any case, Arnold would have had nothing much in common with him. And she so wanted to keep her new friend to herself. What a way for a respectable matron to think!

Once she had made her plans for dinner with Mrs Bramble, Dulcie put on her coat and hat and ordered the carriage.

'Where are you going, Mother?' Agnes met her in the hall.

'Out.'

'I am aware of that.' Agnes laughed. 'Perhaps I would like to come with you, if you are going shopping – I am in need of new gloves.'

'I'm not.' Dulcie was almost at the door.

'Then where?'

'Nowhere interesting.' She had opened it.

'You are so mysterious. Where?'

She was almost through the door. 'Oh, Agnes, I almost forgot. The Prestwicks are dining with us this evening.'

'Mother!' Agnes's wail must have been heard in the centre of town. 'Why didn't you tell me?'

'I'm sure I did.'

'Well, you didn't and I'm dining at the Markhams'. You knew I had arranged it.'

'I must have forgotten. It's difficult to know what you want, Agnes. One week it's Robert and the next another young man.' Dulcie was about to climb into the carriage. 'You're too flighty for your own good.'

'Mother.' Agnes appeared on the steps. 'Mother, please stop at the Markhams' on the way and say I am indisposed.'

'Agnes! Whatever next? You expect me to lie for you?'

'Then I'll send a note saying I'm unwell.'

'Agnes, I don't advise you do that. It's a most dangerous thing to do, you would be tempting fate – anything might happen to you. I can't countenance it for a single second. Drive on,' she ordered, and she was smiling as the coach made progress down Hangman's Hill. Arnold intended to change the name of the hill when he became mayor. He and Agnes thought it an inferior address, and wanted to call it Huntsman's Hill, which she found quite ordinary. Although he got his own way in most things she doubted that he would with this: the change wouldn't make him popular with the traditionalists hereabouts. Dulcie agreed with them that he had no right to alter something that had been so for hundreds of years. Change for the sake of change, she thought.

Sometimes she wondered if she disliked things that Arnold liked purely because he did, and that she approved of others because he didn't. It was her own subtle way of annoying him. He was correct in saying that she was different. She was. She felt a confidence in herself that she had not possessed before.

She could pinpoint when the change had occurred: it had been on meeting Edward and his father. It seemed to her as if a barrier in her mind had collapsed, and who she was and what she felt had been set free. Thoughts were piling up in her mind, new ideas and views to which she was giving time. For years her mind had been busy with incidentals – meals to serve, problems with the servants – but now she had found another side of herself, a more logical, deeper-thinking side, which Edward's father had recognised. She was permitting herself to be honest and felt liberated by it. Although, of course, she wasn't.

The carriage pulled up outside the lawyer's office. The coachman was round at her side in a trice, lowering the steps for her, helping her down. She smiled thanks – her husband and Agnes never did.

'Mrs Randolph-Smythe, this is an unexpected honour.'

'Mr Battle?' She shook hands with the young laywer into whose chamber she had been shown. 'Mrs Randolph is quite sufficient,' she said, as she always did. She took the seat he offered as he settled himself on the other side of the very large desk. She wondered if its size made him feel important – he looked like a boy, not a qualified lawyer. 'Might I be assured of your total discretion?' she began.

'But of course.'

'It is imperative that my husband knows nothing of what I am doing.'

'Nor will he,' he said, though she noticed that he frowned as he picked up his pen to take notes. She wished there were women lawyers she could talk to and trust. How much easier it would be to explain her wishes to one of her own sex who would not stand in judgement.

'You don't approve that he is not to know?'

'It is not my place.'

'As long as you mean that.' Here was an unexpected advantage to his youth: she could not imagine herself speaking quite so sharply to a lawyer of her own age.

'I do, Mrs Randolph.'

'I'm glad we understand each other. No doubt you are aware that normally we deal with Munroe, Small and Whitehead for legal matters.'

'Yes, I am. An excellent firm. We are doubly honoured that you are with us here today.'

'I do not wish to deal with them over certain delicate matters. I don't think I could rely on either Mr Small or Mr Whitehead to maintain strict confidence.'

'But, Mrs Randolph, they are men of standing and distinction, true professionals.'

'Your defence of them does you credit. I'm sorry, therefore, to inform you that they are none of these things. Furthermore they owe me a considerable amount of money.'

'But, then, if that is the case surely—'

'They are under the impression that they owe the money to my husband – he let them think he lent it, and now, it would appear, they have lost it. They will feel an indebtedness to him, not me. To them I am a creature of no importance. He will have seen to that, as he does with everyone. No doubt he will use their difficult situation to his own advantage.'

'But how can that be?'

'Because it is how he wishes it to be. And, fool that I am, I have concurred. It had never crossed my mind that I would be cheated. I would never cheat and I presumed he wouldn't. Innocence, you see, Mr Battle, can be danger-ous. Furthermore, my lawyer and my trustees are in London. They handle the bulk of my affairs at my husband's instigation. However, over the years, they have sent me duplicates of every transaction – not that he is aware of this. The lawyers here in Barlton act for my husband, ignorant of the true facts.'

'With such sums as your husband must be involved in, transactions made, papers . . . It would not be possible.'

'I have signed many papers in my married life that I have not read.'

'But, then, you are . . .' He seemed unsure how to proceed.

'I have only myself to blame? Was that what you wanted to say, Mr Battle? May I remind you that I am a woman, a wife? I behaved as I had been brought up to behave, as was expected of me. But things in our world are changing, Mr Battle, especially with regard to the rights of women. And I am most certainly part of that change.'

'But—'

'Mr Battle, are you trying to argue your way out of taking on this commission? You begin every sentence with "But".'

'Not at all, Mrs Randolph. It is my professional loyalty.'

'Which is highly commendable of you. But I suggest you listen to me, and take my advice about Munroe, Small and Whitehead.' She rearranged her hands in her lap. 'Shall I continue?'

'Please do.' The poor man looked anguished.

'My son and his father do not understand each other. My husband is a practical man while my son is sensitive and artistic. He is returning from South Africa and I do not want him to return home where he is made to feel unhappy. I wish to purchase a property for him, here in Barlton, to be put in his name. I wish also to make him an allowance, separate from the one he already receives, to be paid into a bank account that I am about to set up for him. His father is not to know any of this.'

'I quite understand.' Dulcie was happy to see that there was no frown now but, rather, he was smiling. 'There is one thing, if he is living in Barlton, your husband will surely learn of it?'

'Eventually, yes, but by then my son will be settled. It will be harder for his father to bully him into doing as he wishes. My son will realise that he is capable of living alone. You see, he wishes to pursue a career as an artist and his father does not think it an apt pursuit for his son.'

The young man's smile grew even broader and Dulcie wondered if he himself was in a career he did not enjoy, forced there by the other Battle, of Battle, Todsworth and Battle. 'May I confide in you?' he asked. 'I never wanted to go into law. My father insisted.' He said it somewhat sheepishly. 'Perhaps I should not be saying that to a client.'

'I, too, can keep secrets, Mr Battle.' She had no qualms now. 'Have you clients with suitable houses that they might wish to sell?'

'As a matter of fact, I have three. If you would wait a

moment, I will get one of our employees to accompany you.'

'That would be most kind of you. But there is another matter.' Dulcie opened her commodious handbag and removed a sheet of paper. 'This is a new will that I wish to have drawn up. This is what I require you to put into legal terms.'

'Of course, Mrs Randolph.' He accepted the paper and placed it under his blotter.

By the early afternoon Dulcie had found the perfect property for Chauncey in Captain's Keep. It was an old house, built in the Dutch style, overlooking the sandy beach of Smugglers' Point – such a romantic address, she'd always thought. A stone causeway, like a sleek grey ribbon, stalked out into the sea, the waves constantly battering against it, as if trying to wear it down. The harbour was a mere hundred yards away. Chauncey would have the best of both worlds, either solitude or a bustling port.

The rooms were large and the windows allowed in maximum light. There was a small walled garden in which she would build a pond and a fountain for the summer. The drawing-room window hung out over the small front garden, bow-fronted, with some panes of bottle glass. She would have a window-seat constructed so that he could watch the sea and the ships coming and going.

The arrangements to purchase it were put in hand. She left Mr Battle with a list of the modifications she would require. He would arrange for builders and painters to start work as soon as the property had been conveyed.

The manager of Martin's Bank on Gold Street, not the bank her husband patronised, was overjoyed to welcome her and to set up accounts for both her and her son. Then she took the carriage and entered the shop of her husband's rival. 'Mr Markham.'

'Such a pleasure, Mrs Randolph. Tonight your delightful daughter honours us with—'

'I have secret matters to discuss with you, Mr Markham.' Dulcie nipped in the bud the impending sentimental twaddle. 'I don't want Arnold to know anything about my visit or my purchases.'

'A surprise for him?'

'In a manner of speaking.'

Two hours later the furniture for Captain's Keep had been chosen.

'I must apologise that you have only myself for company, Lord Prestwick, Edward. Both my husband and Agnes had prior engagements.'

'I can think of no one I would rather have as our companion. What do you say, Edward?'

'I entirely agree with you, Father.'

'But poor Edward – doomed to have we two old fuddy-duddies for company!'

'Mrs Randolph, I must object. You are nothing of the sort.'

'I see, Edward, so you think your poor old father is.' Lord Prestwick tried to look cross, then hurt, failed miserably with both and laughed.

'Yes, Father, that is exactly so.' Edward was laughing too.

'What great companions you are to each other.' Dulcie had watched the two men teasing each other with approval and affection. If only Chauncey and his father . . . Arnold would have to change out of all recognition to get on with his son.

'There is no one whose company I enjoy more than my father's. We have had some good times together, haven't we, Papa?'

'The best, dear boy. But there is also good fortune in no other guests being present, Mrs Randolph. There is no one to bore with our endless talk of porcelain and related matters.'

All three looked up as the drawing-room door opened and Agnes, looking particularly pretty in a new coral-coloured dress, entered in a swishing flurry.

'Agnes?' Dulcie looked at her, puzzled. Her heart sank with disappointment.

'Poor Mrs Markham is indisposed and, sadly, they had to cancel their dinner. Would it be impertinent and too much bother if I joined you?'

Dulcie stood up. 'I must tell Bee to lay another place.'

'I already have. Oh, Mr Bartholomew-Prestwick, isn't this fortuitous?'

'Most,' he said, bending over her outstretched hand. 'Might I introduce my father, Lord Prestwick, Miss Randolph-Smythe?'

'How thrilling.' Agnes bestowed on him her most charming smile.

2

For three days Lily had stayed at home, the curtains drawn as if there had been a death in the family. She was in a state of shock. This was not what was supposed to be happening. She was meant to be in charge of her own destiny. She was to make the decisions, not him! All her dreams and plans lay in ashes. Now she was in mourning for the loss of her position – and it was just like a death.

Her career might have begun out of necessity but it had become the core of her life. Without it she felt as if she was once again a person of no importance, of no relevance.

On the third day she decided to go to the shop.

'Where you off to in that get-up?'

'I'm going to see Mr Randolph-Smythe, Mother.'

'What good will that do? You'd be better off going out and finding other employment.'

'I shall demand my position back.' Her brave statement merely made Pansy laugh.

'Beg for it, more like,' she spluttered.

'Perhaps demand is the wrong word.'

'Most certainly it is. You'll be sent off with a flea in your ear.'

'I can always say I was in the wrong, ask to be reinstated – very well, beg to be. I'm not like you, Mother, always thinking I'm in the right. I know when to be diplomatic.'

'My eye, you do. You look like an old ewe dressed lamb-fashion.'

'Can you never say anything pleasant?'

'To you? Unlikely.'

'Take care, Mother. One day you may regret these remarks.' She enjoyed making the veiled threat even if it was with less confidence than when she had been sure she could manipulate her future.

But it sailed over Pansy's head. 'See me quivering,' she cackled, as Lily let herself out.

Nothing could have prepared her for the shock awaiting her as she tried to enter the main door of Randolph's Emporium. 'Sorry, Miss Howard, I've strict instructions to bar your entry.'

'Don't be silly, Shepperton. I just want to purchase a few items.'

'No, Miss Howard. You're not allowed to set one foot on the premises.' His voice was raised.

'You need not shout!' She was whispering, not wanting passers-by to hear this conversation. 'Why not, pray? I am no longer employed. I am a member of the public, the same as everyone else.'

'No, Miss. You're not.'

'But I wish to shop, like these other customers.'

'That's the problem, Miss. You're not wanted as a

customer. You're an Undesirable.' His voice boomed. 'You're a Banned Personage. There's nothing I can do about it.' He stood immovable in front of her, in his uniform with its gold epaulettes. She saw the curious stares of the shoppers, heard the whispered asides, and suffered the agony of being recognised by some. She watched them sweep past her and into the shop where her happiest years, she now knew, had been spent.

On the walk home she, who prided herself on her correct posture, walked with her head down, a picture of dejection.

'Your trouble, Lily, is you think you're a big bug when you're nothing but an ant. I've always said it, but would you listen?'

'Stop it! Can't you see I'm not happy?'

'Happy? What's that? The likes of you and me can't expect happiness. All we can hope for is food in our stomachs and a roof over our heads. You, with your carelessness, have cost us that.'

She had lied to Pansy, saying she had been dismissed for making an error in the books. Had she known the true reason Lily's life would have been even more intolerable than it already was.

'I did my best.'

'You! Your best is enough to make a dog laugh. Best! Your best is everyone else's worst. You're worse than useless, you are.'

Lily looked with loathing at the little woman with her white hair, her sweet smile, her peaches-and-cream complexion, the perfect old lady who could spit out venom worthy of a snake. How she longed to shut her up – smash her head in! 'What is to happen to me? Your father will never forgive you this.'

'Me, me, me! That's all you think about. And what would my father have to say about you lying to me all these years? Pretending to me you were my mother when you're not.' It was out. She had hoped to feel pleasure in letting Pansy know she was aware of the truth, but she felt no different, just as angry. 'Making me wait on you hand and foot.' She was looming over the woman, who cowered in the chair.

'Who told you that? Cherry? That evil bitch. She promised me.'

'Why pretend all these years? That's what I want to know.'

'It was your father's idea.'

'How convenient to blame him when he's dead. You expect me to believe you?'

'When it's the truth, yes,' Pansy said, with such dignity that Lily thought it might be. 'He said it would be kinder for you not to know you'd lost your mother. That I was her. I wanted children of my own, but they didn't come. You were like mine to me.' She wiped a tear from her eye, which Lily chose to ignore. 'And then, when he died, I feared if you knew I wasn't that you wouldn't care for me when I was old. That you would cast me out a poor unloved cripple.'

'Is that all you thought of me? That I would behave like that?'

'I was afraid.'

'You? Nothing frightens you. You're a selfish old woman. Had I known the truth I'd have looked after you – not out of love but out of duty. After all, you're my father's widow, I have a duty. And we share a name, if nothing else. But now, with no work, no money, why should I beggar myself for the likes of you? A deceitful, lying old baggage. No longer!' Lily picked up her hat, rammed it on to her head, put on her gloves and picked up her umbrella.

'Where are you going?'

'As far away from you as I can get.'

'Don't leave me . . .' The pathetic wail followed her out of the door, and she could still hear it as she marched purposefully down the street. She should be grateful to

224

the woman, Lily thought. She'd pulled her out of the self-pitying state into which she had fallen. Her head was buzzing with plans again.

She climbed the steep hill out of the harbour area, impervious to the cold wind whipping in from the sea. How dare Arnold treat her in such a fashion? Her anger fuelled her legs, it seemed, as she speedily crossed the town. She passed the church. Why should she allow herself to become so despondent about her work? If she was clever, if she planned properly, she could choose whether or not to have her old position back. She threaded her way through the crowds outside the shops and reached Hangman's Hill. She was virtually running as she sped down one side and up the other.

At Arnold's house she was told that the family were not at home. She crossed the road and waited in the shelter of a bush.

An hour later she watched as a carriage turned into the drive of December Cottage. She waited another five minutes to give Dulcie time to take off her coat and collect herself. Then she crossed the road, moved swiftly up the drive in case she lost her nerve and banged on the front door again.

The same parlour maid, pinning on her cap, opened the door. I wouldn't have slovenly behaviour like that in my house, Lily thought. 'Mrs Randolph-Smythe. I need to see her,' she said.

'Is Mrs Randolph expecting you?'

'Yes,' Lily lied. 'Tell her Miss Howard is here to see her. And it's Randolph-Smythe to the likes of you.'

'My mistress never says Smythe.'

That was interesting: Lily had not known that. She had always had the same name when Arnold was present. Did he know she did not use it? He must. But as she waited she wondered why.

'Miss Howard, this is a pleasant surprise.' Dulcie

swept into the hall with her hand proffered in welcome. 'To what do I owe the pleasure?'

Lily took a step back. There was something different about the woman. She wasn't the usual mouse-like creature. Before, Lily had thought of her as lumbering, but now she sailed towards her, like a galleon. There was a confidence in her that Lily had never witnessed before – in marked contrast to herself for, to her own astonishment, Lily burst into tears.

'My poor Miss Howard, what is the matter? Come, sit. Tea, Bee, please. Please compose yourself, Miss Howard. I cannot understand what it is you say.'

Lily flapped her hands in agitation and, from her bag, produced a newly laundered hankerchief. She was mortified that it was one of her father's and not a dainty lace one. 'I don't know what came over me. Please forgive me, Mrs Randolph,' she spluttered, and was glad she had been corrected by the maid. The tears were unlike her but she saw that they had made Dulcie doubly concerned for her. Perhaps she could use that to her advantage.

Dulcie was unsure what to do with this weeping woman, about whom she knew little, so she fussed about with the tea to give herself time to think and Lily to compose herself. 'Tea will make you feel immeasurably better,' she said, and handed her a cup. 'There, that's better. Now, perhaps, you can tell me what the problem is.' She smiled encouragement.

'I came to you because you've always been kind to me, what with my birthday and Christmas presents . . .'

'Please, they were nothing.'

'They might not have been to you but they meant a lot to me.' Lily bridled.

'Then I'm pleased,' Dulcie corrected herself. Here was a sensitive soul, she thought.

'Your husband has dismissed me.'

'I can hardly believe that – you, of all people?'

'It's the case. I've been feeling very low and not my usual self.'

'I'm not surprised. It must have been such a shock for you, after all these years. Are you sure there has been no mistake? He's always saying what a treasure you are, how he could never manage without you.'

'Did he?' She smiled with pleasure at the kind words.

She was not to know that he had never said any such thing. 'He says you know more about the shop than he does himself.' Dulcie had compounded the first lie. 'And why, might I ask?'

As she gathered her thoughts, Lily had to take time for some discreet nose-blowing and eye-dabbing. Dulcie was a woman of honour. If she told her about Edith she was just as likely to throw her out. But in any case, faced with the woman's concern and kindness, she found she couldn't. She knew about hurt and she didn't want to inflict it on Dulcie. 'I don't really know.'

'But you must. He must have given you a reason,' Dulcie said.

'There was a misunderstanding about some figures. That's all I can think was his reason.'

Dulcie poured more tea. 'So, what do you expect of me? I never interfere with the shop. That is my husband's responsibility.'

'I wanted you to ask him to see me.'

'Why not go to the shop?'

'He won't let me in.'

'Good gracious me.' Dulcie looked at her watch. 'Miss Howard, I'm not sure that my husband won't see this as interference but, well, you've been a faithful friend to us. He should be back here in half an hour. I have guests tonight and preparations to make. If you don't think it intolerably rude of me, perhaps I might see to my duties and you wait here?'

'You're too kind, Mrs Randolph.' She had registered how Dulcie had called her *friend*. Most people would have said servant, or employee, or something equally insulting.

'Now, now, Miss Howard, no more tears. I'm sure something can be arranged.' Quickly Dulcie left the room.

Left alone, Lily helped herself to a sandwich, and then a cake. Feeling much better, she began an inspection of the room. It was just the sort of drawing room she longed for, with its fine wallpaper, the floral pattern and gilt – they were expensive. As was the furniture. And the knick-knacks. She picked up a silver box. Just that would keep her and her mother for a year, she estimated. It was all so unfair, so unjust. She fingered the heavy silk curtains, noted the heavy interlining, the fine braiding. *She*'d have curtains like these one day. And china, like that pretty couple on a swing – Dresden, it said on the bottom. She wondered whether it would be noticed if she pocketed something. She doubted it. There was so much in this room – who could possibly remember the full contents? But she knew the answer: if this were her home, *she* would.

She heard voices in the hall and sat down again, bolt upright in the brocade-upholstered chair. She steeled herself.

'What are you doing here?' Arnold entered the room in a rush. A second later Dulcie fluttered in. 'Who let you in?'

'She was distressed, Arnold.'

'How dare you invite an employee into my house?'

'I would like to point out that it is my house too.'

Lily had been right – it wasn't her imagination: Dulcie *was* different.

'And you, how dare you venture here?' He pointed a finger accusingly at Lily. He wanted to frighten her, but he wouldn't succeed. She'd be like Dulcie: she would stand firm. Think of that whore, Lily told herself.

'I dare because you and I have matters to discuss.' She was relieved that her voice was strong and firm.

'We have nothing to discuss. You have been dismissed and that is an end to the matter.'

'But you are wrong, Mr Randolph-Smythe. I am quite prepared to talk in front of your wife, but I'm sure you would rather I didn't.'

'Miss Howard, this is not how you were before.' Dulcie was looking at her with disapproval.

'I'm sorry, Mrs Randolph, but while you were out of the room I came to some conclusions. I am not going to be put upon, to end up in Queer Street when I have done nothing wrong.'

Arnold snorted with derision. 'I beg to differ.'

'I have not, and you know so. Why should I be punished for your misdeeds?'

'Arnold, what does she mean?'

'Mad talk, Dulcie. The woman is insane.'

'I'm not. Do you want me to continue?'

'There is nothing you can say that my wife is not aware of, I can assure you of that.' He looked so smug that Lily longed to hit him, to wipe that smirk from his face. So she knew about the mistresses, did she? And condoned it? Interesting.

'0-20-64-2-3,' Lily recited, with a dramatic pause between each figure. She saw him blanch and it was her turn to smile smugly.

'Dulcie, you have much to do for tonight, I'm sure. I'll deal with this creature. If she doesn't leave I shall call for the police.' Arnold looked agitated now.

'Evidently you *do* have business to discuss,' Dulcie said, and Lily was puzzled by the quiet little smile on her face as she left them.

'I thought that would make you change your mind.'

'How did you find out that number? No one knows it.'

'You are wrong. I do. Why don't you take a seat? We have much to discuss.'

'I have guests due in an hour.' He looked trapped.

'If we have not reached agreement by then, I fear they will have to wait for your attention.'

'Are you about to blackmail me?' he blustered, but he looked afraid she noted with satisfaction.

Lily laughed. 'Why should I do a thing like that? I don't want to harm you, Arnold.' She saw him relax. 'I love you.' At that she saw him sit up, rigid with astonishment. 'I have loved you since the first day we met.'

'Miss Howard, what can I say? I had no idea. You never—'

'Said? Of course not. I'm a lady, not like some.' She smiled slyly. 'You need not look anxious, Arnold. I realise I'm not good enough for you.'

'Miss Howard, please don't denigrate yourself in such a manner.'

'Lily, please.'

'Lily,' he said, in a way that made her feel quite weak. But she was not so stupid as to believe him: she knew he was playing with her, hoping to make her relax so that he could manipulate her.

'I simply told you to reassure you that I want to help you. I will admit that I came here very confused and my first intention was to tell your wife about Edith. But I decided against it.'

'She does not care what I do. My wife ceased loving me years ago.' He said this with such a tragic expression that, had she not known him as well as she did, she would have felt pity for him. Instead she ignored it. 'You asked how I knew the combination of the safe. You wrote it in a booklet, disguised, of course – but I'm clever, Arnold, I soon worked it out. Now, if I could, so could others, and what I found in that safe, well, that was careless, Arnold. It took me only a few hours to work it out. You have to be cleverer than that. Figures need to be hidden away from prying eyes like mine.' She allowed herself a superior smile. 'You need me, Arnold. My goodness, how badly you need me.'

'I believe I do, Lily.'

'Good. I have a few proposals, and if you are willing to fulfil them, I shall guide you. Between us we can double the money that you have so far purloined.'

'Dear Lily, what an unpleasant word, but I'm all ears. First, perhaps, a little champagne?' And he laughed in the delightful manner she loved. She could not believe this was happening, that it had all been so easy, that everything was happening just as she had planned. No more depression for Lily, she said to herself.

3

Phoebe never caught up with herself. There were endless chores that needed her attention. She had no time to read or practise her writing. Keeping clean was a struggle once again, but she was determined not to return to her old ways. She emptied the bucket of dirty water down the outside drain and looked ruefully at her hands. At Courtney Lacey, when she had been a lady of leisure, they had become so soft and pink. Now her nails were ripped and the skin was raw from scrubbing and washing. Her mother had rubbed ewe fat into hers to make them less rough, but Phoebe's nose had become sensitive, and she simply could not bring herself to do so. She would have to put up with them as they were.

Although she was now with Lester, she was afraid all the time of Mr Orton because he was unpredictable. One day, at breakfast, he might be half-way human, but at any moment he might change, start ranting and roaring as if he were demented. By lunch-time she would be locking herself into the scullery to get away from him and what she had quickly realised were his evil intentions. Every day she tried not to be alone with him.

Phoebe went back into the kitchen and placed her bucket with a clatter on the floor. Mimi looked up at her from the basket and whined.

'Sorry, Mimi, did I startle you?' The dog continued to whine. 'What's the matter, little girl? Where are the puppies?' Mimi's tail beat a tattoo on the floor. Come to think of it, Phoebe hadn't seen them since last night. She took her blanket from beside the back door, threw it over her head and stepped gingerly into the yard. She had to walk with care since the cobbles were covered in moss, and when it was raining like today the surface was as dangerous as ice. She began to call the puppies, stopping every so often to listen for them whining. But there was nothing. She stopped at the pig sty and looked in. The pig and her piglets stared back. The brown collar told her what had happened. She knew that if she looked she would find the other collars too. Collars that Lester had bought for them.

She did not stop to think, nor did she bother to walk carefully but ran across the cobbles, skidding this way and that. 'Where are you, you horrible man? You've killed the puppies!'

Mr Orton was stumbling down the stairs as if his legs were made of rubber. She ran towards him, up the stairs and met him half-way where she punched his chest and kicked his shins. He began to laugh, a loud, booming sound that battered her ears. 'You fed them to the pigs!' This only made him laugh louder. His head was lolling as if he had lost control of it and his eyes rolled in his head. 'They ate everything except the little collars. I hate you. You're evil!' She was crying as she screamed at him, his laughter fuelling her anger. 'I loathe you and your stinking blubber!' His laughter rose to a screaming crescendo, and she stepped back down the stairs. He hadn't heard her, he didn't understand. He was insane. She backed along the passage to the kitchen, picked up Mimi and locked herself into the scullery.

'Phoebe.' It was Lester.

'Go away.' She was still sobbing.

'Let me in. What is it?'

'The puppies . . .' Her weeping intensified as she told him what she had found.

'Shush, shush.'

'We can't stay here. He'll be killing us next.'

'He didn't kill them.'

'What?' She pushed back her hair. 'What did you say?'

'I gave them away. The pigs never had them.'

She sniffed and wiped at her tears with the back of her hand. 'Then why were the collars there?' she asked.

'They must have dropped off. It was dark and I didn't see.'

'Is this true?'

'Why would I lie to you?'

'You promise?'

'Of course. If he'd hurt a hair of those puppies, I'd have killed him myself. Now, come on out and make us a cup of tea, there's a good Phoebe.'

Phoebe had never had a friend before. At Cowman's Combe there had been no one near to her age, and with her father's reputation as a bully, his enthusiasm for converting people to his religion, the girls in the surrounding villages had been too scared of him to get to know her. Dick had been the nearest to a friend she had ever had but he didn't really count because he was her brother, and male: he could not understand her as she wished to be understood.

Lester was different. Although he was a man, he didn't think like one: he was interested in all the things that Phoebe was. She could talk to him of her dreams, and he didn't laugh at her longing for love, a handsome man and a comfortable home. 'You know, Lester, a front door with a stained-glass window that the sun shines through. And lamps with red silk shades, and china that matches and lots of books on their special shelves. And a grand piano with a big aspidistra on the top in a fine copper pot.'

'You play the piano?'

'No, but it would look nice.'

'Shall you invite me?'

'You can live with us, Lester, in the attic. That's where poets should live. My husband will be a kind, sensitive man and he'll understand such things.'

She confided in him about Phyllis. 'You don't think I'm mad?'

'I think it's the most beautiful thing I've ever heard. How I envy you – a companion of the soul.' She had liked that description of Phyllis. And the next day he had given her a poem he had written. It was called 'The Shadow Sister' and it made her cry, for he had put into words exactly what she thought but had never been able to say. She read it every night before slipping it under her pillow and going to sleep. She thought he was a genius, and there was nothing she could not talk to him about, even the most intimate part of being a woman.

He was even interested in her recent attraction to fashion and jewellery, and she never seemed to bore him with her chatter. Unusually in a man, she was sure, he liked nothing better than to brush her hair and arrange it in new and, to her, outlandish styles. 'Like Queen Guinevere,' he would say, as he decorated it with feathers, beads and artificial flowers. 'You need new clothes. You can't live in those for ever,' he said one day, having contrived a particularly lovely hairstyle of cascading ringlets tied with blue ribbons.

Phoebe looked down at her strange attire, and laughed. She was indeed a strange apparition – especially with her hair like this. She still had the flimsy toga dress in which she had danced at the auction, but she planned to cut it up for dusters. Apart from that she had nothing so she had fashioned a skirt from an old pair of Mr Orton's trousers. On top she wore, against the cold, three of Lester's shirts. She had made a pair of sandals from the soles of a pair of his shoes and bound them onto her feet with canvas she had found in an outhouse. 'Hardly Paris's latest.' She grinned at him and twirled around.

'Even dressed like that you're beautiful, Phoebe.'

'Buttering me up so I'll make you a cake, that's what you're about.'

'No, no, I meant it, and your modesty becomes you.'

She dropped him a mock curtsy.

'I'm going to speak to Father about you.'

She was fully aware of it when he did: Mr Orton's shouting echoed about the house, and Mimi huddled fearfully under the dresser. 'Money? For the likes of her? Are you mad, son?'

'It's not f-f-fair on her. She n-n-needs p-p-pretty things.'

'Pretty things? Would they help her black the grate, cook the food, scrub the floor? Have you lost your wits?'

Phoebe jumped at the violence with which he slammed the back door.

'So he said no.' She laughed at Lester's disappointed expression. 'Honestly, my love, I never thought he'd say anything else. I'm not disgruntled.' She was, but she'd never let him know it.

He slumped into a chair at the kitchen table.

'Lester, it doesn't matter. I'm warm and dry here, food in me belly, and that's all I need while I decide what to do. But don't forget you promised me you'd help me write a letter to Dick's regiment. Will you?' But when she turned back from the stove he was no longer in the room.

Ten minutes later an excited Lester returned, with a bundle of clothes in his arms. 'Mother's. They might be on the big side but we could cut them down to fit you.'

'I couldn't do that, Lester.' The very thought of wearing a dead woman's clothes made her flesh crawl.

'Because she's dead?'

'No, silly, what a daft idea.' She pulled a face at him to cover her confusion that he knew what she had been thinking. 'Can you imagine what your father would say if he saw me in his wife's clothes? He'd throw me out with nothing, and then where would I be?'

'And where would *I* be?' He looked at her tenderly. Then he was racing out of the room and she could hear him thudding up the stairs. He made a lot of noise for one as light as he. Five minutes later he was back. This time his hands were full of billowing red silk.

'From your bedroom wall?'

'The very same.'

'But you love your room.'

'I love you more.'

His words took both of them by surprise. 'You want to watch yourself, Lester. You'll be wanting to make babies next!' She turned the moment into a joke.

'I don't know where to begin.' They were in Lester's room, the silk laid out on the floor. 'I was never any good at sewing, you know. There wasn't much call for it where I come from,' Phoebe said.

'It can't be that difficult. We need to make a pattern first, I think.' Lester took some sheets of paper off his desk. 'If we glue them together . . .' An hour later Phoebe stood with a paper pattern of a dress attached to her with pins Lester had remembered seeing his mother use. That foray into her room had been fruitful: he had returned with buttons, ribbon, needle and thread.

Lester was a brilliant dressmaker. Even he, modest to the point of self-effacement, admitted that the dress was a great success. He had made it to fit her like a second skin. The bodice, cut low to show the rise of her breasts, was trimmed with some lace he had found and dyed red, using beetroot juice, from a bottle of pickle they had found in one of the storage cupboards. 'Hope it doesn't

236

run if I get too hot.' She giggled. The skirt was cut straight in the front and he had ruched it behind to make a fashionable small bustle. 'It don't make me look too big?' She twisted round to see herself in the long mirror.

'It's perfect.'

'But when can I wear it?'

'Christmas, of course.'

But she had worn it before then. He had fashioned her a serviceable coat from an old blanket to put over the silk. 'We're going out.'

'Where to?'

'Barlton, for Christmas shopping.'

'Barlton?' She looked scared at the very mention of the place.

'That's over, Phoebe. You're mine now. You'll be safe with me.' They stood looking at each other across the kitchen. 'I want you to look lovely for Christmas.'

To their disappointment Mr Orton, on hearing of their plans, decided to come too. They huddled in the back of the trap, whispering and giggling together. Mr Orton smiled in a self-satisfied manner, presumably at the success of his plan. Phoebe was still wary of him, but the incident of the puppies had never been mentioned again. She was just lucky that she had attacked him on one of his 'cuckoo' days, as she called them. He was a confusing man to have any dealings with: on some days she thought him the maddest person in the world, on others he was apparently normal. There was no warning of which he was going to be. Of the two different people he was she was not sure which she preferred, and had concluded that she didn't like either.

Today, however, he was so pleased with himself that upon their arrival he pressed a florin into Phoebe's hand. 'Buy yourself something pretty,' he said, doffing his hat. Phoebe felt quite weak with shock.

Their first call was at a bookshop in Coxswain's Passage, where Lester had to collect a copy of Swinburne's poems he had ordered. The other books in the shop proved such an attraction for him that he was soon engrossed in them.

'Lester, I want to go and spend my money.' Phoebe tugged at his sleeve.

He looked up from the book he was reading and seemed not to be focusing on her. 'Yes?'

'Then we can meet?'

'Yes, why not?' he said vaguely.

'Lester, if you're going to meet me, you must remember to meet me. You can't leave me alone in this town. You do understand?'

'Of course. Where? By the harbour? There's a lovely beach. We could walk there when all our shopping is done. Here,' he delved into his pocket and produced some money, 'buy us some bread, and we can have a picnic.'

'In December?'

'But the sun is shining. Where's the romantic in you, Phoebe, my love?'

Phoebe enjoyed the town in daylight. She didn't even shudder when she passed the hotel where she had spent the night in fear with Mr Orton. She was not so sure how she would have felt if she had known in which building the auction had taken place. She found a baker and purchased two baps filled with cheese, and two cream cakes, which the assistant put into a box. As she paid for them she felt just like the housewife she dreamed of becoming one day – one who could afford cream cakes sold in boxes.

Across the road from the baker's there was an enormous shop with windows that stretched down the street and round the corner. 'It must be the biggest shop in the world,' she told herself.

'What would you expect in Barlton?' she replied. She spent some time looking in the windows, amazed by the beauty of the contents, longing to buy everything she saw. Did she dare enter?

'Why not?' said Phyllis, who, Phoebe often thought, was braver than she.

Lester's coat must have looked right for the important-looking man in uniform who stood at the doorway saluted her and opened the door wide for her. She decided it would look best if she walked in head high. She went past fabrics and trimmings, past gloves and bags, past china and glass. Then she climbed the stairs, pausing half-way to look down at the shop, the counters and the throng of people below. On the first floor there was another wonderland of clothes. Everything was here.

'May I be of assistance?' asked a smart woman, dressed from head to toe in black with her hair pulled back severely. She sounded as though her mouth was full of pebbles and Phoebe had to ask her to repeat herself.

'I was just looking,' she answered.

'If you would like to tell me what it is you are looking for?' The woman was still polite, but in a somewhat threatening way.

Phoebe coloured. She could hardly say, 'Nothing,' since she had no money. Was it forbidden just to look or, worse, a crime? Would she be arrested?

'This is too much! Don't you ever listen to a word I say?' Both she and the woman looked towards the other side of the large department where a young, pretty girl stamped her foot and flung the dress she was holding at the alarmed assistant. 'This is rubbish. The alterations are diabolical. I demand better than this.'

How rude, thought Phoebe. The woman who had been with her was fluttering over to the girl agitatedly. 'Miss Randolph-Smythe, I am so sorry—'

'As you should be.'

She needs a slap, thought Phoebe, but now that the assistant had been distracted she made her escape.

Downstairs again, and to the back of the shop, she found a department selling men's clothing. She was not sure if it was seemly to enter, but upon seeing a middle-aged woman there with her daughter, she ventured in.

On one counter she found the ideal gift for Lester, a lovely Paisley handkerchief so large he could wear it as a cravat. She nearly fainted at the price of it and had little change to show, but she had the shop's bag, elegantly black with a large gold R embossed on it, which, to her astonishment, was free.

She was almost out of the department when her heart lurched in her chest. A million insects crawled over her flesh. She felt dizzy and sick with terror. She had seen, standing in the entrance, and engrossed in conversation, the Arnold who had auctioned her. She searched desperately for another door. There wasn't one. She waited and then to her horror saw that, instead of leaving, he was walking towards where she stood, smiling at her.

Just before he reached her a middle-aged woman bustled forward and barred his way. 'Dear Mr Randolph-Smythe, your opinion on a possible purchase, if you would be so kind?'

'Mrs Fanshaw! My pleasure.' He bowed at her.

Phoebe ran through the shop, bumping into people, nearly tripping, knocking a display to the ground but noticing none of these things.

'Phoebe!' He was following her! Her fear was such that she did not see Lester, in the store's fabric department, calling her.

She brushed past the doorman and raced across the street. A horse reared in terror and a delivery boy went flying. She pounded along, with a stitch in her side. The sea was ahead. If only she could swim! She arrived at the beach and collapsed on to the cold sand. She could run no further.

4

'Mrs Randolph, come and see.'

'What is it, Bee?' Dulcie put down the ornament she had been trying to decide where to place. She crossed the room, which was filled with packing cases, to the bow-fronted bay-window where her maid was standing.

'That poor girl, ma'am, there, by the causeway. Do you think I should go and see to her?'

'The poor little thing. She certainly looks to be in distress. Perhaps . . . No, look, Bee, a young man has just run up and joined her.'

'What if it's him what's upset her? Perhaps she's frightened of him.'

'I don't think so, Bee. He doesn't look like a ruffian, and she's talking so earnestly to him. She doesn't look afraid of him. Ah, he's stroking her cheek, consoling her. She's such a lovely creature, don't you think?' With her usual generosity of spirit, she always acknowledged beauty when she saw it.

'He looks so weak, as if he's about to expire. I'm sure if he swatted a fly he'd fall over. What's a pretty creature like her doing with someone like him?'

'Who can tell with lovers?' Dulcie was smiling indulgently on the young couple, who were now sitting on the sea wall.

'I don't think they are. Leastways, he might love her but I don't think as her loves him.'

'Really, Bee! Why have you drawn that conclusion?' Dulcie chuckled.

'It's the different way they look at each other. I'm sure I'm right.'

'You so often are, my dear Bee. Still, spying on people on the beach is neither polite nor is it going to get this room finished – interesting though it may be.' She bustled back to her task. 'Do you think Chauncey would prefer this Meissen of a girl on a swing, or these?' She held up one of a pair of rearing china horses ridden by a moustached hussar.

'Isn't the swing one more suitable for Miss Agnes? The soldier's more masculine.'

'Do you think so?' She studied the procelain pieces intently. 'But it might remind him of unspeakable horrors he's seen. It's so difficult to choose.' She picked up the delicate, less dramatic ornament.

'Why not leave them both here and let him decide? If we've arranged things wrong for him he'll enjoy sorting everything out.' Bee was placing books with fine morocco-leather bindings on the white bookcases.

'What makes you say that? Do you think he won't approve?'

'Of course he will, ma'am. I didn't mean . . . But . . .'

'But what?'

'I'm not sure of these bookcases, Mrs Randolph. White? Bookcases should be mahogany.'

'I rather like them – it's such a light room and I'm told they're all the rage in London.'

'As you wish, ma'am,' Bee said, in a tone that implied she could never agree. 'Still, it's a fine house you and your husband have gone and bought him. And, if you don't mind me saying, I think he'll be happier here.'

'He deserves some happiness after all he's been through.'

'You're cheerful today, ma'am. I must say, I've been quite worried about you recently. You've not been yourself.'

'On the contrary, Bee, I think that that is exactly what I *have* been – for the first time.' She did not elaborate further. 'Perhaps you're right, it should be the horses.' Carefully she placed the ornaments on the mantelshelf.

'But you're right in that I'm much happier now that I know Chauncey's wound is not so bad and that he will soon be back on his feet.' She stepped back to view the figurines, then moved one an inch to the left and studied it again. Then she moved it four inches to the right.

'You do like things to be perfect, ma'am don't you?'

'Especially my beloved china. Now for this painting. I feel we should have the man hang it *there*, central, and then the four smaller oils to the left and right of it.' She made a note. 'I want him to feel immediately at home when he is carried in. Oh dear,' She sighed. She bent down to one of the packing cases to retrieve yet another ornament. When she stood upright she swayed.

'Please be careful, ma'am. Don't do too much and tire yourself.'

'Don't fuss, Bee. I merely stood up too quickly.'

'You look ever so flushed, ma'am.'

'It's a little too warm in here. I asked for all the fires to be lit. He will need warmth, coming from Africa.' She felt her forehead. 'Quite normal,' she said, even though it felt hot. She had no intention of succumbing to a chill now with so much to do.

'I'll see Mr Chalmers gets it right, ma'am. And is Mr Chauncey bringing a friend with him?'

'Not such much a friend, more a servant. Apparently this soldier saved his life. Chauncey must feel indebted to him.'

'Mr Randolph-Smythe will be that proud of him.'

Dulcie paused in her task, uncertain whether to say what was on her mind or not. 'Bee, sit down for a minute. I've been wondering . . . There is something I wish to confide in you, but I must have your assurance that you will keep my secret.'

'But of course, ma'am.'

'Bee, this house is my secret. My husband knows nothing about it, and I don't want him to be aware that our son is returning or that he is wounded. In fact, he has no idea where he went in the first place.'

'Oh, ma'am!' Bee looked shocked.

'Do you now wish you had not promised?'

'No, ma'am,' but she sounded doubtful.

'I have my reasons, Bee.'

'No doubt you have, ma'am, and I would never question them. It just took me a bit by surprise.'

'You, more than most people, are aware of the lack of friendliness between my son and his father.'

'That's more common than you'd imagine, ma'am, and it will change with time, I'm sure.'

'I'm not. I fear they will never be happy with each other. The point is, Bee, I don't want my husband to know for as long as possible – it is inevitable that eventually he will. It can't be helped. But I don't wish you to discuss this arrangement with any of the other servants. Do I make myself clear?'

'As crystal, ma'am. I won't say a word, as God's my witness.' She crossed herself.

'You needn't be over-dramatic, Bee.' Dulcie was laughing: in all the years Bee had worked for her she had never known her go to church except for weddings and funerals.

'I was wondering, ma'am . . . why not get a day-bed that we can place in this here window? He'd be amused, no doubt, watching the people down below – like we were a moment ago.'

'That's a wonderful idea. I shall call in on Mr Markham immediately. A chaise longue, do you think?'

'Bit feminine for a wounded soldier. I was thinking more on the lines of something in wrought-iron, like that bench you've got in the garden.'

'You're so sensitive, Bee. That will be just right. It shall be my task this afternoon. And the young couple, are they still there?'

Bee peered out of the window. 'They've gone.'

The owner of the ironworks she visited knew exactly what was required. Drawings were made and the day-bed would be delivered within the week. Dulcie had enjoyed arranging Chauncey's house for him. Sadly, he would not be here for Christmas but she was pinning her hopes on the boat docking in time for New Year, such an auspicious one: a whole new century lay ahead of them.

The carriage stopped in front of the stationer's. The writing paper and cards she had had printed for Chauncey were ready for her. She had to be so careful to ensure she dealt only with tradespeople who were new to the town, or whom she had not patronised before and hopefully didn't know her husband. Mr Markham had been the exception, but since he had fallen out with Arnold over the right to sell furniture, Dulcie was sure he'd been waiting to get his own back – even though Robert and Agnes were sweet on each other. She could not have anything delivered to December Cottage and arouse suspicions there.

She knew it was silly to try to keep this secret – it couldn't last – but she wanted her son to be hers alone for a time so that they could enjoy each other's company in peace. If he was in the cottage there was always the chance that he would storm out again, and she could not risk that. There was another reason too: she wanted to annoy Arnold. She looked forward to his mortification when he found out what she had done and that others knew but not him.

'Mrs Randolph? It is! I thought it was you. What joy!'

'Lord Prestwick, how lovely to see you.'

He was bowing over her hand. It was such an elegant movement for one as portly as he, she thought.

'Would it be too forward of me to ask if you might care to take some refreshment with me?'

'I can think of nothing I would rather do.' In truth, she had been looking forward to getting home and removing her stays and shoes. But Lord Prestwick . . . For him they must wait.

'If you wish to dismiss your coachman, I can take you home.'

'How very kind you are.' She handed her packages to the coachman. 'Give them to Bee, please,' she told him. Then she took Lord Prestwick's arm and they walked towards the Moll tea-shop. She hoped some of her more malicious acquaintances would be there: it would be wonderful to be the source of some interesting gossip for them rather than the usual petty spite they reserved for her.

Her satisfaction was huge when she introduced him to two particularly malign matrons. 'They are eaten up with envy that I am taking tea with you,' she confided, once they were seated.

'Why?'

She leaned close to him. 'Because *they* don't know any titled people.'

'Do I detect a modicum of malice in your words, Mrs Randolph?'

She was mortified at what appeared to be a rebuke, but then she saw the twinkle in his eye. 'No, Lord Prestwick, you're wrong. It's not a grain of malice, more a barnful.'

This amused him so much that his rumbling laugh rattled around the room. All eyes were immediately upon them. It was his turn to lean forward. 'I've observed that my title is always of more interest to those who don't possess one. Present company excluded, of course. Now, how about more of these delicious cakes?'

'That would be lovely,' she said. How different he was from Arnold, who would never have ordered them, or would so have disapproved of her eating them that her pleasure would have been destroyed. 'Would you make sure that there's some of that lovely chocolate cake, the one with the maraschino cherries?' she asked, her mouth watering at the thought.

Eventually it was time to leave, and she felt sad. She smiled and nodded to her female acquaintances. 'You must come to dine when my friend the duke arrives,' Lord Prestwick boomed, as they passed the women. Outside on the pavement he whispered, 'Not that I know any dukes.'

Dulcie was still laughing when the carriage drew up at her home.

In the hall on the table, for all to see, were the packages from the stationer's with Chauncey's name and new address on the front. She scooped them up, annoyed that the coachman hadn't followed her instructions. She could hear Arnold in the drawing room wih Agnes. Had he seen them, and if so, how was she to explain herself?

For one of her size, unused to running up the stairs as fast as she was doing, the effort was almost too much. She was puffing and panting when she reached the top and had to lean against the banister to catch her breath.

She sat at her dressing-table to remove her hat and winced when one of the pins caught in her hair. She was flushed and perspiration was running down her face. She picked up a fan and wafted it, which helped a little.

Such behaviour was ridiculous, she told herself. Arnold had to know sooner or later about Chauncey. And why had she worked herself into such a state? It was *her* money and she could do what she wanted with it. After all, Arnold had indulged himself with it long enough. This made her smile, until she felt a sharp pain in her chest. Martyr as she was to indigestion, she should never have had that second slice of cake. Then the pain worsened, until she felt as if she was held in a vice. Suddenly she felt woozy, she felt . . . She tried to stand, but collapsed heavily on to the floor.

'Ma'am!' She heard Bee's anguished cry, and was vaguely aware of her maid's arm about her as she drifted into a merciful blackness, which took away all the pain.

'And what do you think you're doing?' Pansy Howard stood in the door to Lily's room.

'I'm packing.'

'And might I ask where you're going?'

'You might, but I don't choose to tell you. Suffice to say, I've somewhere else to reside.' She paused to allow this information to sink in. 'Without you,' she added. Pansy said nothing, neither did she convey any emotion by so much as the twitch of an eyelid. Lily shook out the new red petticoat she had bought. This was unnecessary but she wanted her to see it and be jealous of such fine undergarments. Still there was no reaction. She folded it and added it to her other new underwear. She felt wonderfully feminine in such concoctions of silk and lace. She couldn't wait for Arnold to see her in them.

'Tart's knickers, that's what that lot is.' Pansy could keep silent no longer.

'None of your business, Moth – Pansy.' Never again would she besmirch that word by using it to this woman.

'And what's to happen to me?' There was a distinct quaver in Pansy's voice, which often developed when she was looking for sympathy.

'Quite honestly, Mother,' it didn't register with Lily that she'd forgotten her resolution already – 'I do not know. Neither do I care.' She was folding her latest blouse, bright blue with a black trim. She had promised herself that she would no longer wear drab colours – moth colours, Edith had once called them snidely.

'But, Lily, I've looked after you, cared for you all these years. How can you be so stony-hearted?' Pansy attempted to take her hand, but Lily brushed it away. 'How can you bring yourself to desert me after all I've done for you?'

'And what was that precisely?'

'When you were alone in the world I was there for you. I was young when your father died but I didn't desert you. Many would have.'

'You stayed so that you could spend my money. That was the only reason. And when that was gone you needed me to support you. Remember who you're talking to. I know the truth.'

'No, you don't. It's all lies. The shares went down, I never spent the money. I worked my fingers to the bone for you.'

'Rubbish!'

'I did. Ask anyone. I loved you, looked after you the best way I knew.'

'Whining will get you nowhere, Pansy.'

'Called me Mother a moment ago, didn't you? That shows how you think of me.'

'I did not.'

'Yes, you did. Care and responsibility isn't like a kitchen pump. It carries on, you know, through thick and thin – as I should know.'

'Not with me, it doesn't.' Lily hauled the leather case off the bed. She crammed the last of her dresses into a trunk, and sat on it, pulling the leather straps tight through the buckles. 'Damn!' she said, as the lock sprang open again. 'Can't you help me? I need your weight on this. I'm not heavy enough.'

'Me? I weigh less than a gnat.'

'You try my patience.' Lily looked at the woman she had thought her mother with a ragbag of emotions. She was angry, resentful, happy to be rid of her, yet at the back of her mind she knew she would miss her. 'If you must know, I'm not deserting you, and I don't need any lectures about facing responsibility. You're my father's widow so you can stay here and I'll pay the rent.'

'So generous,' Pansy sneered. 'And what am I to do for food?'

'Don't forget the sherry you go to the public house for.'

'Cherry lied.'

'She told me the truth. I was about to tell you, if you'd just listen, that I'm prepared to give you an allowance, provided you don't demand more or *whine*.'

'Where have you got all the money from to do this?' Pansy looked suspiciously at her. 'You haven't gone and stolen something?'

'Don't be ridiculous, I'm not a thief.'

'Then where? You could hardly be on the—' Pansy stopped.

'On the game? Was that what you were about to say? I suggest you're more careful, Mother.'

'There! You said it again!' Pansy cackled triumphantly. 'You can't just wash your hands of me. And, no, that's not what I was going to say. You're a good girl, I know that better than most. You wouldn't shame your family in that way. Never.'

'So, what were you going to accuse me of?' Lily was not prepared to let up.

'I was worried you might be on the make. That you might have some information on that Arnold.'

'Are you accusing me of blackmail? How dare you?' Lily puffed herself up with indignation.

'I was worried for you. If you did something like that you'd be in danger.' She sounded as if she had spoken in earnest.

'Danger?'

'You could end up in jug, or with your throat slit.'

'Mr Randolph-Smythe a murderer? Oh, really!' But a shiver slipped down her spine. She remembered the gossip she'd heard about the sudden deaths of his in-laws. 'I've never heard such rubbish. He's too fastidious to slit a rabbit's throat, let alone mine – that's if he had cause, which he doesn't.'

'I didn't mean he'd do it personal, like. No, he'd pay someone to do it for him.'

'I'm in the fortunate position of being able to save him

a lot of money so he has promoted me. And as an expression of his appreciation he has given me a sum of money. Satisfied now?'

Pansy stood back to let her pass. 'If you expect me to believe that, you must take me for a simpleton,' she muttered.

'What did you say?'

'He's lucky to have you,' Pansy lied.

Lily was in the sitting room of her new home from which French windows led out down two stone steps to the small garden. Her knowledge of gardening was scant but, come the spring, she would endeavour to make it a romantic bower.

She looked about her with satisfaction at the furnishings – solid, highly polished mahogany. The glass gas mantles were finely engraved. Velvet curtains hung at the door to the hall, and brocade at the window, held back by heavy gold tassels. The walls were papered in a design of roses and ivy, and above the mantelshelf, also draped in velvet, was a triple mirror. It had shelves on two sides with ornaments positioned on them. Her drop-leaf desk in the corner opened to show a satisfying array of drawers; she had yet to find the secret one. Above it was a glass cabinet full of learned-looking books. A fire glowed in the ornate iron grate, and sparkled on the highly polished fire irons.

When she had stepped into the three-bedroomed semi-detached house, she felt as if she had finally come home, that this was what she had been waiting for during the bleak, miserable years. It was what she deserved. It was what she had been born to.

Of the many properties Arnold owned she could not recall having seen any details of this one. Had he purchased and furnished it just for her? At the idea she reeled with joy. For the time being it was 22 Cedar Road, but she intended to change that – The Cedars or, perhaps,

The Gables had a better ring to it. It was a shame it was simply a road: an avenue would have been much more suitable.

The house was not in the most prestigious part of Barlton – she hadn't expected that, of course – but it was away from the harbour, the street was leafy and its residents respectable. It was only a short walk to the centre of the town, ideally placed for shopping. There was a park at the end of the road, with a bandstand, where she could go on Sundays and in the evenings when spring and summer came.

Lily settled back in the well-upholstered easy chair with a contented sigh. She even had a maid to do her chores. What more could she want? Arnold! She laughed softly at her thoughts, which were not nearly as audacious as she had once regarded them.

Through double doors she could see the dining room, with a round table that seated six easily. Above it was a pink chandelier – Italian, she was sure. She frowned. She'd read that it was not chic for drawing room and dining room to be interconnected: it pointed to a lack of space – and thus money, social standing. Still, she cheered herself with the thought that if her plans came to fruition, the unfortunate arrangement need bother her for only a short time.

She wondered who had lived here before her.

She would need a study, of course, but the breakfast room would do for that: there she would do her secret work for Arnold, away from prying eyes. It was imperative that the incriminating papers she had found in the office be put away safely. She had made sure the maid could neither read nor write so that there was no risk of her snooping. All the same she would ask him to have a safe installed.

There was much she needed to discuss with him. She had no intention of relying on his charity for long: everything must be properly agreed – the ownership of this house for a start. She would demand that it be put in her name. Then, in a couple of years when she had saved enough from the commission he had promised her, she would sell it and buy a larger house, detached, further up towards Hangman's Hill. She'd employ a cook, maybe even a coachman.

What percentage her commission should be was another matter to discuss. Perhaps it would be better to have a constant retainer, a regular income that could carry on until she died. There were so many decisions she had to make. He didn't know any of this. There was no point in discussing it with him until she had decided what she wanted to do. The amount it was going to cost him would probably come as a shock, but it couldn't be helped. 'You shouldn't have been such a bad boy!' She giggled. This was a heady time and she would savour every moment of it.

'Yes?'

The maid popped her head round the door. 'Your trunks are here, Miss.'

'Miss Howard, if you don't mind. And push those curls back under your cap. I can't be doing with unruly hair.'

'Yes, Miss Howard.'

'Send the man upstairs with the trunks and tell him not to damage the paintwork.'

The clock chimed the half-hour. That was strange, Arnold was late. Was this a sign that he was still not aware of her importance? If that was so then she would have to explain it to him in the strongest terms. He would not be disrespectful to her, that was certain.

6

Phoebe was upstairs, about to change out of her precious red dress, when she heard an almighty crash in the kitchen below. She rushed downstairs and met

Lester in the passage. He had also been alerted by the noise.

Mr Orton was sprawled on the kitchen floor, attended by an anxious Mimi. 'Is he dead?' Phoebe asked apprehensively. She had never seen anyone dead and had hoped she would never have to.

'Drunk, more like.' His son prodded him with the toe of his shoe. There was no response.

'Are you sure?'

'Look, he's breathing.' He pointed to Mr Orton's chest, which was rising and falling.

'I think he's ill.'

'He's that, all right. And it's his own fault. I've no sympathy with him.'

'What ails him?'

'He has a weak heart and—'

'And what?'

'I'd rather not say to a young woman.'

'Why not?'

'It's not fitting.'

'Such a mystery you make of it. Do tell.' But to her surprise, Phoebe couldn't persuade him. 'He told me he was an egg once. Has that got something to do with it?' Lester felt his father's temple. 'Is he going mad? What's wrong with him?' She stamped her foot, but still Lester didn't answer. 'Then don't speak to me,' she said, trying to sulk – she couldn't – it wasn't in her nature and, in any case, she was too worried, although why she should be was a mystery to her. 'Look at Mimi. He's horrible to her and yet I swear she's close to tears with worry. It's not right, is it?' They stared at the recumbent form, both unsure what to do next.

'I think we should call the doctor, Lester. He looks really poorly to me,' Phoebe said.

'It's the drink,' Lester said eventually.

'But he wasn't drunk when we came in, we'd have noticed.'

'I thought he was.'

'He looks worse than he did when we found him.'

Lester shrugged. 'It's happened before and, no doubt, it will happen again.'

'Lester! He's your father!' Even as she spoke she wondered if she wouldn't behave in exactly the same way if it were her own father lying there.

'I suppose you're right.' With an exaggerated sigh he put his coat back on. 'I'll have to walk. The horse is almost done in.' He headed out again into the cold night.

Alone with the man, Phoebe decided to fetch him a pillow and a blanket from his room. Once there, she wished she hadn't entered it. Since she had been in the house she had offered to clean it and change his bed linen, but he would not allow her across the threshold. Now she could see why. It was disgusting. Newspapers were stacked everywhere, and on the floor there were several boxes of cockle and mussel shells. Why? There were piles of dirty clothes and bowls with mouldy food. His bed looked like a repository for dirty rags. The pillows were caked with grease from his head. The sheets were grey and stained. There was a pervading smell of mice, mixed with the acrid stench of male sweat and stale urine. She rushed across the room to open the window, then went to her own room to change out of her dress into her everyday clothes.

Then she collected the bedding she needed from a spare room. 'You're a filthy old sod, aren't you?' she said, as she covered him. Lifting his head, she shuddered at the greasy feel of it. 'I shouldn't think you've washed your hair in a month of Sundays. Dirty old bugger!'

Back in his room, she pinched her nose with one hand, bundled the dirty clothes into a large pile and stripped the bed. There was no way she could let the doctor or anyone else see the state of this room, but the old man couldn't stay on the kitchen floor indefinitely.

It took her two trips to haul the linen down to the

scullery. She piled as much as she could into the copper, then poured in several buckets of water to which she added a handful of grated green soap. She lit a fire underneath, prodded the clothes about to dissolve the soap and added some more just in case there wasn't enough. Then she filled the bucket again with hot water, added more soap and climbed the stairs with broom and cloths to tackle the filth.

'He can't be left.' The doctor bent over Mr Orton but did not touch him. Phoebe couldn't blame him for that.

'Dog – out!' Imperiously he pointed at the back door.

'Yes, Doctor.' Phoebe scuttled this way and that, in awe of the man who had arrived with a large black bag full of frightenting instruments. She had never met a doctor before: when her family had been ill it had been the hedgerow plants that cured them, not a trained man.

'He should be moved.'

'He's too heavy for me,' Phoebe said.

'Lester?'

'He's not strong enough either.'

'Someone has to.'

'Can't you help me? I could take the other side.'

'*Me* ?' The doctor sounded astonished.

'I don't see anyone else in here.'

'Don't be impudent. Where's Lester?'

'I hope he's gone to get someone to help us.'

'Orton – has he had his way with you?'

'Certainly not!' Phoebe squeaked.

'Good. Sometimes they do. They see young girls as a cure.'

'I see,' she said, but she didn't understand a word he was saying.

'You read?'

'Yes,' she said, with understandable pride.

'He's taking the mercury I prescribed?'

'I wouldn't know.'

For the first time, he touched Mr Orton: he lifted his upper lip to show his gums, which were a remarkable purple colour, and nodded his head as if satisfied by what he saw. The old man's breath was fetid and Phoebe jumped back. 'Egg white and water. Mixed together.' He placed a small dark bottle on the table and wrote on the side of it. *Ipecacuanha.* He produced a feather from his case.

'Yes?' She looked doubtful. The doctor mimed putting it into his mouth. 'I see.' She didn't. Then he added a bottle of cascara. She understood that. The doctor was packing his bag. 'A moment, please. Let me see if I've understood properly. I'm to give him the eggs, then the ipecack – or whatever it's called. Or the other way around?'

The doctor tore a sheet of paper from his notepad and scribbled instructions for her. 'Have I got to tickle the back of his throat with the feather to make him sick? And give him the cascara so that his bowels open? It will be a pleasure,' she said, with irony.

The doctor snapped his bag shut. 'Tomorrow.' He was out of the door.

'A moment. Do I pour this stuff down him while he's asleep? Or should I wait for him to wake?' But he had gone.

Lester returned with the farm labourer, Oz. The debate as to how best to move him took some time. 'I'd best be carrying him meself. Don't think you'm up to it, Mr Lester.'

'If you wouldn't mind, Oz.'

With a fine amount of huffing and puffing and an even choicer string of expletives, Oz manhandled Mr Orton over his shoulder and they got him to his room. It took all three of them to strip him.

'I ought to wash him,' said Phoebe, who wanted to do no such thing but thought she should.

'He'll catch his death,' Oz objected.

'Let's just get him into bed and forget it all until the morning.' Lester sounded so cold.

'I'll ask my wife to give you a hand.'

'That would be very kind of you, Mr Oz,' Phoebe said, unsure how to address him.

Once Mr Orton was in bed and covered with the blanket, Phoebe turned his head to one side, in case he was sick. She thought she ought to sit with him but she compromised by leaving the oil lamp on and the door ajar.

In the kitchen Oz and Lester were drinking cider. Judging by Oz's colour this was not the first of the evening. 'You'd be better off if the old fellow never came round, Lester.'

'I don't like him, Oz, but I can't bring myself to wish him dead.'

I could, thought Phoebe, but at least Lester was now behaving more like a son.

'If he croaks, what will you do?'

'Be happy.' Lester smiled.

Well, almost a proper son, Phoebe thought.

'Good ambition that, my boy. Well, I'd best be on my way. At least you'll have some peace now, girl.' Oz put on his large hat and stomped out of the kitchen.

'Just look at the mess his boots have made. Cows' muck everywhere.' She stood up to clean the floor.

'Phoebe, sit down, I want to talk to you.'

'What did he mean, that I'd have some peace now? He doesn't think – no! He couldn't be thinking that I'm with your father? I'd hate anyone to think that. It's disgusting.'

'I don't know what he meant. Does it matter? Look, Phoebe, I never showed you what I bought you.' He took a large package off the dresser. 'Open it.'

Inside, there were three bolts of cloth: a green satin, a blue tweed and a pink cotton. 'For me?'

'I want you to look pretty. Now I know how to, I want to make you some lovely clothes. I've ordered a sewing machine. I thought I was going to have to hide it from the old man, but he need not know.'

'These came from *his* shop?'

'Randolph's? Yes.'

She pushed the bundle across the table towards him. 'I want nothing of his.'

'But they aren't his any more, they're mine, and I'm giving them to you.'

'It's just I don't want any contact—'

'Phoebe,' Lester took her hand, 'I do understand, you know.'

'I doubt it.'

'Yes, I do. I know what it is to be afraid.'

'Of course.'

'If the old man dies, am I to refuse his money because he hated me and was cruel to me? No, I shall enjoy it all the more, knowing how my wasting it would have annoyed him. My only regret is he won't see me. But I can make you look like a princess, and show Arnold Randolph-Smythe what a superior person you are.'

'Could you?'

'Yes. My father's going to die. I met the doctor in the yard and he says it's only a matter of days. He says I should have him committed to the asylum.'

'Will you?'

'I'll think about it.'

'What ails him?'

'I'd rather not say.'

'But you must. If I'm to help with him—'

'Very well, but I'd prefer it if you didn't say anything to Oz. He's fast approaching the final stages of something called the general paralysis of the insane.'

'He's mad.'

'Yes.'

'I thought he was.'

'The past three or so years.'

'It must have been horrible for you.'

'It wasn't as if I loved him.'

'If it helps you I'll look after him.'

'I can't expect you to.'

'As I said, not for him but for you. If you don't want to send him away. Everybody would know then, wouldn't they?'

'You're very kind. Neither of us deserves you.'

'Don't be silly!' She pushed him playfully.

'Everything will change. Soon I shall have money and I shall sell this farm. Then you and I can go anywhere in the world we want. We could buy a house in Italy, or perhaps go to America.'

'I'm not sure I'd want to,' she said, feeling a little apprehensive at the way he was planning their future.

'Of course you will. You're mine. Where I go you go – just like in the Bible.'

'But—'

'I suggest you listen to me, Phoebe. There are no buts.' She was shocked at the cold way he was looking at her. His moods this evening were changing all the time. Perhaps it would be best to agree with him.

'It sounds lovely, but I wouldn't want to impose.'

'You? Impose on me?' He laughed at the very idea. 'I love you, Phoebe. My Phoebe.' He smiled at her with such a gentle expression that she wondered if she hadn't imagined the coolness of just a moment ago. 'I want to protect you, spoil you. Love you.'

'But, Lester, it wouldn't be possible, as you explained to me.'

'Perhaps I couldn't love you in the way you would wish me to, but I do love your soul.'

'That wouldn't keep me warm at night!' She laughed.

He hit her. She looked at him, startled, then tears stung her eyes.

'Phoebe, forgive me, I don't know what came over me.

I adore you. I want to marry you – keep you safe, keep you mine, always.'

'Lester!' was all she said, and dread touched her.

7

'You promised you'd come the evening I moved here and you didn't.' Lily was trying to be prettily petulant but she sounded merely waspish. 'It's Christmas Eve and only now have you condescended to visit.' That was worse. 'Perhaps you have been too busy?' Better. 'You must not continue in this manner, Arnold, I don't like it.' Oh dear, she thought, but she couldn't help herself.

'It could not be helped.' He went to the sideboard in the dining room and poured himself a large measure of whisky. Lily frowned. This was her house and he should have had the courtesy to ask. Maybe she should lock the tantalus. He hadn't even asked if she wanted a drink.

'An apology might be forthcoming. It is customary when there has been such a lapse of manners.'

'My wife is seriously ill.' He swung round to face her. Were those tears in his eyes?

'I'm so sorry,' she said automatically, while thinking that this was the best news she had heard in a long time. 'She will recover?'

'The doctor will not commit himself. I could hardly leave her within an hour of her collapse to come and see you, could I?'

'She collapsed?'

'For days I kept vigil at her bedside.' He shook out a handkerchief and dabbed at his eyes.

'Collapsed, you said?' she persisted.

'Her heart.'

'All that weight. Have you not noticed among your acquaintances that the more self-indulgent they are the more likely they are to have a seizure?' Lily brushed down the bodice of her skirt, ensuring that he noticed how neat her own waist was.

'You mean fat?'

'Arnold, you could not possibly expect me to describe your wife in such a vulgar manner.' She fluttered her eyelashes at him. She had painted them with a paste of soot and a little water and the result was pleasing: they were longer, thicker, and enhanced the grey of her eyes.

'She is most certainly stout and has been getting short of breath recently.'

Better and better, thought Lily. 'Then it's serious?' She had difficulty keeping her pleasure out of her voice.

'It's been dreadful.' He sat down abruptly and closed his eyes. She was sure he was acting, and he didn't have to pretend to her, of all people. Why did he do it? Perhaps Dulcie wasn't ill at all. Perhaps he was deceiving her with another woman and trying to throw her off the scent? She had to find out. Meanwhile, she would pretend to believe every word he said. 'When you didn't come I nearly went to the shop to see what was happening.'

'They would not have let you in.'

'Have you not told them we are friends again?'

'No.'

'Arnold, why ever not?' She felt a frisson of anger.

'I haven't been to the office for days,' he said.

'Arnold, is that wise?' She pursed her lips into which she had rubbed beetroot juice – another experiment. She had read of it in the *Ladies' Journal*.

'How could I? What sort of impression would that have given?'

'You're here now.'

'I shouldn't be but I couldn't delay a moment longer.'

'Oh, Arnold,' she said, flitting across the room to him and sinking gracefully at his feet. But he stood up and went to replenish his drink, leaving her feeling foolish.

She hauled herself up, and surreptitiously adjusted her corset, which was digging into her.

He returned with his drink but this time he sat down on the opposite side of the fireplace in an upright chair.

'I don't understand why it should be unwise for me not to go to my office,' Lily said. Then she added, 'You look most uncomfortable there. Come back.' She patted the easy chair.

'I'm content here. You were saying?'

'All your papers are there. What if someone else saw them?' Defeated in her attempts at seduction, she returned to matters in which she had more confidence.

'What if they did?'

'You can be so heedless. I know I'm more intelligent than most people but there is always a possibility that others might draw the conclusions I have. That could be disastrous for you.'

'What? Having two people blackmailing me?'

'Arnold! How could you say such a terrible thing to me? I'm trying to help you because I care for you.' She laid her hand on his arm.

'May I offer you refreshment?' he asked. To her disappointment he did not pick up her hand as he was supposed to but stood up to pour himself yet another drink.

'Lemonade would be nice. Thank you'. She collected herself. She must not be too pushy, or she would frighten him. 'I shall go to the office myself in the morning and collect together everything that is compromising,' she said.

'No.'

'You shall write me a note to give to that unspeakable Shepperton who was so rude to me the other day. You must dismiss the oaf, Arnold, for my sake.'

'I shall do no such thing. Neither will you go to the office in my stead.'

'Arnold!'

'It would be most unwise.'

'How could that be so? Then you will go and bring the papers here.'

'I shall not.'

'If you have a safe installed, I can care for them.'

'Dear Miss Howard, you are not listening to me.' His voice was soft suddenly, and thrilled her.

'Lily, please,' she said, widening her eyes and fluttering her eyelashes again. 'If you don't want to do that, I shall return to my position and take care of them there. Oh, Arnold, there is so much I want to point out to you, how much cleverer you can be with me to help you'

'No. You will not return.'

'Arnold! Why not?'

'It would not be wise.'

'Have a care.' Was he never to take her seriously? 'I need to work, Arnold. My brain needs challenge. I can't just be your plaything.'

Arnold spluttered, then had a coughing fit. Lily fetched him some water. 'Forgive me, Lily.' She clasped her hands to her meagre bosom. 'You don't appear to understand. I want you to be happy – you need never work again.' His smile grew broader as he spoke as if he was about to break into laughter from sheer joy.

She felt her heart-rate increase alarmingly. 'How kind you are.'

Then he got up, and before she knew what was happening, he was kissing her, his arms holding her so masterfully. She thought she would faint from the sheer intensity of her joy. Then he said, 'Forgive me, I must return to my wife.' She had not had time to recover before she heard the front door slam and then the sound of his dear feet on the pavement outside.

'Oh, Arnold,' she sighed in a dream. She wafted over to the mirror which hung over the mantle. 'Oh Arnold! No!' She screamed as she saw her soot-streaked face.

Alone Lily found Christmas Day intolerable. After a meagre lunch, she magnanimously gave the maid the rest of the day off and visited Pansy, who was in the public house up the road.

She hadn't even had the grace to look ashamed, thought Lily, as she walked home through a light sprinkling of snow. Nor had she been overjoyed with the silk handkerchief Lily had given her: instead she had pointed out acidly that she had given Lily that handkerchief five years ago.

Everything would be different next Christmas. Then she would be entertaining a large party. Why, she would even have a ready-made family – she would be a stepmother, perhaps even a mother herself. The thought made her feel dizzy with emotion. She quickened her step but instead of turning into Cedar Road, she continued on her way to Hangman's Hill.

Of course, it was inconvenient that Dulcie was still alive. But he had said she was extremely ill.

As she walked she peered into the windows of the houses, seeing the families within, the decorations, imagining their merriment.

If Dulcie didn't succumb . . . It was not a pleasant thought. She had to die! It would be better for everyone, including Dulcie, who, after all, was not happy. It would be a release from her misery. And yet . . . She was such a kind woman . . . It would be a shame. 'No,' Lily said emphatically. Sentimentality must not interfere with her plans.

If Arnold had any sense he would make sure she died. After all, if the rumours about him were true he would know how to go about it.

The houses on this road were so grand. Suddenly it struck her that there was no street lighting, just as there was none where she had lived with Pansy. Yet there was good illumination on Cedar Road. She had almost reached Arnold's when she thought she had found the solution. Down by the harbour nobody cared what befell the residents at night, and up here there was no need for lighting since the inhabitants did not walk the streets: they stayed in their houses or drove in their carriages.

She walked past Arnold's house purposefully, as if she had all the right in the world to be there. Which, of course, she did. There were more lights in his house than in any other on this road. Of course, Arnold had electricity. Nor did he mind how much of it he burnt, for as she looked up she could see that there wasn't a window in the house from which light was not blazing. Such a display of wealth! Why, it was no doubt costing him ten times more than gas. Such finesse! Such riches!

It was called December Cottage, a ludicrous name for such a large, beautiful house. She had once asked Arnold why.

'It's always had that name.'

'But why have you not changed it, Mr Randolph-Smythe, a man of your standing? The Grange, or The Hall would be so much more suitable.'

'I couldn't agree with you more, Miss Howard, but my wife feels it would be bad luck to change it.'

'Like a ship?'

'I presume so. You ladies are often a mystery to we mere men.'

Lily was still in a daze from last night. When she had gone to bed she couldn't sleep for excitement. That he should have kissed her! It was the culmination of so many years of dreams that she had never thought would come true. That he wanted *her* was little short of a miracle. She was not pretty, but much could be done, these days, and she had a trim figure.

At the top of the hill there was a bench in memory of a long-dead alderman and she sat down to rest for a while: it was a steep hill. She had much to offer him – knowing how to behave for one thing, not like that execrable Edith. She was highly intelligent and could be of use to him in so many ways. Would he stray? He was the sort of man who couldn't resist a pretty face and well-turned ankle.

Suddenly a carriage was racing up the hill and swerved into Arnold's gateway. The doctor.

Ten minutes later she sauntered down the hill, just in time to see the doctor leave. It couldn't have been that bad, then: he wouldn't have been away so quickly if Dulcie was dying.

Lily had always believed in being prepared. She was sure she had seen a rat in the cellar of her new house: she would have to visit the chemist for some advice.

Six days later Lily was restless. She had bought the paper every day and turned first to the births, marriages and deaths. Every day the notice she longed to see wasn't there. She had sacked the maid for burning a saucepan, breaking a cup and for what she regarded as insolence: the girl would keep calling her 'miss'. As if she was a shopgirl!

'Good riddance to you!' The girl had screamed. 'At least the last bitch was a bit more pleasant than you, and we had a few giggles.'

Lily threw her bag of possessions down the stairs. 'And what does that mean?'

'His last fancy-girl. Still we could hardly call you that, could we? You're more like a fancy-crone!' She'd laughed.

'How dare you?'

'I dare as much as I want.'

'I shall give you no recommendation.'

'I don't need one. I'm going to Miss Edith's to look after her and her new fancy man!'

'New?'

'Yes, and he's a swell, not like that Arnold. After all, what's he but a tradesman?' And with this the girl had slammed out of the front door.

Lily had been rendered speechless by this information. She had thought he had purchased this house for her, furnished it for her. She had thought he had rid himself of Edith for her. Now she knew that it was he who had been dropped. She needed to confront him. He would pay dearly for this.

The restlessness worsened. She was lonely, she realised. If she wasn't seeing Arnold because of Dulcie, and if he wouldn't let her work in the office, she would find herself another position. She turned to the situations vacant, and saw the perfect position for her.

On New Year's Eve she attended for her interview. 'I've an appointment,' she told the clerk on the desk. 'Miss Howard, to see Mr Battle.'

8

Dulcie, reclining on a chaise longue in her boudoir, could hear voices in the hall below. 'Bee?' she called to her maid, who was readying her bed in the next-door room. 'Bee, who is making that noise?'

'There, there, ma'am. Don't you fret.' Bee appeared in the doorway and came over to fuss with the fur cover that should have been over Dulcie's legs. She had pushed it off because the heat from the fire was intense.

'I am *not* fretting. What a strange word to use.' Dulcie grabbed at the cover Bee was rearranging. 'Leave that! I'm sweltering.' She was not sure what had made her so irritable, but she was tired of doing nothing and it was New Year's Eve – with no news of Chauncey. Then seeing Bee's expression, she was ashamed of herself. 'I'm sorry, Bee, I shouldn't have snapped at you, but I heard that exciting noise and you expect me not to be curious. Go and see who's downstairs.'

'I'm sure it's just the master and Miss Agnes, getting ready for the Assembly.'

'At least I shan't be attending that. Bee, see who it is.'

'Now, you know the doctor said you're to be kept quiet. If it's anyone it'll be young friends of Miss Agnes, and you don't want them up here, do you?'

'I might. If I'm kept much quieter I shall think I'm dead! I'd forgotten about the Assembly. You know, Bee, illness can sometimes be a blessing.'

'We don't want many more blessings like that, thank you, ma'am.'

'I did give everyone a scare, didn't I? And ruined Christmas into the bargain.'

'You couldn't help that, ma'am.'

'New Year's Eve. Where has this year gone, Bee? And all the years before? Imagine, a new century dawning and we privileged to see it.' She watched her maid pottering about the room. They had been together for so long now. Bee had been with her through all her disappointments and sadness. New Year's Eve – it should be exciting but she felt melancholic. 'I think we should have champagne at midnight, just you and me, Bee. What do you say? It is cause for a celebration.' Perhaps then she would be able to enter into the spirit of it.

'I'd never say no to a glass of bubbly, ma'am. But I find New Year a sad time. You have to say goodbye to the old, and even if it's not been a good one I worry what the new one will hold. And how can we be celebrating with all those poor souls in South Africa and under siege? Don't bear thinking about, the goings-on and all. Seems wrong to me.'

'Of course you're quite right, Bee.' She hadn't thought of that. How selfish of her, just because she knew her son was safe.

'All the talk is of change in the air, what with the old queen so frail these days, but I don't want nothing to change, ma'am. I want us all to go on in the old ways.'

'The old ways? No, Bee, not for me. I'm looking

forward to as many changes as possible.' She permitted herself a small, self-satisfied smile.

Another roar of laughter floated up from downstairs. 'I recognise that laugh.' She sat up. 'Give me a mirror, my hairbrush and the peignoir with lilies-of-the-valley embroidered on it. My scent too. Then go and see who it is in case I'm wrong.' Bee handed them to her and left the room. Within a minute she was back.

'It's Mr Edward and Lord Prestwick.'

'I thought it was.' A broad smile appeared on Dulcie's face. 'How lovely. Please fetch them up.'

'Here, Mrs Randolph?' Bee's lips were pursed in disapproval.

'Yes, Bee. And give a good spray of scent. Is it musty in here? Does it smell of the sickroom?'

'Smells as sweet as springtime, ma'am. I've seen to that. But do you think you ought? Don't want you to get overexcited.'

'You're turning into a difficult old woman – just go! I look forward to some company.' She peered into the mirror and brushed her hair. At least it looked a little better, thicker, when it was loose. She pinched her cheeks to get some colour into them, plumped up her cushions and settled back contentedly. She looked up at the knock on the door, but was disappointed to see Arnold.

'Do you think this is wise?'

'What, Arnold?'

'Entertaining in your boudoir – and a peer of the realm to boot.'

'I think it's perfectly reasonable. I shall have Bee to chaperone me and I am respectably clothed.'

'I'm not sure that I want my wife to receive gentlemen in this manner.'

'Poppycock!'

'It's not seemly.'

'How on earth would you, of all people, know what is seemly?'

'These past few weeks, Dulcie, you have been quite unpleasant and irascible.'

'I shan't apologise.'

He looked perplexed. 'But the doctor insisted you should rest.'

'He's a fool. I'm so much better. I look forward to receiving *my* friends.' As she stood up she felt faint, but after more than a week in bed it was hardly surprising.

'What are you doing?'

'I shall change my robe and sit in that chair. Is that seemly enough for you?' She forced herself to walk without a hint of a stagger towards her dressing room. 'Send Bee to me, if you would be so kind, and ask Lord Prestwick to be patient.'

With Bee's help she changed into a loose velvet gown, and had her tie back her hair into a plait.

Ten minutes later Lord Prestwick exploded into the room. He had not ventured further than three feet before a side-table went flying, scattering bibelots in every direction. 'My dear Mrs Randolph, such an oaf I am. Such a clod.'

'It's the stupidest of tables, Lord Prestwick, most unstable. And Edward, what a joy this is.'

'I was just saying to Mr Bartholomew-Prestwick, Mama, how wonderful it is that we shall all be at the ball. Such excitement.' Agnes appeared from behind Edward, swept across the room and kissed her cheek. 'Dearest Mama, you look so well tonight,' she said, and sank elegantly into a chair.

'We can't be late, Agnes. Remember, you're helping me to host this Assembly.' Arnold was looking at his watch.

'A minute, Papa, please. I'm so excited to see our new friends. I'd no idea you were attending, Mr Bartholomew-Prestwick, or you could have been one of our party.'

'I did not know I was to be here until yesterday. My uncle wishes to see me.'

Dulcie wondered if it was her imagination or whether the young man had given her husband a stern look. 'Has a problem occurred with the purchase of your uncle's property in Gold Street?' she said, with a sudden flash of inspiration.

'Dulcie?' Arnold's question mirrored his surprise.

'The property you have already boasted is yours?'

'Boasted? How could you say such a thing?'

'Admittedly you haven't told me but, then, you never do.'

'Dulcie, dear heart, you are embarrassing our guests and shaming our daughter.'

It was you I wanted to shame and embarrass, she thought. But she enjoyed Arnold's thunderous expression. He was even blushing slightly. However, she was distressed to see Lord Prestwick looking equally put out.

'Come, Agnes, we must be leaving,' Arnold said, looking agitated and – for the first time that Dulcie could remember – awkward. 'I shall look forward to seeing you two gentlemen later, and especially to talking with you, Edward.'

'Shall you dance with me, Mr Bartholomew-Prestwick?'

'It would be an honour, Miss Randolph-Smythe.' He stood up and bowed elegantly.

'À bientôt,' she said, and the door closed behind them.

'I seem to lose all discretion in your company, Lord Prestwick. I must apologise. It was an unpardonable comment for me to make.' She hoped she hadn't shocked him out of wanting to spend time with her.

'I'm not sure to what you refer, Mrs Randolph,' he said, with the merry twinkle in his eye that she so liked.

'You are more courteous than I. Thank you. A drink, Lord Prestwick, Edward?'

'How very kind.'

'Champagne?'

'To say goodbye to 1899? A splendid idea.'

'Bee, could you arrange that for me? And if you would bring me the little parcel on my bureau . . .' She took it from her maid and looked shyly at Lord Prestwick. 'A small memento.'

'For me?'

'But of course.'

'May I open it now?'

'I had intended it as a surprise for Christmas, but tonight seems just as appropriate.'

She watched eagerly as, like a child, he tore impatiently at the wrapping. He lifted the lid of the box it had covered and peeped inside. 'My dear Mrs Randolph, what have we here?' He took out a red bowl with a gold rim.

'Isn't that . . . ?'

'Yes, Edward, it is. This, dear, clever lady has found a replacement for the piece of my Pouyat dinner service you broke when you were three.'

'Which one of us should thank you most?' Edward smiled at his father's pleasure. 'You are most generous, Mrs Randolph.'

'Not at all. A dealer with whom I have a connection in London had found this and I just happened to mention . . .' She made it sound as if it had happened by chance when in fact she had written to every dealer in porcelain, every auction house and museum just to track down this one piece. The dealer, suspecting its importance to her, had charged her twice its value. But no matter, she thought. It was worth every penny just to see the expression on her friend's face.

'But we're tiring you. Perhaps we should forgo the champagne and leave?' Lord Prestwick stood up.

'No, please, spare me five more minutes. I have been so weary of being confined to bed. I think that my doctor, while a kind man, has immobilised me unnecessarily.'

'Better to be safe than sorry.'

'Perhaps, Lord Prestwick, but I might die of boredom instead.'

'I had heard you were in a coma.'

'How ridiculous! I fainted. I should not have had that second slice of chocolate cake the last time we met. There is no doubt in my mind that that was the problem.'

'I am relieved to hear it. But you will miss the Mayor's Assembly.'

'And I'm glad of it.' She laughed. 'For years I have pretended to enjoy the company of those I don't like and with whom I have little in common. My New Year resolution is not to do anything that irks me.'

'How wise you are, Mrs Randolph. Perhaps I shall make that my resolution too. And if I am not one of those who are irksome to you, perhaps I could refuse the invitation to the Assembly, which, like you, I do not wish to attend.'

'You? Irksome to me? I never heard such rubbish. Perhaps instead you would care to join me for supper? A light meal, I'm afraid – the staff have plans of their own on such a momentous night.'

'Better for me.' He patted his girth, laughing. What a simple, happy man he is, thought Dulcie.

'I envy you both, but I promised my uncle . . .' Edward got up to go.

'I know I behaved badly a moment ago. But I need to know this. What has my husband done, Edward?'

The young man looked trapped and glanced at his father.

'He's cheating Kendall Bartholomew out of a rather large sum of money,' Lord Prestwick told her.

'Father!'

'I think Mrs Randolph has a right to know, Edward. You see, Mrs Randolph, when Edward tried to see your husband about it he was told you were dying of a heart condition and so, out of respect, we stayed away. Prior to this he could get no appointment at his office. Then I met your doctor, an old friend of mine, who told me you had been unwell but that you were on the road to recovery. Tonight I resolved to find out for myself how you were, using the New Year as an excuse.'

'I had an infection of my lungs. I had been overdoing things for a couple of weeks and a cold developed, that was all.' No doubt Arnold had been telling everyone what he wanted to happen to her! 'Has he bought the property in Barlton?'

'He has and he hasn't.' Edward began a long explanation of the deal that his uncle and Arnold had agreed on, unfortunately for Mr Bartholomew, with a handshake. 'A considerable sum of the principal was due on December the first, Mrs Randolph.'

'Was it not rather unwise to leave everything to the handshake, Edward?'

'My uncle insisted against my better judgement. He said he had had many financial dealings with Mr Randolph-Smythe in the past and had no reason to disbelieve him. And for a gentleman, of course, a handshake is binding.'

But Arnold isn't a gentleman, she thought. 'You were wary, though?' she asked.

'This is difficult, Mrs Randolph. He is your husband.'

'Our conversation is in confidence, Edward. Whatever you say, if it is the truth I shall not hold it against you.'

'Very well. I did not trust him. I had heard rumours. But that was all.'

The poor young man looked ill with worry.

'And now your uncle is blaming you?'

'How on earth did you know that?'

'It seems to me the logical conclusion. Some people, if at fault, will always find someone else to blame.' Arnold and Mr Bartholomew were obviously of a pair. 'My advice to your uncle is to sue my husband.'

'Sue him?' Edward's voice rose in astonishment. 'But the scandal!'

Dulcie shrugged. 'If it has to be, then so be it. But I don't think it will come to that. The threat will be sufficient. I am sure that if you do, Arnold will find the money very quickly. And if he does not I will pay your uncle myself. Thank you for being so open with me, Edward.'

'It was hard.'

'Of course, but truth is usually best. Now you should be off to the dance – and don't worry. It will all be resolved.' She smiled brightly at him.

'You're a wise woman, Mrs Randolph.'

'Not really. If I was I would not have been duped for so many years. But the worm is turning, even if a little late in the day. Now, Lord Prestwick, I have a particularly fine Château Latour '72 from my father's cellar. Perhaps you would enjoy it before we have the champagne?'

'As I said, Mrs Randolph, you are a wise woman!'

'Is it presumptuous and too conventional of me to wonder if you might call me Dulcie?'

'It would be an unsurpassed honour, provided you will call me Theo.'

At one in the morning, after Theo Prestwick had left, Dulcie gladly allow Bee to fuss over her as she helped her to bed. She was tired. She lay in the darkened room, listening to the sirens of the boats in the harbour, the cheering from the town, the fireworks. Without doubt this was the happiest New Year's Eve she had ever enjoyed. But there was more. Dulcie knew she was in love – she had thought she was but now she knew for certain. Sadly, nothing could ever come of it because she was married – and who could love her? But loving him was enough to make her happy. And she could dream. In her dreams she was beautiful, slim, vivacious, and there was no Arnold. She was free to love and be loved.

Phoebe was attacking the parlour. In her opinion all parlours smelt the same – musty stale air, mothballs and mice. Always mice! At least, all the ones she knew did. If she closed her eyes she could imagine herself back at Cowman's Combe.

'Do you want to go back there, then?' she asked herself.

'No!'

'Then what are you going to do?'

Phoebe pushed hard at the harmonium that stood in the corner of the room. It was heavy. The music stand was made of ornate fretwork and she wondered how to get at the dust lodged in its swirls and curlicues. That was another puzzle: how could a room that was never used become so dusty? The vicar's wife had a harmonium like this. She would know how to clean it.

She pushed the harmonium back into its place, then sat on the little stool that matched it, and found that the seat revolved, getting higher. If she went fast enough and high enough would it shoot her out of the roof and away?

'Away.' She sighed. That was all she ever did about getting away: she sighed, dreamed, planned, then did nothing. She was afraid to run, but she was fast becoming afraid to stay. It was Lester. He was different from when she had first come here. He was constantly losing his temper, not just with her but with Maudie, who helped Phoebe care for his father, and Oz, her husband, who helped him. She'd seen him hurl a chair across the room because it was in his way, and rip a cupboard door off its hinges because it was stuck.

She wondered if it was worry about the father he professed to hate. In Cowman's Combe one of their neighbours was always saying how she hated her husband and longed to screw down his coffin lid. When he died she followed him a week later, broken by grief. Perhaps Lester was the same.

'Or he's frightened old man Orton's left his money to some fancy lady.'

'That could be so, Phyllis. You never know.'

She turned the stool in the opposite direction until she had lowered herself, then lifted the lid of the instrument, placed her feet on the two large pedals and pumped her legs up and down. The bellows wheezed and whistled, and still working her legs, she put her hands on the keys, fingers splayed, and pressed down. A discordant note issued forth, so she tried a second and then a third.

Lester appeared in the doorway. 'What on earth do you think you're doing?'

'Playing.' She laughed. 'Don't I make a lovely noise?'

'Not on that you don't.' He crossed the room and smashed down the lid, catching her fingers before she'd had time to remove them.

'What did you do that for? You've hurt me,' she wailed sucking her fingers.

'That was my mother's most precious possession. No one touches it, ever!' He was shaking.

'You should have told me,' she shouted. 'I won't touch the blessed thing again.' She ducked as Lester raised his hand. 'Don't you dare!' she yelled. 'No one hits me.' She jumped up from the stool and faced him. His complexion was mottled, his eyes were glistening and looked wild.

'Then behave yourself,' he snapped.

'I was cleaning it. I didn't know it was a holy relic.' Anger was making her reckless.

'Get out of here.'

'With pleasure.' She flounced past him, ran up the stair, past the old man's room, then on up to the attic. She slammed the door, heaved a chest of drawers across the room and wedged it against it.

That was the second time he had hurt her. Their friendship had disappeared: now he argued with her, gave her orders. Why had he changed? Was she to blame?

Five minutes later there was a tap on the door. 'Phoebe, I want to talk to you.' He sounded quieter, more in control.

'Well, I don't want to talk to *you*!'

'Please.'

'There's nothing to say.'

'I'm sorry I shouted.'

'You did more than shout.'

'I wouldn't have hit you.'

'How can I believe that when you have just slammed that lid on my fingers? Go away, Lester. I don't wish to see you, or talk to you.'

She heard him slump on to the floor and what she took to be his head bang against the door. Then he began to cry. She rolled her eyes. What a child he was. And he wanted her to love him.

She lay down on the bed. After he had declared his love for her she had moved out of his room and into this tiny one, high in the eaves. He had not wanted her to leave his.

'If you love me, as you say, and we sleep in the same bed, something will happen,' she had explained.

'But if you love me you would want it to.'

'How could I when I don't love you?' The first time she had said those words he had winced. She had felt guilty that she didn't, and sorry for him that she couldn't. Now he was constantly pleading with her to change her mind, so she felt no compunction in saying it.

'I told you I'd marry you,' he had said one evening, when she had rejected him once more.

'How can I vow to love, honour and obey when I know it would be lies? And in God's house! How could you ask me?' She had been proud of that, thinking how pleased her father would have been, which made her smile to herself. But Lester demanded to know why she smiled.

'Do you want to control what I think?'

'You're mine. You do, say and think as I want.'

'I belong to no one, and especially not to you,' she had yelled bravely.

'Yes, you do!'

That time she had stormed out of the kitchen, for once having had the sense not to argue with him. But she had resolved to hide her smiles in the future.

About half an hour later she heard him shuffle away. She could not go on like this. Next time he might hit her and, skinny as he was, she knew that temper gave strength to anyone. She also knew, from her experiences with her father, that violence increased, never the reverse. She had hoped to wait for better weather: the first week in January, with snow threatening, was hardly the best time of the year to be on the road.

'At least you'd have some nice clothes to take with you.'

She looked at her fine new dresses hanging on the wall. 'I couldn't take them.'

'Why not?'

'It wouldn't be right. And, in any case, I don't want to be beholden.'

'How will you get employment, dressed like a tramp?'

'Something will turn up. It nearly always does.'

Without meaning to she fell asleep and awoke to a tapping on her bedroom door. 'Go away,' she shouted.

'Are you sure?' asked a woman's voice, bubbling with laughter.

'Is that the time? I'm sorry, Maudie.'

'I'll make a start.'

Phoebe splashed some cold water on her face from the jug on her washstand and rubbed it dry. The towel was rough against her skin, and she remembered the softness, the sweet smell of the towels at Mr Bartholomew's. 'One day,' she said.

'When beggars can ride!' Phyllis answered.

Maudie Cheeseman was already at work in Mr Orton's bedroom. She came twice a day to help Phoebe clean him. Lester had refused to help, as he had rejected the advice to send his father away to be nursed properly and declined to say why he had changed his mind. Without the large, good-natured woman, Phoebe had no idea how she would manage. It was never a pleasant task but Maudie made it bearable.

'Sorry, Maudie, I fell asleep.'

'Not like you, Phoebe, to be nodding off in the afternoon. Had a swig, did you?' She pulled Mr Orton towards her, so that Phoebe could wash his nether regions.

'I don't like the taste of it.'

'I couldn't face this job without a good dollop of gin in me. It'd do you no harm, girl.' She yanked him over, using her considerable bulk to steady him so that Phoebe could roll up the undersheet. She put a clean one in its place. Although he was conscious, Mr Orton said nothing. He was being given large doses of laudanum to keep him quiet since no one could deal with him when he was raving. 'That Lester was acting peculiar again. Said he didn't know where you were. How could he not know that?'

'I had to lock myself into my room, Maudie. Look.' She held up her bruised hands.

'You want to watch him – he might look like a milksop but they often have more strength than you know. I'll do the heavy stuff here – you can't, with your hands like that.'

'But why is he changing?'

'I can't be sure, but my Oz reckons he's taking too much of that there opium stuff. He has mad dreams. Oz has seen him dancing naked in the garden. Said he was a fairy.'

'And Mr Orton here thinks he's turned into a pig.'

'I couldn't have described him better meself.' Together they rolled him on to his back.

'Heaven above, I think he gets heavier.' Maudie wiped the sweat from her brow with her apron.

'Before that he thought he was an egg, then a rabbit. What a family!' Phoebe laughed.

'It's the madness. Dreadful disease, this. And now his legs have given out. Still, that's probably a good thing otherwise we'd never keep him in here. He'd be after you, that's for sure. They go mad for a bit of quim, dirty old buggers like him.'

Phoebe was wide-eyed with horror. 'Maudie, you don't think they've got the same thing? That Lester will go the way of his father?'

'He's not like other men, if you knows what I mean.' Maudie bustled about collecting the dirty linen. Phoebe averted her face. The smell was appalling. 'Did you talk to Lester about all these newspapers? Will he let us throw them out? You can hardly swing a cat in here.'

'He says no. His father will be furious when he gets better.'

'He's not going to get better. Are you, my handsome?' Maudie asked, as she tried to spoon the gruel Phoebe had made into his mouth. He kept turning his mouth away from the spoon. 'If you don't eat you'll be a goner even sooner. Now, then, you great baby, open wide for Maudie . . .'

'I'll take these down to the scullery and put the kettle on.' Phoebe took one last look round the cluttered room. No matter what they did in here it always looked a mess.

As she lit the copper she acknowledged that she was worse off here than she had been at home. To have to look after a man she did not like was the hardest thing of all. She knew she would do anything for Edward, but Mr

Orton – God help her, there were days when she entered his room hoping he was dead.

'He wants to marry me.' Phoebe put the tea on the table with a bottle of Mr Orton's whisky. She had found it in a cupboard and kept it for Maudie, who enjoyed a drop in her tea.

'Who?'

'Lester.'

'Have you accepted?'

'No! I couldn't.'

'When the old man pegs it, he'll be worth a pretty penny. You might never find a better opportunity.'

'I don't love him.'

'Phoebe, love don't keep you warm in winter, or feed the kids. It never lasts. You mind my words. But money! Now you'm talking.'

'I couldn't marry just for money.'

'Then you're a fool and I never thought that of 'ee.' Maudie took a noisy sip of her tea. 'That warms the cockles.'

'But he can't . . . you know. He wouldn't . . . I'd want children.' She was bright red with confusion.

'Wouldn't stop him making babies, as far as I've heard. And him being as he is, he's likely to leave you alone most of the time and that would be a good thing. I wish my Oz would – he thinks of nothing else. He's on at me all the time, morning, noon and night.'

This confidence made Phoebe blush even more – she did not want to think about ungainly Oz and large fat Maudie with their old bodies together.

'Take my advice,' Maudie went on. 'Marry the milksop. Enjoy his money. I would.'

'I don't like it here. I want a different life.'

'Daydreams never fed no one. Think on it, my girl. How are you to get this better life? You've nothing, no one. But I has to say that if you do go and marry him you'd be advised to have someone live in. After the puppies . . . well . . . God knows what he might get up to.' Maudie sucked her teeth and nodded sagely.

'The puppies?'

'I weren't going to tell you, but my Oz saw him do it.'

'Do what? Who?'

'Young Lester. Hurling them puppies in to the pigs. Said their barking got on his nerves. Wicked, it was. There was nothing my Oz could do – gone in a trice they were. But the noise!'

Phoebe put her hands over her ears to shut out the hateful words. She felt sick with fear.

'Which reminds me, and I should have told you sooner, I'm packing this in.'

'You're going to stop helping me? Oh, Maudie, you can't.'

'I'm afraid I must. Oz has got a better position, way over near Widecombe. We'm moving next week.'

That night, in bed, Phoebe began to cry. No Maudie! Two mad men. She couldn't bear it.

'I've no money.'

'Steal some.'

'That would be wicked.'

'It would only be taking what's owed you.'

She crept down the stairs on tiptoe and into Mr Orton's room. She knew exactly where to go. Maudie had found the money hidden under one of the piles of newspaper. She took some coins, she had no idea how many, and stuffed them into the pocket of her corduroy skirt. As she turned she was aware, in the light from the oil lamp, which was always on low, Mr Orton's black, beady eyes glowering at her. He made an animal-like noise and windmilled his arms.

'I'm sorry, Mr Orton, but you owe me this. I haven't taken it all. I have to go. I have to try . . .' What was the point? He didn't understand. Aware that the noises he was making were getting louder and would surely wake

Lester, she raced out of the room and down the stairs two at a time. From beside the back door she took the blanket she used as a coat. 'Sorry, Mimi, you can't come,' she said to the dog, who was jumping excitedly at her feet. But how could she leave her now that she knew about the puppies' fate? 'Come on, then.' She scooped the little dog into her arms, opened the back door and, before she could think any more, raced into the blackness.

She ran as fast as she could. After ten minutes she had to rest to catch her breath – the dog was heavier than she had thought. She lowered Mimi to the ground and sat on the bank. Then she looked back to where she had run from.

The sky was rose-red. The farm was ablaze.

10

At Christmas and the New Year, Dulcie's longing to see Chauncey had reached a peak. She had then to deal with her own bitter disappointment when he had not come. Now, a week later, she was despondent and tormented with worry, convinced that something awful had befallen him. 'What if the ship has sunk?'

'We would have heard.' Bee replied in her practical way.

'Or his train has been wrecked?'

'That would be in the newspapers to be sure. Now, ma'am, don't fret so.'

'Perhaps he's been set upon by robbers, murdered!' At this her eyes filled with tears.

'And may be the fairies have taken him.' Bee laughed, but Dulcie could not join in. 'Now come, ma'am. Chauncey is a fine, strapping lad; he'll take care of himself.'

'I should be in London to meet him.'

'And what would be the point when you don't know when he's coming?'

'I should go to his regiment. I can't just sit here and do nothing.'

'And make yourself ill again? You're not fit to go rushing about the country. What if you did, and he arrived and found you prostrate? Think of the worry you'd be to him.'

Bee was right, there was nothing she could do. But she couldn't sleep, and failed to concentrate on anything. Every noise made her jump. Every ring on the doorbell, every rattle of the knocker found Dulcie peering anxiously into the hall.

And then, despite listening as she sat in her room, bent over her household accounts, Dulcie did not hear the door open and shut.

'Mama.'

She thought she was dreaming, how often she heard his voice?

'Mama.'

Dulcie looked up and blinked. Disbelieving what she saw. 'Is it you?'

'Dearest!' Chauncey stood his arms held open in greeting.

Dulcie, tears cascading down her cheeks, rushed towards him. 'I thought you were not coming. I thought you were dead. My Chauncey!'

II

'Chauncey! My dear child.' Dulcie put her arms round her son and held him tight, as if she would never let go of him. 'I've been so frightened. The worry . . .'

'I'm sorry, Mama. Dry your tears now. I'm back.' She could not find her own handkerchief so he used his, dabbing gently at her face. 'Forgive me, I should never have rushed off in the way I did. I was selfish – I wasn't thinking.'

'Dear boy, I understand, and you have suffered far more than I. Let me see. Where are you wounded, and how badly?'

'It is healed and there is nothing to see. Really, it is no longer a problem.'

'Then why do you limp?'

'I was shot in the leg. It was next to nothing.'

'Dear God, and they told me it wasn't serious.'

'Compared with some I've seen, it wasn't.' His face was bleak as he remembered.

'Sit down, my darling. Tell me just this once, and I promise I will not bother you again for details and awaken those images that I'm sure you wish to forget.'

'It isn't a subject I care to talk about, but you have the right to know.' He closed his eyes as if preparing himself. 'God, I was so lucky. I had been in Ladysmith, but before the siege. Patrols were going out all the time to find the Boers – fiendish fighters.'

'I hate them.'

'Don't, Mama, they were fighting for what they think is rightly theirs. In war, I can no longer see who or what is right or wrong. It is all bad! But let me finish. There were some papers needed delivering to Durban – the corporal who should have gone was taken ill and I was sent in his place.'

'You should not have been – you're not a professional soldier.'

'That is very true, Mama,' he smiled ironically, 'but I volunteered.'

'So brave.' She clutched at his hand.

'But I was just playing postman, and no one expected we would be attacked. I couldn't even do that well.'

'I won't hear you say such things about yourself.'

'But had I not gone, had I not made such a mess of

things, I would still be there with those poor trapped souls.'

'Then thanks be to God you weren't.'

He was looking past her, as if she was no longer there, as if he was not seeing the paintings on the wall. 'I wish I had been there,' he stated simply.

'How could you?'

'Because now I feel like a traitor.'

'Why should you think that? I shan't let you. It was meant to be. You've returned. You're wounded. What more could be expected of you?' The words poured out of her in a torrent. She was pacing the floor, lifting his damaged leg on to a footstool, pouring him tea.

'Mama, please don't fuss. Just sit down, will you?' He sounded angry.

'I don't mean to annoy you. I want to look after you, keep you safe.' She turned her head away so that he could not see the tears in her eyes, then forced herself to sit down with her hands in her lap. 'I'm sorry, Chauncey.'

'And I am an unappreciative son. I'm sorry too, Mama. We're going to have to get used to each other again. I fear I might be different.'

'Just your leg.' She smiled brightly while fearing that that was not all. 'You were saying?'

'There were Boer raiding parties everywhere. We got lost, my fault, and we walked right into an ambush. Two of my men were killed outright and two wounded, apart from me. Had it not been for one of the others, I would not be here. He threw himself at them, fought like a tiger, killed them, but he, too, was wounded, worse than me, in the head. The bullet remains lodged there, it was too dangerous for the doctors to try to extract it.'

'He must have a medal . . . I must write to him too. Is he poor? Will he need help?'

'Poor as a church mouse, but a splendid fellow, and you won't need to write. He's here and I intend to look after him. The war has changed him. He was as brave as a lion but now loud noises, violence – they make him ill.'

'But where is he? I shall help you care for him.'

'I left him at the King William.'

'I'll send the coach for him.'

'He wouldn't come, he's a modest chap. He wouldn't want to impinge on my homecoming. In any case he is ensconced with the biggest breakfast you have ever seen and a pint of ale, with another lined up.'

'The inn by the harbour? How convenient.' She smiled to herself.

'Our luck held. We were found by another platoon who bandaged us up. There was a train – it was late, trouble on the line – and we were put on it. We travelled to Durban – not the most comfortable ride. The heat, you understand, it's the hottest part of the year there . . .'

Dulcie wanted to stop him. She needed to hear the facts, not about the climate, but she controlled herself. He had to tell her in his own way.

'And then more luck. The *Sumatra*, a hospital ship, was at anchor in Durban. We had the best treatment possible. That ship being there saved my leg. Now do you understand my guilt? All that luck for us – why? For it didn't end there. Another ship was setting sail a few days later for England, with a doctor on board.'

'How fortunate.'

'Was it? I'm not so certain. Had I stayed on the *Sumatra* perhaps I would be fit enough to help now, maybe not to fight but in another capacity.'

'No, Chauncey. No!' Dulcie clapped her hand over her mouth. 'I couldn't bear any more worry. You have no idea of the agony of not knowing where you were, how you were.' She began to cry yet again, which was so unlike her. 'I'm sorry,' she said.

'What a mess I've made of things! You're the last person I would wish to hurt,' Chauncey said.

'I promise you I haven't been like this all the time.

Afraid, yes, fearfully so, but I could control it and now you are here, safe, it's as if all the tears I refused to shed have returned with a vengeance.' She managed to smile. 'But please continue. I have to know.' She was desperate, yet frightened to hear.

'As it turned out we were given no choice in the matter. We were simply carried on board. There were some kind women who had travelled to be near their sons. Having lost them, they cared for us.' Now his eyes filled with tears. 'They were like saints.'

'Perhaps you were a comfort to them,' she said, although she was certain that if he had been killed nothing would have eased her pain. 'I must have their names and write to them. And the leg?' She had to know the extent of the damage.

'It was my knee. I was told later there had been a risk of amputation.' Dulcie cried out and clutched at her heart. 'But the doctor saved it for me. It's stiff and might remain so, but when I think of what might have been it's nothing.'

'I shall write to him too. So many people to thank.'

'After that, there is nothing to tell. We came home.'

'You have taken me by surprise. The regiment told me you would be home for the New Year.'

'We were delayed by bad weather in the Bay of Biscay. It couldn't be helped.'

'I had made arrangements to be in London. But when—' She stopped: she did not want him to worry about her.

'When what, Mama?'

'Nothing.'

'Yes, there is. Tell me.'

'Absolutely nothing.'

'She was ill, Mr Chauncey,' said Bee, entering the room with the bowl of soup that Dulcie had insisted on, even though he had declared he was not hungry. 'Feverish, she was.'

'I had a bad cold. Nothing more.'

'She had an infection of the lungs, Mr Chauncey,' Bee said defiantly. 'Burning up with fever, she was.'

'Bee, don't bother him with trivialities.'

'Are you better?'

'Much. It was a lot of fuss about nothing. I needed a rest, that was all.'

'I'm glad to hear it. Imagine if I had come home and you were . . . Mama, I can't even say the word.'

'Dead? I would have refused to go to my Maker until you were safe here.' She laughed. 'Now, eat this delicious soup.'

'Thank you, Bee.' He smiled at the maid as she left them.

Dulcie watched her son spooning the soup, obviously hungrier than he had thought he was. He had changed. He had been thin when he left; now he was muscular. He had tended to paleness; now he was brown from the sun. The mousy hair he had inherited from her was lighter, almost blond, and his hands, once so slender and fine, were calloused and rough. There had been uncertainty in his demeanour before; now there was strength.

'How is Agnes?' he asked.

'In love.'

'With Robert? Poor man.' Like Dulcie, he was wary of his sister.

'No, an Edward Bartholomew-Prestwick.'

'Then poor him. Is he nice or a rogue?'

'He is charming. She set her cap at him and I doubt there is much the fellow can do. He danced with her several times at the Mayor's Assembly. Of course, in my day that would have compromised them but now such behaviour is unremarked.'

'You're sounding like an old dowager, Mama,' he teased. That was nice, she thought, that was more how it had been. She would not discuss the war again and she would make sure others didn't.

'Will they marry?'

'Agnes thinks so.'

'And this Edward?'

'Undoubtedly he will have no choice in the matter. He has great expectations.'

'Then Father will be pleased.' As always when he spoke of Arnold, there was a bitter twist to his mouth.

'I have tried to point out that expectations have a nasty habit of disappearing into the mist, but she won't listen.'

'And how are you, Mama?'

'Very content. I have a new friend who shares my interest in porcelain.'

'Who is she?'

'She is a he.' She laughed at his evident surprise. 'Lord Prestwick.' She enjoyed saying his name.

'A noble friend. You move in illustrious circles, Mama.'

'A dear friend.'

'And Father does not object to your friend?' He placed the tray on a side-table.

'Of course not. Why should he? He has his circle of friends and I decided it was time I had mine.'

'But he's a friend of Father's too?'

'Not at all. In fact, they don't like each other very much.'

'Mama!' He looked anxious. Perhaps her new-found decisiveness was sounding in her voice.

'Not that either have said so,' she added hurriedly.

'I'm pleased. I was concerned for you, that was all, that Father . . . Well, you know how possessive he can be.'

'Is he? I never thought.'

'Mama, I don't wish to upset you but . . .' He glanced out of the window.

'Yes?' Her heart raced. Had he found someone? Would she like her?

'I don't wish to hurt you, but I can no longer stay under Father's roof. I arrived at this time of day on purpose, knowing he would be at the shop. I don't wish to see him. I can never again live under the same roof as him.'

'Dear one . . .'

'Somehow I shall find an occupation. Clerking, perhaps. I am aware that I cannot make a living from my painting.'

'Not to begin with,' she said proudly.

'Perhaps I will have to go to London.'

'But—'

'You see, Mama, I intend to make a home for us both. As soon as I can afford to, I shall send for you. And—'

'Chauncey! Would you listen to me for one minute?' She was smiling broadly. 'You have a new home here in Barlton.'

'I want nothing from Father.'

'No, I—'

'But how could I afford . . . I don't want to be an embarrassment to you, Mama. No, I shall go.'

'I hope not. All is arranged, and you will have a sizeable income. And it was *I* who purchased the house for you. And *I* who made the other necessary arrangements.'

'You, Mama? But how?'

'Everything we own is mine. It always has been and it always will be.'

He sat bolt upright in the chair. 'I'm sorry? Would you say that again?'

'I think you heard me.'

'But if that is so, why did you never say?'

'Because when my father died and I inherited his fortune, I promised Arnold I would not.'

'And he let you?'

'He had his pride.'

'Pride! This makes the way in which he has treated you even worse.'

'In fairness to him, he has tripled my fortune.'

'And how much has he stolen?'

'How shrewd of you. A great deal. But it does not matter to me. By so doing he has inadvertently allowed me to act in a manner I would never have thought myself capable of. I see it as his reward for increasing my fortune.'

'But no one knows? Does Agnes know?'

'No, but she will eventually, and I have begun to let others know – in my own way.' She smiled.

'What has he done to make you change your mind?' he asked.

'Two things. His attitude to you meant that you put yourself in grave danger, for which I can never forgive him. Then he humiliated me once too often. I decided I could no longer live with my promise.'

They had toured Captain's Keep from top to bottom and Chauncey had professed himself entranced with every inch of it. 'And the decorations, Mama, they are perfect, so modern.'

'I didn't think you'd want the clutter I have. And I have to say I find these new styles, with their clean lines, most attractive. I thought I might have to go to London, but Mr Markham is a great enthusiast for this man George Walton.'

'The day-bed is wonderful, but there is no one to recline on it.'

'I thought you might be worse than you are. It was for you.'

'How about it being for you, Mama? Why don't you move in with me?'

'Chauncey, that is so kind of you. I admit, I did think about it, and how delightful that would be. But what if you married? Where would I go then?'

'Anyone I married would have to love you as much as I do, and want to live with you.'

'It might be an onerous task for a young woman. It

wouldn't be fair, I couldn't promise not to interfere.' She was proud that he had offered. 'In any case, I love December Cottage. It has been my home for longer than my father's house. I could never leave it. No, if anyone is to leave, it shall be your father.'

'Mama, you've changed out of all recognition.' He was laughing. 'What if he won't move?'

'I know things about him. I'll make him move.'

'Take care, Mama.'

'Bah! What can he do to me that he hasn't already done? I'm not afraid of him. He may have many faults but he's never been violent to me.' They were standing at the window of the sitting room, which Chauncey had likened to the captain's cabin window in a man-o'-war. 'Ah, look, here comes Bee with your soldier friend.' She was scurrying along the road with a giant of a man. Even at this distance Dulcie could see his broad smile: his teeth were so white against skin that had darkened far more than Chauncey's had. She was glad she was to meet him, glad she would be here when her son asked him if he would like to stay and be his manservant while he painted: he had been born to paint and become a great artist.

'Mama, let me introduce my saviour to you. Mama, this is Dick Drewett.'

Chapter Five
January 1900–April 1900

I

Several times during the long night it struck Phoebe that history, or at least her own, was repeating itself. Here she was, almost six months since she had run away, trudging along an unknown track in the dark, unsure of where she was going or what she would do. It only needed a Mr Bartholomew to arrive in a coach and the circle would be complete. Just thinking of that man made her shudder.

When she had seen Point East Farm ablaze her immediate reaction had been to run back and help. But when she had seen the fierceness of the blaze she had stopped herself: it was unlikely anyone would survive that, and what could she do to help?

She had seen a lone figure rushing back and forth across the yard in an understandable panic. Was it Lester? Was he hurt? Should she return? Then a group of men had appeared, formed a line and passed buckets of water from one to another. From her vantage point it looked a hopeless task.

When the flames began to lick at the roof, she called Mimi and turned her back on the scene. She could watch no more. Mr Orton must have been burnt to death and, though she had not liked him, she wouldn't have wanted him to die in such a dreadful way.

'Come on, Mimi. We'd better keep moving.'

As she walked she congratulated herself on bringing the dog with her: if she hadn't Mimi would have died in the fire, and the darkness was not as frightening with the little creature trotting beside her.

The fire had been her fault – it had to have been. She was responsible for Mr Orton's death. There was no escaping this conclusion, which haunted her. The memory of the old man in his bed, his lamp beside him, arms flailing, was as sharp as if she was still there with him. She should have moved the lamp to a safer distance from him. There was no escaping the fact that if she hadn't been in the room, he wouldn't have woken and become so agitated at seeing her steal his money.

A thief! A murderess! That was what she was. What if she was found and accused? She saw herself in prison, then in the dock, saw the judge place the black cap on his head ... 'No!' She shouted to the sky. The money she had stolen felt heavy in her pocket. It was cursed. *She* was cursed. She began to run as if by running and removing herself as far as possible from the scene, she could escape the thoughts tumbling in her head. Black, bad thoughts.

She sat down beside the track and began to dig with her hands, but the soil was as hard as rock. Instead she collected some stones, as Mimi watched her closely. She put the coins into the ditch, which ran alongside the path, and piled the stones on top. She wanted none of Mr Orton's money. Then, still racked with guilt she continued on her way.

Phoebe's stomach was rumbling. At least last time she'd had the sense to pack some bread and cheese. In the half-light, Mimi froze, her nose twitching, her flanks shivering with excitement. Phoebe watched as she stalked a young rabbit, pounced and, in that deadly movement, had her breakfast. 'Lucky you, Mimi.'

Walking on the track, little used and stony, was difficult. She had stumbled twice, and feared she would twist her ankle, so when she reached a road she decided to risk walking along it. After a little while she saw a signpost, which told her Barlton was only seven miles further. She could be there by mid-morning if she didn't linger.

Then what?

Something will turn up, she told herself. It had in the past – in the shape of sinister Mr Bartholomew, the auction, mad Mr Orton and his equally mad son. 'It can't get much worse,' she said aloud.

As dawn broke, late since it was still January, coaches and carts appeared on the road so she was no longer isolated. There were many, like herself, on shanks's pony, none smartly dressed but rather, like her, wearing an odd medley of clothes. Some had sacking thrown over their shoulders so there was nothing unusual about the blanket she wore.

It puzzled her that there were so many people about. Perhaps she should forget about Barlton and follow the crowd. With so many others walking, she was surprised when a farm cart stopped just ahead of her and the burly driver shouted to her. Be careful, she told herself. She and Mimi had to run to hear what he was saying: 'Want a lift?'

'Yes, please,' she said, but only because a plump, apple-cheeked, smiling woman, presumably his wife, was sitting behind him on a bale of hay. The past few months had taught her caution.

She picked Mimi up and placed her in the cart, which was full of sacks of potatoes. 'Don't want no dog pissing on my 'taters,' he yelled.

'I see.' She put Mimi back on the ground, and began to walk.

'Ain't you getting in?'

'No, thank you, not without my dog. She's very small and she might not keep up.'

'What?' he bellowed at her, cupping his ear.

'I want my dog with me,' she shouted back.

'No skin off my nose.' He whipped up his horse.

The woman thumped him between the shoulder-blades. 'Don't be such a mean old grump, Cyril.' She was shouting too. 'You get up, me dear, hold the little dog on your lap,' she said, in a more normal tone. 'It's not safe, a pretty young thing like you walking alone. I told Cyril to stop.'

'It was very kind of you. Thank you, missus,' Phoebe said, once she was settled among the sacks. By now she was so hungry she was wondering what a raw potato might taste like.

'Come far?'

'No, just back there.' She pointed vaguely to the west.

'You'm look tired out.'

'I was late to bed.' She felt herself blushing. Why was lying so difficult?

'I see,' the woman said, in a tone that implied she didn't believe her. 'Going to the market?'

'Is that why so many people are on the road?'

'I'd have thought, since you didn't come far, you'd have known the third Wednesday in January's always a big market in Barlton.'

Phoebe did not dare look at the woman in case she saw her confusion. 'I'm not from these parts so I wouldn't be knowing.' She felt that was a good answer and allowed herself to relax.

'Then what parts are you from?'

'Cornwall,' she said, without thinking.

'Well, now, ain't that interesting? You don't sound Cornish.'

'I know. But I've been educated.' She said this to cover her lack of accent, but with pride.

'Well, now, b'aint done you much good, judging by them clouts you've got on.'

'I fell on hard times.'

'Sad. A man was it?'

'No.'

'There's a surprise. It usually is, specially with a pretty

little thing like you. Where in Cornwall are you from then? Somewhere I knows?'

'I doubt it. We lived isolated, like, just over the border.'

'Really? Near Saltash?'

'No.'

'Bodmin?'

'Yes,' she said uncertainly.

'Long way from the border, then.' She studied Phoebe intently.

Phoebe looked away to avoid the stare but when she glanced back the examination was still in progress. The woman's eyes were so small that they looked like raisins. This thought made her smile.

'I shouldn't think you'm got much to smirk about, have 'ee? You'm not Cornish at all. That's what I think.'

'It don't bother me what you think,' Phoebe said, with rather more courage than she was feeling.

'I tell 'ee why – I'm Cornish, from Sennen. So why you'm lying?'

'Because you were being so nosy.' She tossed her head defiantly.

Her companion found this amusing. 'Fair enough. Can't abide not knowing what's what.' She laughed and didn't look nearly as threatening. 'Fancy a rock cake?' She held open a bag to Phoebe, who gratefully accepted one. She needed no persuading to take a second, which she shared with Mimi. 'Run away, have you? Husband, was it? Wish I could run from *him*.' She nodded towards her husband, who appeared oblivious to their conversation.

'I ran away from my father. He beat me.' It seemed better not to explain the rest, and easier not to lie.

'Bastards.' The woman spat over the side of the cart. 'Mine did too, so I married too young to get away from 'ee. Out of the frying pan and into the fire. Men are always lamming out with their fists. You know why?'

Phoebe admitted she didn't. ''Cause they can't talk, that's their trouble. *He* used to hit me, until one day I hit him back, on the head with the chamber pot. Not had no trouble since.'

'Was it full?'

'To the rim.'

They both laughed. 'Doesn't he mind you telling me?'

'Deaf as a post. So, let's start again, you come far?'

'Dartmoor.'

'That explains why you look so tired. What's your name?'

'Phoebe.'

'And?'

Did it matter if she knew? 'Drewett.'

'Well, Phoebe Drewett, take my advice – if you'm going to lie make certain you know what you'm lying about.' She smiled broadly.

'I will. But perhaps I won't need to again.'

'A body can't get through life without a bit of lying here and there. So what do you plan to do now? You'm got to be careful, you know – lovely young girl that you are.'

'I know what's what.'

'What will you do?'

'Look for work. I'm not afraid of it. I can work on the land, cleaning, I don't mind what I do.' She said this eagerly. Perhaps . . . ?

'Pity we don't need no one, but us don't. Times are hard, what with the rents due and all. Otherwise I'd suggest you come back along with us.'

'That would have been nice.' Half of her was disappointed they didn't need her but the other half was glad: she could too easily be back where she started, if she wasn't careful.

'But tell you what. Hold on.' She prodded her husband. 'Cyril,' she shrieked, 'wasn't old man Folgate wanting help?'

'Thinking of working there yourself? That would be good news!' He laughed as loudly as he spoke.

'No, this young lady, her needs work.'

'We'll go by that way.'

'Thank you so much,' Phoebe said.

'It's a laundry. Hard work and the pay's not much but you never know your luck.'

Half an hour later they drew up in front of a ramshackle building overlooking the sea. Even from outside Phoebe could smell the sickly sweet fragrance of boiling soapsuds: it reminded her of washdays when her mother had been alive. But she didn't like the acrid smell of bleach at all. At least, it was close to the water. 'There you are, girl. Good luck.' They waved cheerily at her as they left.

She had hoped they would come in with her to introduce her, but she was probably being unreasonable. After all, they had gone out of their way to bring her here.

'You stay there. Mimi,' she told the dog, and ventured inside the building.

It was large, and women were bustling about shouting one to each other over the noise of the boilers, which hissed, snorted and shuddered alarmingly. Young girls were stamping on washing in great wooden tubs, singing at the tops of their voices. In a corner, children were playing a noisy game. Two of the older women were engrossed in a screaming match. The mist of steam was everywhere so that it was impossible to see to the far side of the room, nor its total size.

'Excuse me?' Phoebe tapped a woman's shoulder. 'Is there work available here?'

'Up there.' She pointed towards a flight of iron stairs. Phoebe climbed them carefully: the air was so damp that they were wet and dangerous. She knocked on a door, the top half of which was made of glass.

'Enter.'

Sitting at the desk, with a set of old-fashioned mutton-chop whiskers, was one of the men she had danced for at the auction. Her instinct was to run, but she could not afford such a luxury.

'Come in, dear. Shut the door.' He spoke softly and held out a large hand with smooth pink fingers. The thought of them touching her made her shiver with horror.

2

Lily had quickly settled to work in the office of Battle, Todsworth and Battle. Her experience had acquired her the position – that, and the glowing reference she had written for herself on Randolph's Emporium writing paper – she had had the foresight to take some with her when she was dismissed. Even Arnold himself would have had difficulty knowing if it was his signature or not.

Not that Lily approved of the way her new office was run – she could see many areas in which improvements could be made. But it was enjoyable to be the only female member of staff.

She had been employed to assist the chief clerk, and Mr Battle the senior partner. However, she was not entirely happy with either Smallwood, the clerk, or Mr Battle. Although she was invariably cheerful and charming with them, she wondered if they were aware of her expertise – they treated her as they would a maid. She was mortified to discover that Mr Battle had not wanted to employ her but had been overruled by Mr Todsworth, the middle partner. She soon knew why: he was a bully, and he was lecherous. Now she never entered his office without leaving the door open.

Young Mr Battle, as he was known, had been away at the time of her interview. He had returned in triumph with a typewriting machine. Since no one in the office could work it, Lily had offered to demonstrate her skill with it. While she tapped away at a letter for Young Mr Battle, the other partners decided she should help him; neither of them was prepared to use such a noisy contraption.

Lily was used to working for the top man and was not pleased to have to work for the most junior, but there were compensations. Young Mr Battle did not smoke cigars as the others did incessantly; Lily liked the manly smell, but had discovered that too much made her feel ill. Neither did Young Mr Battle hawk, sniff and grunt as the other two men did, and he was invariably polite. That could not be said of the others – they would have to learn differently if she was to stay. That was the luxury Arnold had given her: she didn't *have* to work. She would stay only if it suited her.

She did not like being referred to as the Typewriter: a *senior* clerk with typewriting skills was how she preferred to describe herself – though she dreamed of the day when she would be called a secretary. 'Why, Mr Battle, I am hardly a machine,' she had teased him, in her new arch and flirtatious manner.

'How could I be so rude, Miss Howard? I must remember.'

Lily smiled her number-three smile at Young Mr Battle. She had a repertoire of smiles that she practised in front of the mirror. Number three was flirtatious but dignified: it served to say that she liked him, and if he liked her . . . it was always wise to have an insurance policy in case Arnold did not come up to scratch and she had to jump ship.

She often watched Young Mr Battle as he passed her desk – Henry was his name. Of course he was a trifle young – she preferred older men, like dear Arnold – but he wasn't younger than her: thirty-five, she had ascertained. He carried a little too much weight for her liking, but that could easily be rectified . . .

Lily might have been happy but for Arnold's neglect. 'You never come when you say you will.' She pouted.

'I have so little free time, with Dulcie to consider. I have to make sure someone is with her at all times.'

'Is she no better?' The woman was so annoying and disruptive to her plans.

'Worse. She has become a pathetic creature. You would not wish me to be cruel to her, surely. How can I leave her when she is *in extremis*?'

'Would it not be wise to seek a second opinion?' Perhaps Dulcie was malingering.

'I could take her to London. She has the best doctor in the West Country, but there I would find the best in the whole realm. How good of you, Lily, to suggest it.'

She had regretted the idea when he talked of going for two weeks, and taking his wife to several doctors.

'I'm sure one would be sufficient.' She was exasperated.

'No, I shall consult half a dozen. Then I and everyone else shall know I have done the best for the mother of my children.'

Lily hated it when he spoke of Dulcie so lovingly. It was as if he was telling her, in a roundabout way, that he loved his wife and would stay with her. Impossible! she told herself firmly. She poured him another drink, and a large sherry for herself. 'I've an idea,' she said brightly, as she handed him the glass. 'I could go to London too. When poor Dulcie is confined to her sick-bed you will be so bored. We could go to the theatres, the opera, dine out. Oh, yes, what fun we could have!'

'That would not be a good idea,' he replied, far too hurriedly for Lily's comfort. 'What if Dulcie discovered our liaison? What if my friends learned of our arrangement?'

'Why? Are you ashamed of me?' She was far too incensed to remember to sulk prettily. What *liaison*? What *arrangement*? she thought.

'Whatever made you say such an unpleasant thing? How could I be? But, dear Lily, you have to understand my position. If a hint of our secret ever got out I'd never be mayor of Barlton. It is my life's ambition. Don't you want me to achieve it?'

'If I'm your lady mayoress,' she said boldly, mollified a little by '*our* secret'.

'Divorce would preclude that.' He downed the remains of his whisky.

'There are other ways.' She smiled her number-two smile: soft, dreamy, sensual.

'What can you possibly mean?'

'She might die.'

'Lily!'

He looked so shocked that she had regretted mentioning it, but the sherry had loosened her tongue. 'You said she is no better. Of course I don't *want* her to die, but I think it is a possibility that you must keep in your mind, Arnold. She *may* not recover. Who's to say? I am only thinking of *you*, and the shock to your system, to your sensitive mind.' Time for number-one smile, brimming with love, the one she never had to act when looking at him. She congratulated herself on the speed and skill with which she had turned an unguarded moment to her own advantage.

He kissed her then, one of his long, hard, searching kisses. She clung to him, aware that when he did this he was about to leave. And she hated him going, leaving her to fill the empty evening alone.

'I must go, Lily.' Gently he untangled her hands from his lapels.

'So soon?'

'One day, Lily. One day soon . . .'

'What, darling Arnold?'

'Shush.' He put his finger on his lips.

'When shall I see you again?'

'As soon as possible.' He blew her a kiss and was gone.

The front door shutting was the bleakest sound she had ever heard, followed a close second by the sound of his footsteps growing fainter on the pavement.

After he left she poured herself a restorative brandy. And then another. Perhaps it was as well she didn't see him every day or she would be a captive of the demon drink, to be sure, she thought, and laughed as she poured a third. She needed the sensation the brandy gave her. His presence, his caresses, his kisses excited her to an alarming degree, and this was how she calmed herself.

If he was to stay, she dreaded to think what she might do. Would she lose control? It was a heady thought. Although she told herself she was a woman of high moral principles who would not succumb to him, she knew she lied to herself.

It would, she presumed, be easy to persuade him to take her to bed. *Bed!* Her mind reeled and she had to pick up her ivory fan to cool her hot face. But that was not the route to take. He respected her now: if she succumbed he would despise her as he did the *fancy* women in his life. Then she would be no better than the unspeakable Edith – and look what had happened to her! She had conveniently forgotten that Edith had left Arnold.

After a fourth brandy she went to her lonely bed. Disrobing proved so complicated that she thought she would have a little rest first. She tried to read but the words jumped about on the page. Perhaps she needed new spectacles. She lay back on the pillow to find the ceiling revolving in a most peculiar way. Which was when she was sick.

In the morning, Lily was aghast at the state of her bed linen and her clothes. It must have been something she had eaten – why, she still felt ill, with a dreadful headache. She regretted not having employed a new maid as she stripped the bed and divested herself of her soiled clothing. Perhaps she should not venture out – but today was her first full day of working with Young Mr Battle. She had thought things over carefully and was pleased now to be his full-time assistant. She couldn't have him thinking her unreliable.

She had a hurried strip wash and, by dint of walking very fast, was in the office only fifteen minutes late, which was still fifteen minutes before the partners were due.

She had picked a small bunch of snowdrops from her garden, which she placed in water for his desk. She arranged his cup and saucer on a silver tray, made some coffee and put the macaroons she had baked yesterday on a plate. Then she waited for him to arrive.

Lily enjoyed the day. Mr Battle was a considerate man and spoke slowly and distinctly as she noted down what he required. 'Should I use a word you don't understand, Miss Howard, just interrupt me. The same if you find difficulty with spelling a particular word.'

'I'm sure that won't be necessary, Mr Battle.' She had a dictionary beside her typewriting machine.

The documents he required her to type took rather longer than she had anticipated.

'I will get faster as I become used to your ways, Mr Battle.'

'I'm sure you will, Miss Howard. However . . .' He was reading the beautifully laid out letter she had just finished. 'I see you have written "in the event of" when I thought I had said "in the event".'

'Yes, I corrected it.'

'Why?'

'I didn't think you would want something incorrect leaving your chambers.' She felt rather hot around her tight white collar.

'It was not incorrect. I decide what is written, Miss Howard, not you.'

'Then I apologise. Shall I redo it?' Her colour rose.

'No, cross out "of".'

'Thank you, Mr Battle.'

In her own office she pounded away at the keys of the machine.

'There, Mr Battle. I thought it best to rectify my error.' She put the corrected letter in front of him for his signature.

'That wasn't necessary, Miss Howard.'

'But I think it was.'

'As you wish ... Miss Howard, I quite forgot. The flowers. Such a kind thought.'

'Just because this is a place of work I see no reason why beauty should be banished.'

'Quite so.'

'My previous employer always enjoyed my little touches. Mr Randolph-Smythe said I made his place of work a veritable home from home.'

'You worked for Arnold Randolph-Smythe? I did not know that. I was not told.' He was frowning most alarmingly and he looked agitated.

'I had good references from him. Perhaps you did not read them?'

'My partners told me they were excellent.'

'Is there a problem, Mr Battle?'

'No, nothing. I was surprised that is all.' But just as she was leaving he called her back. 'You do understand that everything that happens in this office is confidential?'

'Like the confessional. Yes, Mr Battle.'

'It would be instant dismissal if anything was said,' he reminded her.

'Of course, Mr Battle. Is there a problem?'

'No. Good night, Miss Howard, and thank you.'

As she put on her hat and coat to leave, Lily thought this over. He was lying. Undoubtedly there was a problem. What did Mr Battle know that Arnold should not? How interesting ...

'If I might be so bold, there's a question I need to ask you.'

'I shall answer it if I am able.'

'Why, dear lady, is there such sadness in your eyes?'

Dulcie looked up with surprise at Theo Prestwick's question. 'Is there? I didn't know . . .' She was flustered: it was such an extraordinary thing for him to ask. They sat on the sheltered balcony of his house enjoying the sun, which was doing its best to shine. 'Given that it is February, we should be grateful for this feeble sunshine. It's better than none,' she said, more to marshal her thoughts than as a reprimand.

'Forgive me, Dulcie. That was unforgivable of me. You are quite right to change the subject.' He looked sad now, she noticed, but embarrassed too. She would have liked to put out her hand and take his to reassure him that she did not mind his asking, but convention forbade such an intimate gesture.

'It was not deliberate, I can assure you. I was merely trying to hide my confusion.' She smiled at him to show she spoke the truth. 'It was a surprising question. I am not sad, I assure you. I have been sad, but not any more. I have no cause.'

'Then has past sadness marked you for ever? I do hope not. I would give what little I possess to remove all memory of it.'

'As you do, dear friend. I bless the gods every day that we were fortunate enough to meet. You have given me such pleasure with your company. The talks we have, the discussions . . .'

'And the arguments!' He laughed in that all-consuming way he had. A distant rumble began in the lower regions of his stomach rose up, swelling his belly, enlarging his barrel-shaped chest, all the time gathering force so that when it erupted it was a loud noise of untrammelled joy, and his whole body shook with mirth.

Just to hear him made her chuckle too. She remembered their argument. A few days ago they had found they could not agree on the nature of selfishness, and the argument he had referred to exploded upon them, without warning. They had even shouted at each other, but when she had thrown a pencil at him they had been reduced to a wobbling mass with laughter at the absurdity of it.

'Even our arguments are fun!'

'I begin to think we were meant for each other. If only . . .'

Her mind reeled as the meaning of what he had said registered with her. 'Dangerous words, "if only", dear friend. Almost as perilous as "Do you remember?" . . . from what I hear,' she added. She had no pleasant memories from her relationship with Arnold.

He leant forward and took her hand. Although he often did so, she felt a jolt of excitement at his touch. 'No, Dulcie, I think often in that way. And you can't stop me. I can have my dreams and I treasure them.'

She looked at him shyly. 'I dream too.'

'Dearest lady.' He lifted her hand to his mouth. 'I had dared to hope that you . . . liked me.'

'I do, Theo, most sincerely.' She would have liked to tell him she loved him but she could never behave in such an unseemly fashion.

'The gods are unfair. Both of us have known unhappiness, and now, when it could be so wonderful, there is nothing we can do about it.'

'But we can see each other, enjoy each other's company, as we do.'

'I long for far more.'

Dulcie was almost certain that she was dreaming this conversation, that she was hearing these words only because they were what she longed to hear. She was misinterpreting them, she must be.

'You have never said before that you were unhappy. I presumed you'd had an idyllic marriage.'

'No, more's the pity. I know one should not speak ill of the dead but, you see, it is impossible to be happy with a Bartholomew. They are an accursed family.'

'I had no idea.' She had heard rumours of Mr Bartholomew and his insatiable liking for women – or, rather, young girls, but she did not like gossip and never repeated it.

'She was not as melancholic as her brother. He's a recluse, you know. Many think it is because he's an albino and does not like to be seen, but his father was the same, and he wasn't pale. He simply doesn't like people. He derives no enjoyment from them. My wife rejected company too, and disliked venturing out.'

'Perhaps she was shy.' And suffered as I have, she thought but did not say.

'Not my wife. She could command a room in a trice.'

How fortunate for her. Dulcie thought, with envy.

'But she found fault with everyone until finally she had either antagonised or could find no pleasure in anyone. She simply stopped seeing people.'

'And you are such a gregarious man. It must have been hard for you.'

'I made my own life, dear lady, had my own friends. But I have often wondered what it would be like to have a soul-mate. No, we were wrong for each other, but my father was keen on their money, and her father was keen on my title, so it was arranged. If I had been allowed to choose, who knows?'

'But even when one does choose, a catastrophe may still occur,' she said, with heartfelt feeling.

'Sometimes, looking back, I wonder if she only loved her brother – she certainly didn't like me. The Bartholomews are a clever clan, he especially. A classical scholar of note, or so I'm told. She, too, always had her head in a book. I don't know my Plato from my patella.'

'That's not true. You are a most cultured man.'

'My wife didn't think so. She was always comparing me with Kendall and finding me wanting. What I can never understand about him is that he has money and all those lovely possessions, yet is so miserable. If I was rich you'd never find me so wretched.'

'You would use it to the full, enjoy every minute.'

'I would.'

And you shall, dear man, she thought. 'And Edward is his heir,' she said.

'More's the pity.'

'Why do you say that?'

'I feel he doesn't like his uncle – not that he's ever said so to me, he's far too discreet. But I sense it. And, in my opinion, it's not right to kow-tow to a man of whom you don't approve. No amount of money is worth that, wouldn't you say?'

'I agree. Approve, you say?'

'There's nothing I can put my finger on, but I think Edward knows something, doesn't like it, and is wondering what to do about it.'

'And he won't eventually confide in you?'

'Never. My son can be pig-headed where loyalty is concerned.'

'I should not worry. If he takes after you he will undoubtedly do the right thing.'

At which point the French windows to the drawing room opened and a pink, flustered Agnes appeared, with a sheepish-looking Edward behind her. Dulcie's heart sank. Did that look mean that he had proposed? If so, he was making a dreadful mistake and there was nothing she could do about it.

'What on earth were you two doing outside in this weather? You'll catch your deaths, and we don't want that, do we, Edward?'

'Most certainly not.'

'Did you have a nice walk?' Lord Prestwick asked Agnes.

'Very, thank you. But Edward complained too soon that we had gone far enough.'

'And how far had you gone?'

'To the view at the top of the hill. I wanted to go much, much further, down the other side and out into the country. He was bored with me.' She displayed her pretty pout and Dulcie found herself thinking that perhaps all was not lost.

'Agnes, I did not want to risk tiring you.'

'How could I ever be tired in your company, Edward?' Her eyelashes fluttered, and Dulcie had to admire the ease with which she turned the conversation with a pretty compliment.

'Tea, everyone?' Lord Prestwick was on his feet.

Dulcie had noticed a fleeting frown on his face when the young couple appeared. Perhaps he, too, was concerned by Agnes and Edward being together. He was such a shrewd, sagacious individual. Had he seen through Agnes's pretty manners to the petulant child beneath? 'Tea would be lovely, Theo,' she said.

'Why did you insist on leaving so early? We could have stayed at least another hour,' Agnes said, in the carriage bearing them home. As always, Dulcie was sad to have left Theo, but she had feared they might overstay their welcome. As usual they had left long before convention required.

'We have a long way to go.'

'An hour and a half at most.'

'We had been there long enough. One doesn't want people to tire of one.'

'Stuff and nonsense. They were enjoying me being there. You can see how Lord Prestwick delights in my company. Why, Mother, I think he has taken quite a shine to me!'

'Isn't he rather old for you?' she said, in as normal a voice as she could manage. She felt quite ill at the implication of what Agnes had said.

'He'd be dead all the sooner!'

'Really, Agnes, what a wicked thing to say.'

'It's perfectly reasonable. Why not? I could make his last days very happy.'

'He's only fifty.'

'*Only!*'

'He has no money. I thought you were intent on marrying someone well provided for.'

'It isn't necessary. Papa has money, and Lord Prestwick doesn't have any, so he would like that. And he's a lord so I'd be a lady, and I'd like that.'

'It takes rather more to be a lady than simply marrying a lord.' She did not try to keep the waspishness out of her voice.

'Why, Mother! If I didn't know better I'd think you were jealous of me.' She laughed gaily. 'How amusing that would be.'

Dulcie looked out of the carriage window. She knew she had coloured, and feared Agnes seeing it, for if she did she would make her life intolerable. Her knowing how Dulcie felt would besmirch her harmless dreams.

'Stop!' Dulcie banged on the partition which separated them from the coachman. 'A moment.' As soon as the coach drew to a halt she hurriedly dismounted. Beside the road, slumped on the ground, was what seemed at first to be a bundle of rags, but Dulcie had seen it was a person. Gently she touched it. 'Don't be afraid,' she said to the startled, tear-stained face, which she could now see belonged to someone young who might have been pretty once. Such sadness in the world. Dulcie sighed. 'I am here to help you, not hurt you.' Dulcie called her coachman to assist her. Together they helped the woman to her feet, where she swayed uncertainly. 'My dear, let me take you to a home I know of. There's no cause for alarm. It is a most respectable establishment set up to help such as yourself. What's your name?'

'Rosie Grainger, madam.'

'Then you come with me, Rosie. You need some soup and a warm bed.'

'Thank you, madam.' And Rosie began to sob with relief.

From inside the coach Dulcie took a rug to wrap around her. 'You get up beside the coachman, there's a good girl.' Satisfied Rosie was settled, Dulcie climbed back into the coach.

'Honestly, Mother, I sometimes think you care more for your waifs and strays than for me. She could have been a robber.'

'She doesn't have the strength to rob anyone.' Dulcie ordered the coach to proceed.

'She is no doubt alive with lice.'

'To be sure.'

'Don't you care about me?' Agnes moved further away from her mother. 'Picking up dross such as she when I am with you.'

'Which is why I sat her outside. I thought you might object and I was right. Do you have no humanity?'

'Me? Of course I do, but I don't see the point in helping a girl like that. She will only disappoint you as so many of them do.'

'And maybe she won't. Maybe we can give her a new start in life.'

'No doubt she has only herself to blame.'

'We don't know that, Agnes. Anything could have happened to explain her sorry state. You are lucky, Agnes, you should be grateful and show some compassion.'

'No doubt I shall when I am as old as you but for the moment I am not interested.'

They rode in silence for a couple of miles. Dulcie was fully aware that no matter what she said, she would never change how Agnes felt, just as Agnes would never persuade Dulcie to stop what she was doing.

'I just don't understand Edward, Mother.' Agnes said, evidently no longer interested in moaning about the young woman. 'I gave him opportunities without number, but we were only gone a quarter of an hour. What is a girl to do with such little time? I flirted. I was helpless. I complimented him – all the things that normally work so well. He just talked about the view and the buildings we saw.'

'Perhaps he was trying to tell you something.'

'What?' Agnes leaned towards her eagerly.

'That he is not interested in you in the way you wish him to be.'

'That's a horrid thing to say!'

'It might be the truth.'

'But of course he wants me. He just hasn't realised it yet,' Agnes said sulkily. 'You wouldn't understand these things, anyway, but Papa will.'

'Undoubtedly,' she said with a wry note that Agnes did not notice.

'Papa will arrange everything. I shall persuade him to settle a huge sum of money on me, so much that either Edward will see sense or I shall marry his father. There! I feel so much better now that I know what I must do.' Agnes sat back against the soft leather upholstery of the carriage with a smug expression.

Perhaps it was that look or perhaps it was her own intentions with regard to Theo, or perhaps even that she was changing as much as she hoped . . . Dulcie folded her hands in her lap and took a deep breath. 'I shouldn't rely on that. There is something I should have told you years ago about money. It would have made a big difference in your attitude towards me.' She smiled at that. 'You see, Agnes. The money . . .'

Dulcie waited calmly in her boudoir for the storm to break. She had heard Arnold return, late as always. She had heard Agnes rush down to the hall to meet him. She had heard the slam of a door. She could not hear what was said, but she could well imagine.

Arnold's footsteps were heavy and rapid as he climbed the stairs. There was no knock on the door before it swung open violently.

'What do you mean by this?' He stood in the doorway, menacingly.

'I thought it was time she knew.' As Dulcie faced him, her composure deserted her.

'What about the promises you made me?' He was shouting.

A tearful Agnes emerged at the side of him, plucking at his sleeve. 'Papa, say it's not true!'

'Agnes, please leave us. I have matters to discuss with your father.'

'I shan't go. I've every right to hear why you lied to me.'

Dulcie stood up. 'I did not lie. I spoke only the truth.'

'Papa! Tell her to stop. Tell her to cease these untruths.'

'No, Agnes, you stop! Get out!'

'Papa!'

Without more ado, Arnold took her arm, pushed her out of the room and slammed the door.

'The promises?' He stepped towards her threateningly.

Dulcie quailed. She had never regarded him as a violent man, but perhaps that was changing too. She forced herself to stand tall, her head held high, while her heart pounded and she could feel the blood coursing through her veins. 'Had you kept your promise to me, I would have kept mine to you.'

'What? Explain.'

'Your affair.'

'Over the years you have condoned my actions – not

for my comfort I am fully aware but to ensure that I left you alone at night. Isn't that nearer the truth, *wife*?'

'Rather, it is the other way round. I would have been a dutiful wife to you in that respect, had you wanted me.'

He looked her up and down. 'Hardly surprising that I did not,' he said softly, which, after the shouting, she found even more alarming. She ingored the insult – he had not been able to hurt her feelings for a long time.

'You promised me you would not embarrass me with any friends of ours, that you would keep your activities to girls I did not know and would never meet socially. Your liaison with Sophie humiliated me. I decided that my vow was no longer valid.'

'And you are happy to destroy my daughter's faith in me because of your own snivelling selfishness?'

'She loves you. Nothing I say will alter that. That is, if she truly does love you more than she loves herself.' She enjoyed saying those words.

'You are evil.'

'No, I am not.'

'Are you about to say that I am?'

'No, Arnold. You are not evil, you are weak.'

'After all I've done for you!'

'I am the first to admit what you have achieved. I have nothing but admiration for your work and how my fortune has grown because of you. But I would have preferred it, Arnold, if you had not systematically stolen from me over the years. You have amassed a tidy sum. Agnes will want for nothing.'

'Then why tell her?'

'Because, Arnold, I no longer wish to live a lie. She had to know, as does Chauncey.'

'I'm amazed you kept it for so long from that weakling.'

'He . . .' She had been about to defend her son, tell Arnold of his courage, but then he would know Chauncey was here.

'Not up to defending him? Well, there's a surprise.' He stepped towards her and, before she could move, grabbed her arm. Slowly, he twisted it behind her and yanked it. Pain shot through her shoulder as if she had been pierced by an arrow. 'You will apologise to Agnes. You will say you lied.'

'I shall do no such thing.' The arm was wrenched and she cried out with pain.

'Oh, but you will, Dulcie. You most certainly will,' he said. 'You will continue to live with our lies. You see,' he bent forward so that he was whispering in her ear, 'if you don't, I shall kill you.'

4

Phoebe thought constantly about how long she was going to work in the laundry. From the first day she had hated being there.

Since she was the most recent recruit, she was given the worst tasks. She had to clean the lavatory, which was infested with rats. If a drain was blocked, she had to delve into it and remove whatever was obstructing it. The water in the coppers, buckets and sinks had to be checked first thing to make sure it had not frozen overnight; if it had, the ice had to be broken. The clatter of the wooden paddle combined with the shouting of the women so early in the morning was almost too much for her.

Phoebe was not alone in disliking working there. Everyone did. A thick mantle of discontent led to rows between the women which, in a second, could escalate into screaming, vicious fights. Furthermore, there were Mr Folgate's roving hands to look out for.

A bitter, salt-laden wind howled in from the sea and through the tiniest cracks in the dilapidated building to torment them further. Often, it was colder inside than it was out. The constant dipping into water, the harshness of the soda and bleaches meant that the women's hands were chapped and often bled, while their cracked lips were sore, and chilblains itched. The others rubbed in mutton fat for some protection and to ease the pain. Once Phoebe would have done the same, but now she longed for scented balms.

When Phoebe had released the water from its icy shroud, it slopped and cascaded everywhere: the floors were always wet. She was deafened by the clanking of the machinery and by the sound of wooden clogs on the cobbled floor.

'Watch how you walk,' she'd been advised on her first day.

'Them floors are that uneven, you could break your ankle.'

'Best look out for chilblains.'

Those had been virtually the only friendly words spoken to her in the three weeks she had been there. All the other workers were from Barlton and had known each other from birth; they had no time or need for her. They were members of two families, the Skeltons and the Tomlins. For roughness and unpleasantness there was little to choose between them.

Since all the members of both families worked here they brought their children too. A couple of old women, the grandmothers or great-grandmothers, were supposed to look after them, but by ten in the morning they were invariably drunk on cider and incapable of looking after themselves, let alone the little ones.

The children worried Phoebe. She had to look around carefully before she moved anywhere so that she did not trample on one. Worse, they were always in danger of scalding by hot water or burning by the irons. She seemed the only person concerned for their safety.

'Would you like to learn to read and write?' Phoebe had asked, on her second day.

'No,' the children chorused. She hadn't tried again.

After three or four hours the atmosphere became so hot that often she thought she would faint. Rivulets of sweat trickled down her back and between her breasts. She was always afraid that she smelt, even though at the end of every day she stripped and washed herself thoroughly.

'Would it be possible to have a kettle of hot water, Mrs Purt?' she had asked her landlady on the first night.

'This bain't no hotel. I'd have thought working at that there laundry you could do your dhobing there. I don't want no smell of boilding clothes in my establishment. If there's one thing my husband can't stand it's the smell of washing.'

'It's to wash myself.'

'Hot water once a week and that'll be threepence extra.'

'I can't afford that.'

'Then you'll have to go without, won't you?' And Mrs Purt shut the door that led to her private quarters at the back of the boarding-house.

Phoebe always climbed the dark, narrow stairs with caution: the threadbare carpet was a death trap – almost as bad as the loose linoleum in the passage, which she had tripped over several times. On her first day, the sash had broken and the window had crashed down. She had asked for it to be mended.

'Serves you right, letting the cold into my house in this weather.' Mrs Purt did not dispense sympathy.

'I needed some fresh air.'

'Then you should have gone out for a walk.'

Phoebe's room was at the top of the house below the eaves. It was small – which, given the cold, was probably just as well. It will be steaming in summer, she thought. No matter, I shan't be here. Although she didn't know how she was to extricate herself from these lodgings.

She had a bed, whose mattress she preferred not to inspect too closely, a chest of drawers on which stood her wash-bowl and jug, a small stool and a candle. For this she paid two shillings a week, and a shilling for Mimi, the only creature she could talk to. This left Phoebe with less than a shilling a week to feed the two of them. Most nights they went to bed hungry. Times without number she regretted leaving Mr Orton's money buried beside the road. She had wondered once or twice about going to find it, but her conscience would not let her. She should not have taken it and only evil would befall her if she used it, of that she was certain.

As if her lodgings and the work were not bad enough she also had to contend with Frank Folgate – Mr Fumble Fingers, as everyone called him behind his back. She was often aware of him watching her from his office. If she happened to glance up she would see him, through the steam, licking his lips as if in anticipation.

'Don't I know you?' he'd asked one day, on meeting her in the passageway that led to the furnace room where the sheets were hung to dry when it was raining.

'I don't think so, Mr Folgate.' She stood rigid as a podgy hand with a large gold ring touched her cheek.

'Such a pretty little face, haven't you?'

'Thank you.' She had to say something.

'I'm sure I've seen you somewhere.'

'No, Mr Folgate. I'd have remembered you.' She ducked and wove her way out of his clutches.

She was always careful not to be the last to leave at night. He'd have raped her then, she was sure. She had heard two of the women talking about just such an incident.

'I'd set you on him, Mimi,' she told the dog.

A ditch ran along the laundry wall, dry and protected by an overhang. The first time Phoebe had left Mimi there while she worked she was frightened that the dog might run away, but she never did. 'My most faithful friend.'

Even the best-laid plans can go wrong, though. One

evening just as it was time to leave one of the Mrs Skeltons ordered her to repack a basket: the contents did not tally with the laundry book. 'That's for Mr Randolph-Smythe.'

'Who did you say?' Phoebe was sure that the cobbles had shifted beneath her feet and held on to the lid of the large wicker basket for support.

'You heard.' The woman moved away, but Phoebe stopped her. 'What you up to?'

'Please, I need to know. Is he the man who owns the big shop?'

'Yes.'

'Does he ever come here?'

'Of course he don't. But he's one of Fumble Fingers's most important customers, so don't muck it up.'

'I'll try not to, Mrs Skelton.' As always, she smiled brightly in the hope that the woman would be friendlier. She wasn't.

Phoebe got down on her hands and knees to count the linen sheets, pillowcases, chemises, petticoats and napkins. Wherever she went in these parts it appeared she was destined to hear of that man. Just his name frightened her.

'What if I met him face to face?' she asked herself.

'Ignore him,' Phyllis answered.

'Easier said than done.'

She admired the fine embroidery on one of the pillowcases. How soft it was. How sweet-smelling. Just like at Mr B—

'Don't think about *him* either!'

There was a clattering on the metal staircase that led to the office. She froze in her task.

'Is anyone there?' Mr Folgate called.

She held her breath.

'I heard voices.' He stepped into the cavernous room. Perhaps he wouldn't see her. 'Ah, it's you.'

'Yes.' She scrambled to her feet. She felt safer standing up.

'Who were you talking to?'

'Myself.'

'I don't believe you.'

'It's the truth. I often do.' She backed away as he advanced towards her.

'You shouldn't lie.' He wagged a finger at her.

'I didn't.'

He looked down into the basket. 'And what are you doing, with no one else here?' He was smiling.

'Sorting this basket for Mr Randolph-Smythe.'

Mr Folgate stood transfixed. He frowned, he was thinking, helped by one of the fat fingers outlining his full red lips. She could see a trickle of saliva oozing from the side of his mouth. Just as if she was a leg of mutton, a steak pie, she found herself thinking.

'That's where I know you from! Of course. Old Orton! He took you!'

'I'm sorry. I know no Mr Orton.' She would have backed further away except there was nowhere to go: she was pressed against the wall. 'No!' she said, in a squeaky voice, as he loomed over her.

'Poor old Orton. Well, he's not to know – not when he's locked away as he is.' And he lunged at her. She screamed as loudly as she could, even though she knew there was no one to hear. His arms were round her, and his spittle sprayed over her as she tried to escape him.

'What the—' He yelped and sprang away from her, bellowing like a wounded bull.

'It's a huge rat!' Phoebe shouted and, with a twist and a turn, she was free. 'Mimi!' she screamed. The two escaped from the building and ran like the wind until they reached the safety of their little room.

That night Phoebe barely slept. There was no escape in this town from the instigators of her problems. She had to move away. She'd go to Exeter. Mr Randolph-Smythe would not bother her there, and she could forget the Ortons. She would build a new life.

First, she had to brave Mr Folgate. He owed her money and she owed Mrs Purt. If she tried to leave without paying her landlady, Mrs Purt would have the police on her before she had reached the edge of the town.

The next morning she knocked on the office door. 'Come,' she heard the hated voice say.

'Mr Folgate, if you wouldn't mind—' She did not finish her sentence. A policeman was standing in the office. Folgate had told on her. She was about to be arrested. They'd think she'd murdered Mr Orton. She sank on to a chair since her legs were incapable of supporting her.

'Phoebe Drewett?'

'Phoebe, yes, Drewett, no. Yes . . .' she stammered. The policeman loomed over her and she stood up abruptly. That's better, she told herself, even though her eyes only reached the top button of his tunic.

'Now, miss, which is it?'

'Yes, that's me – or, rather, it was.'

'Quite the little riddler, aren't you? Mr Folgate here says you're one for telling lies.'

'I never do.'

'But you just have, Miss Phoebe Drewett, even if you then decided to tell me the truth. Now, why would you do a thing like that? You've nothing to worry about.'

'Haven't I?'

'Not that I know of. Or is there something you should be telling me?'

'I don't want my father to know where I am.'

'I see. And why might that be?'

'I don't like him.'

At this the policeman laughed. 'Well, that's honest enough and no mistake. Run away, did you?'

'Yes.'

'How old are you?'

'Seventeen.'

'You don't look seventeen.'

'That's what everyone says, but I am.'

'Then if you are you've every right to be wherever you want. But why Barlton?'

'It seems a nice town.'

'Have you been anywhere else?'

'No.'

'Are you sure?'

Phoebe closed her eyes momentarily. She looked at Mr Folgate. He was sitting at his desk behind the policeman, mopping his brow in an agitated way. 'I stayed awhile with Mr Bartholomew.' Why shouldn't she mention him? What had he done for her but almost ruin her?

'The Mr Bartholomew out at Courtney Lacey? That's a grand place. What happened? Didn't you suit?' The policeman and Mr Folgate waited for her reply. 'Cat got your tongue?'

'Yes. I mean, I didn't suit.'

'And then what happened.'

'I lived at Point East Farm. I was the housekeeper.' No one had called her that, but it would give her standing and respectability.

'You know Mr Orton, then?'

'Yes.'

'Which one?'

'Both.'

'And how did you get a position like that at your age?'

'I answered an advertisement. I can read.' She was aware that the lie was making her blush. And she did not know why she had not told the policeman the truth – fear that it might get her into trouble, she supposed. For someone in her position there was not much justice.

She could see Mr Folgate exhaling with relief.

'Do you know where the son is?'

'No.'

'Pity.'

'Why?' she felt bold enough to ask.

'He's run away too. I'd hoped you'd gone together. Seems he tried to kill his father and stole his money. Set fire to the house, he did, with his poor old father confined to his bed. Fortunately for him, one of his workmen saw the flames and rescued him. But, given the state of his mind, he wasn't aware of it.'

'The poor man.' Phoebe sat down with a bump. It hadn't been her fault at all. She felt light-headed with relief.

'Still, if you hear of him, you'll let us know?'

'Of course.'

'Thank you for your time, Mr Folgate.' He collected his truncheon and, with a steady tread, left the room. They heard his great boots ringing on the iron steps of the staircase.

Phoebe turned back to face Mr Folgate. She was not frightened now, but he was. 'Nice of me not to tell the policeman about the auction and your part in it, wasn't it?'

'Will you say anything in the future?'

'Maybe I will, but then maybe not. And perhaps the policeman would like to know about Mr Randolph-Smythe and all the others.' She hadn't the least idea of who the others were but a plan was forming in her mind.

'It would be the ruin of me.'

'As it nearly was of me.'

At least he had the grace to look ashamed. 'You can triple my wages and never lay a finger on me ever again, and I'll promise never to say a word.'

Mr Folgate could do nothing but agree.

'There's just one thing. Did you call the policeman?' Phoebe asked.

'No, I didn't.'

'Then who did? Who knows I'm here, my name? Who called the police if it wasn't you?'

'I don't know, and that's the truth.'

But as she ran down the stairs, elated, Phoebe realised it must have been the farming couple who had brought her here. And the woman had seemed so nice. No one could be trusted.

As she reached the laundry all the women stood and cheered.

'So you're one of us!' one of the Mrs Skeltons shouted. They advanced on her and clapped her on the back. One offered her a sweet, another a piece of bread. That was all it had needed for her to be accepted: to be thought a criminal, just like them. She had to laugh.

5

Lily was considering setting herself up in business. She could not make up her mind between Howard's Offce Custodians or Miss Howard – Office Custodian. Of the two she felt the latter was more dignified. She would offer clients a comprehensive inspection and advice on their office security. Her experience of how simple it was to unlock fiscal secrets held in an office, both at Randolph's Emporium and at Battle, Todsworth and Battle, showed there was need of such a service.

She had not uncovered any secrets that indicated fraud at the solicitors', but it was early days. She had found out a few interesting facts about some of Barlton's finest citizens, but nothing she felt inclined to use yet.

The idea for the business had come to her when she had found a list of clients and their assets. Such a simple, stupid error to have compiled it but not secured it. The clients would be unhappy to discover that by dint of opening a safe – an easy task, with her acute hearing and memory for numbers – she now knew how rich or poor they were. She'd have thought that Mr Cooper, the butcher, would have had more, but he did go rather often to Newton Abbot on 'business' but in fact for the races. No doubt that was where his takings went. And how right she had been, when working in the shop, to chase Mrs Fanshaw's account: for all her airs and graces, she was teetering on the edge of Queer Street. She had warned Arnold but he had not believed her.

If she, an amateur, could uncover so much knowledge from just two businesses, how many others might need her advice? Barlton was a small town, it contained at least a dozen potential clients. And she could open a branch in Exeter where the possibilities ran into hundreds. If she went to London . . . Well! She felt faint with excitement.

'You see, Pansy, I could offer them so much assistance. How to keep secrets . . . well, secret. How to hide that which needs to be hidden from prying eyes.'

'Like yours?' Pansy said archly.

'I am observant. I am moderately intelligent. And if I can find out important details, so can others.'

'*Moderately!* Not like you to be modest, Lily.' Pansy's smile was sly, Lily noticed. She would ignore the barbs: rising to them only made her appear vulnerable, which she wasn't, because Pansy did not matter to her any more.

'I hoped you'd be interested in my little scheme.'

'At least you could stop being someone's fancy woman.'

'How many times do I have to tell you? Arnold is a friend.' More's the pity, she thought wistfully.

'This looks like a kept woman's house, if you ask me. All them frills and furbelows.'

'Pansy, I invited you here because I feel sorry for you.' And I couldn't stand another Sunday on my own with no one to talk to, she thought, but she would never admit *that*.

'No need to feel sorry for me. Best thing you ever did,

leaving. Got me strength back, can walk a mile now and not get puffed. A new lease of life, you've given me.'

'I'm happy to hear it, but sorry you couldn't have found a use for your legs all the years I was burdened with you.'

'Burdened! Now, that's not a nice thing to say to your old mother.'

'But you aren't my mother, are you?'

'The only one you've ever known, and you can't take that away from me.'

Pansy settled back in her chair. 'This venture of yours, how will you finance it? You'll need a tidy sum to rent premises and take on staff.'

'Initially I can work from here.'

'And who'd believe you were a professional person?'

'I hadn't thought of that. It wouldn't do at all. However, I wouldn't need staff to start with. Anyway, perhaps clients would be happier dealing with just me.'

'What sort of secrets can you find?'

'Well, who's stealing and how much.'

'What if it's the boss?'

'If he had partners or shareholders, I would feel duty-bound to point out to him that his actions were discernible.'

'Or tell the others, if he was a horrible old cove.'

'Perhaps.'

'Or the one who'd pay you the most for such information.'

'Really, Pansy! Do you want to hear my plans or not?'

'I'm listening. I'm giving you my valuable opinion.'

Lily controlled her irritation. 'Should he have no others to whom he is beholden, he can hardly be stealing from himself, can he?'

'But you could file away the information for a rainy day, in case a situation arose when it might be useful?' That arch look again.

Lily rolled her eyes impatiently.

'You can take that expression off your face. I was only pointing out possibilities. If you won't listen, why ask my opinion?'

'You're right, Pansy. I'm sorry.' She hadn't meant to apologise, it had just slipped out – old habits.

'If you look at all the eventualities, make plans for them, you're not going to be taken unawares, are you?'

'Correct again, Pansy.' And, of course, she was.

'It sounds interesting to me. I wish you well, Lily, I really do.'

'Thank you, Pansy.'

'But do take care. Do a little too much digging around and you might end up in danger.'

'Really, Mother! You have such an imagination! I *would* be careful. In any case, there are other avenues. I could help friends of mine.

'Arnold, you mean. You haven't got any friends.'

Lily winced. 'For example, I know that Dulcie Randolph has an income of twelve thousand a year.' She had been longing to impart this juicy piece of information.

'Twelve thousand pounds!' Pansy screeched. 'I never knew such money existed! What does she want with all that? You couldn't spend it in Barlton, no matter how hard you tried. All that money and she looks so miserable all the time. I'd be grinning from ear to ear all the days God gave me. Does she get it all from that shop? No, that's his. Where from, then?'

'You must never tell a living soul this but . . .' Lily leaned towards Pansy '. . . it's all hers. Always has been. I knew as much before, but not the details.'

'But he prances around as if it's all his,' said Pansy. 'I hope she keeps him on a tight rein – but of course she doesn't! He's got you.'

'Why do you have to be so spiteful?'

'I was just teasing.' Pansy laughed, but as if she was wondering if she had gone too far.

'It's strange how often you claim that the hurtful things you say are teasing.'

'I said I was sorry. I really *am* interested – especially in where all that money comes from.'

'It's not just the shop. She owns property in London, she has stocks and shares, interests in a coal mine, a cotton mill. She's a very rich lady to be sure. But the odd thing is, I found all this out in the office of the solicitors I work for. But she and Arnold have always dealt with Munroe, Small and Whitehead. Why is she instructing Mr Battle?'

'It don't take a genius to work *that* out.'

'What?'

'Any chance of some port?'

'Pansy! You won't tell me until I give you a drink?'

'That's right.' Pansy winked. Lily poured the port, and Pansy settled back in her chair. 'She's made another will, cut the bugger out. That's what she's gone and done, and good luck to her, says I. I've always thought that Arnold was a shifty toad.'

'He isn't.' But Lily was distracted now. Why hadn't she thought of that? She hadn't been able to read any of the wills in the office because they were kept in the large safe, a really strong Chubb, which she had not been able to open.

It was time for Pansy to leave. Lily was so grateful for her insight that she gave her the bottle of port.

'Lily, you look even more scrawny than usual. Not getting your oats as frequent as you want?'

'Mother!'

'You want to watch that man. He's got another fancy woman. Saw him with her only last week. Prancing and mincing along they were, no shame. And her such a respectable-looking woman – quite shocking.'

'You say these things to hurt me.'

'Truth often is painful. Can't be helped. It's best you know.'

'Not lies, it isn't. He loves me.'

'Don't be so daft. What's there about you to love? Just look at you.'

'I'd like you to leave now. And you'll never see another penny from me.'

'Suits me.' Pansy fumbled with the buttons on her coat. 'I never enjoyed being beholden to you.'

'But what will you do?' This was all wrong. Pansy should be crying and begging her forgiveness by now, Lily thought.

'You're not the only one with a fancy man. I've got one too. But mine wants to marry me.'

Lily's mouth was still open with astonishment when the front door slammed.

6

'Mother, what a lovely surprise! But you look so tired. Sit down.' Chauncey rushed out of the room and shouted down the stairs, 'Dick, some tea for Mrs Randolph.' He was a whirl of movement as he plumped cushions, moved books, closed the window, led Dulcie to the sofa and found her a footstool.

'Still doing half a dozen tasks at the same time, just as you always did. How lovely to see you moving so well.' She settled herself on the sofa. 'But I'm not an invalid, you needn't fuss.' She pushed away the stool with her foot.

'Then why are you looking so peaky? You don't look after yourself properly.'

She was laughing. 'It is normally I who say that to you. I must be getting old.'

'I worry about you.'

'Then don't. I haven't been sleeping well, that's probably the reason.' She was touched by his concern.

'Why?' He swung round from drying a handful of paintbrushes.

'I've so much to think about. I can't stop planning and running over things in my mind when I should be sleeping.' She said this in a light-hearted way. She had no intention of telling him that she lay awake at night going over and over the dreadful scene with Arnold, which would always haunt her. He had many faults, but violence towards her had not been among them until now. That night he had not been play-acting: he would have killed her if she hadn't retracted her statement to Agnes – and how humiliating that had been. Agnes was barely speaking to her, which she could understand, but Arnold carried on as if nothing had happened and she found that even more chilling. Chauncey was the last person who should know of such threats and unpleasantness. He was hot-headed, would take matters into his own hands, and she loved him far too much to put him at risk.

'If that's all then why is that smile you're giving me not in your eyes?'

'What an imagination you have!' She inhaled deeply. 'How I love the smells of linseed oil and turpentine.'

'Strange tastes you have, Mama.'

'Not at all. When you were away, the least hint of them and it was as if you were in the room with me.'

'There were no lilies of the valley where I was so I didn't have the luxury of being reminded of you. Not that I needed any stimulus. You were always with me, all the time. How's my delightful sister?'

'Much the same,' she said. 'Very cross that her young Edward hasn't asked her to marry him.'

'Wise man. I'd like to meet him and warn him.' Chauncey crossed the room to the long table that held his paints and drawing materials.

'I had thought to ask you if I might bring him and his father here to meet you one afternoon.'

'I would be pleased – but you don't have to ask me, it's your house.' He settled himself on a chair opposite her, pad and charcoal in hand.

'No, Chauncey, it's yours. I keep telling you so. What are you doing?'

'Sketching you. I'm going to do a portrait of you. I did the last when I was sixteen. I want to see if my technique has improved. Otherwise I shall become a fishmonger.'

'The portrait was perfect. There was no need for improvement.'

'You talk like a mother.'

'How else am I to talk? I *am* one.'

She laughed gaily. It was a good idea to have come, even unannounced, which she would never normally do. The contrast between here and December Cottage, with its atmosphere and her fears, was stark. 'May I move?' Already she felt the need to stretch.

'A little, but if you could stay silent – just for five minutes?'

She felt most resentful of her need to get out of her home, which she loved so much. Had he ruined the house for her? Would she always be afraid there? Would *she* have to move out? Never! Why should she? She must stop being afraid, she must learn to ignore Agnes and her moods, she must . . .

'I didn't ask you to frown.'

'Was I? I'm sorry.'

'What's wrong, Mama? You would tell me if something was worrying you?' He had laid down his sketch-pad and pencil.

'Of course I would. There's nothing. Your return home, safe at last, has made me blissfully happy. May I see?' He handed her the lightning sketch he had done. She did not recognise herself in the dumpy little woman he had drawn. There was a stiffness in the pose, the set of the mouth. But he was an artist, and, no doubt, he saw people as they were and not how they hoped they were.

'It's very good, you're an excellent artist. But you have drawn the worry that you, wrongly, think I have.'

'I draw and paint what I see.'

'May I?' Dulcie began to turn the pages of the pad. He was so talented, she knew, and not because she was his mother. 'These are interesting.' She pointed to a series of drawings of a young woman.

'She walks her dog on the beach most days.'

'How interesting.' Dulcie smiled at him. 'Are you perhaps a little smitten?'

'No, of course not. She's a good subject, that's all. Sometimes she sits as still as a rock for minutes at a time – a perfect model. I'd love to know what occupies her so.'

'She's pretty but the poor soul looks like a tramp.'

'She does, rather. I'm thinking of buying her a coat. It just seems to get colder – one would never guess spring is round the corner.'

'How kind of you, but perhaps I should give it to her. She might be offended if a man did.'

'You think of everything, Mama.' They looked up as the door opened, then Dick, walking backwards appeared, balancing a tray precariously. 'At last. You took your time, Dick!'

'Sorry, Mr Chauncey, it's the crusts. I have a struggle to cut the bread neat. I hope you'll forgive me, Mrs Randolph, but this sort of work is new to me.' The strapping boy held the plate of sandwiches awkwardly in his large hands. The cress was sticking untidily out of the sides, half the egg had already fallen out, and he hadn't been entirely successful with the crusts. 'They look positively delicious.'

'The cake is bought, I'm afraid, Mrs Randolph. Cakes are a bit of a problem for me.'

'Cake-makers are born not taught, so don't bother yourself with them. And a bought cake is always so reliable, I find. Shall I pour?'

They held their breath as Dick transferred the tray to

the table in front of Dulcie, weaving his way between the furniture, tripping over his boots. 'Sorry.' He grinned, which wiped the frown of concentration from his face, and she saw how good-looking he was. She began to pour the tea. 'There's a slight problem, Dick.' She had to control herself not to laugh. 'There doesn't appear to be any tea in the pot, just water.'

'Oh, lawks! I'm sorry. So sorry!'

'Stop saying sorry, Dick, you buffoon. Do it properly this time.'

'Yes, Mr Chauncey.' Dick was bright red as he picked up the teapot.

'Take the water jug too. That'll be cold by the time you've organised yourself.'

'Sorry, Mr Chauncey.' He picked up the jug spilling water over the table, missing Dulcie by a fraction. 'Sorry.'

'Dick!' Chauncey yelled.

'Yes ... Mr Chauncey. Thank you,' he said, since Chauncey was holding the door wide open for him.

'You shouldn't be so stern with him,' Dulcie said, when Dick had left the room. 'It will take him time to learn.'

'He's used to it. He was a soldier. Everyone shouts at everyone else in the army. Unless you're Lord Roberts. He'd think I was ill if I didn't.'

'I can't agree. He will learn faster if you don't. And why not get a girl in to help out? Did you see his hands? He's used to manual work, not serving tea in a drawing room. I don't think he'll ever be a satisfactory manservant.'

'I couldn't desert him.'

'I'm not suggesting you should, but find him something else to do. What about the garden? Perhaps he could grow vegetables. My Mr Wilshire has retired and he could help out at December Cottage. The new man is not nearly reliable enough.'

'I'll discuss it with him. This afternoon he's going home to sort some problems out. He'll be gone for a week, and he can think then what he wants to do. Ah, you managed it this time, Dick. Sorry I was such a grump with you.'

'You said *sorry*, Mr Chauncey.' Dick smiled broadly.

'My son says you're going away for a few days, Dick. That's nice.'

'I doubt it will be, Mrs Randolph. You don't know my father.'

'A difficult man?'

'Very. We don't see eye to eye about anything.'

'I told him I had the same problem.' Chauncey laughed cycnically. Dulcie frowned. She couldn't approve of him talking about such personal matters with Dick: it would only confuse the poor boy further – one minute a servant, the next a confidant. In her experience it never worked. One could so easily lose their respect. Another of those changes, she supposed, that everyone was talking about. 'His father's a religious zealot, isn't he, Dick?'

'He is that.'

'Maybe you can give Dick some advice, Mama.'

'It would be my pleasure, if you think I would be of any assistance, Dick.'

'Well, it's where to begin. When we returned here, Mr Chauncey kindly offered to write to the local vicar's wife for me. I'd written to her before, just to let the family know I was safe. We said I was back, and that I'd be coming home, like, and could she let my sister, Phoebe, know. Well, we got a reply what told me Phoebe ran away last year. About August time, her said. No one has seen hide nor hair of her since. I don't know where to start looking for her or what to do.'

'Has your father been searching for her?'

'I doubt it. He was probably the reason she ran away.'

'Dick's worried. They were close, weren't you, Dick?'

'I love her,' he said simply.

'See, Mama, not a bit like Agnes and me!'

There! Again! It was true that he didn't get on with his sister, but he should keep it to himself, not tell others. Confiding in such a way . . . Her thoughts screeched to a halt. Was she not guilty of the selfsame thing with Theo Prestwick? But at least he wasn't a servant. The very thought made her smile.

'Have I said something amusing, Mother.'

'No, dearest. Just a silly thought I had. And nothing to do with your problem, Dick. How rude you must think me – you must be so concerned. One reads such dreadful stories in the newspapers. Now, let me think.' The two young men, one sitting, one standing, awaited her advice. 'A reward. That's it. You need to post a reward. One in the newspaper, and perhaps a few fly-posters about the place. Describe her to my son. He could do a likeness of her to illustrate it.'

'How could I draw someone I've never seen? And how much do you think the reward should be, Mama?'

'Five guineas? Ten? I'm not sure what sum would be appropriate.'

Dick looked crestfallen. 'It don't matter which, I haven't got either.'

'Perhaps your father would help. Even if he was the cause, he may wish to make amends.'

'That's true.' But Dick sounded doubtful.

'You could discuss it when you go home to see him.'

'Yes – I've got to find out what happened. And I have to see that my little brother is all right.'

'I have a solution. If your father won't help you I will arrange for you to have the money.'

'I couldn't presume on your generosity, Mrs Randolph, it wouldn't be right.'

'I didn't mean as a gift. If you could come to my house and help in my garden the reward could be in lieu of wages. What do you say?'

'That would be very kind of you. I like gardening.'

'Better than making sandwiches?'

'Oh, yes, Mrs Randolph. Sandwiches is hard work!'

7

People were such fools, Lily thought, as she watched Old Mr Battle check the number of the Chubb safe against the number he had written in the notebook he kept in the inside pocket of his jacket. She had plans to search it, should he ever take it off – most men, when in a rush, changed at their place of work. But in case he didn't, and certainly he looked too old and desiccated to have much of a social life, she had an alternative idea.

Recently she had spent hours learning how to read numbers reflected in a mirror. In the office there was an intricately engraved silver mirror, Venetian, she thought, almost opposite the large green safe on a bureau. She had been moving it slowly, inch by inch, so that no one would notice, until the wheel of the safe door was clearly visible in it. She had to hope no one registered her removing her spectacles – like many who needed spectacles for reading, Lily had perfect long sight. By dint of moving it and aligning it, she had acquired the first four numbers of the combination. She might not need to resort to pickpocketing.

'I trust you are not watching, Miss Howard,' Old Mr Battle quavered.

'Of course not, Mr Battle. As you see, I have my back to you.' In the mirror she saw him looking over his shoulder. Suspicious old fool, she thought, then had to suppress a laugh. Since the last two numbers were the same, she now felt triumphant that she knew them all.

Over the month she had been working here she had made a practice of staying late: catching up with her work, she told everyone. This was a barefaced lie since she was always up to date with everything she did.

Sometimes she even offered to help those less efficient than herself, who had a backlog. There were nights when the partners worked late and, to her annoyance, there seemed to be no set pattern to this. But the delay worked in her favour for the caretaker was used to seeing her about the place after office hours. And since she was charming to him, he was always helpful.

It was a stormy February night and she wished the wind would die down – if someone came she might not hear them. But she had to act. She was beginning to feel that time was against her.

She had pleaded with Arnold to spend more time with her, but he continued to do exactly as he pleased. Once he had come twice in a week; the longest he had stayed away was three weeks. When he appeared he might stay an hour or two, or merely five minutes. Sometimes he delivered papers to her and barely spoke. Sometimes he accepted a glass of wine or whisky. When they talked it was always about business. This annoyed her but, no matter what she did or said, she could never steer the conversation on to personal matters. Once or twice when she had nearly succeeded she had noticed how edgy he became, how swiftly he made an excuse to leave.

She couldn't bring herself to think he did not care about her; she dared not think he meant nothing to him. Such thoughts were locked firmly away. He needed organising, she needed greater control, more regulation. She needed . . . him.

He had other women. There were times when she could smell them on him, which made her feel sick with frustration and jealousy. Pansy had been right.

He constantly told her that Dulcie was still ill. Then, last week, Lily had been asked to deliver some papers to a client, a request that normally would have offended her but, with the first hint of spring in the air, she had been glad to be out in the fresh air. She was enjoying herself until, in Gold Street, she saw Dulcie, looking in the pink of health and hurrying along at a spanking pace.

He had visited that evening; it was one of those when he dallied for a drink. She had waited until he was on his second whisky. 'I saw your wife today, looking remarkably fit for someone so close to death's door.' He coughed and spluttered, then pretended the drink had gone down the wrong way. She patted his back, pleased at the chance to touch him, allowing her hand to stray upward until, just for a fleeting second, she could stroke his hair.

'You saw who?'

'Dulcie. Your wife,' she said, with marked sarcasm, and marvelled at how swiftly her mood and feelings could change when she was with him. 'Very pleased with herself she looked too.'

'But I don't understand. When I left her this morning she was so weak. I'd had a dreadful night, hardly any sleep. She can't keep anything down, you see.'

'You don't have a professional nurse for her?'

'She likes me to be close.' She had to admire the meek, modest expression he adopted. She loved him so much when he was being wicked.

'Well, she's made a miraculous recovery, or she's pretending to be ill when she isn't.'

'Why should she do something so devious?'

'To get your attention.' She, of all people, could understand Dulcie employing such a ruse. Perhaps if she tried the same ploy he might take more notice of *her*.

'She has always had my attention, all the years of our marriage.'

Liar, she thought. She hated him speaking in such fond terms: it emphasised that, no matter what, Dulcie was his wife and Lily wasn't. 'Perhaps you are lying to me.'

'Me? Lie to you? Why should I do that? What would be the point?'

'I don't know. Perhaps your are stringing me along.

Perhaps you want to stay with your wife and not be with me.'

'Lily, you know that's not true. You know I rely on you so very much.'

'You never tell me you love me.'

'It would not be right. I'm a married man.'

'And if you weren't?'

'Well, then I would be free.' He placed his glass on the table beside him. 'Is that really the time? I have to be at a lodge meeting in five minutes.' He was on his feet.

'Can you not miss it, just this once? I've cooked you a lovely meal.'

'Soon, dear Lily, we shall have all the time in the world, you and I.'

'But, Arnold . . .' He kissed her forcefully, which made her feel as though her insides were melting, and then he was gone.

After he had left she poured herself another drink, and found her hand was still shaking. More of those kisses, and she knew she would throw decorum to the winds, would beg him to take her . . .

Ah, such dreams! She sighed as she heard the last person but one leave the office.

'Just us left, as usual, Miss Howard. All right if I pop over the road to the post office?'

'Of course, Thomas. Be as long as you wish.' She smiled at him. 'If you wouldn't mind?' She handed him a coin.

'You're a pearl, Miss Howard, and no mistake.'

She waved him on his way, but not to the post – that was their little joke: he'd be swilling down the beer she'd just paid for at the Admiral's Arch. She always asked him to bring her back a small cherry brandy so that he would think he had information about her and thus that he could trust her not to tell on him. She congratulated herself on how devious she could be.

The huge door of the heavy safe would weigh a ton,

she thought, but it swung open easily. She was overcome with excitement when she saw the contents: boxes upon boxes of documents, bags of sovereigns, piles of bank-notes and what looked like a stack of jewellery cases. No, she told herself, don't touch the money or the baubles. You've plenty and, if you're right, you'll soon have even more.

Her instinct – natural enough, she reassured herself – was to dive in and sort rapidly through the papers, but logic told her to memorise where everything was. Even though the three partners had access at all times to this safe and it would be difficult for them to swear to exactly where things were placed, it would be foolish of her to take the risk.

'Be methodical. This may take time – days, even.' She removed a box, careful not to disturb the contents. What a mess! There was no order here, no sensible system, no filing. The box contained wills. She sifted through them. Many of the names meant nothing to her, but every so often she came across one she recognised and peeped inside. Well, Mrs Fanshaw should be making a new will and no mistake. Either the poor woman was not aware of what a mess her finances were in or she lived in a dream. Mr Markham, she read, had thousands, and left most of it to the poorhouse. There would be disillusioned relatives. She wondered if they would contest his will – she would if she were them – and who, in law, could do so. She paused. That was a new idea. Why shouldn't she become a solicitor? She had the brains. After all, there were now women doctors, not that she would ever consult one: she would not be sure she could trust them, far better a man's healing hands. It was an interesting idea . . .

Meanwhile she returned to her task. How she would love to organise this safe properly. Have the wills in alphabetical order so that she would know exactly where she needed to look. She laughed to herself. How inconsiderate of the partners not to make her task easier.

She glanced at her watch. Thomas, the caretaker, would be vacating the public house fairly soon, and she had not found Dulcie's will. What she did find, which would be of immense help to her, was a box containing the pristine parchment sheets used for writing wills. She took one. When she found Dulcie's she would make a new one and destroy the original; so simple. She would take the risk that no one would have counted how many remained there.

Five minutes later when Thomas returned Lily was working diligently on a letter. 'Did you have a convivial time, Thomas?'

'Very pleasant, Miss Howard, thank you very much. And here's your little treat.' He winked as he placed the glass containing her cherry brandy on the desk in front of her.

'You wouldn't tell on me, Thomas, would you?' She fluttered her eyelashes.

'Our secret, Miss Howard.' He winked at her, which she found most offensive. 'You shouldn't be still working.'

'Just this one letter for Young Mr Battle, then I'm off.'

'I hopes that lot appreciate you and no mistake.'

It was not until three attempts later, in March, that Lily found what she was looking for. Dulcie's will had been placed in a box on which some fool had written 'Trusts'. Such inefficiency! She undid the ribbon and read it with mounting fury.

Pansy had been right. She had cut out dear Arnold completely. The evil creature had merely left an annuity for her daughter, her own flesh and blood – a large one, to be sure, but was it fair? Otherwise every penny went to her son. The woman didn't deserve to live.

She made careful notes. Dulcie's full name – Dulcie

Maud Augusta – the names of the executors, and most importantly, the witnesses with their addresses. She glanced at her watch and saw she had ten minutes left. She rushed to her desk and grabbed a piece of tissue paper. Concentrating as hard as her racing heart would allow, she traced the signatures. That done, she closed the safe and scanned the room to make sure she had left nothing out.

In the doorway she bumped into Thomas.

'You don't normally work in here, Miss Howard?'

'I needed a certain law book.'

'Haven't found it, then?' He nodded at her empty hand.

'I've just put it back, Thomas.' She smiled at him.

'Of course, I should report this to the partners.'

'What on earth for?'

'That's my instruction. *"Anything untoward."* That's what Old Mr Battle told me.'

Lily forced herself to laugh gaily. 'Well. I've never been thought of as *untoward* before. How very amusing.'

'Well, I should.'

'And perhaps I should tell him about your little trips to the Admiral's Arch. After all, that's a little "untoward", wouldn't you say, Thomas?'

'And what about you then and your little tipple?'

'But he knows, Thomas. Gave me a little present of cherry brandy himself.' She bestowed on him one of her superior smiles, the one that would tell him who was in charge. And who could blackmail whom.

8

It was a good thing that no one could read her mind: what a shock they would have, thought Dulcie, as she descended the steep stone steps into Chauncey's kitchen.

She quite shocked herself with her frequent immodest thoughts about Theo Prestwick. So silly of her. The bottom of these stairs was too dark, she thought, they needed better lighting here or someone would break their neck. She must investigate the possibility and cost of having electric lighting installed. It was so much easier, cleaner – a wonderful invention.

'Mrs Milner, I think we should ask Dick to hang a lantern outside at the bottom of the stairs. It's very dangerous.'

'I was thinking that only this morning. I'll ask him the minute he returns.'

'Is he still away?'

'Yes, Mrs Randolph. He's still with his family – a slight difficulty, I gather.'

'I understand.' Dulcie respected such discretion on the part of the new cook-general she had found for Chauncey. If there was one thing she loathed it was gossip below stairs.

'I've been wondering what sandwiches you'd be wanting, Mrs Randolph?'

'Gentleman's relish, but with toast, most certainly. And the smoked salmon, with just a hint of cayenne.' She checked the cake. 'Such fine chocolate icing. Lord Prestwick adores chocolate cake.'

'And I took the liberty of baking some shortbread too.'

'He will be delirious with joy. Are you settling in, Mrs Milner?'

'Very comfortable, thank you very much, Mrs Randolph.'

'My son is so happy with your porridge. I told him we needed to find a Scot, since only your countrywomen truly understand porridge.'

'Like a Yorkshirewoman makes the best puddings.'

'Exactly. Now, I've asked my coachman to bring down the Worcester tea service – it will have been washed, so there's no need to do it again, but I would ask you to take great care of it. You've found a girl, I hear?'

'Ethel. She's doubling as parlour-maid and kitchen-maid. I told Mr Chauncey I didn't think she was up to it, but he said to train her. Easier said than done, in my opinion.'

'I'm sure we can teach her, Mrs Milner. It will be a good opportunity for her. Chauncey tells me she came from the waifs' home. I'm involved with it, you know, and I always try to find employment for them, if I can.'

'Very well, madam. But I'm not sure she could be trusted with fine china.'

'She should learn. I really must find Chauncey some good china of his own. Perhaps if I spoke to her?'

'Ethel!' Mrs Milner shouted. At her call a small, emaciated girl appeared, looking scared. She looked barely old enough to have left home, let alone be working. She stood awkwardly, her dress crumpled and none too clean. 'Ethel, this is Mrs Randolph what is employing you. Now, you listen to her and no cheek, mind.'

'Hello, Ethel, how do you do?'

The child looked close to tears as she mumbled a response and wiped her hand down her dress.

'Don't sniff,' Mrs Milner said sternly.

'Now, Ethel, I have a very important task for you. When my china arrives, I want you to unpack it with care, carry it to the drawing room a few pieces at a time – there is a table outside the door where it can be left in preparation. After tea, each piece is to be washed separately and rinsed in the second sink. Dry it gently – imagine it's a baby.' As she imparted this information Ethel looked even more wan and frightened.

'Are you sure she's to be trusted, Mrs Randolph?'

Ethel's lip quivered.

'I'm sure she is, Mrs Milner. Aren't you, Ethel?'

'I'll do my best, m'm.'

'You'll do more than that, my girl!'

'I'm sure you will manage it beautifully. Has she some decent clothes, Mrs Milner?'

'I purchased a uniform for her, only I didn't want her wearing it in the scullery.'

'Quite so. Still, I think we can run to some new clothes for her kitchen work, too.' She smiled at Ethel, who, evidently unused to such kindness, looked close to tears again. 'Do you think you can carry the tray into the drawing room? And the cake-stand? And not hurt yourself?'

'I will, Mrs Randolph. I promise.'

'Excellent.'

As she bustled back upstairs Dulcie wished that dealing with people she met socially was as easy as talking to her servants. But, of course, that was at the core of her liking for Theo: he was so easy to talk to – he never made her feel dull or half-witted.

It must have been at least the third time that Dulcie had plumped up the cushions. 'Honestly, Mama, if I didn't know better I'd have thought either the Queen or a beau was about to arrive!'

'Such a tease you are, Chauncey!' She lowered her head and straightened a paperknife so he could not see her face and the high colour it had acquired. 'Did I hear the bell?' She walked quickly to the window. 'Yes, it is they.'

The meeting, so long in the planning, was about to take place. The delay had been caused because Theo had been to France. Dulcie had felt bereft when she'd heard he was going – and she would have liked so much to accompany him. But at last they were here.

What if they didn't like each other – the two most important people in her life?

'Lord Prestwick and Mr Bartholomew-Prestwick, Mrs Randolph.' Ethel announced them, with a neat curtsy, as if she had spent all her life doing so. Dulcie wished Mrs Milner could have seen her: kindess often had such satisfactory results.

'Welcome, welcome, dear friends.' Her excitement apparent for all to see, Dulcie approached them with her arms wide in welcome. 'Come, meet my dear son.'

Even as the introductions were made it was obvious to her that all would be well. The liking was instant, just as she had felt it would be. There was so much for them to talk about, the war, art, porcelain. Chauncey and Edward in particular took to each other. How nice for him to have a friend, older, but near enough to him in age.

'And where do you live, Lord Prestwick?'

'I have a small house in Exeter in Mont le Grand. The name of the street is much grander-sounding than the residents to be found there.' One of his laughs rumbled up. 'But it suits me, and your mother has graciously visited me there.'

'On several occasions, and always such a pleasure.'

'As it is for me when I visit you.'

Dulcie saw an almost conspiratorial look pass between the young men. What could it mean?

'I'd have presumed—' Chauncey stopped abruptly.

'Presumed I'd have a great estate?'

'No, nothing like that. I presumed that . . .'

Theo and Edward looked interested in whatever it was Chauncey was trying to say.

'I . . . That . . .'

'Yes?'

'Well, yes. I had supposed you would live in a great house.'

'As lords should.' To Dulcie's relief another of Theo's laughs engulfed him. He had not taken offence. Soon they were all laughing, just as Ethel appeared with the tea. 'Such a cake! And shortbread! Just look at those wonderful sandwiches. Your mother spoils me, Mr Randolph-Smythe.'

'Randolph is sufficient, if you would be so kind.'

'Like your mother?'

'Yes.'

'Then I am assured I shall like you especially well.' Theo's eyes twinkled.

As she dismissed Ethel, Dulcie saw that the girl looked as if she was about to faint with relief. 'Well done,' she whispered to her, before she scuttled from the room.

'I like your straightforwardness, young man,' Theo went on. 'I know most people wonder about my circumstances but never dare ask. So I shall tell you. The reason I do not live as the world assumes I should is, like so many of my class, the damned corn laws.'

Dulcie nodded. She should have thought of that.

'They have led to the arrival here of cheap corn from America. That, coupled with the failed harvests around 'seventy-five, was the trouble. This country changed, twenty-five years ago, and prosperity deserted those of us who relied on the countryside.'

'I'm so sorry, sir.'

'No need, dear boy. Our own fault. We should have seen it coming. Industrialisation, better wages in the cities, that's right and fair. The future lies with clever chappies like your father – giving the population what they want – and the other clever coves who make things.'

'Poor Theo,' Dulcie said softly.

'Stuck in the past, that was my problem. No head, you see, to look into the future. Tenant farmers couldn't pay the rents. I lowered them, which didn't give me enough to run the estate. I kept selling bits and bobs of land, but eventually there was nothing for it but to sell, lock, stock and barrel. Lost some pretty things that way, I can tell you – things that would have gladdened your heart, dear lady. Still, no point in crying over spilt milk. It's done and there's an end to it. And, estate or no, this is the best shortbread I've ever tasted.'

'I'm so sorry. And who bought it?'

'My brother-in-law. Clever family, the Bartholomews. They're in cotton up in Lancashire. Not that my wife was happy for people to know that.' Dulcie was aware of a shade of bitterness in his voice as he spoke.

'So, in a manner of speaking, it's still in the family,' Chauncey remarked.

'I don't regard the present incumbent in that way. I probably shouldn't say so but your mother, I think, is aware of how I feel. But one day Edward here will inherit. That is, if he's a mind to it.'

'Are you not happy to be your uncle's heir, Edward?' Dulcie asked.

The young man looked down at his feet and shuffled them.

'I embarrass you, I apologise.'

'No, it's not that, Mrs Randolph. It's to be beholden to someone . . . It can be difficult.' He looked even more upset.

'I can imagine. More cake, everyone?' Dulcie saw that he was discomfitted and that there were unresolved matters afoot, which were best not pried into. She rang the bell, for something to do, wishing she had not been so forward. 'Thank you, Ethel. If you wouldn't mind . . .'

Very slowly and with infinite care Ethel removed the tea things, putting them on the table outside as they had arranged. Suddenly there was a crash. Dulcie sat upright but said nothing.

A minute later, Ethel, eyes streaming, shaking with fear, appeared in the doorway. 'I'm sorry, I'm so sorry . . .' was all she could say.

'There, Ethel, never mind. I'm sure it was an accident. Just get a dustpan and brush.' Ethel, still crying, rushed from the room. 'These things happen,' Dulcie said, and smiled.

*

'I approve wholeheartedly of your friends,' said Chauncey, as they mounted the steps after seeing them to their carriage.

'I've never really had a friend before, one I can relax with, who seems to understand me and has the same interests.'

'Shame you're both married.'

'Chauncey, what a thing to say! In fact, he's a widower.'

'Is he?' Chauncey grinned at her. 'Did you not think that Edward was upset when the conversation turned to this Bartholomew?'

'It was all my fault. I should never have asked. I feel so ashamed.' Dulcie resumed her seat.

'I don't think he held it against you. I asked the wrong question too.'

'Theo did not mind, and I'd wondered myself. But it must be hard on the boy. He is likely to inherit that great estate while his poor father has lost so much. And although Theo's house is charming it is very modest for such as he.'

'Have you any idea why Edward reacted as he did?'

'There is much rumour and gossip about Mr Bartholomew. He's prosperous, which annoys many, and he keeps himself to himself, which annoys others. It must be hard for Edward if he has heard the same rumours. After all, he is his uncle.'

'Lord Prestwick doesn't like him.'

'So it would seem, but you will learn that there are often undercurrents of jealousy and resentment in families. And he's not of his blood. It makes a difference.'

'Agnes is my blood, and I don't like her.'

'Chauncey!'

'Shall you tell me what you know about this Bartholomew?'

'No, Chauncey, and you should know better than to ask me.'

'How tedious of you, Mama.' He wandered over to the window. 'Come, it's the girl I've been drawing.'

'Why, I've seen her before, with a young man. Chauncey, she looks so sad. What do you think has happened to her?'

9

'You were right, Pansy. She has changed her will, the evil bitch!' Lily was hardly through the door of her mother's house.

'You never used disgusting language like that before.'

'Maybe I didn't, but you did.' Lily looked about the dingy room with distaste.

'Quite the little lady you used to be. Living in sin isn't doing you much good, is it?'

'I am not *living in sin*. I don't know how many times I have to say this to you, but Arnold is my friend. He is repaying me for a service.'

'So you say!'

Lily, who had been about to sit down, stood up again. 'Whenever I try to be friendly, you always say something offensive.' Her hands were on her hips, ready to do battle.

'How can the truth be *offensive* ? Unless you're riddled with guilt, of course.'

'What have I got to be guilty about?'

'Lusting after another woman's husband and deserting me.'

'That's a matter of opinion. I would hardly call the allowance I make you desertion.'

'Tea? With a nice nip of whisky?'

'Thank you.' She sat down. Pansy had admitted defeat: offering tea was her way of calling a truce. Lily was glad of that: she hadn't come here to argue.

'You never used to drink. Signed the Pledge, didn't you?' This was less an accusation than curiosity.

'Must be all that living in sin I'm supposed to be doing.' She managed a smile, and Pansy chortled. While Pansy made the tea – *there* was a difference, she'd never done it before – Lily settled back in her chair and wondered how best to approach the subject she had come to discuss. But now that she was here, she was having second thoughts.

It was true that she was drinking more: she was lonely and found that several port and lemons in the evening cheered her no end. She had never thought she would miss Pansy, of all people, but she did. Her relationship with Arnold was a great disappointment to her. She wanted to trust him but she was finding it difficult to do so. If he could lie to her about Dulcie and her health, what else was he lying about?

Pansy fluttered about the room fussing over Lily, which was a new and rather pleasant experience.

'Pansy, why did you pretend you were unable to walk when you've stronger legs than I have?' She spoke gently to show that she was not about to argue.

'Silly, wasn't it?' Pansy poured the tea, then added a generous measure of whisky. 'Fooled you, though, didn't I?' She gave a sly smile. 'Promise not to laugh? I wanted . . . affection.' Suddenly her eyes filled with tears.

'Oh, Pansy.' Lily took her hand. 'I'm so sorry. I'd no idea.'

'You were always so busy. I knew you didn't want to be stuck with me. I'm sure I would have scarpered if I'd been put in the same position. But you're a good woman. I knew that if I pretended to be an invalid you'd stay. And you did. Till that Arnold got at you.'

'I've room enough in the new house for you.'

'You, me and a maid? In that shoebox?'

'I sacked the maid weeks ago.'

'Why? Have you lost your senses? You'll find another, of course?'

'I don't think I will. I didn't know how to deal with the girl. I felt awkward with her, someone there in the house every hour of the day and night. And I hated the idea of her looking through my drawers.'

'Why? What are you hiding?' But it was accompanied by a grin. 'Give me a maid, I'd know how to handle her. Never heard anything so silly in my life.'

'So what I was wondering – why I came is . . . Would you like to come back with me? Get out of this hovel?'

'Lily, love, I can't. I told you, I've a beau.'

'I thought you said that to annoy me, that it wasn't true.'

'It's true. A nice man too. He's got no money, works in the dockyard, but he suits me. He likes a laugh. It wouldn't be right, not under your roof. You know, the hanky-panky.'

'Mother, you don't!' Lily blushed to the roots of her hair.

'And why not? Don't want to be nailed in my coffin without an adventure or two!' A soft expression came over her face. 'I know I'm not your mother, and I know I wasn't very good as it was, but I love you, Lily, and I did my best. And I'm so happy when you call me Mother, not Pansy.' She lifted her skirt and, from her bloomers, removed a large handkerchief and blew noisily into it.

Both women dissolved into floods of tears, and Lily, for the first time ever, realised she loved Pansy too. But she collected herself. 'I don't mind what you do under my roof, so will you come?'

'It isn't that simple. I told you, my fellow wants to marry me, and I've decided to say yes. He's retiring soon and his mother left him a nice little cottage out Courtney way.'

'You – in the country?'

'I was raised in the countryside.'

'That doesn't mean you like it.'

'With the right man I could be happy anywhere. I'm sorry, girl, but there it is. No point in me moving to yours, then moving out again in a month.'

At this information, Lily burst into tears once more and appeared unable to stop. 'Lily, what on earth – what's the matter?' Pansy knelt on the floor in front of her. 'Tell me, let me help you.'

'You can't,' Lily hiccuped.

'Everything's possible. Now, pull yourself together, Lily. What's wrong?'

'I'm so lonely.' Lily sobbed even harder.

Pansy, who had initially been sympathetic, now looked exasperated. From a drawer she produced a pile of newly laundered handkerchiefs, which she put in front of Lily. 'If there's much more of this, you're going to be needing them.'

'I knew you wouldn't understand!'

'To be honest, I don't. You couldn't wait to be shot of me. Now you're lonely and want me back because it suits you. Don't you think I was lonely too, when you left?'

'I'm sorry.' Lily looked up pleadingly.

'You should have thought all this before you went.' Pansy was sitting opposite her now, hands folded in her lap, lips pursed with disapproval.

'I don't understand. One minute we're friends and I think you want to help me. The next you're cross. What am I to do?' Lily wailed anew. 'I want you to love me!'

'And what about Arnold? Don't he love you?'

At the mention of his name the volume of Lily's bawling rose. Pansy stood up again, shuffled across the room and slapped Lily hard across the face. 'Pull yourself together, do!'

Lily's howling ceased.

'That's better. Such a caterwauling. Now, tell me.' Pansy listened intently to the litany of Arnold's shortcomings. 'You were thinking straight at the beginning.

Remember when you told me your plans? I respected the clear way you were thinking, so do that again. The first thing is to have that house put in your name. You've this information on the will—'

'I should tell him?'

'No! Why would you do that?'

'He should know.'

'Don't be stupid! That's the last thing to do. If you tell him it's out of the bag, done with. Hint at it. Hint there's a big secret you know that involves him. It's a perfect opportunity for you. Imply that if he signs the house over to you, you'll tell him. As soon as the papers are altered, you can tell him if you want, or not. But change the locks and, if you'll take my advice, have nothing to do with him.'

'But I love him!'

'You don't. You love the excitement of knowing him, the unknown.'

'I hoped if I told him about the will he'd be so cross he'd divorce Dulcie and marry me.'

'Heaven above, girl! You've less sense than I thought. He's not going to divorce her – think of the scandal. Half the town would stop patronising his shop. He'd never be mayor. If Dulcie croaked, or if he rubbed her out, it would be the same. He isn't going to marry you, ever. If she died, or he murdered her, he wouldn't settle for someone like you. He'd have all the money he needed to buy the prettiest girls on the planet.'

'But he wouldn't. I've the proof. She's left everything to her son. He wouldn't be rich. Only if I destroy the will.'

'And you're sure there isn't a duplicate?' Pansy looked at her with a sly expression.

'Is that possible?'

'Yes. In a case like this I should think it highly likely. I'd have one, if I were Dulcie. Wouldn't you? Let me think a minute.' Pansy frowned deeply. 'That's it!' She looked triumphant. 'You need to put the will you took somewhere safe. Here, for instance. Then you can tell him ... He'll search for Dulcie's copy and then if he doesn't find it you've got real bargaining power.'

'Mother, you're so clever!'

'I'm only thinking what's best for you. As a mother should.'

Lily had Dulcie's will spread out in front of her on the dining-table. She never tired of reading it and wondering what it must be like to have so much to leave anyone. She was still congratulating herself on her trick. She'd spent hours practising the writing to be found on the front of the document, flowing and flowery. She replicated the writing on the spare document she had stolen, leaving everything to Arnold – she had enjoyed doing that, almost as if it were her money. This she had placed in the office safe last night, keeping the real one. Her mother was right. She would hide it in her house: it was the last place he would think to look.

The sound of footsteps on the street outside made her jump. She'd recognise his tread anywhere. Hurriedly she folded the precious will, placed it in an envelope and hid it at the bottom of her work-basket as his key grated in the lock. Seconds later he was in the room, giving her a modest peck on the cheek, his usual salutation.

'What a pleasant surprise – after so long! Another week gone by. Why, it'll soon be April. Before we know where we are it will be summer.' She knew she was nagging, and she had resolved not to, but she couldn't resist doing so.

'Is there any good reason I should come if all you're going to do is act as my wife?'

'Forgive me, Arnold. I spend so much of my time alone.'

'Your choice. I supplied you with a maid.'

'She wasn't to my liking and, in any case, I can hardly

spend my time conversing with a servant. What on earth would we have in common?'

'Then you must learn to deal with being alone. For myself I can't think of anything more pleasant.'

'I have employment, Arnold.' She feared he would be angry.

'Really? Doing what?'

'Much as I did for you.' She was disappointed at how uninterested he sounded. She had so hoped he would rant and say that no woman of his would work.

'Who with?' Did she detect a spark of interest?

'Battle, Todsworth and Battle.' Yes, he was certainly interested now: he'd folded the newspaper he was about to read.

'Perhaps . . .'

'I could find out interesting matters for you? I already have.'

'And what has my clever little Lily discovered?'

'You can't be cross with me one minute, then sweet the next. It's deceitful.'

He pulled her towards him and kissed her.

This had the usual effect on her. She was eager to please him. 'Mr Markham is retiring. His business is for sale. He has cut his son out of his will.'

'Markham – Robert? Are you sure?'

'Positive. I read it with my own eyes.'

'Then it's a good thing my daughter has lost interest in him and turned to young Edward. Now there is a man with prospects worthy of Agnes.'

'I agree. He is a fine, upstanding young man. Why, he is so much more manly than Robert Markham.'

'Anything else?'

'Nothing for the moment,' she lied, giving herself an imaginary hug. 'Except . . .' She outlined her plan for her business. The more she talked, the more she was convinced this was a wonderful idea. 'What do you think?' she asked.

'Rubbish!'

'Pardon?'

'There would not be enough business in this town. Old Briggs, the debt-collector, does a good trade in gossip for a consideration, and a lot less than it sounds as if you will be charging.'

'I'd hoped you would be my partner.'

'No, thank you. I've more sense than to go into business with a woman.'

He flicked open his newspaper as if she was not in the room. It was too mortifying.

'How is your wife?'

'No change, the poor creature,' he said, from behind the paper.

'Why do you lie, Arnold?'

'I'm not.'

'Afraid I might go and tell her that you still owe Mr Bartholomew money over that property in Gold Street?'

'How do you know that?' He looked startled, then seemed to collect himself. 'You would, in any case, be wasting your breath since she knows.'

'She might. But does she know that the large sum of money she paid out has not yet found its way into Mr Bartholomew's bank account? I doubt that.' She was guessing now but, knowing him as well as she did, she was confident she was right.

'Busy little Lily, aren't you? Not at all like the lilies of the field.' He smiled complacently, pleased with his little joke, by which she, having heard it a thousand times, was not amused. 'You still haven't told me how you came by such information, not that it is true.'

'Oh, but it is, Arnold, as well you know. Her lawyer, you see, happens to be the man I work for.'

'That's not possible. We share the same lawyer.'

'You might have once, but no longer. You say she has been so ill, but not so bad that she can't visit your son in the house she has purchased for him.'

362

She had to admire the way he shrugged his shoulders as if he didn't care. 'I'm pleased the boy is well lodged.'

'Not so bedridden that she didn't go and see Mr Battle weeks ago to change her will.' She threw caution to the wind, determined to shake him, to make him notice her.

The astonishment, shock, then fear on his face were a pleasure to see. 'I should sit down if I were you, Arnold. You look quite pale. We've much to discuss and plan. Haven't we, Arnold?'

'It would appear so, *dear* Lily.'

10

Phoebe had been working at the laundry for three months. The last few weeks had been happier now that she had been accepted by the Skelton and Tomlin families. Mimi no longer waited for her outside in all weathers, for one of the women, kinder to animals than the others, had fashioned a bed for her out of old blanket scraps and tucked it away in the drying room. The little dog was always warm and less anxious since she was closer to Phoebe.

The experiences Phoebe had endured in the past months had changed her. She was lonely and would have liked to make friends with the other women but she had nothing in common with them. She did not want to spend her precious earnings on drink. She was appalled by the way they fought, and was disconcerted by the way the younger girls talked about men from morning until night. She knew that several were not averse to going to the back of the laundry with them and were paid for the services they performed. She found this sad, but the girls laughed, pocketed the money and said what fools men were. She longed to have someone with whom to discuss books and pictures, and to confide her dream of travelling. To be able to talk of dresses, scents and pretty things. She began to wonder if the changes in her were irreversible or would she, if stuck permanently in this situation, always feel isolated and alone.

However, a mutual respect existed between them. The other women liked her spirit, even if they had been disappointed to discover that, after all, Phoebe had committed no crime. They admired her education, although she had protested that she was only at the beginning.

For her part, she valued their irrepressible high spirits and their unquestioning loyalty to each other, and wished she had someone to defend her in the way they looked after each other.

Since she was earning more, Phoebe squirrelled away every penny she could muster. She still had her plans: she and Mimi would go to Exeter and find their fortune, perhaps even London . . . As always, she acknowledged, they were vague, and the oddest thing was that, despite everything, Barlton had a hold over her. It was as if this town was the key to her future – that somehow, somewhere, she would be dressed in silks and satins and living in a house that had a bath with running water.

Having learned to read and write she had no intention of allowing her skills to lapse. 'Would you like me to try to teach the children their letters?' She asked Mirabelle Skelton and Ruby Tomlin, the matriarchs of the clans. 'Only if they want to. You can't make them learn.'

'Yes, you can,' declared Mirabelle, and waved her large hand meaningfully.

Phoebe thought there was little point in trying to explain that learning did not work like that. A class was arranged, once more in the drying room, for Mr Folgate never ventured there. Of the six children Phoebe taught, two were clever and eager, two were stupid and eager, and two, both boys, made it clear they had no wish to learn anything. She ignored them and concentrated on the others.

She had never taught anyone before, but she soon found she enjoyed it. An idea formed in her mind that, if only she could learn more, she could become a governess. Then she learned of a library, recently opened in Barlton by a rich benefactress, to enable the poor to have access to books. She set off to find it. It was in a small building tucked away behind the high street, much in need of a lick of paint. She paused in the hallway to inhale, with pleasure, the smell of the books, which she could see in the rooms to either side of her, neatly arranged in coloured ranks on plain wooden shelves. One room said 'Reference Library', on a white card pinned to the door, the other 'General Library'. Which one did she need?

She knocked on the glass-panelled door, and when no one responded she pushed it open. A woman leaped to her feet. 'You, out! We don't want tramps in here.'

'I'm not a tramp.'

'Then why do you look like one?' Everything about her was grey, Phoebe noticed.

'Because I have no money.'

'Exactly. Come here for warmth, have you?'

'I wouldn't get very warm from that.' She pointed to a meagre coal fire. Only a wispy tendril of smoke showed that it was still alight.

'Rudeness will not help you. I shall not be persuaded. Out!'

'I've come to look at books.'

'You're not touching them.'

'But it says outside, "Books for the Poor". I can read, if that's what's bothering you.'

'I'm not in the least bit interested if you can or you can't. What concerns me is that you're dirty. No doubt if I came close enough I would find you smell, but I shan't be doing that, I might become infested.'

'What gives you the right to be rude to me?'

'Out! Now! This instant!' The woman's voice rose with every word.

'I *can* read.' Phoebe backed away from her out into the hall. The woman followed. 'And if we're talking about dirt, just look at your fingernails and compare them with mine.' She held out her hands for inspection. Though they were rough from the soda and soap, her nails were shining, pink and clean. 'See? I wouldn't like your filthy hands touching me!'

'You rude little slut!'

'I'm no such thing. I'll have you know I'm a good girl. I want a book to look at. It says for the poor over the entrance and, as you said, that is what I am, so the books are for the likes of me!' She was pleased with how well she had expressed herself, not raising her voice, not shouting, which was what she really wanted to do.

'My patience is at an end!' The woman was so angry that she was shaking. Red blotches had appeared on her grey cheeks.

'Is there a problem, Sally?'

They looked up. A plain and very plump woman was descending the stairs. Her nose reminded Phoebe of the one on the bust of a Roman emperor at Courtney Lacey, but her other features were rather small. Her appearance was not helped by a wart in the centre of one cheek, with a single whisker growing out of it. But she had the most beautiful brown eyes, the kindest expression and a warming smile. In a flash Phoebe had noted the shine of silk, the softness of cashmere, the glint of gold, and the scent of expensive perfume. She found herself longing for all those things again.

'Dulcie, this girl will not leave. I have asked her to several times. She is insolent.'

'Were you?' Her expression was serious, but there was merriment in her eyes.

'Yes, I was, but only after she had been rude to me.' Phoebe stood her ground. There seemed no point in lying, for, despite the kind expression, Phoebe sensed that this woman would see through any falsehood.

'And what did you say?'

'After she accused me of being a tramp, a slut, dirty and flea-ridden, I told her I didn't want her filthy hands touching me. That's all.'

A small smile flickered about the woman's mouth.

'I never did, Dulcie. Can you imagine me saying such a thing?'

'She did.'

'You want to borrow some books? Can you read?'

'Yes.'

'That is the purpose of the library, Sally, lest you've forgotten. Now, come with me.' Dulcie led the way back into the reference library. 'What was it you were looking for?'

'I don't know.' Phoebe heard an unpleasant snort of derision from the woman. 'I want to learn more, but I don't know where to begin.'

'Perhaps an encyclopedia might help you. Sally.' Dulcie flicked her fingers. Phoebe admired the action: not too authoritative – rather, an unconscious show of who was in command.

Sally Ebberton scuttled off, rather like the colourless crab Phoebe had seen the other day on the beach.

'You walk on the beach with a little dog, I think?'

'Yes.' Phoebe was surprised and somewhat alarmed.

'My son has a house close by. We like to watch the sea, and the people passing. We weren't prying.'

The accompanying smile made Phoebe relax. 'Watching people, making up stories about them, can be fun. And I love the sea,' she said.

'It never palls, does it?'

'It's different every time I go there. It soothes me.' Phoebe saw that the woman was looking at her with interest.

'Do you go to walk the dog or be soothed?'

'Both. I find that the restlessness of the waves is

calming when I'd expected the constant movement would lead to agitation. It's always a puzzle to me.'

'You are so young to have problems.'

'Surviving, that's my main one.' She laughed almost apologetically, as if she regretted saying it. 'Still, we get by, Mimi and I.'

'Read me this.'

Phoebe took the book, which had been pulled at random from the shelves, and opened a page. She felt nervous suddenly and knew she was reading badly, stumbling here and there on unfamiliar words.

'That was very good. I hope you don't feel insulted by my checking. You see, Miss Ebberton was merely guarding the books, if a little overenthusiastically. On occasion people have claimed they were readers only to steal the books, presumably to sell them. Can you forgive her?'

'I would like to, but I doubt it.'

'I see. It cannot have been nice to be called a slut. May I ask your name?'

'Phoebe.'

'Have you no other?'

'I'd rather not say.'

'Even if it means you can't have one of the books here?'

'Yes.' Phoebe fought to cover her disappointment.

'Then you must be either badly hurt to keep it secret, afraid you will be discovered, or you are a criminal.'

'I'm not.'

'I believe you. I suggest you study the encyclopedia, find a subject that fires your interest, then go to the other room and talk to Miss Gatling, the librarian there. She will show you the books that might be of use to you. I shall prepare her for your visit, so there will be no risk of another unfortunate incident. I would hate it if you thought this was a horrible place and stopped coming. I hope you enjoy the book she will find for you.'

'Thank you, you've been very kind.'

'Now I'm afraid I have to go. I've an appointment.'

'Thank you,' Phoebe repeated, wishing she didn't have to leave. 'Please, ma'am, who owns this library?'

'I do,' Dulcie said simply, as she left.

Having found the library Phoebe was happy. Several times a week she climbed the steep hill from the harbour, and borrowed another book. After her sixth visit, Miss Ebberton, whom Phoebe had found she liked and had forgiven, suggested that she might borrow three books at a time: she was so careful with them and always brought them back before they were due.

One day she returned to the laundry with her precious bundle of books in a hessian bag that Miss Ebberton had given her for carrying them and to keep them safe. She always put them on a shelf above Mimi's bed. Already she was looking forward to settling down with them tonight. After much consideration she had chosen two subjects. She was learning about the Romans and she enjoyed poetry – if nothing else, Lester had kindled that interest in her. The other was a big tome of household management, which for Phoebe was sheer indulgence.

'Thanks, Ida,' she said, as she took her place at the great ironing table, which was her latest promotion. Ida Skelton and a couple of the others always made sure she was not missed when she went to the library: it was closed by the time she finished here. If Ida and the others wanted to slip away she replaced them.

'Old Fumble Fingers wants to see you.'

'No!' Phoebe went ashen. 'He knows I slipped out then.'

'I said you had a bad stomach and were in the thunderbox. He wasn't going to go looking for you there, was he? Not with the rats.'

As she climbed the metal staircase to Mr Folgate's offce her heart was beating violently. She made herself calm down. What did it matter? She knew too much for him to dismiss her, she was sure. And if he did, she'd just get work somewhere else, though it would not be easy. She tapped on the door and opened it at his command. When she stepped in her legs gave way.

'Hello, daughter,' said her father.

Phoebe had fainted, not that she was aware of it, but when she came round, on the floor of Mr Folgate's office, two of the women were fussing over her and the acrid smells of sal volatile and burning feathers were in her nostrils.

'Get up, Phoebe,' her father ordered. 'She's acting, sir. She's as strong as an ox. She's never fainted. It's not in her nature. She's biding her time, aren't you, girl, planning what to do.' He prodded her with his foot and she moved sharply away. 'See that, Mr Folgate? Sly as a box of monkeys is this one.'

'She's got a bit of spirit, that's for certain,' said Mr Folgate, a hint of admiration in his voice.

'And a merry dance you've plagued me with, you idle spawn of the devil.'

There was a sharp intake of breath from the women at her father's choice of words and she saw them cross themselves. Now she was aware of the faces peering at her from the doorway, through the large window. They all looked anxious.

Slowly Phoebe got to her feet. She did not take her eyes off her father, ready to jump away from any blows he might aim at her.

'You don't seem pleased to see your father, Phoebe. That's not very nice, is it?'

'You don't know him as I do, Mr Folgate.'

She stepped back as her father's hand swished through the air. There was a trickle of applause from the women outside. Despite the danger she was in Phoebe smiled.

'You can take that smirk off your face.'

'How did you find me? I didn't want you to. I never wanted to see you again.'

'Do you see what I have to contend with, sir? Shocking, isn't it? Evil she is, evil ways, and no doubt been keeping evil company.' He turned to face her. 'There are God-fearing people round about. A couple found you after a suspicious fire – no doubt your work. They told me.'

'Your father had kindly put out a reward for you, as any parent would. You should be grateful,' Mr Folgate added.

Phoebe laughed harshly. 'Not him, that's for sure. Put up money for me? It's not in his nature!' She dodged another blow. 'I'm not going back with you. You've no right to expect me to. I hate you!' She was shouting now, hysteria in her voice.

'See, Mr Folgate? What did I say? She's in league with the devil. Hating her own father! Not natural, is it?' Before she could avoid him he had grabbed her arm. 'Thank you, sir, you've been most co-operative.' She hated the way he said "sir", in such a false, ingratiating manner.

'These are her earnings so far this week.' Mr Folgate had a neat pile of coins on his desk.

'That's my money!' She wriggled in his grasp. 'Don't you dare touch it.'

'You don't own anything.' He further tightened his grip. Phoebe began to fight, but he was too strong for her. He pressed her against the wall as he finished counting the money. Suddenly Mirabelle, Ruby and a couple of the others rushed into the room.

'You let go of that there maid,' Mirabelle demanded.

'Or else,' Ruby added menacingly.

'She's my daughter, I've every right—'

'She belongs to herself. You've no right—'

Ruby had hold of his arm and she was as strong as he was. She twisted it behind his back, while Mirabelle

371

prised open his fingers, bending them back, forcing him to release Phoebe. His face was distorted with pain.

'Run, girl!' Ruby ordered.

Phoebe scuttled for the door, oblivious to the pain in her wrist. 'Mimi!' she shouted, as the women parted to let her pass. She slipped and slithered down the iron staircase. Behind her they closed ranks, blocking the way.

'Run!' they were shouting in unison. 'Run!'

She could hear her father bellowing and Mr Folgate ranting, but she dared not look back. She clattered out of the building followed by Mimi, and ran helter-skelter through the streets. She'd no idea where to go.

Dulcie and Chauncey were taking tea, which Ethel had set for them in the large bay window. They were watching the weak spring sun sparkling on the water, hoping the porpoises would appear as they did if the sea was frisky.

'What is that commotion, Chauncey?'

'There's a mob down there. A man's running and shouting. It's most amusing, Mama. He's being pursued by a tribe of fierce-looking women, and they're all shouting too. Let me open the window. We'll hear better.'

'Really, Chauncey, a street brawl? I'm not sure I want to hear that.' But she couldn't resist a peep. 'Chauncey, look! It's the young girl in your drawing – she came to the library. She looks terrified. The poor creature!'

'Is it she? What's he doing? You're right. He's chasing her.'

Before she could stop him, Chauncey was racing from the room. 'It's not our business,' she called, but either he did not hear her or he ignored her. Dulcie leaned out of the window.

'Leave me alone!' She heard Phoebe cry. 'Dear God, please make him leave me!' Dulcie put her hand to her mouth as she saw the girl backing along the causeway.

'Oh, the poor girl. The dear sweet creature.' She clutched at her throat as she saw the large, heavy-set man, step on to the causeway and follow her, his hand raised. Phoebe retreated further, clutching the little dog to her.

'No!' Dulcie called out of the window. 'Don't!' But it was too late. Phoebe kissed the dog and placed it carefully on the causeway. Then, without a backward glance, she jumped into the bitterly cold sea. Without hesitation the dog leaped in after her.

II

Dulcie covered her face with her hands. She dared not look. But then she had to. She peeped through her fingers in time to see her son rushing across the road, his limp barely perceptible in the drama of the moment.

'Dearest, don't!' she cried out, even though she knew he could not hear. She took her hands from her face and steadied herself against the window-sill, dizzy with anxiety. Surely he would not be so rash? But even as she asked herself she knew that he would. He was brave. He was selfless. She should be proud of him. Instead she felt angry that he was about to risk his life. The girl was floundering in the water, disappearing under the waves, which, as Dulcie watched, were growing larger.

The group of screaming women who had followed her were blocking Chauncey's way and he was struggling to get past them, but in the mêlée they seemed unaware that he had come to the rescue. Several times he almost lost his footing. Two of them were jumping up and down on the edge of the causeway, waving their arms impotently.

Dulcie picked up a shawl and hurried out of the house, clutching it close against the chill wind. She moved as fast as she could to join the noisy crowd. Their aggression was centred on the large man who was barring their way.

If one of the women darted too close he battered them with a stave he was holding. It did not stop them venting their spleen on him in language that, had she not been so distressed, Dulcie would have found distasteful, but fear had made her deaf. Of Chauncey there was no sign.

'Chauncey!' she called repeatedly. She stepped on to the causeway, ignoring the slipperiness of the stones. Her way was blocked by the man, who threatened her with the stick too.

'Excuse me.' Dulcie had to raise her voice for him to hear. 'Will you let me pass, pray?' She hoped that politeness might have more effect than abuse.

' "They that are after the flesh do mind the things of the flesh . . ." ' He stood four-square in her path. His eyes lifted to the heavens as he brandished the stave, then focused on her.

'If you don't mind?'

' "But they that are after the things of the Spirit . . ." ' he proclaimed.

'Be that as it may, let me pass.'

' "For to be carnally minded is death," ' he bellowed.

Dulcie gave him a mighty push. 'Go and preach elsewhere!' she shouted, as he lost his balance and toppled over. Dulcie rushed past him, but nearly lost her footing on the wet surface and forced herself to slow down. She did not look back, so did not see the women descend upon Phoebe's father to lambast him.

Half-way along she saw Chauncey. He was swimming against the waves to the end of the causeway, where there were steps. 'So brave, Chauncey!' She had cupped her hands around her mouth to shout. 'Courage, my son.' She walked along beside him, willing him on. If only Dick had been here instead of at December Cottage working in the garden – they needed his strength.

At the end she looked down to see, on the steps, the little dog, looking more like a rat now, whimpering and shivering. Gingerly Dulcie descended, hanging on to the guard rail, and scooped it into her arms. 'Chauncey will find her. Don't you fret.' She was rewarded by having her face licked. 'There, Chauncey! There! I see her!' She pointed to where, ten yards out, she could see the young woman. Her son, never a strong swimmer, had been tiring, she knew, but her call gave him a new burst of energy and he quickened his stroke. As she watched, Dulcie held her breath. She saw him reach the girl and lift his arm in triumph. He needed help now – or he would drown. Dulcie hurried back to the women. 'My son . . . he has her . . . needs help!' She was breathless. No one noticed she was there. The women were engrossed in venting their rage on the man who lay sprawled on the stones. 'Will no one listen to me?' she screamed.

A couple of the women glanced at her. 'He's found her. My son . . . Drowning . . .' She pointed back along the causeway. The gaggle turned and raced along the stones. Dulcie followed them, then knew she couldn't stand and watch her son drown. There was nothing she could do, for she was unable to swim.

She looked down at the man spreadeagled on the grey slabs. His nose was split, his mouth was bleeding, bruises were forming on his forehead and his eyes were swelling. If her son died this man would be to blame. But if the two young ones perished, that mob would kill him. She prodded him with her foot. 'I suggest you remove yourself from this place forthwith. If you don't, I can't guarantee your safety.'

'She's my daughter.' He was sitting up, a sorry sight, and she saw that he was crying.

'Then why was she running away from you with a look of sheer terror? Be gone.'

He scrabbled to his feet. 'I love her,' he blurted out, between his sobs.

'I do not know if that is true or if she loves you. If it is so, it is a strange way to show love. If my son saves her I shall take her home with me and care for her. If you wish you may call and reassure yourself of her well-being, and I shall ascertain whether she wants to see you. My address is December Cottage, on Hangman's Hill. Anyone will direct you there. Now, as I suggested, go!'

The huge man lumbered away in the direction of the harbour. Dulcie stood and prayed. She was not a religious woman, but she found a vehement and passionate belief today. Her eyes were closed for fear of what she might see. The dog, which she still clutched, struggled in her arms suddenly and she opened them.

The women were trudging along the causeway towards her. Between them they carried the girl, her arms dangling. The relief when she saw her bedraggled son walking behind them was too much for her and tears streamed down her cheeks as she hurried to him.

'Your son's a hero, ma'am. No mistake,' a woman said to her.

'I know,' she said, with pride. 'The girl?'

'She's all right, thanks to him. Exhausted, that's all.'

'But, Chauncey, you're freezing.' She put her shawl round him.

'Don't fuss, Mama.'

'I don't know how not to.'

They reached the roadside. Even soaked, her hair like so many eels, the girl was ethereally beautiful, but she looked terrified.

'He's gone, my dear. I sent him away,' Dulcie told her.

'Thank you so much.'

'You came to the library.'

'Yes, I did. And you were kind to me then ... I'm sorry ...'

'Not now, my dear. You're exhausted. There's time enough for explanations. I suggest we go to my son's house for a warming drink and dry clothes. And then, Phoebe, we shall go to my own house and I'll care for you there. If you ladies could perhaps help this young woman?'

Dulcie fussed about organising, suggesting, requesting. No one responded, and she realised that the women were eyeing her suspiciously. They took hold of the girl again in an almost proprietorial way. 'We can look after her,' one said defiantly, and a murmur of assent rose from the others.

'I'm sure you can. But I think she would be more comfortable with me. I mean her no harm.'

'She's had bad experiences.'

'I understand. Your care for her is most commendable.' The doubtful looks persisted. 'Perhaps you would all accompany us. Then you can check for yourselves how safe she will be.' Dulcie was not sure why she was suggesting this or why she wanted the young girl to come with her, just that there was an aura of innocence about her that she wanted to protect. In any case, she thought, wasn't this why she was involved with the home for waifs and strays? The only difference here was that she had never taken any of the others into her home to be cared for.

The women huddled together, muttering and arguing, but finally agreed. The motley group, carrying Phoebe, helping Chauncey, crossed the road and entered Chauncey's house.

The murmurs of disagreement disappeared as the women looked about them at the decorations, the furniture, the fabrics, with awe. They stood mutely, not sure now what to say, how to behave.

They were even more astonished when Dulcie, in the hall, picked up the telephone earpiece and wound the handle to be connected to the exchange. 'Barlton two three, please.' She smiled reassuringly as she waited for the connection to be made. 'Bee, is that you? I'm at Mr Chauncey's.' She was shouting into the mouthpiece. 'If you could please order the coach and send some dry female clothes . . . No, not for me . . . Find something of Agnes's . . . I expect them at six this evening . . . And

377

air the attic-room bed.' She replaced the earpiece. 'Such a wonderful invention, isn't it?' The women did not look sure. 'I was speaking to my maid, making arrangements. It would not be seemly for your friend to remain here unchaperoned with my son,' she explained. That statement reassured them.

Phoebe was carried upstairs. She protested she could walk but her friends would not allow her to. Dulcie showed them the way to the bathroom.

'I think it would be beneficial for Phoebe to take a hot bath. See? She is shivering. I shall find a dressing-gown of my son's for her to wear. Are you all friends?' she asked, as she led them along the corridor.

'We work at the laundry, with Phoebe.'

'I see. Here we are.' She opened the bathroom door for them. 'You should find soap and towels . . .' She had to smile as she heard their exclamations of astonishment at the bath and running hot water. Poor creatures. If only everyone could have what they enjoyed and took for granted. She laughed as she heard Phoebe say that she was quite capable of bathing herself, and didn't they know how to light a geyser?

In the kitchen Dulcie asked the cook for tea and cakes and told Ethel to dry the dog, then fetch the women down for refreshment.

Their wages must be meagre, thought Dulcie, as she watched them consume the food, fighting over it. 'Ladies, ladies, there's plenty for everyone, and Mrs Milner will make sure that no one goes hungry. Anything left over can be parcelled up for you to take with you. If you would be so kind, Mrs Milner?'

'As you wish, Mrs Randolph.'

Dulcie found her son in the sitting room, slumped in a chair. 'You shouldn't have jumped into the sea, Chauncey, you might have drowned.'

'I didn't stop to think – but even if I had, I'd still have tried to save her. She's lovely, Mother. Like a mermaid, a fey spirit.' His face was alight with enthusiasm . . . and was there something else?

'Chauncey, take care.'

'Of what, Mama?'

'We do not know anything about her.'

'I know she is the most beautiful creature I have ever set eyes on.'

'I do wish Dick had been here to help you.' Abruptly she changed the subject. Her son looked bewitched, or was it simply tiredness? 'My dearest, you ran as if there was nothing wrong with your leg.'

'I know – strange, isn't it? It hurts like billy-o, now.'

'Should I get the doctor for you?' She was fussing again. 'I'm sorry. You can decide that for yourself, can't you?'

'I think I'm about capable, yes.' He was grinning. 'Come in,' he called, to a quiet tap on the door.

'Excuse me. Only I didn't know where to go. And I heard voices. And I know it's not proper . . . Especially . . .' She pointed to Chauncey's dressing-gown, which was all-enveloping and thus her modesty was secure. 'Perhaps I should go to the kitchen, if you would show me the way?'

Even in the over-large Paisley dressing-gown, her hair still wet, hanging loosely over her shoulders, Phoebe looked attractive in the light from the oil lamps. But there were dark smudges of weariness beneath her eyes, her complexion was too pale and her bare feet, just peeping out from below the robe, were tinged with blue.

'Of course you must come in here.' Chauncey was already on his feet and arranging a chair for her.

'This is Phoebe, Chauncey.'

She watched as her son and the girl shook hands solemnly. 'I can't thank you enough. It was stupid of me, but—'

'You were afraid?'

'My father wanted me to return with him. I didn't want to go.'

'The man who was chasing you?'

'Yes.'

'Might I enquire why?'

'He's cruel to me. He beats me. He hates me!'

'The brute!' Chauncey looked distressed.

'He told me he loved you,' Dulcie said softly.

'If he does then I want none of his sort of love.'

'He wants you to go home.'

'That was no home. It was a prison.'

'But your home is always your home.'

'I apologise, ma'am, but there's more to a home than bricks and mortar. If there's no real love, it's just a building. I've learned that.'

'And you so young . . . Oh, the sadness . . .' Dulcie felt immeasurably sorry for her. 'And such wisdom. You don't have to go with him. I have told him I shall take you home with me until you recuperate, that I will ask what you wanted to do and that I will respect your wishes.'

'You're so kind. It's like I'm dreaming all this. At any moment I'll wake up and you'll be gone.'

'We're real, aren't we, Mama?' Chauncey was beguiled – Dulcie could see it written on his face.

'My friends said my dog was saved. I was so afraid she had drowned.'

'Such a brave little creature. She's in the kitchen being dried.'

'She's called Mimi. Such love she showed me.'

'If only people could be so devoted.' Dulcie looked up as the door opened. 'Thank you, Ethel.'

The maid placed the tea tray on the table, which was already laid with a fine embroidered cloth. 'Will that be all, ma'am?' Ethel blinked, then blinked again. 'Good Lord above! Is it you? Is it Phoebe?'

'Ethel!'

Phoebe rushed across the room, tripping over the dressing-gown, and fell into Ethel's arms. They squealed and squeaked with such pleasure that the others smiled benevolently on the reunion.

'Are you well, Ethel? What happened to you?'

'Dreadful it was.' Ethel shuddered and glanced her employers. 'I don't want to talk about it, not here.' She blushed. 'But I'm fine now. The master and his mother are angels to me.' She smiled shyly at them. 'And you?'

'Better not to ask.' Phoebe had taken her seat again, rather suddenly, and Dulcie wondered if perhaps she should be lying down.

'You know each other, that's nice,' said Dulcie. 'How?'

'We met when we were about to be sold, didn't we, Phoebe?'

'*Sold*?' Dulcie and Chauncey spoke in unison.

'Ethel, did you say you were *sold*?'

'Yes, ma'am.'

'Like the old-fashioned hiring fairs? Surely not in this day and age?'

'No, ma'am, not really.'

'I am most glad to hear it.'

'Not at a fair, at an auction after the boxing.'

'*Boxing*?' Again Dulcie and Chauncey spoke in unison: How idiotic we must sound, Dulcie thought. 'An auction?' she asked.

'Well, it was, and it wasn't, ma'am. Some wanted maids, like me. Some were looking for . . . It's not nice to talk about, ma'am.' Ethel blushed the colour of beetroot.

'You need say no more. And don't fear, Phoebe, you are safe now. I promise you that.'

Bee had arrived with the clothes and Phoebe had gone to change, ready for the journey to December Cottage. While she did so, Dulcie summoned Ethel. 'I would prefer it if you were not here, Chauncey, while I talk to her. It might be difficult for her.'

Alone, Dulcie waited, seething with indignation, arguing with herself that she must have misheard.

'Now, Ethel, sit down and tell me everything. I shan't be cross but I have to know.'

'Yes, ma'am.' Ethel picked at her index finger. 'I've only been twice. It was more for the pretty ladies, girls like Phoebe.'

'I see. And you say they are sold for bad purposes?'

'I think so, ma'am. Some go to London, I do know that they go to ... Well, you know, them special places what gentlemen go to ...'

'And ... ?'

'I've heard some get sent abroad, like.'

'Where to?'

'I don't know, ma'am. I don't really know what abroad is. But I did hear as it was good business ... ma'am.'

'Do you know who bought Phoebe?'

'Yes, a horrible old man called Horton, or some such. It was him and another man. They were fighting over who was to have her. But I don't know his name ... Only a bit of it.'

'Which is?'

'I can't remember.' Ethel was taking a strong interest in her finger again.

A thought was forming in Dulcie's mind and her heart sank. 'There's just one thing, Ethel. When Phoebe is in the room, or you are talking to her, would you be so kind as to refer to the master as Mr Chauncey only, and me ...' She thought for a moment. 'You will refer to me as ma'am, or simply Mrs R. Do you understand?'

'Mrs R?' Ethel looked puzzled.

'Yes, I would prefer that.'

'I'll try ... Mrs ... R.' She giggled as the door opened.

'Well, just look at Phoebe. You look lovely in pink, my dear, doesn't she, Ethel?'

'She do, Mrs R!' Ethel giggled again.

Chapter Six
April 1900

I

The following morning when Phoebe sat up in bed it struck her that she had awoken once before in a strange house, room and bed. She had felt the same then – curiosity mixed with uncertainty – but this time there was no fear. Her welcome here bore no comparison to the abrupt, rude manner with which the housekeeper at Courtney Lacey had received her. Here, Phoebe had met only with courtesy, kindness and concern for her well-being.

It was the prettiest room: it was as if she was in a snowflake. The half-tester bed was painted white with faint silver detail on the finials. The curtains were of sheer muslin embroidered with small flowers, which from her books she knew were edelweiss. Perhaps the bed was Swiss – Mrs Lingford would have been proud of her for knowing that. The ceiling was painted with clouds against a pale blue sky so that, with the whiteness of the fine cotton sheets on the bed, she could imagine she was floating on one.

The dressing-table was cream and silver, as were the chairs, which were upholstered in either white silk or a blue that was slightly darker than the ceiling. There was a wonderful scent of lilies of the valley, and she knew she was safe here.

The bedroom at Courtney Lacey, luxurious as it had been and filled with priceless furniture, was menacing in a way that this light, airy room could never be. She knew which she preferred.

'This is the loveliest room I've ever seen,' she informed Bee, the maid, who had brought her a tray of breakfast on which was a silver cup full of primroses, 'and that is the prettiest tray.'

'Are you rested?'

'Yes, thank you. I ache a little but that will soon pass.'

'From what I hear, you're lucky to be alive. But for Mr Chauncey, who knows? Them aches is from the cold and the long swim.'

Phoebe laughed. 'I don't think you could call my dog-paddle swimming.'

'When you've finished your breakfast, there's a bathroom along the corridor – second door on the left. When you're dressed – I've left out clothes for you to try on – my mistress would like to see you downstairs in the morning room.'

'Of course.' The happy feeling deserted her. No doubt the kind woman who had rescued her would want her gone. She couldn't blame her. She had looked a tramp yesterday and that was not all: they probably thought she was trying to kill herself. Who would believe that she had been running away and that fear of her father had made her jump, unthinking, into the sea? Suicide would never be acceptable in a God-fearing household, as this one must be. 'Is she nice?'

'Mrs R? Salt of the earth she is. A kinder woman you'll never find.'

'Why is she called Mrs R, it's silly.'

'She likes it.'

'What should I call her?'

'Why, "ma'am", of course.'

Phoebe dallied over her bath, the longer to prolong her visit. Often in the past weeks she had dreamed of a bath like this, with sweet-smelling soap and huge soft towels. Now she was enjoying the second in twenty-four hours, but soon it would be just a dream again. Perhaps it would have been better if this family had not found her: it would be hard to return to her dismal lodgings after such luxury.

'Feeling sorry for yourself isn't going to help,' she found herself saying.

'Why have you suddenly come back? There's nothing to be frightened of here.'

'Maybe there isn't, maybe there is.'

'Fiddlesticks!' Phoebe rose from the bath. She dried herself, selected a talcum powder, which she used too liberally and had to clear up, not wanting to make work for anyone else. Then she patted scent over herself, carnations it said on the bottle. She sniffed the air appreciatively.

The sun was shining so she chose a pale yellow linen suit, with gilt buttons and black silk frogging on the bodice, and a white blouse with a high collar. Her dearest wish was that perhaps they would let her keep it, but she had to smile at how incongruous she would look if she turned up at the laundry in it.

Shoes were more of a problem; the ones left out for her, a particularly smart pair of buttoned black boots with a neat heel, were too big and she had lost her clogs in the sea. How would she explain that to Mr Folgate? She buttoned the boots and felt her feet shifting about inside them. 'Whoever these belong to they must be a giant.'

She went down the stairs warily, hanging on to the banister. It was hard to walk in shoes several sizes too big. In the hall she found four closed doors.

' "Curiouser and curiouser"!' she said to herself feeling, like Alice in the book she had borrowed from the library. She tapped on the first door and, when no one answered, she opened it gingerly. It was the dining room, which was empty, the table not yet cleared. The second door led into a man's study, which smelt of cigar smoke and books. Immediately she thought of Mr Bartholomew and closed it.

At the third her knock was answered. As soon as she entered, Phoebe was engulfed in a hysterical welcome from Mimi, looking smart from her bath and brushing. The lady, at her desk with a woman who must be her cook beside her, smiled broadly. 'Phoebe, good morning. We shall have to buy Mimi a collar and lead. I trust you slept well?'

'Yes, thank you.'

'How charming you look.'

Not sure what to say, Phoebe blushed at the compliment.

'If you would be seated I shall be with you shortly. Now, Mrs Bramble, where were we?'

As the two women discussed the menus, Phoebe looked about at an entirely different room from the one she had woken in. It would have been impossible to squeeze another piece of furniture into it. Mrs R was on the stout side and she wondered how often she knocked things over. The walls were covered with a pretty red, green and gold wallpaper, not that she could see much of it for all the paintings, drawings and photographs. She would have liked to inspect them more closely but thought it would be impolite. She sat with her hands folded demurely in her lap, and wondered how she could persuade this kind-hearted woman to keep her.

'There. That's finished.' Dulcie closed her recipe book, tidied away a few papers, then turned her attention to Phoebe. 'Now, I should like to invite you to stay here as long as you wish, as my guest. Of course, that is only if you wish to do so.'

'Oh, I wish, ma'am,' Phoebe said, without hesitation.

'Perhaps it would be expedient to ask what I propose?'

'I'll do anything. I can clean. I've watched how to polish silver, and I've read Mrs Beeton and I'm good with laundry – I've learned a lot about starching and I know about lace. I don't think my cooking would be to your liking, but you've got a cook, haven't you?' Phoebe knew that she was talking too much and too fast, but she was so relieved and excited that she couldn't stop. 'And I can write and you know I can read. Oh, no!' She put her hand over her mouth, her eyes wide with alarm.

'What is the matter, Phoebe?'

'My library books! I left them in the laundry! Mr Folgate will shout at me, and he'll never let me have them back. I've no money to replace them or pay the fines – my father took my wages, and there's that notice in the library that you must—'

'Don't worry. Mr Folgate will let me have them back, I assure you.' She leaned forward to pat Phoebe's hand comfortingly. 'I want you to tell me all about yourself. I shall be honest with you, Phoebe, you intrigue me.'

'I can't imagine why, ma'am.' Phoebe laughed. 'There is little of interest to tell you,' she lied. There was no way she could tell this respectable woman what had happened to her: it would be too shocking for her to hear. 'I told you why I ran away. You see, my father thinks the devil is in me, but he isn't.'

'I never for one moment thought he was – that's if he exists at all.'

'I wasn't trying to kill myself – nothing so wicked. I was trying to get away from him and the sea was the only place left to go. I want to live, honestly I do!'

'I'm sure you do, Phoebe. I saw it all happen so I know that panic made you act so. You still don't wish to see your father? I thought it was best you had time to think about it, in case you changed your mind.'

'I'd rather not, thank you very much.'

'Working in the laundry must be hard.'

'It is, but the women there, when they were used to me, were nice enough. I had lodgings, just by Trotter's Hill. Not very nice, but enough for Mimi and me.'

'Where did you find Mimi? She looks like a pedigree dog to me.'

'I rescued her. Her puppies were fed . . .' Phoebe placed her hands over Mimi's ears '. . . to the pigs,' she whispered. 'I was afraid the same might happen to her.'

'And where did this most unfortunate occurrence happen?'

Should she say? 'Point East Farm. It burnt down. No one was killed,' she added, a little too hurriedly.

'Did you run from there too?' The smile was reflected in Mrs R's eyes.

'Yes, I did.'

'Might I ask why?'

'Because of the P-I-G-S.' She spelt out the word, not wanting Mimi to hear. 'The father was violent and I was afraid of him. But also because the son wanted to marry me.'

'And you didn't want to marry him?'

'No. I didn't love him.'

'But Mr Orton is very rich. It would have been a good match for you.'

'You know him?' Phoebe's heart plummeted. Now Mrs R would change her mind and ask her to leave.

'He's an acquaintance, more my husband's friend.' Was it her imagination or did Mrs R give her a rather piercing look? 'A good match,' she repeated. 'Don't you think?'

'Some people might see it like that, but I didn't. I could only marry for love.'

Dulcie smiled. 'That can be disastrous too.'

'That's what someone said to me once, but it's a risk I'd rather take.'

'Have you met this great love?'

'Yes, but it's just a dream. He's far too grand for the likes of me.' She smiled. What a strange interview this was: every question so far had been most personal.

Perhaps Mrs R was simply nosy, as the woman in the cart had been.

'We all need dreams.' Dulcie smiled wistfully. Phoebe wondered what that meant in someone as *old* as she. It couldn't be about love.

'I have to ask you an impertinent question, and I quite understand if you do not wish to answer and are offended by my inquisitiveness, but I can assure you I do so for a reason.'

Phoebe's mind raced. She was aware that she must be careful: she must be sure she didn't say anything that would shock this kind lady too much. But on the other hand she was wondering if she knew already. Perhaps if she hinted at the adventures she had had, Mrs R might be even more kindly disposed towards her? It was difficult to know what to do.

'Please ask. Then I shall decide if I want to answer.' She hoped fervently that she did not sound impertinent: it was difficult to know what to say and in what tone. She felt as if she was in a conversational maze, like the one in the garden at Courtney Lacey, which made her think of Edward and smile.

'My dear, your father seemed to me to be a rather rough and ready type of gentleman. How shall I put it without sounding too offensive? A "son of the soil" might be a good description.'

Phoebe thought it a very good description. 'Yes, he is.'

'Then why is it that there is a finesse about you, a delicacy of movement, of manners and a correct way of speaking, which is at odds with your father?'

'I don't mind answering that. I'm educated, you see.' She said this with her customary pride.

'Might I ask where?'

'At Courtney Lacey.'

'Mr Bartholomew's establishment?'

'The same.'

'How did you come to be there?' She was frowning deeply as she spoke, and Phoebe wondered if she knew him too. Was she cross that Phoebe knew him or . . . No, that could not be possible, a respectable lady such as she would not know . . . Phoebe was attempting to marshal her thoughts. She took a deep breath. 'When I ran away Mr Bartholomew found me and he rescued me. He took pity on me and gave me nice things and he had a lady, Mrs Lingford, and she was my instructress and she taught me how to behave and how to eat and read and write, and we looked at books and she taught me kings and queens and geography, and I know the Latin names of all the plants in the garden, and I know how to get out of the maze and to converse, and I never eat peas with my knife.'

'So many accomplishments.' Dulcie clapped her hands and laughed. Mimi wagged her tail, as if she, too, was enjoying the conversation. Then Phoebe saw that the frown she thought had gone was flickering across the pleasant face. 'And, Phoebe, how best to put this?' She studied her garden for what, to Phoebe, seemed an age. 'Were you . . . harmed in any way? Were you afraid? Are you damaged?'

'I was often afraid. I worried, you see, about what a grand gentleman like him would want with me.'

'As you would.'

'As to the rest, I danced for him. That was all.' And she blushed as she spoke.

'I expect you like dancing?'

'Oh, yes, very much, I do.'

'Then we must make sure you do some dancing while you're here, mustn't we?'

Phoebe did not have time to reply before the door opened and a young woman, who looked vaguely familiar and was about the same age as herself, stepped into the room.

'I'm sorry, I didn't know you had someone with you, Mother,' she said. She didn't sound in the least bit sorry. Then she stared at Phoebe, long and hard. 'Who are you?'

'Agnes, manners!' Dulcie reprimanded her.

'And what are you doing in my clothes?'

'I gave them to her.'

'They're not yours to give.'

'You had put them aside as no longer wanted. I didn't think permission was required,' Dulcie said coldly.

'I'm so sorry, I'll take them off,' Phoebe said, with dignity. She might have guessed the pleasantness wouldn't last.

'You keep them, Phoebe. Agnes has a multitude of clothes. Let me explain, Agnes. This is Phoebe, the daughter of a friend of mine. She has come here on a visit. Perhaps you will be friends.'

'Not in my frocks.'

'Agnes, don't be so petty!'

'And what a scruffy dog.'

'She's adorable. She's called Mimi.'

'She smells!'

As Phoebe listened to mother and daughter, she remembered where she had seen the girl. She'd been showing off and rude in the large shop in Barlton – the shop that had filled her with terror since *he* was there, the man she feared most, even more than her father. This girl would never be nice to her or accept her – let alone be her friend. Phoebe was certain she was listening to her future enemy being rude to the kind lady.

'No! Oh, really, Mother. She's got my shoes on too. It's too bad.'

'You can have them, if you wish.' Phoebe bent down and began to unbutton them. 'They're much too big for me, you see. I've only got small feet, and yours must be enormous.'

Dulcie had a great deal to think about. Events had taken her by surprise. She did not wish to say anything to anyone until she could be sure of her facts. The spreading of rumour and gossip was such a dangerous pastime.

Dulcie had insisted that Phoebe take a rest after luncheon. It had not been an easy meal, with Agnes sulking and monosyllabic. Now, alone in her morning room where she did so much of her thinking, she began methodically to take stock and, hopefully, reach some conclusions.

Her desire to help Phoebe was based on her instincts and the warmth she had felt towards the girl when she had first seen her on the beach with the young man, presumably Lester Orton. It would be pleasant to have a companion, even if there was such a marked difference in their ages. The child had been taught well, and she would like to finish her instruction.

She had an idea, perhaps too far-fetched but one she could not shake away, that she could make Phoebe indistinguishable from any well-brought-up girl. Then perhaps she might make a good marriage and need never be frightened again. Dulcie knew about fear and how demoralising it was. She might not know about physical terror, as undoubtedly Phoebe did, but she knew the fear of not being accepted, the dread of making a fool of herself, of being laughed at behind her back. She didn't want Phoebe's youth to be damaged as hers had been, and for her to wait until her forties to gain courage.

The disadvantage of living in a small town was that everyone knew everyone else's business and disseminated it, but it could sometimes be turned to one's advantage. It was useful that she had heard, years ago, of how badly Cynthia Orton had been treated by her husband – for now she knew that Phoebe had spoken the truth about Orton. Dulcie had gone out of her way to befriend Cynthia – a sweet woman: they had both had difficult, domineering husbands who were also philanderers, and had been a source of comfort to each other. She had visited Point East Farm on several occasions, and could not say she had enjoyed it for there was such an air of desolation about the house.

'Why does he keep you so short of money?' she had asked Cynthia, with unusual temerity, one day.

'Because he believes whatever is his belongs to him, and whatever is mine is his also.' She had tried to smile but the large bruise on the side of her face prevented it.

'Fortunately my father had the wisdom to protect me financially.'

'But, Dulcie, you let the whole world think everything belongs to Arnold.'

'One day, Cynthia, I am sure I shall break free.'

'I shall probably be long buried by then.' Her friend had spoken lightly, but sadly had been proved right – within the year she was dead. Of pneumonia it was said, but Dulcie had always felt uncomfortable with this diagnosis. She might not have succumbed, but for the beating she had received from her husband when he had cracked her ribs and pleurisy had set in.

Why didn't Dulcie and other women like Cynthia band together? Why didn't they have the courage of their sisters in London who were beginning to ask for more rights? Had the relentless instructions from their own mothers on what constituted a good wife taken root in them so deeply that they could never change? For some time the talk was all of change, a new century. A new king, everyone said, would soon be on the throne, a new beginning. But what was new in most women's lives?

That child Phoebe wouldn't be like her – or Agnes, come to that. They would strike back; they would run. Dulcie was certain they would never tolerate husbands like hers and Cynthia's. Or, once settled, would they become like their own mothers, obedient and cowed?

Not Phoebe, she thought. Lester Orton had wanted to marry her, she had said. He had been a better prospect than his father, Dulcie thought – then shuddered at the idea of a young girl forced to be intimate with the old man. And Lester as a husband? She had always thought him strange. When she had heard of the farm burning down, she had not been surprised to hear that Lester was the suspected arsonist.

But there was only so much she could ask Phoebe. These were such delicate matters, subjects that, even on her own, she did not like to contemplate.

It had been wise of her to instruct Ethel and the other servants not to refer to her by her name. She had no proof, but instinct told her that Arnold had had a hand in Phoebe's fate. She moved restlessly in her chair. She knew he was capable of anything, but auctioning young women like cattle? Was he so very evil? She had to know. And if Orton was involved, who else in this small town was? Did she entertain others just as guilty? Were there no decent men?

Of course there were: Theo Prestwick for one and, she was sure, Edward too. She regarded her instincts as sound – but were they? She could hardly call her life a success where people were concerned.

With Theo there was yet another problem: Kendall Bartholomew. He had hinted at evil; he had said he worried about his son being involved with him. Did he know of the rumours she had heard?

When she had been told that Kendall Bartholomew collected young women like some men collect butterflies, she had thought it could not be so. Such people inhabited the sort of novel she had sometimes thought she might like to read but never did for fear it might corrupt her. Really, sometimes she had such bizarre notions. As if a book could *tarnish* one. Then she had been told that

Kendall Bartholomew cast them aside when he had tired of them – having used and abused them, no doubt.

She had to find the Lingford woman of whom Phoebe had talked with such warmth. But where to begin? She pulled down the front of her writing bureau. Inside it looked different somehow. She checked, but everything was there. She must have put her address book back into a different cubby-hole from the usual one. That was probably it. She slid her paperknife into the silk lining at the back of the book, and extricated a business card. It belonged to a Mr David Corbin, a private investigator. She had thought of commissioning him to follow Arnold and report when he was with other women, but she had decided it would be undignified. Anyway, what would she do with the information?

However, this was different. She penned a letter and rang for Bee. She didn't trust the young maid, Jane: she never knew with staff whether her husband had bedded or bribed them, or both. 'Take this to the address on the envelope straight away, Bee. Please would you wait for the reply? And ask Jane to bring me some tea.' She sat back in her chair. She felt a lot better now that she was doing something.

There was still one big problem she had to surmount: she had to tell Phoebe whom she was married to. If she was right and they met here . . . She did not want the child to be so frightened that she ran away again. And yet . . . Dulcie had to know for her own peace of mind, although what she would do with such knowledge she had no idea. Somehow she had to find out and protect Phoebe. If Arnold had been involved in her downfall it was Dulcie's bounden duty to help her, heal her and reform her.

And where should she move Phoebe if she refused to stay here – and who could blame her if she did? She could not possibly go to Chauncey's house, and she could not leave her alone here either. What a pass she had reached in her life!

She shook herself. The first matter to be dealt with was a practical one. Shoes for Phoebe.

3

In his black frock coat and pinstripe trousers, Mr Corbin looked more like a respectable businessman than an investigator. Only the diamond glinting in the pin that kept his neatly tied cravat in place gave the game away. From her assiduous study of books on etiquette Dulcie knew that diamonds should never be worn before luncheon.

'It is kind of you to come at such short notice, Mr Corbin.'

'My aim is to please, at all times, Mrs Randolph-Smythe.'

'Mrs Randolph is sufficient.'

'I understand.' He gave her an alarming wink.

They were in the morning room, the spring sunshine pouring through the windows. In the better light she saw that, in fact, the jacket looked musty and the trousers were in need of pressing. She felt sorry for him, but wondered how successful he could be if his clothes were in such a state.

'I need to trace someone. I have no idea of her whereabouts. Is it possible?'

'Everything is possible, Mrs *Randolph*.' He winked again.

'Mr Bartholomew of Courtney Lacey – I presume you know of him?'

'Very much so, Mrs Randolph.' Another insufferable wink. It would be easier to deal with if he wasn't so respectably dressed: she would never have expected such behaviour from a gentleman.

'Coffee, Mr Corbin?'

'That would be most welcome, Mrs Randolph.'

When Dulcie handed him the cup and saucer she saw that his hand was shaking. Would he be reliable if he drank to excees?

'I trust you have credentials for the work you do?' she asked, with a smile: she was not prepared to offend him yet, but she needed to check.

'Twenty-six years in the Metropolitan Constabulary. Retired with the rank of inspector – homicide. I have my references with me.' He picked up the leather folder he had placed on the floor and withdrew a sheaf of documents. 'My time in the police force, you will understand, Mrs Randolph, is the reason why I am so successful at the work I undertake. I have contacts, you see, in many of the forces around the country. You cannot serve as long as I did without accumulating many sources.' His eyes flickered.

'Then why are you here in Barlton, Mr Corbin, with such a fine record? I am sure that there cannot be much work for you in this quiet backwater.'

'You'd be surprised, ma'am.'

'And do you employ others?'

'Most certainly not. Much of my work is confidential. I prefer to be the only person who knows what my clients want and thus can confidentially offer a highly personalised and discreet service.' Wink!

There was an air of dignity about him, despite the shaking and the worn clothes, and an eagerness to please. She liked him instinctively, even if she deplored the wink. She would give him a chance. 'I am searching for a Lynette Lingford. She had been living at Courtney Lacey in the employ of Mr Bartholomew. I have no idea where she resides now. But she has five children and an aged father-in-law. I doubt that she has gone far.' As she spoke he was scribbling in a notebook.

'Is this a delicate matter of a matrimonial persuasion?'
The wink again.

'Mr Corbin, is there something in your eye?'

'My eye?'

'It would appear that it is troubling you. Perhaps you need a lotion to soothe it.' She looked suitably concerned.

'No, Mrs Randolph. It is merely a twitch that has disturbed me of late.'

'You should see a doctor, Mr Corbin. It is somewhat disconcerting.'

'I shall, Mrs Randolph, the minute I leave here. Thank you for pointing it out to me.'

Dulcie knew then that this man, with his immediate understanding of such subtleties, was ideal. 'Were you asking if this has anything to do with my husband? If so, the answer is no. I simply wish to talk to this person about another matter, that is all.'

'Then I shall start my searches forthwith.' He stood to leave.

'I am not sure of the procedure, but perhaps . . . for your expenses . . . ?' Dulcie looked at him questioningly. If she was right he would have little money to spare, and if she helped him, he would return all the sooner with results for her.

'That is most considerate, Mrs Randolph. Helps the wheels turn . . .' The wink had returned.

Dulcie opened the drawer in her bureau where she kept her cheque book and loose change. 'If you would . . .' That was most odd, she thought. Her petty-cash book was not on the top where it had always been.

A minute later, in the hall, as he was putting on his overcoat, he turned to Dulcie. 'I had a case once concerning a Randolph family. I wonder if it was connected with you in any way.'

'It's not an uncommon name. But, no, my family has never had any contact with the police.'

'Of course not. This was a case of suspicious deaths, a

husband and wife, a respectable couple. He owned a shop in Whitechapel, if my memory serves me right, but nothing was ever proved. Poisoning can be a difficult crime to solve unless one is on the scene immediately. It has always bothered me. Well, Mrs Randolph, I'll bid you good day, for the time being.'

He must have thought Dulcie rude, but she could not see him to the front door for the simple reason that she was unable to move. As the door closed she sat down heavily on a chair by the hall table. He's left his gloves, she thought inconsequentially. Surely not! Black thoughts scudded this way and that in her mind like so many trapped birds. Arnold was immoral, she knew, but surely even he—

'You look like you've seen a ghost, ma'am. Are you all right? Do you want some smelling salts?'

'No, Bee. I had a bit of a shock, that is all. Where is Phoebe?'

'In her room. She and Miss Agnes had a disagreement. I don't think it's going to be possible for her to stay here, ma'am.'

'Why not?'

'I don't think they're going to be friends,' Bee said stoutly.

'You mean Agnes doesn't want her here, but there's nowhere else for the child to go. Agnes will just have to accept that I decide who is to be a guest in my house, not her.'

'Yes, ma'am.'

Later that afternoon Dulcie had hoped to remain silent in the carriage on the journey into town for she had so much to think about. Phoebe was looking about her with great interest. Nothing, it seemed, escaped her watchful eyes. Dulcie had decided to suggest she accompany her since she did not want her exposed alone to any unpleasantness with Agnes.

'Will your husband mind me being in his house?'

'It's my house too, and he spends little time with us.'

'When shall I meet him?'

'Tomorrow. The following day is his birthday. He is away on business until then.' He had gone with Sophie Franks, Dulcie thought. No doubt all their circle knew now but she no longer cared, perhaps because Chauncey was back in Barlton . . . or perhaps because of Theo . . .

'Your daughter told me she is engaged to be married. When is the wedding?'

'I have no idea. I was not even aware that she had a fiancé.' Dulcie had not meant to sound sharp. 'No doubt she will tell me in her own good time,' she added, to dilute the acid in her tone.

'Are we going to see your son?'

'Later, perhaps, but first I must visit my lawyer.'

It was strange how a passing remark had made her take stock in a way she hadn't before. Ideas she had aplenty, but nothing certain. It had been this child, only yesterday, when she had said she could never marry Lester: 'Why should I live a lie, just for convenience and what other people might say . . .' Phoebe's words which she had later said, jolted Dulcie. For all her tender years the girl had more sense and morality than most people she knew. But Dulcie was honest. She had wondered then if it had simply been what Phoebe had said or her dream that, if she were free, Theo might ask her to marry him. He might be like so many men she had observed over the years who flirted and said the most outrageous things to married women who were unlikely to make demands on them. Was he like that? She hoped not. But there was only one way to find out, she thought. She must make herself available.

They drew up outside Mr Battle's offices in the broad avenue on which the trees were just coming into bloom. 'Just look at the blossom. It'll be summer before we know where we are.' She was making conversation because she had hardly spoken to Phoebe during the journey. 'Will you wait in the carriage or come in with me?'

'I'd prefer to come with you.'

When Phoebe was installed in the waiting room with a copy of *Punch*, Dulcie was welcomed by Young Mr Battle.

As she settled herself into the chair before his desk, she felt oddly nervous.

'And how may I be of help to you, today?' he asked.

'I want a divorce from my husband.'

Mr Battle laid down his pen and studied his blotter. 'Have you thought about this long and hard, Mrs Randolph?'

'Of course.' It was last night that she had finally decided, but her feelings and her thoughts had been leading to this for years.

'Might I ask on what grounds?'

'My life is intolerable with my husband. He has many mistresses. I find I can no longer live with the humiliation.' She was not sure of this, but she had to say something.

'Divorce is more complicated than that, Mrs Randolph. No doubt many wives would seek it if it was so simple.' She did not like being spoken to if she was a child. 'Adultery by your husband is not sufficient grounds for you to sue him for divorce. It has to be coupled with another offence to be admissible. Unless . . .' There was a long pause, which seemed to go on and on. 'Could his adultery be of an incestuous nature?'

'Of course not. What a ludicrous idea!'

'Is he physically cruel to you?'

'Does he beat me? Fortunately never.' Twisting her arm the other night would not be sufficient. 'He has threatened to kill me.'

'Were there witnesses to this statement?'

'No, just the two of us.'

'Matrimonial banter?'

He was laughing again, and she wondered if she was quite as impressed with this young man as she had first thought. 'I have no idea what you mean.'

'Quite so.' He coughed. 'Have you grounds for thinking he has committed bigamy rather than adultery?'

'No.'

'Is there or have there been . . .' He coughed. Oh dear, thought Dulcie, he was about to ask her something of a personal nature. She wished he was not quite so young. '. . . acts between you of a bestial or . . . unnatural nature?'

'We have not shared a bed for twenty-two years.'

'Ha-ha!'

'If I was unfaithful, what then?'

He brightened. 'That would be a different matter. Your husband could sue unconditionally.'

'Is that fair, Mr Battle?'

'I did not write the act, Mrs Randolph. Have you . . . ?'

'Have I committed adultery? Oh, really, Mr Battle!' The laws in this land were ridiculous. Something should be done about them. 'Then what *can* I do?'

'Perhaps ask your husband for a judicial separation.'

'That would do.' She sounded as if she was shopping and had just spied a bargain. 'What is involved in such a matter?'

'I would draw up a deed that you and your husband, having consulted his firm of solicitors, would sign. We could agree what allowance your husband would make for you.'

'I have already explained that is not relevant to us.'

'You would release him from responsibility for your debts.'

'Mr Battle, I am not in the habit of having any.'

'Quite so. Of course, in your case there is no problem

with children since they are of age. Otherwise, naturally, your husband would have custody of them.'

'Why *naturally*, Mr Battle?'

'Because it is the law, Mrs Randolph.'

'Which of us would remain at our home?'

'You would have to find other accommodation.'

'I don't want to do that.'

'Then there is a problem.' He frowned as the door burst open. 'I said I was not to be disturbed, Miss Howard.'

'I'm so sorry, Mr Battle. Mrs Randolph, what a pleasant surprise.'

Dulcie sat as if she was made of stone. 'What are you doing here, Miss Howard?'

'I work here. Did you not know?'

'I had no idea.'

Mr Battle was on his feet. 'Really, Miss Howard, this is unforgivable. Please leave us.' He waited until the door closed again. 'I am so sorry, Mrs Randolph. Now, where were we?'

'You did not tell me that that woman was employed here. She used to work for my husband.'

'I have only recently learned that myself.'

Dulcie was shaking with agitation. She stood up. 'I can no longer deal with you. She will tell him everything I have consulted you about. He will know about Chauncey, he will—' And then, so unlike her, she burst into tears. 'My will!'

'I can assure you on that, Mrs Randolph. It is perfectly safe. Look.' He strode across the room and opened a panelled door behind which she could see a gleaming metal safe. He wound the large wheel on the front. A series of clicks followed and then the huge door opened. Mr Battle emerged triumphantly, holding aloft her will. 'You see?' He showed her the front with her name on it. 'Safe as houses. Only my partners and I know the combination of that safe. Your secrets are sacred to me, Mrs Randolph.'

From the desk she picked up the notes he had been making and stuffed them into her handbag. 'I think it would be better if you thought about my position. If we are to have a further meeting, I would prefer it to take place at my son's house.'

'As you wish, Mrs Randolph.'

'And anything pertaining to me is to be locked away in the safe. I do not want that woman knowing anything of my affairs. Is that understood?'

'Perfectly, Mrs Randolph.'

Dulcie was angry as she swept out of the inner office. Lily stood up: 'Mrs Randolph—' she began, but Dulcie swept past without a word. Lily's eyes narrowed.

'Come, Phoebe. We are leaving.'

An astonished Phoebe leaped to her feet, smiled politely at Lily and virtually ran after Dulcie to the carriage.

4

Outside the office Phoebe and Dulcie stood on the pavement. Phoebe was concerned about her companion's high colour and agitation.

'Mrs R, is there anything I can do? Have I upset you?'

'I'm not upset,' she said, and looked at Phoebe so intently that she wondered if her face was dirty. But then there was a hint of a smile. Phoebe hoped she wasn't mad like almost everyone else she had met recently. 'Of course not. Me! Upset? Never!' She took a deep breath. 'Come, my dear, into the carriage.'

Phoebe climbed in behind her, and the coachman tucked the blanket around them. As if they'd be cold in here! she thought.

'Agnes is being so difficult about you wearing her

clothes that I thought it might be a good idea if we bought some for you.'

'It's very kind of you, Mrs R, but I couldn't possibly impose on you.'

'It would be my pleasure. It can't be pleasant for you to wear someone's cast-offs. I should have thought of that before.'

'I don't mind. I just wish your daughter didn't.'

'I shall enjoy making you look your best.'

'Perhaps if you had some material, I could make myself a frock?'

'You could, although I have a competent dressmaker – unless, that is, you are talented?'

'Not really. I once knew someone who was, though.' She was thinking of Lester.

'We can buy ready-made garments. Then you won't have so long to wait for them.'

'You're the kindest person I ever met.' Phoebe would have liked to kiss her there and then, but she refrained.

'Good gracious me! You can't have met very nice people.'

'I haven't,' Phoebe said quietly.

'The emporium,' Dulcie ordered the coachman.

As they clip-clopped along Phoebe watched the people hurrying by on the pavements. She saw the well-to-do, she saw the poor. Only yesterday she'd been one of them, yet today she was in a fine carriage about to have clothes bought for her. Life was truly astonishing, she thought, as the vehicle slowed to a halt.

A man in a uniform was holding the carriage door open for them, saluting, bowing, lowering the steps in a fine display of servility that Phoebe found funny.

'Thank you, Shepperton.'

She began to follow Dulcie but then, on seeing where they were, she shrank back into the carriage. 'Do we have to go in there?' She felt sure her face was as white as a sheet.

'Not if you don't wish to.'

'I don't mind not having clothes.'

'But I mind. Madame d'Or,' she ordered instead, as Shepperton helped her back in.

Phoebe felt foolish. If she was going to stay in Barlton it was inevitable she would one day run into *that* man. How could he hurt her if she was with other people? Mrs R was obviously well-to-do: she would protect her. 'We could go back if you want, Mrs R.'

'No, no. We're nearly there.'

During the next two hours, Phoebe learned what it was like to be an indulged daughter. Finally, she decided, it was better if she did not say she liked something: if she did Mrs R insisted on purchasing it for her. She was measured for three gowns – morning, afternoon and evening – and from Madame d'Or's range of ready-made clothes, she had two suits, one linen, the other tweed, two day dresses, a dress for the evening, underwear, blouses, hats, gloves and shoes.

As she sat in the carriage waiting for Dulcie, who had undertaken an errand of her own, Phoebe began to worry. While they had been shopping she had allowed excitement to supress her fears. Now they had rushed back to torment her. She shouldn't be so trusting. If only Phyllis hadn't deserted her she would have been more cautious.

'Mrs R, I don't wish to sound ungrateful, or to offend you, but might I ask why you are doing this for me?' she said, when they were being driven back to December Cottage.

'How sensible of you to ask. I am not in the least offended – a young woman should be careful, you read such dreadful stories. To be honest, my dear, I'm not sure. I'd seen you once before on the beach outside my son's house, but the next time I saw you, you had changed. You looked so wan and sad. I wanted to help

you, I suppose. And then, when that dreadful man . . .
Oh dear, Phoebe, please forgive me, I should not speak of
your father in such terms.'

'Please, don't apologise, he *is* dreadful. You speak only
the truth.'

'I just wanted to rescue you. And perhaps because I am
selfish.' She smiled shyly.

'Selfish? You?'

'When you are ugly like me—'

'You're not ugly!'

'Phoebe, you need not flatter me. I know I am.'

'But you aren't. You're not pretty, I agree.' Phoebe put
her hand over her mouth. 'Forgive me! That was so
rude.'

Mrs Randolph smiled at her honesty.

'What I wanted to say was that you're a good person
and it shows in your face. Just look at your eyes! No one
has eyes that shine with such kindness as you, and when
you smile it's as if all the candles in the room were lit at
the same time. And your voice is so sweet and pleasant.
Oh, no, I envy you.'

'Well I never!' She looked dumbfounded. 'Thank you,
Phoebe, that was a pretty speech. I was told once I had
sad eyes.'

'Were you? I see no sadness in them.'

'Then maybe it's gone. There's a pleasant thought.
What I wanted to explain was that I did not want to see
beauty such as yours go to waste. I wanted to make you
look perfect.'

At this Phoebe huddled in the corner of the carriage
and tears sprang to her eyes. 'Phoebe, what is it? What
have I said?'

'A memory of a horrible time.'

'Dear child, you're safe now.' She put out her arms and
cradled Phoebe. 'I think, my dear, you should cry. You
will feel so much better if you do.'

Dulcie and Phoebe returned elated from their shopping expedition.

'I want to dress immediately,' Phoebe declared.

'Then you must do as you wish! I shall be in the morning room, I've a visitor waiting.'

'Isn't that funny? Afternoon in the morning room.' Phoebe was laughing as she picked up some of her parcels.

'I'll ask Jane to carry up the rest for you.'

Dulcie watched Phoebe race up the stairs, dropping boxes and giggling uncontrollably as she picked them up only to drop them again. How quickly the moods of the young changed. No one would have guessed that ten minutes ago the girl had been sobbing her heart out. And what a happy spirit she was, in such sharp contrast to Agnes. This morning, buying the clothes for her had been a real pleasure. The child had taken such joy in the purchases, but Agnes could find no pleasure in anything. It was evidently the result of too much indulgence, and Dulcie had to admit she was as much to blame as Arnold. She had given her everything she had ever wanted . . . to ingratiate herself with her, to try to gain her liking. Just as she had with that creature Sophie. What a pathetic woman she had been.

'Mr Corbin, I had not expected to see you for some time.'

'We professionals, Mrs Randolph . . .'

'Of course. And I see you have had tea? Another cup, perhaps?'

'That would be greatly appreciated, I'm sure.'

'Have you found the party?'

'I have, Mrs Randolph. It wasn't too difficult a task. The lady in question is residing close to Cowick Street in Exeter. She is employed as a seamstress at Pinder's, in the high street. Hard times, by the look of things, Mrs Randolph.'

'Oh dear, the poor soul. More cake, Mr Corbin?'

'I'd never refuse, Mrs Randolph.'

'There was one other thing, nothing to do with me, you understand, just idle curiosity. Mr Corbin, I've been doing some research into my family, and I was interested to hear the other day that you were involved in a case – poisoning, I think you said.' She was appalled anew at the idea. 'It was the name. Could you tell me more?'

'You know what they say, Mrs Randolph.' He tapped the side of his nose with a large finger, but he did not wink at her. 'Curiosity killed the cat.'

'Don't even say such a thing, Mr Corbin. Is it very ghoulish of me, do you think?'

'Nothing like. I always find great interest in such matters. If I was given a guinea for every time I was asked about the Ripper, I'd be a rich man.'

'You worked on that dreadful case?'

'Yes, Mrs Randolph, I was there.'

To her shame, Dulcie found that the next half-hour sped past as she sat enthralled by his tales of horror and gore. 'And I can do better than that for you, Mrs Randolph, if I might be so bold. I've a book of cuttings – all my cases. If you would care to see it, I can bring it here for you.'

'Why, Mr Corbin, that would be fascinating. And does it . . . ?'

'The poor Randolphs? Yes, it does.'

'Will the truth ever be known?'

'Mrs Randolph, from my experience, these matters are generally resolved. It might take time, but deathbeds are handy places for confessions, you know.'

She didn't, but she acknowledged his remark as if she did.

The door of the room burst open. 'How dare you ask my maid to look after that slut you've foisted upon me?'

'Agnes, really! I do apologise, Mr Corbin.'

'I understand. I've a daughter of my own.'

'And what does *that* mean?' Agnes swung round.

'If you could remember the cuttings?'

'My pleasure, Mrs Randolph.' Mr Corbin was backing out of the door, which he shut with alacrity.

'That was intolerably rude of you, Agnes.'

'And it was rude of you to ignore me.'

'You weren't here so I did not think that asking Jane to carry a few parcels up the stairs was of great importance.'

'Carrying parcels! She's dressing her, gossiping and giggling up there. It's not right!'

Dulcie had sat down at her desk and was calmly making a note in her book of the address Mr Corbin had given her. She always found it best to duplicate things at the earliest opportunity.

'You're not even listening to me!' Agnes stamped her foot.

'What is not right?' Dulcie asked calmly.

'That she's here.'

'She needed help. I gave it to her.'

'How commendable, Mother. But do you have to bring your waifs and strays home with you?'

'If I wish, yes.'

'Well, I don't know what Father will say.'

'He already knows we have a visitor. She's so pretty that he won't object.'

'That's a horrible thing to say. I shall tell him you said it.'

'As you wish.'

'Ever since you lied to me he's not been pleased with you.'

'As I have not been particularly pleased with myself.'

'That you lied?'

'No, that I apologised.'

Agnes did not seem to register what Dulcie had just said.

'When's Papa back from London?'

'Tomorrow. I presume he won't want to miss his

birthday.' And then what will I do about poor Phoebe? she thought.

'Why are you spending his money on a stranger, lavishing things on her that she can't possibly appreciate?'

'Don't you have enough, Agnes? Aren't you spoilt sufficiently that you cannot allow another person some good fortune?'

'It's not right!'

'So you keep telling me. Sometimes, Agnes, I feel quite sorry for you.'

'Me?'

'Yes, it must be so difficult always to be so unpleasant.'

Phoebe had rushed downstairs to show Mrs Randolph her new dress and overheard Agnes. She stepped forward as if to enter the room, then decided she might make matters worse. She raced back up the stairs, to her room beneath the eaves where she felt safer. She sat on her bed. Her pleasure in her new clothes had evaporated.

'What's up, Miss?' Jane, who had been tidying the room, asked.

'I've just overheard Agnes and her mother arguing about me.'

'You don't want to take no notice of her. She complains about everything, she does. Right spiteful little madam she is, and no mistake.'

'I was so happy.'

'And you carry on being happy. *She* didn't buy them for you, Mrs R did. She wanted you to have them. It would be downright rude if you gave them all back.'

'Still, I can't stay here any longer, can I?'

'Why ever not?'

'If Agnes doesn't like me.'

'Get on with you. She doesn't like no one. You stay. I would, just to annoy her.'

'She says she's engaged but her mother says she isn't.'

'She'd like to be but the fellow's got more sense, seen right through her, I reckons. He's too good for her, that's for sure. Gracious me! Did you hear her screaming for me? Best be going.' She made for the door, then turned back. 'Your dog, Mimi, the gardening boy's taken her for a walk.'

'That's kind of him.'

'Isn't it? Lovely, he is. Big and so good-looking . . . I'm coming, Miss Agnes!' she called. 'Keep your hair on,' she muttered.

Left alone, Phoebe pondered what to do for the best. Was Jane right or were here own instincts? If she left, where could she go? Perhaps she should stay a week, then see.

There were strange goings-on here, to be sure.

When she had entered the lawyer's chambers she had nearly fainted when the clerk welcomed Mrs *Randolph*.

'That wouldn't be Randolph-Smythe?' she had asked the clerk, when she was alone with him.

'No, that's Mrs Randolph. No Smythe,' he had answered, to her intense relief.

The wait had been enjoyable, rather like she imagined the theatre. A woman had stalked in – you couldn't call it simply entering: she had opened the door with a noisy flourish and swept in, head held magisterially high. 'You are?' she had asked Phoebe imperiously.

'With Mrs Randolph. I was told to wait.'

'Mrs Randolph?' The woman had sounded surprised, and pulled what appeared to be an engagement diary towards her. 'It's not in the book.' She glared at Phoebe.

'I'm sorry, but the book is nothing to do with me.'

'Don't be impertinent.'

'I wasn't aware I was being so.'

'Why was I not told?' The woman had burst through the door of the other office.

'Who's she? Does she always hurl herself through doors without knocking?'

'Thinks she's the Queen of Sheba,' the clerk replied, laughing.

'She doesn't look much like her, not with that wig.'

'We've often wondered in the office if Lily's hair was false.'

'Oh, yes, most definitely.' Phoebe spoke as if she knew everything there was to know about hairpieces, but modesty made her add, 'I think.'

'Are you related to Mrs Randolph?'

'No, I'm just a visitor.'

'Really, only I was wondering . . .' The young man's face had turned quite pink, but Phoebe was never to know what he was wondering for at that moment Lily reappeared, looking cross. Phoebe would have loved to ask why she was so angry.

Everything was odd, she decided, remembering the happenings this morning. But even if it was, she didn't want to leave. What if she gave Agnes one last try?

She knocked on the door of her room. 'May I come in?'

'If you must. But don't stay long, I've a headache.' Agnes was sitting at her dressing-table, holding a hair-brush and staring vacantly at her image.

'Would you like me to do your hair?'

'I'm not looking to employ a second maid. Jane suits me very well.'

'I offered because of your headache.'

'Then brushing it would only make it worse.'

'Do you think so? I find it soothing.'

'Then your head isn't as sensitive as mine!' Agnes turned back to her mirror, studying her face intently. Jane entered the room, a pink silk dress held in front of her. 'There you are! I rang for you ages ago.'

'I'm sorry, Miss. This took longer to press than I thought.'

'It's such a pretty dress. It will suit your colouring,' Phoebe said.

'I've changed my mind. I'll wear the blue.'

Phoebe saw Jane controlling her exasperation. 'Yes, Miss.' She bobbed, disappeared into the dressing room with the pink dress and emerged with a blue one.

'Are you going out to dine?' Phoebe asked.'

'I shall be meeting my fiancé. It's imperative I look well.'

'Of course. Let me help you – I'm very good with hair.'

'All right, but don't tug whatever you do.'

'Have you been engaged long?'

'What business is it of yours?'

'None. I was just making conversation.'

'Then don't. I can't imagine that anything you have to say could possibly be of interest to me.'

'As you wish.'

'I do.'

Phoebe rewarded her with a vicious yank. Agnes yelped, and Phoebe apologised. As she worked she looked about the room. It was furnished in a manner any girl would love. Agnes was beautiful, she was engaged and she had every reason to be happy, so why was she so horrible, bad-tempered and spiteful? She must be very sad inside, Phoebe concluded.

5

Just before leaving work Lily entered Mr Battle's office to tidy it, as she did each evening. It was an easy task since he was not disorderly, unlike Arnold, whose office sometimes looked as if there had been a snowstorm. That, of course, was because he was a genius and had no time for mundane tasks.

A cursory look at the desk showed her there were no papers pertaining to Dulcie's visit of the afternoon. No matter. She smiled to herself as she turned to the safe, spun the dials and swung open the door. She searched it, but found nothing.

The papers must be somewhere. Mr Battle could not be keeping her affairs in his head – he didn't have the brain capacity for that. Where, then? The bookcase. She stood in front of the shelves for some time, imagining herself hiding something there. She would secrete it in a book with relevance to Dulcie. Wills – she scanned for anything by someone with a surname that began with W. Finding nothing she repeated the exercise with R, then S and, finally, D. Still nothing. What about the reference books? Making wills – she shook several but no papers fell out. Acts of separation – that lifted her heart. Still nothing. Divorce! She could barely breathe with excitement. Would Dulcie go so far? Disappointment followed swiftly.

Then *where*? He must have made notes, he always did, in his spidery hand.

Perhaps he had thrown them away. She emptied the wastepaper bin on to the floor, knelt and searched diligently through the screwed-up papers.

'Lost something?' The caretaker stood in the doorway, an insolent smile on his face. How long had he been watching her, *lusting* after her, no doubt. She had to control herself. He must not become her enemy – he knew too much.

'An address. I must inadvertently have thrown it away.'

'Not like you, Miss Howard.'

'No, it isn't, is it? But, then, we all make mistakes, Thomas, don't we? Some more than others,' she added significantly, but doubted if he had the wit to understand the veiled threat.

'Just call me when you've done, then, Miss H, so as I can lock up.'

There was no point in looking further: this was just rubbish. She dusted the desk, removed the blotting paper, threw it away. She collected the large bottle of ink from her own office and the small funnel she used to decant it into the inkwell.

Of course! How silly of her. She retrieved the blotting paper, folded it neatly and placed it in her bodice.

'I'm away now, Thomas,' she called.

Always a fast walker, Lily was home in double-quick time. First she made herself some tea and added a nip of whisky. Forgoing food, she settled down to study Mr Battle's blotting paper.

She stretched it flat on the table, then angled a small hand-mirror section by section over it. She was fortunate that it had not been too busy a day: apart from Mrs Randolph and one other client he had spent most of it in court. When she made out a word she wrote it down, and added incomplete words, even single letters. Two hours later, she had a page of jumbled words.

Randolph ... *Pr----r -y.* That was simple enough. Property. *Ad--t-ry.* *Bestiality* nearly had her falling off her seat. Not her dear Arnold. Oh, the wicked woman! Of what was she accusing him? She didn't deserve to live, that was sure. There was much more. *Separation* had evidently been discussed. *Debts*, she made out, but it was not clear whose, Dulcie's or Arnold's. He was too clever to have any so they had to be hers and then, according to the law, they would be his responsibility. It was all wrong, poor Arnold. If she owed money it was doubly disgusting, given the amount she had.

Oh, this was so exciting, like a giant game of anagrams – Lily had always been skilful with them.

Sleep was out of the question. Over and over it she went. If Dulcie was planning divorce then Lily's dreams would come true. Dulcie couldn't possibly stay in Barlton – no one would speak to her, she would not be socially acceptable – but that was to Lily's benefit; she wouldn't want the woman here, queening it with her good works.

Lily had plans for charitable ventures of her own – for

December Cottage too. She would knock it down and start again, build a house along Arts and Crafts lines. It was not nearly grand enough for Arnold. Perhaps they could buy an estate in the country. Could they afford it, though? After all, despite the fortune Arnold had acquired, the bulk of the money was still Dulcie's. And there was another thing she hadn't thought of until now. Would Dulcie's wealth make a difference to how she was regarded by the citizens of Barlton? Lily frowned. The rich could do anything and get away with it.

Lily thumped her pillow at the injustice of life. Of everything. Of Dulcie . . . She had to do something about that woman.

In the morning, in the better light of day, she found yet another word: 'Set---ment.' Settlement. There was not an inkling of doubt in her mind now: Dulcie was planning divorce. Arnold had to be told: he had to make contingency plans, more money had to disappear – he would need Lily to hide it for him, in companies within other companies. Eventually even he wouldn't know where it was. But she would. 'Oh, most certainly I shall,' she said, as she let herself out of the door.

Her first call was at the office where she sought out the senior clerk.

'I shall be late today. Would you be so kind as to explain to Young Mr Battle? My mother has been taken seriously ill. I have to go to her.' Since she never missed a day and worked longer hours than anyone else, her story would not be queried.

Then she raced down Hangman's Hill, up the other side, and was breathless when she arrived at December Cottage. She gazed at it as she waited for the doorbell to be answered. It might be pretty, it might look like a doll's house, but it would have to change. And those hedges between the garden and the road would have to go: no one could see in. There was no point in luxury if no one else could see it.

'Miss Howard for Mr Randolph-Smythe,' she announced imperiously to the half-witted girl who opened the door.

'He's not here.'

'Of course he is. He never leaves before seven forty-five. I know.'

'Not today. He's gone away.'

'Where?' Lily felt sick with apprehension.

'He didn't tell me.' The girl laughed.

'When? This morning?'

'Who are you, asking all these questions? I'll get Mrs Randolph for you.'

'That won't be necessary,' Lily said hurriedly, twirled round and set off down the drive. It might be unseemly to run but she had no choice – she had to find him. Where had he gone, and why? Then she stopped. It was his birthday tomorrow, she'd already bought him his present. He'd return today, surely. He would never miss his birthday – the staff always made him a presentation. She must go to the station, meet every train. He would come home with her and they would spend the whole evening, the whole night, working out what to do.

During the previous sleepless night Lily had made other resolutions too. She would allow him to take her – she had made him wait too long.

Lily purchased a platform ticket, and haunted the station. As she did not know where he had gone she had to meet every train. The morning dragged by, then half of the afternoon. Some of the railway staff were giving her strange looks. A policeman had even asked her if she was all right. The impertinence.

She was pinning her hopes on the London train, which was due at four forty-five, and never late. Ten minutes before it arrived she checked herself in the mirror in the ladies' waiting room – a mistake: she looked dishevelled and wild-eyed with exhaustion.

At last the train was steaming into the station. The platform was full of people, which was annoying: with so many she might miss him. There was so much luggage on the platform that it would be difficult to run after him if she had to. She saw several people she recognised from the shop. None remembered her, or they pretended not to. She'd have such fun not inviting them when . . . She had positioned herself where a porter had assured her the first-class carriages halted.

One by one they passed her. No sign of him. The throng was even greater now, as people welcomed others alighting from the train. He was not here! She ran along the train frantically, checking again. And then she saw him – embracing Sophie Franks. She stood in the shadows of the booking hall, her eyes on the carriage. They broke apart, and he helped her down from the train, Sophie looking to left and right, with such a guilty face.

'Afternoon, Mrs Franks,' Lily said, as she swept past her. She was no better than a tart, marrying poor old Mr Franks for his money.

Arnold was moving along the platform towards her, and suddenly he wasn't there. He couldn't have passed her – it was impossible. She went back along the platform, looking in doorways. Had he seen her? Was he playing games with her? Suddenly he was there. She put up her hand to wave to him. He was beckoning with an urgency that took her breath away. She increased her pace as much as the hordes would allow, and saw him duck into the doorway of the parcel office. She was almost there.

'Arnold,' she said. But he did not hear her. He was kissing another woman. But he had seen Lily, for he moved slightly to show her that it was Edith he was embracing with such passion. Then he looked straight at Lily and winked.

What was that noise? she thought. And why were all

these people skirting round her with looks of anger, pity, amusement? And then she realised: *she* was making the noise. She was screaming out her anger and pain as her remaining sanity crashed into a thousand pieces.

6

It was not yet ten but Phoebe was already in the garden. She had much to worry and think about. Yesterday she had helped with the preparations for the party. She had watched intently and learned a lot from her hostess about how to make arrangements. What had impressed her most was that though there were staff to help her Mrs R checked and supervised the details herself. That, Phoebe had decided, was how she would be when she entertained guests. When she had woken she had been looking forward to the day – but no longer.

Since there was a chill in the air she had chosen the fine tweed costume Mrs R had given her. It was in shades of lavender and sea green, and with it she wore a dark lavender blouse with a high neck and tight sleeves buttoned at the wrist. Normally this would have thrilled her and she would have taken pride in it, but not now.

Much earlier, for she had been up since six, she had experimented with her hair. Agnes's always looked pin neat, which might be because she didn't have Phoebe's curls. She'd flattened her hair, used combs to hold it smooth and had been longing to show Mrs R. But it didn't seem important now.

She had seen him on the landing!

She had stood holding the banister for fear she would fall – her legs felt as if they were made of rubber. She felt sick with terror, bleak with fear.

'Hullo, and who are you?' he had asked.

'A friend of Mrs R.' Dare she hope he had not recognised her?

'Are you now? And don't you mean Mrs Randolph?'

'She says to call her Mrs R.'

'How strange of her. Don't I know you?'

'I don't think so, sir.'

'Are you sure?' His intent stare had been difficult to endure. 'Are you staying here?'

'For the time being.'

'How pleasant for us all, a visitor.' The way he had said the words made them sound anything but innocuous. 'I remember, my wife did tell me.' He hadn't touched her, but she felt almost as if he had. She shuddered.

'Are you cold?'

'No, sir.'

'I look forward to our becoming better acquainted.' He smiled such a charming smile, then entered a room. She was left clutching the banister while her mind told her, 'Run!'

Afraid to go for breakfast, since surely he would be there too, she had gone back upstairs. In case she was alone in the house with him, she pushed a chair against the door and lay on the bed, careful of her clothes.

Over an hour later, she'd felt a headache coming on: she would get up and go out. She had been cautious as she went down the stairs looking around her, for what if he lurked in the shadows? There were voices in the morning room, so she had let herself out into the garden.

She paced round the large garden, and then again, trying to work out what to do and what to say. There was a small summer house in which she sat on a wooden bench, having first wiped the seat with her handkerchief to protect her new clothes.

He was here, and he was Randolph-Smythe, and her benefactress was Randolph, and he'd referred to his *wife*, and he'd called her a *visitor* – which must mean he lived here! The thoughts jostled in her head. Why had the woman lied? But then she hadn't actually *lied*. Yet the clerk at the lawyers had said that Randolph was her name, surely she wasn't involved in the use and abuse of young woman? Had Mrs Randolph been setting a trap for her? But she had such kind eyes.

Nothing made sense.

It wasn't so much that she felt betrayed: in the past months she had discovered that danger lurked everywhere for girls such as she. Rather, she was hurt for she had trusted the woman. In the three days she had known Mrs Randolph, she had grown to love her, and had been sure that Mrs Randolph was forming an attachment to her.

Mrs Randolph evil? It was not possible.

The best thing to do was leave – say nothing and just go. But then she looked up at the house, remembering how secure she had felt here. She didn't want to throw away her chance to improve her life . . . but not in *that* way.

'Why can't I make any sense out of it all?' she asked herself.

'Because you're panicking. He might not even be staying here.'

'Then what was he doing *upstairs*?'

'Well, if he does live here, and he's her husband, and his daughter is here too, what can he do to you? Nothing, that's what.'

'Maybe this is a house of ill repute!'

'Stop seeing the worst in everyone. Calm down!'

Having Phyllis back steadied her. But it was alarming too: it meant that she was really afraid.

Logic told her that if he recognised her it was he who should be afraid. She knew so many bad things about him, things he wouldn't want his wife to know, and certainly not his precious daughter . . .

'That's better!'

Phoebe jumped as a small object hurled itself at her with untrammelled joy. 'Mimi!' She scooped up the dog and cuddled her. She'd ask Mrs Randolph if she could take her to bed with her, say she was frightened of burglars. Mimi would defend her.

'Phoebe? Is it you?'

She looked up from the dog and shaded her eyes against the sun. A large man was striding across the lawn towards her. She knew that walk: only one person . . . 'Dick? Is it you? Is it really you?' She feared she was dreaming or, worse, hallucinating.

'It was last time I looked in a mirror.'

'Dick!' Mimi was dropped unceremoniously to the grass as Phoebe flung herself into her brother's arms. 'Oh, Dick. I've needed you so much.' And then she burst into tears.

At the window of the morning room Agnes watched the scene. 'You said I shouldn't have called her a slut. As usual, Mother, you're wrong. Just look at that disgusting exhibition! She's virtually devouring the gardener!'

'How wonderful,' said Dulcie, sure she knew why.

'She's not dining with us! Especially now.'

'But, Agnes, I promised her.'

'Honestly, Mother, you can be so strange. You don't know this girl, yet you treat her as an honoured guest.'

'She has a charm that I find attractive.'

'She might steal the silver, murder us in our beds.'

'I hardly think so. I just want to give her a start in life. We have so much, and we should help others.'

'A fine sentiment, but why does it have to be in our house?'

Dulcie returned to her list, which apparently infuriated Agnes even more since she slammed a book on the table. Dulcie was searching for her india rubber, which was not in the cut-glass tray where it normally was, and ignored her. This evening's celebratory dinner party would be a nightmare if Agnes continued in this mood.

'Come,' she said, to a diffident tap on the door.

'Mrs Randolph, oh, Mrs Randolph! You've no idea what has happened!' Such was Phoebe's excitement that she didn't even realise that she called Mrs R by her name.

'Really! Is there no escape?'

'Agnes! What has happened, Phoebe?'

'This,' Phoebe held the door wide and a sheepish-looking Dick appeared in stockinged feet. Dulcie noticed the large hole in his sock. She must buy him some more. 'This is Dick.'

'Yes, I know.'

'My Dick.'

'Phoebe is your sister?'

'Yes, Mrs Randolph. A miracle, that it is.'

'I couldn't believe my eyes when I saw him striding across the grass. I've longed for him so much.' Phoebe was holding on to her brother as if he might disappear again.

'Were you not told of our excitement? How Phoebe was rescued from the sea?'

'And Dad's clutches. Mrs Randolph saw him off,' Phoebe put in.

'I knew nothing. I came straight here when I returned from Father's – there's them shrubs you wanted planted, they've got to be in this month or else it'll be too late. I arranged it with Mr Chauncey, honest, I did.'

'I'm sure you did. And do you know—'

'Chauncey! Did he say *Chauncey*? He's here? Where? Why did you not tell me?' Agnes's eyes blazed with fury. 'How could you? My own brother! I hate you!'

'Don't you talk to your mother like that. Have you no respect?' It was Phoebe's turn to be furious.

'You mind your own business! You disgust me!'

'You don't know how lucky you are to have a mother, especially this one. And you speak to her in that manner! Well, I find *that* disgusting.'

'I'm going to telephone my father about this.' Agnes's intention to leave the room in a flurry was thwarted when she had to wait for Dick to manoevure his way further in to give her space.

'I'm sorry, Mrs Randolph. I shouldn't have spoken up like that.'

'It was very kind of you to try to help, Phoebe. Of course Agnes had every right to be angry with me, I should have told her that Chauncey was home, and safe. But . . . it's a long and complicated story and I shan't bother you with it. I can assure you, I had my reasons.'

'I'm sure you did, Mrs Randolph.'

'I have news for you, Phoebe. I received a note this morning that a couple who gave you a ride in their cart were claiming the reward for finding you.'

'The police already knew where I was. They'd already been to them. But wasn't that amazing, Mrs Randolph? Dick told me my father really did put up a reward for me. Me!' She smiled broadly. 'He doesn't normally spend a halfpenny if he can help it!'

Dulcie looked at Dick and, with an almost imperceptible shake of her head, warned him not to say anything about where the money had come from. She didn't want to spoil Phoebe's pleasure at what she thought her father had done.

They all looked at the door as it burst open and a tear-streaked Agnes hurled herself into the room. 'I hate you both!' she cried. 'He knew too, and he didn't tell me either.'

'Knew what, Agnes?' Dulcie asked, but she knew what the answer would be.

'That Chauncey was back in Barlton.'

Dulcie had a headache so intense that she could not even bring herself to study the folder of past crimes that Mr Corbin had delivered this morning. Instead she asked Bee to put it in the bottom drawer of her desk for safe-keeping and to make sure it was hidden by her house-keeping ledgers.

She lay on the *chaise-longue* in her boudoir with the curtains drawn. Agnes was still in a nasty temper, banging doors. What worried her, however, was how long Arnold had known about Chauncey and why he had not said anything to her, even if it was simply to shout his displeasure. It was ominous.

And then there was Phoebe. Her reaction at the shop had alarmed Dulcie. Why should she have been so frightened? Unless . . . She forced herself to confront the idea. Unless Arnold was involved with the auction of young women. But why should he be? He had never been short of women chasing him – it wasn't as if he was old and fat, like Mr Orton who had to buy his pleasures. Or was money at the root of it? Money, the accumulation of it, and her husband were always intrinsically linked. However, she must not let her distrust of him make him out to be worse than he was: it would not be fair.

Now Phoebe had her brother's protection she could move into Chauncey's home – but Chauncey was a little too interested in her. Although she liked Phoebe, Dulcie was not sure she wanted her to be involved with her son. She still knew too little about her.

It was evident that she could not stay here, though. Not only was there her concern about Arnold, which would not go away, there was Agnes too. But if Phoebe left, if she never met Arnold, how was Dulcie to know the truth? For her own peace of mind, she *needed* to know.

And it was a mystery why Agnes was so jealous. Normally she had no time for Dulcie, was rude to her, and had, no doubt, longed to tell her she hated her, which she had managed today. Whatever Dulcie had spent on Phoebe in no way affected what she would spend on Agnes. So why?

Edward. It had to be him. Agnes, while pretty, was no match for Phoebe's fey quality and her beauty. Was she afraid he might take a shine to Phoebe? If only she and Agnes were closer, Dulcie would tell her that it was pointless to pursue him if he did not want her. She could tell her how hard, how depressing it was to love someone when they did not love you in return.

What to do? She wondered if she had always been so indecisive, or if Arnold had made her so with his hectoring, carping and endless criticism. There had been that glorious period only three months ago when she had bought the house, changed her will – defied him. But she had done nothing since for fear of him. She could not forget the expression in his eyes when he had threatened her with death or stop thinking about what he might do if he found out she had made a new will. But how could he? It was safe at the lawyer's. Or was it? Lily was devoted to Arnold . . . But Mr Battle had assured her . . .

If only she could cancel this dinner, but it had been planned for so long – Arnold's forty-ninth birthday. And still she had not resolved the problem of what to do about Phoebe.

'Yes?' She hoped it wasn't Agnes. She had seen enough of her today.

'May I come in? Would I be disturbing you?' Phoebe peered round the door.

'No, my dear. It will be pleasant to have you to talk to. Sit here.' She patted the chair beside her.

'Would you like me to massage your head, take the pain away?'

'I wish you would.'

'Then lie back, close your eyes, and think of nothing – that is, if you can. I never can. Thoughts keep popping in and out of my head like blown blossom.'

'What a lovely idea.' She closed her eyes, as instructed, and Phoebe positioned herself behind her, then began to massage her temples. Round and round went her fingers, and round and round went the blossom in Dulcie's mind. Eventually the massage ceased and she shook her head, as if testing it. 'I do believe my headache has disappeared. That was so enjoyable, my dear. Truly.'

'My mother taught me. She said she thought sometimes she was a witch and it was a good thing she'd been born when she had or she'd have been drowned in the village pond.'

'What a dreadful thought.'

Phoebe sat down on the chair beside Dulcie. 'I've made up my mind what I should do, Mrs Randolph.'

'And that is?'

'I have to go. I can't stay here. I seem to upset Agnes, which is a shame since I would love to be her friend. But I understand. She doesn't want to share you with anyone and I don't blame her. If you were my mother I'd kill anyone I thought was trying to take you away from me.'

'But you're not.'

'I know. But Agnes doesn't, does she? She's jealous, and that is why she's so cross all the time.'

'I'm not sure I want you to go. I would miss you.'

'You wouldn't have had that headache if it hadn't been for me. If your son doesn't mind, I could stay there for a little while. Then Dick and I thought we might look for positions together somewhere. He would do the gardening and odd jobs and me the housework or cooking – as long as it's simple fare. And then, if we got places perhaps with a small cottage, we could send for our younger brother, Jim. He shouldn't be alone with our father. But, you see, there's just one thing.'

'Which is?'

'If you could write us testimonials. We couldn't get anywhere without them.'

'The most glowing ones I've ever penned. I had hoped you'd accompany me to Exeter tomorrow. There's someone I need to see there, and I hate to travel alone.'

'Exeter? Oh, Mrs Randolph, yes! I've always wanted to see Exeter. People say it's enormous.'

'Then we shall leave first thing in the morning by railway.'

'A railway train!' Pheobe's excitement was mounting.

'Then, when we return, I shall speak with my lawyer and find a cottage to rent for you and your brother. Would you like that?' Solved, and so neatly!

'Mrs Randolph, what can I say? I should be so happy!' And, throwing caution to the wind, Phoebe leaped up and kissed her. Mrs Randolph did not seem to mind a bit. 'But, Mrs Randolph, about dinner tonight? I'm upsetting Agnes so it's better if I don't attend.'

'I invited you.'

'I don't want to cause any more trouble. The truth is, and please don't take this wrong, but if she's nasty to me, I can't always be certain I won't be nasty back.'

Dulcie turned her head to hide her smile. Agnes was about to get her own way again. It really was so unfair. 'Very well. If you won't attend the dinner, why not join us afterwards for refreshments and dancing?'

'Dancing! Oh, I love to dance!'

'Any more excitement, Phoebe, and I think you'll burst!' Dulcie was laughing.

7

It was impossible for any of their guests to notice that anything was wrong, Dulcie thought, with satisfaction, as she sat in her usual place at the head of the table. Arnold was being over-polite to her, had deferred to her, had even paid her a couple of compliments, but that was his custom when they were entertaining or when other people were about.

Tonight was different for her in that this was the first large party she had organised when she had not had sleepless nights over the detail. She was happy that the food, drink, flowers and entertainment were up to her normal high standards, but if they hadn't been, she wouldn't have cared.

Agnes was glittering with youth and charm. She could

turn it on at whim. Dulcie watched the young men fawning over her, and marvelled that people could not see what she was really like. Dulcie prided herself on reading people the first time she met them.

There were twenty at dinner and another thirty had been invited for afterwards. She looked along the table at the faces of her guests, some of whom she had known for years, and decided that, with two exceptions, she would not mind if she never saw any of them again.

'You are thoughtful this evening, Dulcie, or is it that I bore you?'

'Theo, how could you dream such a thing? I'm sorry if I seem distant. I was thinking that I needed to find resolve somehow.'

'Then you are making decisions?'

'Yes, Theo, I think I must.'

'I trust they are the ones I hope you will take.'

'And which would they be?'

'Now, Dulcie, I cannot influence you. It would not be fair.'

She was enjoying this teasing conversation, such a new experience for her, when suddenly Theo was monopolised by Mrs Williams, a tedious matron who sat on his right. How unkind – she'd never thought such things before ... Sophie. And there she had had one small triumph: she had refused point-blank to invite her.

'Where are the Frankses?' she had heard a woman ask.

'A surprising omission. Isn't Sophie one of Dulcie's dearest friends?'

'Like sisters. Well, they were ...' An arching of eyebrows, a supercilious smile. Dulcie could have said something, but she didn't: people might think she cared, and that would never do.

When she had done the placements she had seated Edward several chairs away from Agnes, but while she had been changing, Agnes had crept into the dining room and altered the plan. Now, he was beside her, and she had shot Dulcie such a triumphant glance when they had taken their places.

At the moment she was flirting outrageously with the man sitting beside her and the two opposite, but Edward seemed unaware of her, deep in conversation with Juliet Parson, who was interested in art so he wouldn't be bored.

'We were saying?' Theo was able to concentrate on her again.

'I shall inform you in due course. But now, dear Theo, I fear you must excuse me.' Dulcie stood. 'Ladies, please . . .' She led the way out, followed by the other women.

Phoebe was in the drawing room waiting for them. She had on the pretty evening dress Dulcie had purchased for her. It was a lovely coral colour, which, with her dark hair, suited her beautifully. Since she had come to know the girl Dulcie had thought of her as a child, but now she looked like a woman.

'What's *she* doing here?' Agnes hissed.

'She's a visitor in my house and I invited her. Now, please desist from your silly vendetta. I compromised and did not have her dine with us. Ah, Mrs Parson, refreshment? Phoebe, be a dear, please get some more lemonade for our guests. We have finished what there was.'

'That Edward Bartholomew-Prestwick is an interesting young man. Tell me more, Dulcie.'

Olive Williams's intervention could not have come at a better time for immediately Agnes was concentrating on their conversation: the Williamses were dangerous since they had three daughters whom they were hoping to marry off.

'Isn't he? And interested in so many things.'

'He talks intelligently on the arts and politics, yet he rides to hounds and has a good knowledge of the land.' This was of prime importance to Olive. 'I can't think why I've never met him before.'

'He lives in Exeter.'

'In a city? Poor fellow. No land?'

'They used to own Courtney Lacey.'

'*That* Bartholomew! And *that* Prestwick! I see!' Dulcie smiled at the avarice in Olive's face.

'He's most entertaining company.' Agnes was staking her claim in no uncertain terms.

'You know him well?' Olive enquired.

'We have seen much of each other since the Mayor's Assembly.' Agnes, Dulcie saw, looked smug.

'Ah, thank you, Phoebe. Olive, might I introduce my young friend Phoebe Drewett?'

'Any connection with the Drews of Chagford?'

'Unlikely.' Phoebe grinned at the idea. 'But I am from Dartmoor, Cowman's Combe.'

'Cowman's Combe!' Olive looked astonished. 'Nobody lives there.'

'I did.'

'Phoebe, some of our guests need attention,' Dulcie rescued her, 'perhaps you could talk to them. Such a sweet child,' she said to Olive, as she watched her move elegantly across the room.

'But that's a hamlet. Only peasants live there.'

'But she is one! Didn't you realise, Mrs Williams? You know my mother – always bothering with waifs and strays. Now she's bringing them into our home.'

'You're so kind, Dulcie, an example to us all.'

Agnes scowled.

'You must be so proud of her, Agnes,' Olive Williams continued.

'I am.'

It was Dulcie's turn to look smug.

Phoebe was handing chocolates to a particularly deaf and difficult woman, who was laughing for once.

'Ah, the gentlemen!'

Arnold strode in, the epitome of a gracious host. Dulcie was quickly at his side. 'Arnold, you haven't met our guest yet. Phoebe, might I introduce my husband to you?' She watched closely for any reaction on either part.

'Welcome to our home.' Arnold proffered his hand. Phoebe made a show of the fact that she had glasses in both hands, so could not shake his hand. Was that deliberate, Dulcie wondered.

'But we've met, Mr Randolph-Smythe.'

Dulcie looked from Phoebe to her husband. Was that a frown on Arnold's face? She was sure he looked uncomfortable.

'We have?'

There was no doubt of it: Phoebe was smiling. 'On the stairs, this morning!' She laughed.

Dulcie felt weak with relief.

'But of course. I must have been half asleep. Forgive me.'

Phoebe did not look afraid. All that worrying for nothing. At last, thought Dulcie, she could concentrate on other things but especially Theo. How she missed him even when she knew he was in the next room! 'Here's Lord Prestwick.' She could have laughed at the speed with which Olive turned and rushed across the room, nearly tripping on the hem of her dress.

Edward had entered the room behind his father, with his usual amiable expression. Suddenly his face changed. He looked astonished and blinked as if he did not believe what he was seeing. Slowly he smiled, with such joy. 'Miss Phoebe!'

'Mr Edward!' Phoebe looked equally happy.

'Oh, Miss Phoebe.' He approached her. 'I never thought to see you again.'

'Nor me.' Her smile had become a wide grin that encompassed her entire face.

'Well, now we know.' Dulcie turned to find Theo standing beside her. 'He told me he had met someone.'

'I could almost wish he hadn't,' sighed Dulcie. Agnes's face was twisted with anger, then distorted by grief.

'Phoebe, you wanted to come to Exeter with me?'

Dulcie had found Phoebe walking in the garden. She looked as if she had been to bed long before two o'clock when in fact they had all retired. How wonderful to be young and to show no ill-effects from such a late night, thought Dulcie. Her own complexion was a little too pink from the red wine she had drunk the night before, and she knew she looked weary.

'If you wouldn't mind my staying here, Mrs Randolph, I am a little tired.'

'You don't look it.' Dulcie was unsure what to do. It would not be wise to leave her here with Agnes in her present mood. No doubt she was staying in the hope that she would see Edward. 'If you don't wish to accompany me, I think it would be better if you spent the day at Chauncey's. Then you can have time with your brother.'

'That would be lovely.'

Dulcie felt somehow that Phoebe had no intention of going there. 'I will drive you down on my way to the station.'

'The walk will do me good.'

'I think I'd prefer to do so.'

'It's very kind of you, Mrs Randolph,' she said, but there was a touch of disappointment in her voice.

A little later Dulcie glanced at her watch. 'I'd come in with you, but . . .'

Phoebe was alighting from the carriage outside Chauncey's house. 'You must not miss your train for me.' She glanced at the causeway and shivered.

'You're safe now.' Dulcie laid a hand on her arm. 'Have a lovely day. I'll call for you this evening.' She looked up at the window to see her son watching them, a broad smile on his face. 'Do explain to my son why I was in such a rush.'

Phoebe did not wait for Dulcie's carriage to turn the corner before she began to run up the road beside Chauncey's house. By the time she had reached the top of the hill, she was panting – like a dray-horse, she told herself. She would have liked to remove her coat but thought it might draw attention to her. She straightened her hat, took a few deep breaths and continued up the high street, nearly breaking into a run past Randolph's Emporium, until she had reached Hangman's Hill.

Why she had run, and so swiftly, she was not sure. She was free to do as she wished, see whom she wanted. Mrs Randolph had made that clear to her. She didn't have to go and visit her brother at Chauncey's. So why had she? 'Habit,' she said to herself, with a grin. She was always running from someone.

As much as she would have liked to see Exeter, Edward was more important. As she walked, sedately now, she smiled to herself as she thought of the night before. Without doubt yesterday evening had been the happiest of her life.

Seeing Edward had been such a surprise, and the way he had smiled when he saw her, the eagerness with which he had stepped forward – she could not have asked for more. At the sight of him all her fears and worries about Mr Randolph-Smythe had disappeared like the early mist on the moor. With Edward close by she would be safe. The only unpleasant thing was Agnes scowling in the background. Phoebe felt sorry for her: how sad to love Edward and see him happy with another.

'She's so cross with me,' she had said to Edward, when he had brought her some lemonade to quench her thirst after they had danced an energetic polka. Their first dance, she remembered dreamily.

'But why? What have you done?'

'She loves you.'

'I don't think so.'

'But she does. She said she was in love, that she was to marry, that you were her fiancé.'

'She named me?'

'No, but who else is there? She's been making sheep's eyes at you all evening.'

'You are mistaken, Miss Phoebe. She loves a Robert Markham. He's not here this evening. That was who she meant. They have known each other for a long time. The whole town expects an announcement any day.'

'Really? Oh, that is nice. I didn't want to upset her and I didn't want her wanting you.'

'Miss Phoebe, I love you so much!'

She had looked up at his words but was disappointed to see him laughing, and to realize that he used that precious word as one does to a dog, or a particular dish, or the setting sun. Not to her as a woman. 'Have I said something amusing?'

'No. Your honesty touches me. There's no artifice in you.'

'I hope not.' She blushed, for she lied: she wore a false hairpiece at the back. And her lips, well, secretly she had added a little rouge. So it could be said she was all artifice.

'Have I offended you?' he asked, seeing her colour.

'The pleat of my hair is false,' she whispered, and turned her back so that he could see. She didn't mention her lips. This only made him laugh the more and she had been glad when the instruments tuned up and another dance was announced.

'If she hadn't had another gentleman, would you have shown interest?' Phoebe asked, as she sipped her lemonade.

'Agnes? No. We have nothing in common. She does not attract me. And in any case I had found the young

436

lady for me. I could not get the thought of her out of my mind. Each night I dream of her beauty.'

At these words Phoebe felt as if her heart was tumbling into the pretty satin slippers Mrs Randolph had bought for her. She felt close to tears, but she wouldn't let him see how upset she was.

'Really? How interesting. And pray who is the lucky girl?'

Edward leaned over and whispered in her ear, 'You!'

It would be for ever a mystery how she had refrained from flinging herself into his arms. Instead she had smiled, she hoped in a sophisticated manner, and murmured, 'That makes both of us, then.'

'You're in love with another girl?' He had pulled a shocked face.

'No, silly, *you*!' She had pushed him playfully and laughed uproariously, which had made everyone look at them.

As Phoebe scurried down Hangman's Hill she hugged herself as she remembered that scene. Then she decided to remember it again, word for word. She could not have gone to Exeter after such a declaration. He would visit her at some time today, she was certain.

In the hall she met Bee. 'What are you doing here, you minx?' But she smiled as she spoke. 'I thought you were spending the day with your brother.'

'I'm tired after last night, and I didn't want to bother Mr Chauncey. He told me he doesn't like to be watched while he paints.'

'I've never heard that before. Still, you're here now and you can help me put away the linen.'

It was strange to be sorting the linen, storing it away in neat piles, when only a matter of days ago she had been washing and ironing the same sheets and pillowcases. What an extraordinary turn of events.

'Why did Mrs Randolph have to go to Exeter?'

'How should I know? She don't tell me everything –

well, she do almost,' Bee added, not wanting to sound less important than she was.

'I was just curious. She's a kind lady, isn't she?'

'That she is. The good works that woman does would fill a book. There's many as have their happiness and their health thanks to her. Nothing is too much trouble. And give! Why, she never stops.'

'You love her, don't you?'

'When I started in service if you'd told me I'd come to love my employer I'd have told you not to be silly. But it's true. You know, when my father was ill, she paid all the doctor's bills. Right as rain he is now.'

Phoebe was astonished that someone as old as Bee should still have a father alive but she held her tongue. 'She should be much happier than she is.'

'You've noticed? The young don't usually have eyes for such things.'

'Sometimes even if she's smiling her eyes look sad.'

'She's better since she met that lord. Not as I approve.' Bee sniffed.

'But he's so nice.' And he was Edward's father so *of course* he was the second most perfect man in Barlton, if not England, if not the world, she thought.

'Is he? You know that, do you? Well, he bothers me. It's money, you see. If you don't have it, it's a problem, and if you do, it still is.'

'I wouldn't think so. I can't think of any problems money brings.'

'You just think about it, young woman. If you were the richest woman in Barlton, how would you know if people liked you for yourself or for the money in your pocket?' Bee looked triumphant.

'But he's a lord.'

'And in the past I knew of some what were as poor as church mice. Times they are a-changing. There's different rich, these days, people what once upon a time wouldn't have had tea with the king-to-be. Now anyone can. All wrong in my opinion, that is.'

'But—'

'And you look at Lord Prestwick's cuffs next time you see him, see how frayed they are. After her money, no doubt, just like the rest.'

'That would be horrible. Still, it's nice for her to have such a friend. She told me he was her best friend. It's not as if he's a suitor, is it? She's married to someone else.'

'Don't even let me start on *him*!' And Bee gave an enormous snort of disapproval. 'What was that?'

'I think it was the front door.'

'Who could it be at this time of day? Go and peep over the banister, see who it is.' Bee was already patting her hair, getting ready to receive someone.

Phoebe's heart was racing in a tattoo of delirious excitement as she tiptoed on to the landing, praying it was Edward come to see her. To her disappointment it was Mr Randolph-Smythe, and she ducked down when she saw Agnes appear from the drawing room.

'Papa, you've got to do something about that girl Mama has taken in.'

'Really? Why?'

'She's not suitable. Last night she was an embarrassment to me, flirting disgustingly.'

'So it's all right for you, but not for anyone else?' He stroked her cheek tenderly.

'Not if it's Edward, it isn't. He's mine and I won't have her dallying with him.'

'Jealous, are we?' He was laughing.

'Of *that* creature? How could you even think so? No, Edward told me last night that he did not know what to do with her, that she was a nuisance and he wished she would go.'

'You've nothing to fear. Women like that girl are for men's amusement, nothing else. Where is she?'

'Gone to Exeter with Mother.'

'Did she say why?'

'No. Does Mother ever tell me what she is about? I'm a person of little significance to her.'

'Hardly. And where are you going? Am I to be left alone?'

'Yes, Papa, I'm sorry. But you lunch here?'

'No, I forgot some important papers this morning. Am I to be told where you are taking lunch?'

'I've an appointment.'

'So mysterious.' He chucked her under the chin as he bent to kiss her.

Phoebe did not believe a word of this conversation. Edward had hardly spoken to Agnes, so how could it be true? She was fully aware that in Arnold's eyes she was for men's amusement – but only if they could catch her. No one had succeeded so far.

How strange to have a father who treated one so; young-looking too. But he still gave her the shivers: too many of her bad memories were bound up with him. She was glad Bee was here and that she was not alone in the house with him.

When Dulcie arrived Barlton station was bustling. Quite a crowd had gathered to catch the train to Exeter. It was already standing at the platform, great clouds of steam gushing forth. The platform was quite an obstacle race as Dulcie made her way to the first-class carriage, past piles of luggage and cartons of produce destined for the city.

'Mrs Randolph,' she heard someone call. She ducked her head. She did not want to meet anyone she knew, not today, not on this mission. 'Mrs Randolph,' the voice persisted. 'Phoebe isn't accompanying you?' It was Edward who, somewhat breathless, had caught up with her.

'Edward! I thought you were staying in Barlton.'

'No, Father wanted to return today. And Phoebe had mentioned . . .'

'She was going to Exeter? She changed her mind.'

'I see.' Poor Phoebe, Dulcie thought. 'Is your father here?'

'Yes.'

'I don't see him.' Dulcie had been looking in the windows of the carriages as they bustled past.

'He's not in first.'

'No?' She was astonished. 'In second?'

'Third.'

'Shall you join me?'

Edward looked embarrassed. How insensitive of her. Of course, they were economising on the fare. 'Then I shall join you, if I may?'

'It's not very comfortable, Mrs Randolph.'

'But it's such a short journey.'

Edward led her back the way they had come. 'Look who I've found, Father.'

Theo looked up from his copy of the *Barlton Globe* and jumped to his feet, dropping his cane and newspaper, and knocking sideways the hat of the woman sitting beside him. Despite his fulsome apology, and a gentlemanly bow, the woman told him in ripe language what a clumsy oaf he was.

'Madam, if you would excuse me butting in,' Dulcie was opening her large bag, 'I have a ticket here for the first-class compartment. Perhaps I might take your seat and you take mine?'

At first the countrywoman looked suspicious, but then she snatched the ticket without any thanks and was off. 'That's better,' Dulcie said, as she settled herself. 'And a window seat too. How fortunate.'

'But, Dulcie, I must protest, this is not what you're used to.'

'Theo, if it is good enough for you it is most certainly good enough for me.' They heard the guard's whistle. 'Always such an exciting moment, don't you think?' She looked out of the window as the engine began to move.

'You know, the first time I travelled on a train, there was no glass in the windows. Do you remember, Theo?'

'I do. And we were all afraid our heads would fall off from the great velocity.'

'Such silly fears we had! And now my husband's motor car travels faster than we did in those days. What an exciting world we live in, something new every day.'

'Is she ill?'

'I'm sorry, Edward. Is who ill?'

'Phoebe.'

'No, quite the contrary. She's fresh as a daisy. She wanted to see her brother.' This was not strictly true, as Dulcie well knew.

'I see,' said Edward looking downcast.

'Are you bitterly disappointed?'

'It would have been pleasant, if she had been here.'

'Don't believe a word he says, Dulcie. He's talked of nothing else all morning.' Theo laughed.

It was a pleasure for her to be with them, but a nuisance too: how could she explain to them that she was about to find and question Lynette Lingford about their kinsman? And what if her fears about Kendall Bartholomew and Phoebe were proved right? How would poor Edward react then? How could he contemplate involvement with a girl who had lost her innocence in such circumstances? Perhaps that would be for the best. She was a sweet, lovely child, but hardly a suitable match for one such as he. Dulcie thought of Agnes and her shattered hopes, how she had longed for Edward. Perhaps marriage to him would make her nicer, less discontented. She'd seen it in the past, nasty girls turning into sweet women with contentment. But, then, she had seen the opposite happen too. Oh dear, it was all such a puzzle.

'If I might ask, what takes you to Exeter, Dulcie?'

'I have to see a friend,' she said non-committally.

'Perhaps you would care to have luncheon with me?'

'How very kind you are.'

It was an uncomfortable journey. Within ten minutes Dulcie was very conscious of the wooden seat, the carriage was not as clean as she was used to, and some of the occupants smelt unpleasant. It was noisy too: the carriage shook and rattled, there was no panelling, no curtains to absorb the noise, and everyone was shouting.

She was glad when even Theo gave up trying to make polite conversation and eventually fell asleep. *Lynette Lingford*. The name was familiar, but for the life of her she could not think why. She had checked in her voluminous address book but she had not written it in there. The thought nagged at her for the rest of the journey.

9

Upon the train's arrival in Exeter, Dulcie said goodbye to her friends. Then, dusty and dishevelled from the uncomfortable journey, she popped across the road to the Rougemont Hotel. There she ordered coffee, and used the excellent facilities in the ladies' cloakroom.

As she rearranged her hair she thought of how times had changed. Only a few years ago, no decent woman would have ventured into an establishment such as this without an escort, but today she had walked in and placed her order, and no one saw it as unusual or shocking. She preferred the liberty of the modern world.

She left the room and asked the hall porter to order a hansom cab to take her to her destination. The hill was steep down through the town and, fearing for the safety of the horse, she alighted at the top of Stepcote Hill but arranged for the man to wait for her.

'There's rough types about so close to the river,' the driver informed her.

'I doubt they'll bother me. I've my trusty umbrella.' And she waved it with its heavy duck-head handle.

Negotiating the steep cobbled steps was quite difficult – they were strewn with rubbish so she had to look carefully where she put her feet and lift her skirt so that it did not trail over the filth. The old houses, on either side of the steps, were of different periods and sizes and appeared to be leaning as if they were keeping each other standing. Children were everywhere, unwashed, uncared-for, playing in the refuse. It distressed her to see such poverty and neglect.

It was an interesting walk, given that there were so many people about and some distinctive architecture to see. She had not known that in this area of the city so much was distinctive and old. The streets could not have changed much since Tudor times, judging by the number of buildings she saw of that period. No doubt they would still be here in this higgledy-piggledy state when another hundred years had passed. There was comfort in such continuity, Dulcie thought.

She needed to ask the way twice and finally found herself outside a house, which, she was quick to note, had clean curtains at the windows and a gleaming front step. She knocked on the door with her umbrella. It was opened a crack and a sweet-faced girl peered out.

'Does a Mrs Lingford live here?'

'Yes, ma'am.'

'May I see her?'

'I'm not sure if she's in. Who shall I say is calling?'

'Mrs Randolph from Barlton, if she would just give me five minutes of her precious time?' She smiled encouragingly since the child looked so uneasy. 'If you would be so kind?' she added, since the child appeared uncertain whether or not to let her into the house. She had noticed that her clothes, though worn, were spotless, and that she spoke well and clearly, without the accent she had expected.

'You'd better step in,' she said, and Dulcie was glad: a small gaggle of curious children were watching her with solemn, hungry eyes.

Dulcie waited in the narrow passage with its worn linoleum and chipped paint. There was an overwhelming smell of cabbage and a strong odour that she hoped was not rats.

'May I help you?' A figure had appeared in the passage.

'No! Why, it's you! My dear Mrs Lingford, how are you?' Dulcie put out her hand with pleasure. 'How long ago is it since you helped me with a couple of placements of young girls? Four or five years at least.'

'It was way back in 'ninety-six, Mrs Randolph.'

'It was your name – I knew that we had met but, of course, not here.'

'I couldn't believe my ears when Ella said—' And Lynette Lingford burst into tears.

'What must you think of me, welcoming you in such a manner?' Mrs Lingford had finally composed herself, mainly with the help of two cups of tea, and Dulcie's soothing voice.

'I think I have found a woman who is distraught and at the end of her tether. Am I right?' Dulcie asked.

'It has been hard.' Miss Lingford was still dabbing her eyes, but sat with a touching dignity.

'Do you wish to tell me, or is it too painful for you?'

'Where to begin? But I am not seeking sympathy. I fear my problems are of my own making.'

'And what would they be?'

'It is difficult to find employment and with so many mouths to feed . . .'

'I heard about your husband, it was most unfortunate.'

'He didn't do it, you know, embezzle all that money. He was a good Christian man. Others stole it and he took the blame.'

'He paid the ultimate price, I hear.'

'I don't think he killed himself. He wouldn't have done that, not with all of us waiting for him ...' Tears threatened again.

'I remember your distress over that child you brought to the home.'

'She wasn't a bad girl.'

'But it is always the female who takes the blame, have you not noticed, Mrs Lingford? So unfair. How many young girls have the strength to fight off a determined man? But she had her baby and he was adopted, and I found her a good position.'

'I've always remembered the work you do for these young girls. You've humanity and understanding. There were many times I felt I should come to you, but it was difficult.'

'I'm sure it was.' Dulcie patted her hand, and hoped she was about to become more forthcoming. She sensed the woman wanted to talk to her but that something was stopping her. Fear? 'I had always hoped you would come back. I felt you would have been so good at working with the girls. When I met you I thought we had the same compassion for them. We could have worked together. But I had no address ...'

A silence descended. Dulcie was not sure how to proceed. Eventually she said, 'Tell me, Mrs Lingford, do you know of a Phoebe Drewett?'

'No! Oh, no, please don't tell me anything has happened to her! Dear Phoebe.' And before Dulcie could say anything she was weeping again.

'Edward is not here?' Dulcie asked, as Theo helped her remove her coat.

'He's had to go to the lawyer's, some business for his uncle.'

'He works hard for that man. I trust he appreciates it, and I also trust it was nothing to do with my husband.'

'As far as I know, it was not. He tells me little but if you were involved I'm sure he would. Shall we?' With his hand he indicated the sitting room. 'You need have no fear about the property in Gold Street. Your husband finally paid. I gather he's making a hotel. A sherry or perhaps Madeira?'

'A sherry would be most appetising. I'd heard rumours myself about his plans.'

At this Theo shook his head and gave a brief ironic laugh.

'You are amused?'

'No, dear lady, puzzled.'

'That I am not privy to his business? It's how he prefers it, and I too. What I don't know can't affect me, can it?'

'Are you disappointed you have only me for company?'

'Theo! I do believe you're fishing for compliments. Thank you,' she said, as she took the glass from him and sipped it immediately, then again.

'Are you distressed, Dulcie? You look flustered.'

'And I drink my sherry too fast but you are too polite to say so.' She smiled at him. 'I have just had a most unpleasant hour.'

'No one hurt you?'

'Good gracious, no. I had to listen to some most ugly information.'

'Is there anything I can do to help you?'

'I'm not sure. In fact, I am uncertain what to do. I need a little time, I think.'

'As you wish, my dear Dulcie.' He poured them another drink and she was shocked by the alacrity with which she accepted it. 'Edward is very taken with Phoebe, I have to say.' He had his back to her as he spoke. Dear man, changing the subject, she thought. Only, inadvertently, he was making it worse. 'But you are frowning, dear lady. You do not approve?'

'I don't know, Theo. She is a sweet child and very lovely, of course, but I wonder if she is suitable. He is such a cultured man, and she, well, she is hungry to learn but it would take her a long time to catch up with him.'

'It does not worry you that she is not socially his equal?'

Dulcie felt uncomfortable for, of course, she had thought just such a thing. 'She isn't, but she is learning how to behave. And, more importantly, she is willing to be told without getting into a huff.' Like Agnes. 'I do believe that soon no one will know she wasn't born to a far greater position than . . .'

'And what was that?'

Dulcie studied her sherry. She did not like this conversation. On the one hand she could see what a mismatch it would be, what a scandal it would cause. But on the other she wondered if, provided one party was willing to change, it really mattered. In ten years who would remember? And if happiness was at stake . . . Still, Edward wasn't her son, he should decide for himself. But what if it was Chauncey? She liked to think she would accept Phoebe but she had a nasty feeling that she would not. How unfair of her, but how natural. She only wanted the best for her son, and was Phoebe the best?

'I have to say, Theo, that I'm ashamed of the way I've been thinking. She's a good girl, kind and sweet. I must fight such prejudice.'

'You're so honest. She's lucky to have found you.'

'I do hope so,' she said, with feeling. 'Her father has a smallholding on Dartmoor, a poor place. They can barely scratch a living, I gather, and he is a beastly man. He beat her and she ran away from him.' She spoke abruptly, as if she felt she should tell but also that she shouldn't. 'Her brother, Dick, helps me with my garden.'

'Dulcie, what a sweet woman you are.'

'Me? What have I said?'

'Most people would have said, "He's my gardener." Or "I employ him." He *helps* you. I find that endearing.'

'After the intolerant thoughts I've been having? Surely not!'

'Why shouldn't you think in that way? It is how we are conditioned to think. It is what Society has taught us. It takes a brave heart to defy convention and Society's rules.'

'But it is so hypocritical. My father was a shop-keeper, as I am. One of my grandfathers was a farm labourer, the other a shop assistant. My mother was a maid. Who am I to stand in judgement? My father was successful, he was rich, and so am I, but it doesn't change who I am inside, does it?'

'Not many are willing to acknowledge that.'

'I tried to change. I tried to fool everyone. I worried about protocol and etiquette. I wanted to appear to be what I was not.'

'And how much of that was at Arnold's instigation?'

The maid announced that their lunch was served, and led the way into the small but elegant dining room. The walls were covered in shelves on which was displayed Theo's collection of porcelain. 'Such a pretty period for china, Regency, isn't it?'

'I have to agree.' He flicked open his napkin. 'I also found it appealing when you said to the poor maid that breaking your china was just an accident.'

He was studying the food on his plate carefully, as if enjoying it with all his senses, which she, in turn, found endearing.

'You know what I had expected? That you did not approve of Phoebe because you would prefer my son to fall in love with Agnes.'

'I can't imagine why you thought that. I hoped quite the opposite.'

'I am so sad that you and your daughter do not get on.'

She looked up from her plate, her fork poised half-way to her mouth. She put it down. 'If I tell you something, will you promise never to tell a living soul, including Edward?'

'But of course.'

'Agnes is not my daughter.'

Theo had just taken a large bite of bread. He spluttered and choked, then coughed so much that she had to get up and pat his back firmly. 'Forgive me!' He was still spluttering. 'How rude!'

'I'm sorry I shocked you so.'

'Do you wish to tell me more? I reiterate my promise to you.'

'I've never told a living soul this. No one. Arnold took me to America for a long holiday – he likes the way Americans do business. He often goes to get ideas for the shop. When he took me, we'd had a difficult time.' She looked down at her napkin. 'I thought it was an opportunity for us to mend our marriage, but of course it wasn't. His mistress – a young woman from a prominent Devon family – was expecting a child. I'm not sure what his plans were, only that he wanted us out of the way in case anything awkward happened – as it did. The mother died. She had travelled to America with us on the same ship, and wherever we went so did she. Innocent fool that I was, I hadn't realised the truth. He simply collected the baby, gave her to me, explained the circumstances and I returned to Barlton, apparently a new mother and supposedly overjoyed with my daughter.'

'And you accepted her?'

'I had no choice. He said he would leave me if I didn't and take Chauncey with him. I couldn't have borne that.'

'My poor dear lady. So you didn't like the child because of who she was?'

'Oh, no. I didn't like the situation, of course, and I felt it was intolerable of my husband to expect me to accept it. But what he had done wasn't the child's fault. It was little different from an adoption, which was how I decided to regard it. But it didn't work. I don't know why

450

but, try as I might, she did not take to me. It was almost as if she knew. The situation has simply worsened over the years.'

'And Chauncey does not know?

'Only you, Arnold and I know. That is all. I'm finding it such a relief to confide in you. It has been such a burden, this secret.'

'I am angry when I see her treat you with such scant respect.'

'But can we blame her? She learns by example.'

'Arnold?'

Dulcie shrugged her shoulders.

'Your husband is an evil man.'

'I have thought about him a great deal, why he is as he is, what has made him so angry with life that he treats people as he does. I have reached a conclusion. I don't think he can help himself. To him his behaviour is normal. He should be pitied,' she added modestly.

Theo took her hand. 'And you, dear lady, are too good. I would never forgive or understand. You have such sensitive fingers.'

'Me?' She laughed and spread them out on the tablecloth. 'I've always thought them too small.'

'I love your small hands and, no doubt, your small feet.'

'Lord Prestwick!' She was teasing him too, laughing, but then she stopped suddenly. 'I have had some alarming news today. I'm glad Edward is not here. I have been trying to make up my mind whether to tell you or not. It's so difficult.'

'Is it about me?' She shook her head. 'Edward?'

'No. Nothing to do with you, but it affects you.'

'Kendall Bartholomew?'

'I'm afraid so, yes.'

'Please tell me.'

'Phoebe was there. I found the woman who cared for her, helped tutor her. She told me many things . . .'

Dulcie began the sorry tale. She left nothing out, even though it embarrassed her to tell much of what she knew to Theo of all people.

'An auction! Women sold at an auction!'

'And I am ashamed to say that my husband organised it.'

Theo's hand banged down on the table with such ferocity that the china, glass and silver danced and rattled.

'Such evil! And in my house! Degrading my family's home. I shall go and see him. I shall go today.'

'Theo, do you think that is wise?'

'But poor Phoebe. Do we know if he ... Dear lady, how shall I express myself to you?'

'Is she a maiden? I don't know.'

'Poor Edward. When he finds out ...'

'He mustn't. He can't be told.'

The door had opened and neither had been aware of it. 'What can't I be told?' He was standing in the doorway, smiling, happy.

As his father told him everything they knew, his demeanour changed. The smile disappeared. His happiness was ravaged.

10

'Are you sure there's nothing more I can do for you?' Phoebe asked Bee.

'Well, you're a helpful maid and no mistake. Let me think ... You could dust the morning room, but be careful because Mrs Randolph loves her ornaments.'

'Are you going out?' Bee was pinning on her hat.

'I've a friend works down the road. She's not been well and her employer is not one of the kinder specimens. Mrs Randolph said I could take her some soup. If you're worried about being alone, I shan't be long.'

'Don't hurry back for me. I shall enjoy dusting the room.'

Which was partly true. She would admire the ornaments while she dusted them. She was not sure about being alone in the house, but she reminded herself that the rest of the staff were in the kitchen. All the same, it would be nicer when Bee or Mrs Randolph was back.

Last night at the party she felt she had triumphed when she met *him* – she didn't like to use his name. She had looked him straight in the eye, and although she had referred to the meeting on the stairs she knew that he was aware of what else she had meant. For all that, she had been happy when he left that morning and alarmed when he returned. He'd forgotten some papers, he'd told Agnes. It crossed her mind that it was odd for such an important man to fetch them himself, but perhaps they were of a personal nature.

It was silly of her to be bothered since Dick was working in the garden. Phoebe had asked Mrs Bramble for sandwiches for her lunch and a jug of lemonade. 'You'd think it was summer instead of a chilly April day,' the cook had exclaimed.

'But I can wrap up warm and the sun is shining. I can be with my brother when he takes his break.'

Dick had questioned her a little too closely for comfort over what she had been doing while he had been away. It was hard for her to make light of all her adventures when she had been so frightened. But she knew she must never tell him the truth. He would have a list of people to kill if she breathed a word of what had befallen her. She had made it all sound like a game.

'Mr Chauncey was a bit worried. He said this Mr Bartholomew is a strange man, that there's a lot of talk about him.'

'You shouldn't listen to gossip, Dick.'

'Was he strange?'

'A bit.' She found it difficult to talk about him for when she did the memories came rushing back.

'Why's your voice gone funny?'

'I've a chill coming.' She coughed to emphasise it.

'How was he strange?' Dick persisted.

'Well, he's no colour in his skin – albino, they call it.'

'Like the rabbits?'

'Exactly. He didn't venture out much in the daylight.'

'Why?'

'I was told the light hurt his eyes. And perhaps if it was sunny he risked being burnt.' She had just thought of that and found it a most satisfactory explanation. 'He was clever. Foreign languages, you know.'

'And what did you do there?

'I helped the housekeeper,' she lied. What was the point in him knowing anything? It was over and done with. 'You like Mr Chauncey, don't you?'

'He's been very good to me. He's an honourable man.'

'His mother says he's a brilliant artist.'

'I wouldn't go as far as to say that. He'd like to be, but he says as hard as he works he can't seem to get any better.'

'But Mrs Randolph says—'

'She's his mother, she would, wouldn't she? Mr Chauncey doesn't like his father.'

'How sensible of him.' She grinned.

'He says the man makes his mother's life hell on earth. And she so nice and kind. He's hoping they'll get a divorce.'

'A divorce!' Phoebe's shock at the idea was in her voice and her face. 'But the scandal!'

'He doesn't care. He wants her to send her husband right away from here. Then he'll step into his shoes and run the shop for her. He says he'd like that. It's in his blood.'

'Then maybe he will, if Mrs Randolph does as you say, but I can barely believe it. Mind you, she'd do well to send that Miss Agnes packing too. Spiteful, she is, and I tried hard as I could to make friends with her.'

'Mr Chauncey hates her too.'

'I can understand him not liking his father, but his sister? I could no more hate you, Dick, than I could fly.' She kissed him to make sure he knew she meant it.

'Mr Chauncey's taken a shine to you.'

'Me? Don't be silly.'

'He has. He told me.'

'But he can't. I don't want him to.'

'I doubt if he can help how he feels.'

'But I love another.'

'Poor Mr Chauncey. Shall I tell him?'

'Don't you dare!'

'Who? Who is it?'

'Mr Edward. And he feels the same way.'

'Phoebe, no. Be careful.'

'I don't know what you mean.'

'Men like them, they want a girl just for one thing. Toffs are different. They play with the likes of you and when they've had enough they cast you aside.'

'Maybe, but it's a risk I shall have to take. Like Mr Chauncey, I can't help how I feel, can I?' And it was something she had allowed herself to think about if only for a minute. It was too horrible a thought to spend more time on – but she kept it at the back of her mind just in case.

'I enjoyed them sandwiches, even if they were a bit on the dainty side.' He stood up.

'When I've finished my chores I think I'll go and have a rest, in my room. That's what ladies of leisure do.'

'You, a lady? That'll be the day,' he said over his shoulder, as he made his way back to the toolshed.

Of all the ornaments in the room it was one of a girl on a swing, her young man looking at her with such love, that Phoebe liked best. She looked at the bottom – Spode, she must remember that. As she worked she remembered the conversation she had overheard between Agnes and her father. Her mother had said that you never heard good of yourself if you snooped on what others were saying. Well, it was true! She hated the way Mr Randolph-Smythe had spoken of her. As if she was a plaything. But, of course, that was what he had wanted her to be. Goosebumps prickled on her arms. And how dare he say such awful things about her to Agnes?

Better to think of what Edward had said. She was sure she hadn't been dreaming.

'You look particularly happy.'

She nearly dropped the piece of china she was holding, and turned slowly to face him.

'Am I to be let into the secret?'

Last night with others about her she had been able to look at him and show no fear. Today was a different matter. 'Cat got your tongue?' He stepped into the room and she took a step away from him. 'That's not like you.' Another movement forward, another back. 'Was that look because you hoped to see me?' At such a question Phoebe screwed up her face in distaste. 'That's not very polite.' Her back was now against a bookcase. There was nowhere further for her to retreat. 'Remember what I told you when you were with Orton? I said I'd have you one day.'

'No!'

'So you *can* speak. Well, I think that day has come, don't you?'

She stepped nimbly to the left, but he followed, as he did when she moved to the right.

'Don't you?'

'There are others here. I shall scream.'

'Do so, if you wish, but I doubt they will hear. The doors are solid in this house.'

Phoebe opened her mouth to shout but no sound emerged. He grabbed her arm, but she twisted and freed herself. Weaving round the furniture she made for the door, knocking a table flying as she did so. Her hand was on the knob when she felt her head jerked back. He yanked her hair violently, opened the door and pushed her into the hall. Still holding her hair he dragged her up the stairs. 'No, please, no,' she wailed. 'Help me!' As the pain in her head intensified so did the fear.

'My daughter wants me to be rid of you. But I don't want that, do you? Let's have a little fun first, shall we?' He pushed her into a bedroom. His mouth was on her and his hands were tearing at her clothes. She struggled hard, but he was too strong for her. She heard her bodice rip, felt his hands on her breasts. 'I like a woman with some fight in her . . .'

He was climbing on to her, pulling up her skirt, his hands touching, rubbing, grasping. She pushed at him, attempting to pull down her clothes. He laughed – this was just a game to him. But the sound angered her, momentarily quenching the fear. With a mighty heave she pulled back her knee and, with all the effort she could summon, brought it up and into his stomach. He rolled off her, holding himself, moaning and swearing. With one leap she was across the room and yanking at the window. She looked about her frantically and saw a bowl, brightly painted with flowers. Before he reached her she hurled it out of the window. 'Dick!' she screamed.

'Too late. I sent him packing. Oh, you're like an animal. I knew when I first set eyes on you that this was how it would be!' Once more he had her hair and was pulling her back to the bed. He tossed her on to it, then hurled himself upon her. She struggled as he pinned her down. She was crying out, screaming, weeping, begging all at the same time, but she could feel herself weakening, the energy seeping away.

There was a sudden roar, and then she could not move. He lay sprawled on her, unconscious.

She felt him being pulled off her and thrown on to the floor. She struggled to sit up.

'Dick!' He was standing over her assailant with a copper warming-pan. 'You hit him.'

'I did.'

'Oh, Dick,' she was laughing, 'you look so funny!'

Then he was laughing too.

II

'Have you killed him?' Phoebe was not laughing now, neither was Dick. The enormity of what had happened had sunk in.

She knelt beside the recumbent form. 'His heart's beating, but his head's bleeding.'

'Let's go.' Dick was heading for the door.

'Dick, no! We can't! He needs a doctor. He might die.'

'You care about him? He was trying to ravish you!'

'I know, and I'm grateful to you, but I can't just leave him, like an animal.'

'There's no one about. If we're quick, they needn't know it was us.'

Dick's face twitched, and Phoebe noticed his hands were shaking. Finally he collapsed into a chair, tremors racking his entire body. 'Oh, you poor thing.' Phoebe was not sure which of the two men to care for, which was in the worst condition. With all her might she pulled at a cover on the bed, trapped by Arnold's body. He groaned and her heart leaped with terror: Dick was in no state to protect her. And what if Randolph-Smythe was not badly hurt?

She tucked the blanket firmly around Dick and tried to soothe him but her voice was tremulous and rose as terror took hold of her again. She knew she had to act or she would be beyond helping anyone, let alone herself. 'I'm going to get help. I'll only be a minute.' Forgetting,

458

in her panic, that her dress was torn and her flesh visible, she ran from the room, down the stairs, and to the back of the house.

'Heavens above, what's happened to you?' Mrs Bramble dropped the bowl she was holding. It smashed into smithereens and the batter she had been beating spread across the floor. 'Good heavens! Jane! Come quick,' she called. 'Sit down, and tell me how you got in that state.'

Phoebe looked down at herself and pulled her dress across her chest. 'Mr Randolph-Smythe . . . He . . .' To her annoyance she burst into tears, which would not help Dick.

'Well, there's a surprise! Dirty sod!' Mrs Bramble spat.

'Gracious me. What's going on?' Bee, her hat still on her head, came rushing into the room and looked at Phoebe in horror. 'Your face, does it hurt?'

'My face?' She put her hand up to her cheek. It came away covered in blood. 'It doesn't hurt, I didn't know.'

'Fought for her honour, it looks like.'

'No!' Bee was appalled. 'I saw this coming.'

'He's unconscious. His head's bleeding, we need to get a doctor.'

'Jane, coat, doctor, now!' The maid needed no second bidding. 'And tell him it's urgent. Tell him to get here as fast as he can . . . Now, Bee, you and I had best go and see what's what.' Mrs Bramble, arming herself thoughtfully with a rolling-pin, marched out of the kitchen, followed by Phoebe, with Bee bringing up the rear.

'What on earth . . .' In the hall they met Agnes, just returned from shopping and removing her hat. 'Just look at the state of you! What have you been doing? Fighting? Typical!' She turned her back.

'I've sent for the doctor.'

'For her? Why?'

'No, for your father.'

'Papa!' She was interested now. 'What has happened?'

She pushed past the others and was first up the stairs and into the bedroom. 'Papa!'

Arnold, the warming-pan raised high over his head, was bringing it down on Dick. From the look of him it was not the first blow he had received. Blood was pouring from his head and his face was covered with it. So were his swollen hands, bruised and cut, which he had held up to defend himself.

Phoebe planted her hands in the middle of Agnes's back and shoved her so hard that she toppled over. Before anyone could restrain her, she was across the room and beating Arnold with her fists, kicking him, and biting him, all the while screaming at the top of her voice.

'Get the policeman. Lock them up!' Agnes shouted, as she attacked Phoebe.

'We'll do no such thing,' Mrs Bramble protested. 'That will only mean trouble after what he's been up to. Think of the scandal – think of poor Mrs Randolph.' Then, with great presence of mind, she picked up the jug from the washstand and hurled the water over them. 'Like you do with fighting dogs!' she said. The shock of the cold water made Agnes and Phoebe let go of each other. They collapsed onto the floor in a heap. Only Arnold looked as if he was about to continue. 'You had better not, Mr Randolph-Smythe!' the cook shouted. Standing on tiptoe, she grabbed the warming-pan as it sliced through the air yet again. The force knocked her off-balance so that she joined the two girls, but the warming-pan clattered across the floor. Bee caught Arnold's arm.

'I think you'd best sit down a moment, sir. Get your breath back.' She was now the calmest of them all. He stopped struggling and sat on the bed, panting, looking with such malevolence at Phoebe and her brother that she had to look away as if she were the guilty one. Dick was sobbing, his head in his hands, blood dripping onto the carpet at his feet. Annie was barking orders to which no one responded but Agnes was shouting loudest of all.

The arrival of the doctor, with a flustered Jane in attendance, galvanised Arnold. 'Thank you for being so prompt.' He stood, swaying alarmingly.

'I should sit down again if I were you, Mr Randolph-Smythe, before you fall over. If everyone else could be quiet?' The doctor looked about him at the women, all of whom were talking at the same time. Dick was wailing. 'Be quiet, I said!' he roared. 'Now, what have we here?'

'These two assaulted me, while I was resting.' Arnold's finger shook as he pointed it at Phoebe and Dick. 'No doubt they are about to burgle us.'

'You lie. *He* was attacking *me*, about to rape me! My brother rescued me.'

'As if my papa would touch you!' Bee restrained Agnes, who looked as if she was about to fly at Phoebe again. 'I told you! Call for the policeman.'

'No, Agnes. That won't be necessary. I shall deal with this personally. The fewer people know the better.'

'Exactly. Keep it a secret, just as you keep everything else secret.' Phoebe spoke up, while Mrs Bramble held on to her.

'Did you hear that, Doctor? You are a witness. Was that not threatening?' Arnold Randolph-Smythe asked.

'You would be advised, young woman, to take care what you say. It might get you into serious trouble,' the doctor said.

'How can I get into trouble if I speak the truth?' Phoebe stood proud.

'Quite easily, Phoebe, when it's them and us, as well you know. Be careful,' Mrs Bramble said softly.

'If you wouldn't mind leaving us, I need to examine Mr Randolph-Smythe.'

'There's no need, Doctor. I'd prefer you to look at my daughter first. That termagant attacked her too.'

'Mr Randolph-Smythe!' Mrs Bramble's shock at the lie was apparent on her face.

'You dispute my word? Do you wish to be dismissed?'

461

The staff sucked in their breath.

'It's Mrs Randolph as employs me, and it would be she what would dismiss me . . . sir.' Mrs Bramble's pause was masterly.

'We shall see about that. You, Doctor, what are you doing?'

'The young man looks to be in the worst plight.'

'I said, my daughter . . .'

'As you wish, Mr Randolph-Smythe. You'd better get these two down to the servants' quarters, then,' the doctor told Mrs Bramble and Bee.

Chauncey opened the door of his house to his mother. Edward and Theo, looking thunderous, stood behind her, and behind them a woman, who was tearful. 'Chauncey, may we prevail on your hospitality?' his mother asked.

'But of course, Mama. Is there a problem?'

'There most certainly is,' Dulcie said as she swept in.

Chauncey led the way up the stairs and into the drawing room. 'Some tea?'

'Could you send for Phoebe, first, please?'

'She's not here.'

'I dropped her off this morning. Don't you remember? I saw you at the window and waved.'

'Yes, but by the time I had run downstairs, she had gone. I just glimpsed her running up the hill.'

'And Dick?'

'He's not here either. He said if I would excuse him he had work to do in your garden, something to do with the roses. Does it matter that they are not here?'

'I have an uneasy feeling . . .'

'Nothing could happen to her if she has Dick with her. He'd die to protect her.'

'I'm just being silly, I know.' Dulcie patted her cheeks. She was suddenly feeling hot and not very well.

'Shall I go, Mrs Randolph? See that all is well?'

'Would you, Edward? That would be so kind of you.'

462

There was a forbidding silence after Edward had left. Dulcie fanned herself with her handkerchief, Theo looked as if he had all the problems of the world heaped on his shoulders, and the woman sat in the corner of the room – as far away, it seemed to Chauncey, as she could get – and cried quietly.

'I wish someone would enlighten me,' he said. 'Mother, what is it? What has happened? You look most upset. And who is this lady?'

'She is Mrs Lingford, a friend of Phoebe's. I'd rather Phoebe was here. There are matters of a delicate nature that I wish to discuss with her. Matters that need verifying before we do anything.'

'And you will not enlighten me, Lord Prestwick?'

'I agree with your mother. We should wait for the young woman.'

'Mrs Lingford? Would you tell me?'

'I fear it is my fault.'

'Really, Mrs Lingford, have I said it was?' Dulcie asked. 'Have I said one word of blame to you?'

'No, Mrs Randolph, you haven't, but that does not stop me thinking that it is. I should have acted, I should have taken advice.'

'Be that as it may, Mrs Lingford, you didn't. There's no point in thinking of what might have been. I understand the predicament you were in.'

'I doubt if anyone else will.'

'Who knows how *they* would have reacted in the same position?'

'You've more strength than me, Mrs Randolph.'

'No, my dear. It's simpler than that. I have more money. It makes life and the decisions one has to take so much easier.'

'You are so understanding.' The tears were falling again.

'Mrs Lingford, I think it might be helpful if you found the kitchen and organised us some tea,' Dulcie said sharply. She was losing patience with the constant weeping.

There had been considerable consternation in Chauncey's house, but when Edward returned with Phoebe and Dick it quadrupled.

'Has a doctor seen you?' was Dulcie's first question. 'Were you set upon by vagrants?' was the second.

'No, Mrs Randolph, but I look a lot worse than I am,' Phoebe replied and tried to smile. 'Dick got a far worse beating than me. His head is split open and I can't stop it bleeding, and he keeps shaking.'

Chauncey was at Dick's side immediately. 'He was wounded in his head. He was warned – the doctor!' He was half-way across the room when Lynette Lingford entered with a tray of tea.

'Mrs Lingford, is it really you? I'm so happy to see you!' The other woman put down the tray quickly. Phoebe rushed into her arms.

Chapter Seven
April

I

Lily could neither sleep nor eat. At night she paced her bedroom and padded down the stairs. She would prepare herself some food and then not eat it. But she drank. The small wine cellar Arnold had started for her was depleted daily. When dawn broke she felt so wretched that she invariably had a small port. Midmorning she needed a restorative. Lunch was beer. And so it went on through the day.

Lily knew it was not doing her any good, but she could not stop. She wanted to sleep, and if she got drunk enough perhaps she might. But if she nodded off it was only for minutes and then she would dream, nightmares that woke her with a start, sweating, muttering. Then she was so afraid of sleep that she fought against it for the horrors it might bring.

There was no one to whom she could confide her misery. Pansy had married, without even telling her, and was in Dawlish on her honeymoon. Consequently Lily rambled to herself, monologues of despair, plans so outrageous that part of her was still sane enough to know they would not work.

Alone in the house with her bitterness, the love she had had for Arnold changed to a corrosive hatred. She wanted revenge.

She no longer looked in mirrors. She was afraid of what she might see. She did not wash. She did not brush her hair. She did not change her clothes. How could he treat her so badly? And with Edith, of all people. But there had been worse. The day after she had seen him with Edith, Lily had received a letter from his solicitors saying that she must vacate her home forthwith.

'Did you get Arnold's letter?' Edith stood on the step, bright and smiling, smug and neat. 'You look a mess.'

'And you look a tart.'

'Did you get the letter?' Edith persisted.

'Yes, I did.'

'So when can I move in?'

'Never.'

'He'll have you thrown out.'

'He can try. He won't succeed.'

'You're a fool, Lily.'

'Then you don't know me, Edith. And good day to you.' She had slammed the door.

That accomplished, she leaned against it and wept uncontrollably. 'All my dreams, all my plans, swept away,' she wailed.

It was time. He had not listened to her, had not believed her warnings, thought he could cast her away like so much rubbish. She would show him.

Lily took a long bath, washed her hair and dried it. She changed her linen, her dress. Then, her hairpiece pinned into place, she set out to confront him.

The front door of December Cottage was wide open. The light streamed out in a yellow swathe that beckoned her, as if the door had been left open for her. She felt as if she was in a dream as she entered and stood in the hall. Around her there was silence. Some doors were open, others were closed.

She thought she heard voices and followed the sound to the kitchen. People were speaking agitatedly. She had no intention of meddling with servants. Not when, very soon, she would be their mistress.

She felt as if she was floating as she made her way back to the hall. She went up the stairs. One night he would lead her this way. One of these rooms would be hers.

Here he would take her. She paused on the staircase, one hand on the banister. What was she thinking? Edith. Her lips set firm and she strode on up. There was no floating now.

It did not cross her mind to knock before she opened a door. This must be Dulcie's room, she thought, all cluttered and feminine for someone with no femininity. That was not nice, Lily told herself. Poor Dulcie! What a cruel life she had had. Another door was locked. From behind it she heard weeping. Agnes? Let her suffer. Hadn't she given enough people pain? One door was open, the bed dishevelled, the covers on the floor. She tutted, went in, picked up the bedspread and folded it neatly. Was that blood?

She was humming as she worked. There was too much to be done in this room, she would leave it: she had other matters to attend to.

Back in the hall she checked the dining room and the drawing room; both were empty. Then she was outside the morning room. Since she had come to see Dulcie, she would go in. Should she knock or take her by surprise? She opened the door.

Dulcie was not there. No matter. She would search the room. What for? If only she could recall! If she started she might remember.

There was no point in going through the desk, not yet. If she had hidden something she would not put it in the most obvious place. Lily was sure that someone like Dulcie would have a safe – especially since she was married to a thief like Arnold. She paused in the centre of the cluttered room. One painting did not match the others: it was bolder, more modern and, what was more, it was raised slightly from the wall. She lifted the frame. How clever she was, how logical.

It took her all of five minutes to get into it. She clapped her hands with glee. This would keep her amused for hours: Dulcie had sheets and sheets of accounts. She must have known that Arnold was purloining her money. Why had she not said anything to him?

'Poor soul, fear of being left alone, no doubt.' Lily sighed. She could sympathise with that.

There were letters – old, faint handwriting, difficult to decipher, from her parents.

There was money in some envelopes, but that didn't interest Lily. A fine calf-leather folder held various documents. A copy of Agnes's birth certificate – issued by the British embassy in Boston. She was about to cast it aside when a name caught her eye. The mother was not Dulcie. Lily groped for a chair. But Arnold was the father.

'You fiend!' she said aloud. Her heart went out to Dulcie.

She wiped a tear from her cheek. She had not been aware that she was crying, but it was all so sad. She thought of Pansy and her deception, of the pain it had caused.

As quickly as she had begun to cry she stopped. The tuneless humming began again and she looked about her brightly, rather as a bird does when it is searching for grubs.

The desk.

Should she begin at the top or the bottom? She'd read once that that was what burglars did, and what was she? A thief of secrets.

A folder had been tucked away in the large bottom drawer and Lily hauled it out. As she read the old newspaper cuttings and the police reports, her heart thudded and there was a ringing in her ears. The rumours she had heard at her aunt's were true. He'd killed them. Was there no end to his wickedness?

'Who are you?'

Lily turned. 'Hello, Agnes. Don't you remember me?'

'No.'

'I've known you since you were a little girl. Are you sure you don't remember me?'

'No.'

'That's a mistake.' Her smile, had Agnes known her better, was chilling. 'I worked for your father.'

'If you're an employee how can you expect me to know you? My father employs many people. And what are you doing in my mother's room? Snooping?'

'I'm also a friend of your mother's.' The empty smile appeared again.

'I would like you to leave.' Agnes was looking less confident.

'Have you been crying?'

'It's none of your business.'

'You can tell me, I won't breathe a word to a soul.'

'I most certainly won't. And if you don't mind . . .' Agnes opened the door wide.

'I don't want to leave.'

'I shall insist.'

'Where's your father?'

'He was here but he left. I don't know where he is.'

'Then I shall wait for his return. He and I have so much to discuss. And so have we, Agnes. You'd be amazed at what I know about you. It might even change your life.' Lily laughed mirthlessly. 'There's the little matter of a birth certificate. And this. Just look . . .'

As if mesmerised Agnes walked back into the room.

'Let me show you and explain.'

A few minutes later Agnes cried out in disbelief and distress, but her agony had only just begun.

2

'There is much we must ask you, Phoebe.'

'Do you have to, Mrs Randolph?'

'Unfortunately it is imperative.'

Phoebe, clutching Mimi, looked at the assembled company. Everyone in the room was staring at her so intently that she was even more aware of her dishevelled state, that the suit she had put on so proudly that morning was creased, torn and ruined.

'So?' Phoebe stared at Dulcie with frightened eyes. How could she tell her what a tyrant her husband was, what a bad man? And he the father of her children. She had been kind to Phoebe when others would not have been. She might be asking to be told, but she had no idea of what she risked learning.

'I don't think I can, Mrs Randolph.'

'But you're with friends here, Phoebe. We all care about you.'

Edward was standing further back than the others, watching, his dear face creased with anxiety. And they thought she could say such things with him there, listening, each word chipping away at the respect and affection he had for her. It would be too cruel, she could not endure it.

'There's nothing to tell, you, honestly. I need to see my brother.'

'The doctor is with him. He has calmed and sedated him, he says there is no danger. But I told you this, Phoebe.'

'I can't remember.' She looked about her wildly. 'Please, I wish to go. I have nothing to say.'

'Phoebe!' Lynette Lingford stepped forward. 'I've told them. There's no need for you to protect anyone.'

'I'm not. I'm not sure what you're talking about.' But she looked even more flustered.

'I was privy to enough. I told Mrs Randolph about—'

'No!' Phoebe pressed her back against the wall, still clutching the little dog, who growled protectively. 'No!' she repeated.

'Perhaps if we asked the gentlemen to withdraw?' Dulcie asked.

'How thoughtless of us.' Theo was already on his feet.

'There's no need. I can go.' Holding her dog close, almost as if she feared they would take it from her, Phoebe moved away from the wall cautiously.

'I cannot abide this.' Edward stood in front of her, barring her way. 'Can you not see that she is afraid? I will not stand by and see Phoebe so upset.'

'Please don't stop me, Edward. Please!' He would not be defending her and caring for her when he knew all there was to know. She wanted to be far away from here: she didn't want the shame of seeing him and him knowing.

'Would you please leave us alone? I think it would be better.'

'But, Edward, in the circumstances—'

'Father, I wish to speak to Phoebe with no one else present.'

'It would not be right.' Dulcie was playing with her string of pearls, as if it were a rosary.

'It is what I wish.'

Reluctantly the others left and they were alone. In the silence of the room Phoebe was certain that the thumping of her heart must be audible to him.

'Dearest Phoebe, sit here. I'm not going to hurt you, you know.'

'I wish I could turn back time,' she said, as she took her seat. He was pulling a small armchair towards her so that he could sit close to her.

'And where would you go?'

'To the day I first met you . . . When I was still . . .' She stopped.

'Still what, Phoebe?' He took her hand. She felt a thrill at his touch and wished she hadn't. It would be easier to say goodbye if she didn't love him.

'Nothing. Silly dreams.'

'I know about my uncle, Phoebe, and his wicked practices. Mrs Randolph told me earlier today. I cannot say how sorry I am that a member of my family treated you so—'

'So if you know, do the others? Does Mrs Randolph?'

'Yes, they do.'

'Then why all that fuss just now? Why was everyone wanting to talk to me, wanting me to tell them things I never want to say, ever?'

'Because everything we had heard was hearsay. There was no proof. You are the proof. If you tell us what happened, we can act. Especially me. Phoebe, is it true? Did he keep you locked up for his own . . . pleasure?' He covered his eyes with his hand.

'Yes.'

'Oh, my God!'

'But I learned so much – to read and write, and how to behave.' She wanted him to know there had been good things too. 'He could be kind,' she said disarmingly.

'For his own ends, no doubt.'

'I think he liked me.'

'Then why treat you as he did? Sending you away to be sold.' His eyes were bleak.

'I disobeyed him. I wrote to my brother when I should not have – not that I understood the secrecy.'

'Mrs Lingford tells me there was a web of intrigue, that it was a business just like any other, that girls were destined for houses of the night. When I think of such a fate for you—' He clenched his fists.

'I did not know that. I was not told.' Phoebe was aghast at the fate she had so narrowly escaped. 'Oh, Edward, those poor girls.'

'That is so like you, thinking of the others and not yourself. Phoebe, I love you.'

They were not the words she had expected to hear. Why was he saying them now, when it was all too late?

'I have longed to say those words to you. When I first met you, I knew you were for me. I had read of love at first sight and thought it a foolish notion, but then . . .'

Such a declaration should have been for Phoebe the most wonderful experience of her life. 'But now? Everything has changed, hasn't it? You look at me differently, I know.' She knew what she had to do, what to suggest, and just pray he wanted her enough. 'I know now that I have no future, Edward, without you. If you could forgive me, I would go with you to the ends of the earth. I'd be there for you and only you, whenever you wanted. Please love me . . .'

She looked at him with such pleading that he cried out, 'My darling, why do you ask my forgiveness? What have you done? I shall never leave you, never desert you. It doesn't matter to me that he had you when rightfully you were mine. I shall erase—'

'Edward, please.' She leaned forward and put Mimi on the floor. 'Edward, he did not.'

He looked up so sharply that she feared he might damage himself. 'What did you say?'

'I danced for him, naked, that was all. While I danced he . . .' She blushed crimson and covered her face with her hands. 'I cannot tell you, I am too ashamed.'

'My dear heart, my only one . . .' He had stood up, pulled her to her feet and was kissing her face. 'That is the most wonderful news.' She wanted him to be smiling, to be happy, but still he looked stern. 'The anger won't leave me. I shall be back for you. Care for your brother.'

At the door he waved to her and blew her a kiss, which she caught and put to her lips.

Dulcie found Phoebe at her brother's bedside.

'He's going to be all right, Mrs Randolph. I was so afraid.'

'Phoebe, how did he get into that condition?'

'Didn't Edward tell you?'

'There was barely time.'

'He fell down the stairs,' she lied.

'I don't believe you, Phoebe.'

'It's the truth.' She looked stubborn. Dulcie decided to question her later.

'Where's Edward?'

'I'm not sure. I thought he would be with you.'

'I had better go and find him.'

Dulcie met her son in the doorway. 'Here's Chauncey to keep you company.'

'Is he sleeping?' Chauncey asked.

'Like a baby. The doctor says he must rest for a good few weeks. If we could stay here, I could help in the house,' Phoebe told him.

'Of course you can. I insist.'

'You are so kind, just like your mother.'

'I hope so. But it's not just kindness, it's . . . You see, Phoebe . . .'

Phoebe put a finger to her lips. 'Chauncey, don't say what I think you're about to say. It might be presumptuous of me but you must know that I love someone else.'

'That's good.' Chauncey smiled. 'I was going to ask you if you could persuade my mother to live here with me. She seems to like you and listens to you.'

'Now I feel foolish!'

'Have you seen Edward?' Dulcie asked.

Theo was standing in the middle of the deserted drawing room, looking worried.

'Theo, what is it?'

'I think the hothead has gone to see his uncle.'

'We must follow him immediately. He must not do anything foolish. Let me get my cape and hat.'

Dulcie ordered the coachman to drive as fast as safety permitted. In consequence it was not a comfortable ride as the carriage swayed and bumped, and the occupants were thrown about. Conversation was difficult so finally neither spoke. Dulcie sensed that Theo was relieved by this for he sat huddled into a corner through most of the journey, deep in thought.

Courtney Lacey was a blaze of light as the coach ground to a halt at the front door, which stood open.

'Should we go in?'

'I would much prefer you to wait in the carriage.'

'But I want to meet this cruel man. Our lives have inadvertently been entwined for years through my home for waifs and strays, and I had no idea.'

'Sometimes there is truth to be found in the most unlikely gossip.'

'I shall not be so sanctimonious in future. Theo, what a wrench it must have been to leave all of this.' She indicated the fine hall with its linenfold panelling, the great sweep of the oak staircase.

'It's been spoilt by that man. It could never be the same again for me.' He turned abruptly. 'This way. This is where he will be.'

Dulcie had to scurry along the corridor to keep up with him as he strode towards the library. As they approached it was obvious why no one had answered their knock: the entire staff were crouched at the door and one of them, with her ear to the keyhole, was reporting to the others what she heard.

'What does this mean?' She had never heard Theo angry before. She hoped he was never so with her.

'Milord!'

'Mrs White, I never thought . . .'

'Sorry, milord.' She gave an unconvincing bob and *en masse* the servants hastened away.

'You are evil incarnate!' They heard Edward shout.

'Oh dear,' said Theo, and they entered the cavernous room. It was in darkness apart from at the far end where Edward stood over the desk. Kendall Bartholomew wore an amused smile.

'If I am so evil, why are you here?'

'To tell you what I think of you.'

'Are you sure you didn't come to inspect who I might have here? Or is it Phoebe you lust for?'

'You devil! Satan! Monster!'

'Running out of words, are you? You were never particularly articulate. And I think I should warn you to have a care, nephew.' At the sight of Theo and Dulcie moving down the long room, he stood up. 'And here's your father with a friend. Come to visit your old home, Theo? See how beautifully I care for it.'

'You have ruined it.'

'You should tell your son to treat me with more respect or you won't fulfil your dream to return.'

'I could never return. This house is tarnished for me. I could never rest here – never.'

'Theo!' Dulcie attempted to restrain him.

'Theo, is it? How intimate. How extraordinary!' He laughed unpleasantly. 'And you are? Will no one introduce us?'

'I'm Mrs Randolph—'

'Not Smythe?'

'He's my husband.'

'Interesting,' said Kendall Bartholomew.

'I intend to tell the world about you, Uncle. I want everyone to know of the evil that resides here.'

'And what about her husband? Edward? Theo? Such strange friends you keep. Shall I tell you about him? Or, rather more fun, why don't you ask him? Get her husband to tell you about the auctions. Ask him about the Paris brothel and about the money he makes.'

Dulcie felt as if the walls of the room were collapsing on to her. She put out her hands as if to fend them off.

'That's too much, Uncle. This lady is innocent. How dare you?'

'A likely story. Though I'd have thought Arnold might have chosen better!'

'That's a dastardly thing to say.' Theo lunged out and hit Kendall Bartholomew hard on the nose. His blood looked stark against his pale flesh.

'You can hardly expect me to leave my will unchanged now, Theo.'

'I don't give a damn what you do.'

'But your son will. He will be the loser!'

'No, I won't. I don't want anything from you, Uncle. I don't want this house, your money. I want to expunge you from my memory.'

'With pleasure, dear Edward. I shall do just as you request.'

3

In the coach returning to Barlton, Dulcie was in shock. It wasn't the revelation of Arnold's nefarious activities that had surprised her but his duplicity. He knew how much her work with unforunate women and girls meant to her, the pride she took in helping them, finding them positions. They had even had them working in the shop, in the house. How he must have enjoyed the joke: she saving the corrupted when he had corrupted them.

She should have investigated the rumours she had heard, proved they were false, rather than presuming they were. She felt such guilt. And then there was poor Phoebe. What would she think of her? Would she stay with them now?

'Don't blame yourself, Dulcie.'

'I don't see what else I can do, Theo. I should have guessed.'

'How? These were matters of which you had no knowledge. No doubt you did not know such places existed.'

'But I did, Theo. And I should have questioned more deeply why so many local girls were involved. There had to be something in the locality, someone – and to find it is my own husband! And then dear Edward having to find out, and losing his inheritance.'

'It was an inheritance that, for some time, he has not wanted. He, like all of us, had heard dreadful rumours, but had no proof. He felt he was entangled in a web of lies and deceit. There were times, he told me, when it was on the tip of his tongue to demand to know, but something held him back.'

'The truth can, too often, be painful and one prefers to hide from it – I, of all people, understand that. And he has the blood of this man in his veins. How frightening that must be for someone as sensitive as he is. But I expect you were proud of him this evening.'

'I was.'

'And now you will never return.'

'Just bricks and mortar.'

'As Phoebe so wisely said.'

Theo moved restlessly in his seat. He had on his face the expression that she now knew meant he was thinking deeply and not necessarily enjoying it. 'Is something bothering you?'

'It's difficult to put into words and not offend you.'

'We won't know unless you tell me what it is.'

'But then I think, Why tell you? Why not let it fade?'

'If there is something else I would rather learn of it now from you than find out about it much later from some other source.'

He took a deep breath. 'Very well. Do you intend to stay with your husband? Please do not answer if you feel I intrude too far.'

In the darkness she smiled. 'That is the one thing I am certain of. I had already consulted my lawyer about a separation because I do not have grounds for divorce. It would be intolerable for me to live under the same roof as such a fiend. No, I shall purchase another property, I'm not sure where yet.'

'There is another matter, which has been bothering me rather more.'

Dulcie looked up expectantly.

'Phoebe.'

'Yes.'

'My son told me earlier, before we left, the state she was in . . .'

'Yes?' But she knew what she was about to hear. 'Arnold attacked her?'

'I'm afraid so.'

'And Dick rescued her? The brave boy. My husband?'

'Dick knocked him unconscious. While Phoebe went to call a doctor, he recovered. That was when he attacked Dick.'

'What can I possibly say to the poor girl, Theo? What words will express my horror?'

'She won't blame you. Why do you think she wouldn't talk to us? She was shielding you.'

'I shall always care for her.'

'Perhaps that won't be necessary now.' And Theo smiled. But then the restlessness reasserted itself.

'What is it now, dear friend?' she asked, in an encouraging manner.

'I dare not say what's in my mind. I'm afraid.'

'You? My lion? Never!'

'You might be cross with me. You might be insulted.'

'Really, Theo, you are a maze of puzzles this evening, quite unlike yourself. I insist on knowing. My curiosity can take no more.'

'I love you.' He sat back on the leather seat. 'There, I have said it.'

'Oh, Theo.'

'Then you're not cross?'

'Why should I be? I love you too.'

'Please repeat that. Please!'

'I love you.'

'Dulcie, I've longed for this moment.'

Although it was difficult in the confined space of the carriage, they embraced as if they would never let each other go.

'I have a suggestion, and this, again, is something I fear may insult you.'

She tapped his hand playfully. 'Now, now, Theo, no more guessing games.'

'I have little money, but if I sold my house and my porcelain there would be some. And . . . we could go abroad, you and I – France or Italy, I thought. Somewhere no one would know us – or know that you had a husband. Change our names. Be different. And I would care for you, look after you. You do realise that I would never bother you? It wouldn't be right if you were not free. But even if you were I'd understand and not pester you.'

'I'd swear you're blushing, Theo. I think it's a wonderful solution. But please don't sell your porcelain. And I should most certainly like you to *bother* and *pester* me.' In the closeness of the carriage Dulcie smiled to herself.

'What are you doing here?'

Lily was sitting in the morning room, calmly planning what was to be. It seemed to her as if the turmoil she had experienced over the past few days had been transferred to Agnes, who had run screaming from this room. Now he was here. Now her future could begin.

'Waiting for you. I am tired of always being alone in the little house, hoping you will come. All your promises, Arnold, you have not kept them, have you?'

'I was not aware that I made you any.'

'But you did. You knew I loved you.'

'Don't be ridiculous, woman.' He poured himself a drink.

'I'm not. One can't help loving someone. But I have begun to wonder if you deserve my love.'

'That comes as something of a relief.' He laughed.

'At the station you saw me and you kissed Edith to annoy me, didn't you?' She wished he would stop laughing. It was very rude. 'And your other mistress had returned with you from your little adventure. She was only just out of the station.'

'I enjoy the frisson of deception, and she accepts she has to share me.'

'Then she can't love you. Someone who loved you would rather be dead than share you, I know that. But, then, perhaps it's not you Mrs Franks likes but your money – or, rather, your wife's.'

'What I have made is mine. I've told you so before. Dulcie knows what I have done, and she understands.' He was looking bored with this conversation.

'What about the will? It looks as if she does understand but not as you intended.'

'What will? You made that up. There is no new will. I've searched this house from top to bottom – I know where she hides things. There is nothing.'

'But there is. I have it.'

'Did you bring it?'

'Really! Do you think I would be so stupid? I have hidden it where you will never find it and . . .' He moved towards her suddenly and she stepped back. She did not like the expression on his face. She began to hum for comfort. 'Someone else knows, Arnold, so if anything should happen to me I have left instructions for it to be returned . . . I think of everything.' She put her hands up to hold him away.

'Dearest Lily, don't back away from me as if you were scared of me. I was going to kiss you, that was all.'

'I don't want your kisses, Arnold. We are talking.'

'Yes, Lily.' He laughed again, as if her dignity amused him. That was not polite.

'I'm not like Dulcie. No doubt you think she forgives you for everything. She's a saint to have put up with you all these years, isn't she? But it strikes me as unfair.'

'She needed me too. I have cared for her. But imagine my life, Lily. You know how hard I work and then to come home to a sulking wife who never understood me.

481

Who found my body disgusting, who never loved me as you do.' He stepped forward. 'Just a little kiss?'

'Just one.' She closed her eyes and pursed her lips. He kissed her. How odd, she thought. She had barely felt him. She began to hum again.

'That's a strange song.'

'It's mine.'

'It's very pretty.'

'Thank you.' She should have known he would appreciate it.

'Would you care for a drink?'

'I should like a sherry. What is that scratch on your face?'

He fingered it. 'A contretemps with a young lady who thinks she doesn't want to bed me, but she will.'

The words slammed into Lily. How could he be so cruel? 'You are vulgar.' She glowered at him.

'Lily, what a thing to say!'

Now she was smiling, her moods flickering like shadows in sunlight. 'Dulcie has begun proceedings to separate from you.' She enjoyed the stupefaction on his face. 'She is moving from here.'

'It is probably for the best.'

'Arnold, you are so right. I have such plans for this house.'

'You won't be coming here.'

That should have hurt her, but she felt nothing. Why?

'Dulcie is talking of getting you out of the shop.'

'She can't do that!'

'Mr Battle seems to think that she can. After all, you have been stealing from her long enough. I heard talk of police proceedings. Oh dear, Arnold, you look quite shaken. You're going to need me so much, aren't you?'

'She won't do any of those things. She's too conventional. And what can you do?'

'Now, Arnold, don't say things you might regret

482

You've had a shock. Would you like me to pour you another drink? You sit there and let Lily get it for you.'

'That's more the Lily I know.' He watched her as she picked up her small bag and went to where the decanters stood on a silver tray. 'Do you know why I'm here?'

'To see me, of course.' He smiled.

'No. I came to tell your daughter the truth.'

He looked up, startled. 'What truth?'

'I told her about the stealing. She didn't believe me.'

'She wouldn't. Agnes is loyal.'

'Then I told her about the auctions. I don't think she understood what I meant.'

'She's an innocent, of course she wouldn't'

'I told her she was illegitimate and that Dulcie was not her mother.'

He leaped to his feet. 'How dare you? How do you know that? And why tell her?'

'I was in the same position. I had a mother who was not mine. I thought I hated her until I found out she was not my mother. Then I realised how much I needed her. I've watched Agnes with Dulcie. She is cruel, unthinking, wicked. I had to put it right.'

'Are you mad, Lily?'

'No, Arnold. Rather, I see myself as justice incarnate.'

'Where are the scales?'

'Always so droll, Arnold, but you look peaky. Here's your drink.' She handed him the tumbler of whisky with a strange smile.

He took a gulp. The smell of almonds filled his nostrils. The pain was instant and intense. He knew he was dying before his body hit the floor.

Chapter Eight
February 1901

Too many changes, thought Dulcie, as she wrapped more of her porcelain in triple layers of tissue paper, not relying on the removal men to do it for her. If anything was broken, she reasoned, she would have only herself to blame. She was sitting at the dining-table on which were arranged her possessions, rather like the displays she had seen at auctions.

Auctions! There were other words in her vocabulary now that she did not like to say or think about. She was working here because she could not enter the morning room after the awful happenings of last April.

April: a month she had always enjoyed, with the scent of spring in the air, a month for optimism and regeneration. Would it ever be like that for her again? She doubted it.

Arnold. She had tried hard to feel grief for the man. She was sorry for the manner of his death: animals were not dispatched with the acute pain that her well-meaning but insensitive doctor had explained Arnold had suffered. Death had been almost instantaneous but he would have known his fate. And for the man himself? She was merely relieved that he was no more. She had no fond memories, only bitterness for what he had done, the nightmare that her parents' suffering had been caused by him, and the nagging unanswered question: if he had not been murdered would he have killed her?

It had been suggested that she should have her parents' bodies exhumed, but what for? If he had murdered them he was beyond punishment. It was better that they were left in peace. She knew in her heart of hearts that he had killed them and blamed herself: if she had not been so stubborn, so much in love, she would have listened to them and never married him in the first place. Then they would still be alive.

'You can't blame yourself, Dulcie, I won't have it. You were not to know he was mad and evil.'

'I acknowledge that what you say is true, Theo, but in my heart it is hard to forgive myself.'

Asylum – another word that made her shudder. That poor woman Lily had been tipped into madness at seeing the man she loved suffer at her hand. When she had visited her in the asylum, Dulcie had been horrified by the scenes she had witnessed, the poor lost souls. And the smell – not only of body waste but of fear. Lily had not recognised Dulcie, which was a blessing since she had felt there was no point in making further visits. Everyone was to blame over Lily. No one had befriended her, cared for her. Her mother or, rather, her stepmother was almost in the same quandary as Dulcie: 'If only,' she had kept saying, just back from her honeymoon. In the circumstances having Lily moved to a home for the insane rather than leaving her in the local lunatic asylum was the least she could do.

Poor Agnes, bereft at her father's death and told the truth of her parentage by Lily. That had been unkind. Punishing Arnold, no doubt. Dulcie had done all in her power to try to help the girl but Agnes blamed her for her father's death. 'I haven't even seen you cry,' she had accused Dulcie.

'I wish I could,' she had answered honestly.

'You lie. You care nothing! If you hadn't been so ugly and horrible to him he would never have sought others.'

The simplicity of youth, Dulcie had thought, as Agnes's words had hit her like arrows.

'You will disown her now, surely?'

'How can I, Theo? She does not know what she says. She is mad with grief.'

Eight months later she was still unbalanced with sorrow, but Dulcie could not find it in herself to cut her off. She was now in Italy, would be in Austria soon and had plans to go to America.

'She should be punished, not have tickets and hotels paid for her.'

'She didn't ask to be born, Chauncey.'

Sometimes Dulcie knew she irritated the others with her attitude, but it was not in her nature to hold a grudge.

'That's the last of your favourites, Mrs Randolph. What next?' Bee was placing the figurine of the girl on the swing, watched by her swain, on the felt they had laid on the table.

'I used to love this one, but I'm not so sure any more, Bee. When I touch it I feel most peculiar. Do you?'

'No, ma'am, I can't say as I do.'

'Then you have it.'

'Thank you, ma'am. I shall cherish it.' Bee looked about the room, whose walls were already denuded of paintings. 'It'll be strange leaving December Cottage.'

'I couldn't have stayed.'

'Gracious, no one expected you to. We'll be fine where we're going.'

'I do have happy memories of this house – Chauncey and Agnes, when they were young, and the parties we gave them. But they are outweighed by the bad ones.'

'You deserve happiness, ma'am. You really do.'

Dulcie looked down at the modest ring on her finger. She had much finer baubles but to her this was the most beautiful jewel in the world. She touched it, a look of wonderment on her face. 'I hope I can make him happy.'

'Ma'am, I've been thinking . . .'

'Yes, Bee?'

'It's not my place . . .'

'Oh dear, that sounds ominous.' She smiled encouragingly at her maid. 'Whatever it is, Bee, you should tell me. We've been friends for so many years. You should feel free to speak your mind.'

'Well, would you please think about yourself and not others all the time? It quite wears me out. What I say is I hope *he* makes *you* happy. Start being a little bit selfish, ma'am. It would do you the world of good.'

Dulcie laughed. 'But I am. I always save the largest strawberry for myself.'

'That's not what I meant.'

'You worry he's wrong for me?'

'Not exactly, ma'am. But I do wonder if it's you he's after or your money.'

'Bee, don't look so distressed. In the circumstances it is reasonable to think of it. However, it's a problem I've had all my life. It's a question the rich always have to ask. It's probably punishment for being rich in the first place. Of course I've thought about it but I don't think it's so in this case. And if there is a small element of it, at least it's getting me what I want, which is him.'

Bee burst out laughing. 'I never thought to hear you talk like that, ma'am and that's the truth.'

What was the truth? She did not know, and she no longer cared. Marriage to Arnold had taught her much, and one thing she now knew was that she would survive.

She pulled the copies of the *Barlton Globe* she had saved towards her and reread the advertisement

NOTICE OF SALE.

On the instructions of the
Honourable Edward Prestwick,
the sale, by auction, of the house, estate,
and contents thereof, of the manor house of
Courtney Lacey, in the county of Devon.
To be held at
The King William Hotel,

When she had seen the notices of the sale she had been overjoyed: here was a golden opportunity to buy everything, lock, stock and barrel, for Theo.

'Why do you study the details, Dulcie, my love?'

'I'm just curious, and thinking now fortunate it is that Mr Bartholomew didn't change his will. Was it guilt, do you think?'

'Dulcie, you're changing the subject. I trust you're not contemplating purchasing the house.'

'Me? Why would I?'

'Because I know you and your generosity. If you are thinking of purchasing one cup and saucer, please, my darling, don't. I have no need of anything from that accursed place. As Edward doesn't either.'

'Because of Phoebe?'

'No, my love, because the house is shamed and neither of us wants anything further to do with it.'

She knew and understood Theo.

'I had thought to purchase Courtney Lacey for your father as my wedding gift to him. What do you think, Edward?'

'Believe me, Mrs Randolph, he never wants to cross the threshold ever again.'

'Neither of you is simply saying that because you don't want me to spend any money on Theo?'

'No, Mrs Randolph. We say it because you would be wasting your money. He hates the place now, thanks to my uncle. And I could never visit you because of what might have happened to Phoebe there. However, if you are interested, there is a house for sale near Cowman's Combe.'

Dulcie had fallen in love with Theo when she had first set eyes on him. Similarly she fell in love with Graceteign Manor at her first sight of it. Untouched since Elizabethan times, it was perfect for them, and not too large – the prospect of being chatelaine of Courtney Lacey had filled her with dread. They could be happy in this house, protected by its ancient walls, which in turn were safeguarded by the steep, wooded valley. It was even better when they learned that Edward had found a house at Tunhill, close enough for easy visiting.

Apart from her beloved china, she was taking nothing from December Cottage. She did not want one napkin, one pillowcase: she would not take her past into her future, for it was a past she wished to bury.

Chauncey had understood how she felt, and wanted nothing either. She had written to Agnes at several *poste restante* addresses asking what she wanted, but there had been no reply. Everything was to be sold apart from some of the furniture, which the young couple who had purchased the house wanted.

She had been upset when Chauncey announced he wanted to give up his art for the shop. 'But you have such talent.'

'Mama, I fear your love for me blinds you to my abilities. I dabble, and I can always do that on Sundays or bank holidays. But an artist? I'm not good enough. If I persist, the frustration of my limitations will drive me mad, I'm sure. I should like very much to take on the shop, if you would trust me to.'

'Dear Chauncey, you will make such a success of it.'

'Now, Mama, don't let maternal feelings get in the way of judgement,' he had teased her.

She could not believe what he had said about his painting. 'What do you think, Theo? Don't you think it's a dreadful waste of a talent?'

'The truth is, no, I don't.'

'Theo!' She was shocked.

'He can draw quite well, and he paints pleasantly, better in watercolour than oils, but as a career, quite honestly, Dulcie, no.'

As she trusted Theo in all other things so she trusted him in this. But she collected together every scrap of paper she could find on which her son had done the merest scribble.

Everything had changed and in such a short time, not just for her but for so many whom she loved. Her life, she thought, was like a giant jigsaw puzzle.

She picked up the sheaf of press cuttings from the *Barlton Globe*, and wondered whether to keep them.

Mysterious Death of English Gentleman

Zermatt, Switzerland

Three-day Search Ends in Tragedy

A three-day search by the authorities ended today when the body of a visiting Englishman was found in a gully on the Matterhorn mountain. The man, Mr Kendall Bartholomew, of Courtney Lacey, nr Barlton, in the county of Devon, an inexperienced mountaineer, had left his hotel on Friday evening, preferring, as his companions explained, to climb at night, and alone.

Foolhardy Night Climb

Fritz Wanger, chief guide with twenty years' knowledge of the mountain, was reported to have commented that if people were so foolhardy, there was little could be done for them.

Authorities Alerted

The authorities were alerted by Miss Rosemary Fenton, a travelling companion of the victim. She had waited for his safe return for nearly three hours. A tearful Miss Fenton proclaimed it was her fault and had she not delayed, the victim might have been found.

Mr Wanger, however, said that no rescue team would have risked the mountain at that time of night.

Was Skin Complaint Cause?

Herr Schramm, the hotel proprietor, claimed that the victim was suffering from a skin condition where he was advised by his medical practitioners to avoid daylight. 'He was very pale,' Miss Fenton told our reporter.

Consul Informed

His Majesty's consul was immediately informed. The family, contacted, were speeding to the site of the tragedy. A funeral will take place at Courtney Lacey, early next month.

Miss Fenton has been given succour by the nuns of the Holy Order of St Cecilia.

Respected Scholar

Mr Bartholomew was a respected scholar and translator of ancient texts. Mr Dingwell of the British Museum, when contacted by the *Barlton Globe*, said the world of scholarship was a poorer place as a result of his death.

The local villagers of Courtney Lacey are, it has been confirmed, planning a fine memorial for their benefactor. 'He will be sorely missed by one and all,' an estate worker has said.

Had he been avoiding the sun, or did he intend to die? Theo favoured the latter notion.

'I trust so, it was the only honourable course of action left to him.'

'At least, if you are right, he died in a manner befitting an English gentleman.'

'I can never regard him as such, my dear. Never!'

Dulcie had decided, out of consideration, that it would be better if she did not discuss the matter with him again.

He became most agitated at the mention of either the man or the house.

There had been an anxious wait for Edward while searches were made for any wills later than the one naming him as sole beneficiary, but nothing appeared and his fortune was secure.

'I am grateful to my uncle for what he has left me, but I cannot divest myself of his name fast enough.' And he had relinquished the name Bartholomew, and the hotel in Barlton, which Dulcie now owned, was called the Victoria, in honour of the late queen. Lynette Lingford was making a great success of running it, and Dulcie never needed to worry: in her she had found an honest perfectionist.

And then there was Phoebe. The young sweet girl who had come as a visitor and changed Dulcie's life. She had not even paused to consider when she had agreed to care for Phoebe's younger brother, Jim. It had been a good decision. He was a charming boy, eager to learn and for Dulcie it was as if she had a young son again.

Phoebe was in a permanent daze of happiness which was a joy to see.

'I think anyone who is melancholy should know you, Phoebe. You always make me smile.' Dulcie had said to her only yesterday when they had sat sewing together in the new house.

'I read a lovely poem the other day:

> "Better by far to forget and be happy
> Than you should remember and be sad..."

'Isn't that lovely? That's my philosophy, I've decided.'
'You don't need a philosophy, you are – happy.'

Dulcie wondered if it was her father she was thinking of. Dead these three months now, struck down in the pulpit of a seizure, as he had ranted at his minute congregation to take care, that death was all around them. And it had been for him! Theo had been quite wicked and had laughed. Dulcie didn't think quite that way.

'Do you think I am wicked that I did not mourn for my father?' Phoebe asked her as if mirroring her thoughts.

'No, Phoebe. Love has to be earned, like everything else in life. He was not good to you. Why should you mourn him?'

'Because he was my father.'

'I have thought a lot about such matters. I'm not sure if it is an instinct we are born with, to love a parent, or whether we are taught it.' She thought of Agnes: she had never been cruel to her, yet Agnes had always hated her. 'I think if you can't feel for your father it is because he destroyed your love.'

'I would hate to be wicked.'

'I don't for one minute think you are.' Dulcie smiled at her.

'You know, Mrs Randolph, I often wonder why I was spared dreadful things happening to me and not the others.'

'That proves what I say. How could you be spared if you were bad? I think your innocence protected you, like a shield.'

'Do you? That's nice. Like a knight's armour! Oh, yes, I like that thought.' She carried on with her sewing. 'Mrs Randolph?'

'Yes.' Dulcie looked up from hemming a trousseau petticoat with lace.

'You're happy?'

'Very.'

'Are you sometimes frightened that you're so happy it can't last? That something awful might happen to punish you?'

'Frequently. Then I brush away such bad thoughts and live for the day.'

'I thought it was just me.'

'One often does when one has strange thoughts.'

The sewing continued. 'Can I tell you a secret?'

'Do you think you should?'

'I'm not sure. But I've been feeling so sad about him and now there's this wonderful news . . .'

'Who? What guilt?'

'Dick. You see he once told me . . .' She blushed. 'Well, he told me that Chauncey rather liked me. And I asked him to tell Chauncey that I loved another and it was such a horrible thing to have to do . . .'

'And?'

'He's in love. Isn't that marvellous?'

Dulcie was not so sure. 'Really? How interesting. Who with?'

'Ella Lingford. Lynette's pretty elder daughter.'

'That is most satisfactory.' Dulcie sat back with relief.

Ella was a sweet child, and clever too. She'd be a good match for him. And she was hard-working, helping her mother with the hotel. It was odd how solutions so often fell into one's lap. What to do with the business had been bothering her, but if they should marry . . . Dulcie looked thoughtful.

That was the greatest mystery of all. Why had Arnold not made a will and left everything he had amassed to his beloved daughter?

'Guilt,' was Theo's conclusion.

'I don't think that word was in his vocabulary,' Dulcie's said. 'Far more likely that he thought he was immortal. Or else he was afraid to, thinking that if he did he would die. Many people are like that, you know.'

'And most inconsiderate of them too. Look at the fuss it leaves everyone with.'

That was true. The muddle of Arnold's estate would take years to unravel, a task into which young Mr Battle had thrown himself with alacrity. Poor Lily Howard would have been an invaluable help to him: she had known everything there was to know.

There. She had gone full circle with her rambling.

'That's finished, Bee. Time to go.' She put on her coat and pinned on her hat. In the hall she looked about her and wondered if she should go from room to room saying goodbye to the house. It was still a lovely home. It was not the building's fault that such awful deeds had happened here. 'Sentimental claptrap,' she said aloud, and scurried out of the door to the carriage for the longish drive to Dartmoor and her new life.

Barlton Globe   25 March 1901

Pretty Wedding at Graceteign Manor

The marriage of The Honourable Edward Prestwick, only son of Lord Prestwick, and Miss Phoebe Drewett, only daughter of the late Saul Drewett of Cowman's Combe, Dartmoor, Devon, took place in the chapel of Graceteign near Widecombe.

Due to the sad losses that both families have suffered in the past six months, the wedding was, of necessity, a small but elegant affair.

The bride walked from her previous home at Cowman's Combe to the church and was led to the altar by her elder brother, Mr Richard Drewett. She was attended by her matron-of-honour Mrs Lynette Lingford, who wore a delightful gown of pale blue organza, and carried a bouquet of spring flowers.

The bride's dress was a becoming duchesse satin, fitted with a small pleated bustle. Her bouquet was a magnificent concoction of lilies and spring flowers.

The ceremony was conducted by the Reverend Mr Benson of Castle Combe, who, as he told the congregation, had had the honour of baptising Miss Drewett.

The organ was played with great accomplishment by Mrs Benson.

A magnificent feast was served at Graceteign Manor, truly one of the great houses and one of the crown jewels of this fair isle. The gracious hostess was Mrs Dulcie Randolph, the fiancée of Lord Prestwick.

Many servants and estate workers attended, as did the staff of Folgate's Laundry, Barlton.

The happy couple were pulled by the aforementioned who insisted on releasing the horses from the carriage shaft and pulling it themselves, to much merriment.

What might have been a sad occasion, was made joyous.

Before departing for their honeymoon, which will be spent in Paris, the bride requested that her bouquet be laid on a grave at Cowman's Combe parish church, with a simple card, written in the bride's own fair hand, 'For Phyllis.' The Honourable Mrs Edward Prestwick would not divulge who Phyllis was.

A great cheer was heard as the happy couple left the estate by the crested gates.

The editor and staff of the *Barlton Globe* respectfully add their best wishes to the young couple.